What People Are Saying about the Left Behind Series

"This is the most successful Christian-fiction series ever."
—Publishers Weekly

"Tim LaHaye and Jerry B. Jenkins . . . are doing for Christian fiction what John Grisham did for courtroom thrillers."
—TIME

"The authors' style continues to be thoroughly captivating and keeps the reader glued to the book, wondering what will happen next. And it leaves the reader hungry for more."
—Christian Retailing

"Combines Tom Clancy–like suspense with touches of romance, high-tech flash and Biblical references."
—The New York Times

"It's not your mama's Christian fiction anymore."
—The Dallas Morning News

"Wildly popular—and highly controversial."
—USA Today

"Christian thriller. Prophecy-based fiction. Juiced-up morality tale. Call it what you like, the Left Behind series . . . now has a label its creators could never have predicted: blockbuster success."
—Entertainment Weekly

Tyndale House products by Tim LaHaye and Jerry B. Jenkins

The Left Behind® book series

Left Behind®
Tribulation Force
Nicolae
Soul Harvest
Apollyon
Assassins
The Indwelling
The Mark
Desecration
The Remnant
Armageddon
Book 12—available spring 2004

Other Left Behind® products

Left Behind®: The Kids
Devotionals
Calendars
Abridged audio products
Dramatic audio products
Graphic novels
Gift books
and more . . .

Other Tyndale House books by Tim LaHaye and Jerry B. Jenkins

Perhaps Today
Are We Living in the End Times?

For the latest information on individual products, release dates, and future projects, visit www.leftbehind.com

Tyndale House books by Tim LaHaye

How to Be Happy Though Married
Spirit-Controlled Temperament
Transformed Temperaments
Why You Act the Way You Do

Tyndale House books by Jerry B. Jenkins

Soon (also available in unabridged audio)

THE COSMIC BATTLE OF THE AGES

ARMAGEDDON

LARGE PRINT EDITION

TIM LAHAYE
JERRY B. JENKINS

Tyndale House Publishers, Inc.
WHEATON, ILLINOIS

Visit Tyndale's exciting Web site at www.tyndale.com

Discover the latest about the Left Behind series at www.leftbehind.com

Left Behind series designed by Catherine Bergstrom
Designed by Julie Chen

Published in association with the literary agency of Alive Communications, Inc., 7680 Goddard Street, Suite 200, Colorado Springs, CO 80920.

Characters in this novel sometimes speak words that are adapted from various versions of the Bible, including the King James Version and the New King James Version.

Library of Congress Cataloging-in-Publication Data

LaHaye, Tim F.
Armageddon : the cosmic battle of the ages / Tim LaHaye, Jerry B. Jenkins.
p. cm — (Left behind series)
ISBN 0-8423-3234-0 (HC)
ISBN 0-8423-3236-7 (SC)
ISBN 0-8423-6560-5 (LP)
1. Steele, Rayford (Fictitious character)—Fiction. 2. Rapture (Christian eschatology)—Fiction. 3. Petra (Extinct city)—Fiction. 4. Armageddon—Fiction. I. Jenkins, Jerry B.
II. Title. III. Series.

PS3562.A315 A76 2003
813'.54—dc21 2002152499

Printed in the United States of America

09 08 07 06 05 04 03
8 7 6 5 4 3 2 1

To the memory of
A. W. Tozer,
who pursued God

Special thanks
to David Allen
for expert technical consultation

SIX YEARS INTO THE TRIBULATION;

TWO AND ONE-HALF YEARS INTO THE GREAT TRIBULATION

The Believers

Rayford Steele, late forties; former 747 captain for Pan-Continental; lost wife and son in the Rapture; former pilot for Global Community Potentate Nicolae Carpathia; original member of the Tribulation Force; international fugitive in exile, Petra

Cameron ("Buck") Williams, mid-thirties; former senior writer for *Global Weekly;* former publisher of *Global Community Weekly* for Carpathia; original member of the Trib Force; editor of cybermagazine *The Truth;* fugitive in exile, San Diego

Chloe Steele Williams, mid-twenties; former student, Stanford University; lost mother and brother in the Rapture; daughter of Rayford; wife of Buck; mother of three-and-a-half-year-old Kenny Bruce; CEO of International Commodity Co-op, an underground network of believers; original Trib Force member; fugitive in exile, San Diego

George Sebastian, late twenties; former San Diego–based U.S. Air Force combat helicopter pilot; underground with Trib Force and Co-op, San Diego

Ming Toy, mid-twenties; widow; former guard at the Belgium Facility for Female Rehabilitation (Buffer); AWOL from the GC; underground in San Diego

Ree Woo, mid-twenties; pilot for Co-op; underground in San Diego

Tsion Ben-Judah, early fifties; former rabbinical scholar and Israeli statesman; revealed belief in Jesus as the Messiah on international TV—wife and two teenagers subsequently murdered; escaped to U.S.; former spiritual leader and teacher of the Trib Force, now teaching the Jewish remnant at Petra; cyberaudience of more than a billion daily

Dr. Chaim Rosenzweig, early seventies; Nobel Prize–winning Israeli botanist and statesman; former *Global Weekly* Newsmaker of the Year; murderer of Carpathia; leading the Jewish remnant at Petra

Abdullah Smith, mid-thirties; former Jordanian fighter pilot; former first officer, Phoenix 216; presumed dead in plane crash; on assignment at Petra

Al B. (aka "Albie"), early fifties; native of Al Basrah, north of Kuwait; pilot; former international black marketer; now member of Trib Force; underground in Al Basrah

Mac McCullum, early sixties; former pilot for Carpathia; presumed dead in plane crash; underground in Al Basrah

Hannah Palemoon, early thirties; former GC nurse; presumed dead in plane crash; underground in Long Grove, Illinois

Leah Rose, early forties; former head nurse, Arthur Young Memorial Hospital, Palatine, Illinois; underground in Long Grove, Illinois

Lionel Whalum, late forties; former businessman; Co-op pilot; underground in Long Grove, Illinois

Chang Wong, twenty; Ming Toy's brother; Trib Force's mole at Global Community Headquarters, New Babylon

Gustaf Zuckermandel Jr. (aka "Zeke" or "Z"), mid-twenties; document and appearance forger; lost father to guillotine; underground in Avery, Wisconsin

The Enemies

Nicolae Jetty Carpathia, late thirties; former president of Romania; former secretary-general, United Nations; self-appointed Global Community potentate; assassinated in Jerusalem; resurrected at GC Palace complex, New Babylon

Leon Fortunato, mid-fifties; former supreme commander and Carpathia's right hand; now Most High Reverend Father of Carpathianism, proclaiming the potentate as the risen god; GC Palace, New Babylon

Viv Ivins, late sixties; lifelong friend of Carpathia; GC operative; GC Palace, New Babylon

Suhail Akbar, mid-forties; Carpathia's chief of Security and Intelligence; GC Palace, New Babylon

KEY LOCATIONS FOR ARMAGEDDON

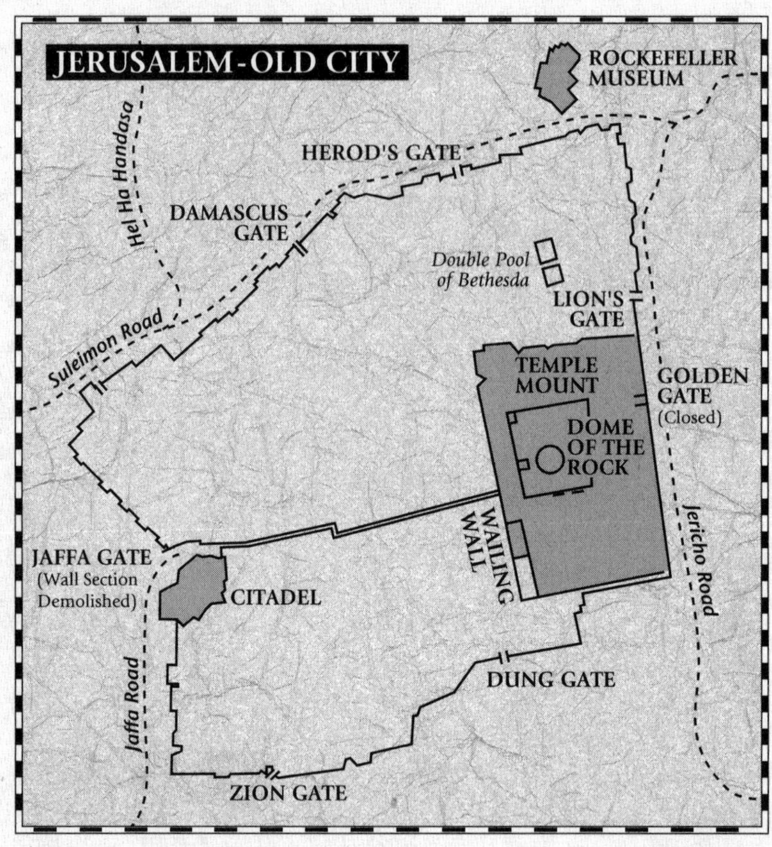
JERUSALEM-OLD CITY
ROCKEFELLER
MUSEUM
HEROD'S GATE
Hel Ha Handasa
DAMASCUS
GATE
Double Pool
of Bethesda
LION'S
GATE
Suleimon Road
TEMPLE
MOUNT
GOLDEN
GATE
(Closed)
DOME
OF THE
ROCK
WAILING
WALL
Jericho Road
JAFFA GATE
(Wall Section
Demolished)
CITADEL
Jaffa Road
DUNG GATE
ZION GATE

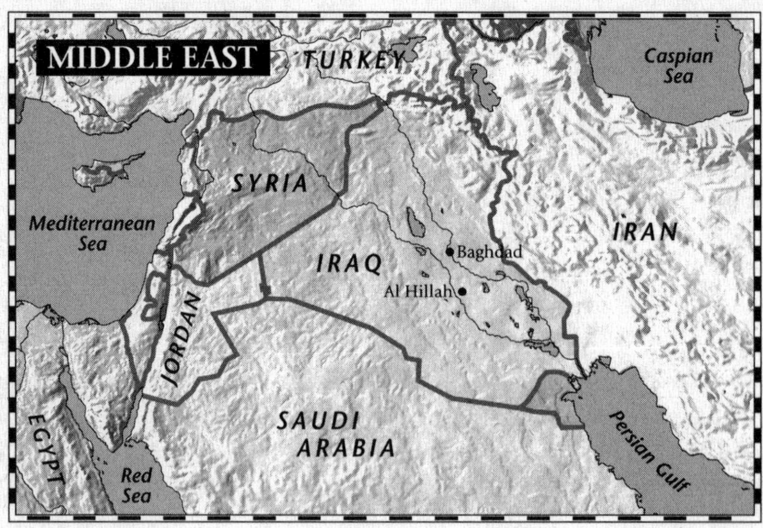
MIDDLE EAST
TURKEY
Caspian
Sea
SYRIA
Mediterranean
Sea
IRAN
Baghdad
IRAQ
Al Hillah
JORDAN
EGYPT
SAUDI
ARABIA
Persian Gulf
Red
Sea

PROLOGUE

From The Remnant

"FOR THE first time in a long time," Nicolae Carpathia said, "we play on an even field. The waterways are healing themselves, and we have rebuilding to do in the infrastructure. Let us work at getting all our loyal citizens back onto the same page with us. Director Akbar and I have some special surprises in store for dissidents on various levels. We are back in business, people. It is time to recoup our losses and start delivering a few."

• • •

The new mood lasted three days. Then the lights went out. Literally. Everything went dark. Not just the sun, but the moon also, the stars, street lamps, electric lights, car lights. Anything anywhere that ever emitted light was now dark. No keypads on telephones, no flashlights, nothing iridescent, nothing glow-in-the-dark. Emergency lights, exit signs, fire signs, alarm signs—everything. Pitch-black.

The cliché of not being able to see one's hand in front of one's face? Now true. It mattered not what time of day it was; people could see nothing. Not their clocks, watches, not even fire, matches, gas grills, electric grills. It was as if the light had done worse than go out; any vestige of it had been sucked from the universe.

People screamed in terror, finding this the worst nightmare of their lives—and they had many to choose from. They were blind—completely, utterly, totally, wholly unable to see anything but blackness twenty-four hours a day.

They felt their way around the palace; they pushed their way outdoors. They tried every light and every switch they could remember. They called out to each other to see if it was just them, or if everyone had the same problem. Find a candle! Rub two sticks together! Shuffle on the carpet and create static electricity. Do anything. Anything! Something to allow some vestige of a shadow, a hint, a sliver.

All to no avail.

Chang wanted to laugh. He wanted to howl from his gut. He wished he could tell everyone everywhere that once again God had meted out a curse, a judgment upon the earth that affected only those who bore the mark of the beast. Chang could see. It was different. He didn't see lights either. He simply saw everything in sepia tone, as if someone had turned down the wattage on a chandelier.

He saw whatever he needed to, including his computer and screen and watch and quarters. His food, his sink, his stove—everything. Best of all, he could tiptoe around the palace in his rubber-soled shoes, weaving between his coworkers as they felt their way along.

Within hours, though, something even stranger happened. People were not starving or dying of thirst. They were able to feel their way to food and drink. But they could not work. There was nothing to discuss, nothing to talk about but the cursed darkness. And for some reason, they also began to feel pain.

They itched and so they scratched. They ached and so they rubbed. They cried out and scratched and rubbed some more. For many the pain grew so intense that all they could do was bend down and feel the ground to make sure there was no hole or stairwell to fall into and then collapse in a heap, writhing, scratching, seeking relief.

The longer it went, the worse it got, and now people swore and cursed God and chewed their tongues. They crawled about the corridors, looking for weapons, pleading with friends or even strangers to kill them. Many killed themselves. The entire complex became an asylum of screams and moans and guttural wails, as these people became convinced that this, finally, was it—the end of the world.

But no such luck. Unless they had the wherewithal, the guts, to do themselves in, they merely suffered. Worse by the hour. Increasingly bad by the day. This went on and on and on. And in the middle of it, Chang came up with the most brilliant idea of his life.

If ever there was a perfect time for him to escape, it was now. He would contact Rayford or Mac, anyone willing and able and available to come and get him. It had to be that the rest of the Tribulation Force—in fact, all of the sealed and marked believers in the world—had the same benefit he did.

Someone would be able to fly a jet and land it right there in New Babylon, and GC personnel would have to run for cover, having no idea who could do such a thing in the utter darkness. As long as no one spoke, they could not be identified. The Force could commandeer planes and weapons, whatever they wanted.

If anyone accosted them or challenged them, what better advantage could the Trib Force have than that they could see? They would have the drop on everyone and everybody. With but a year to go until the Glorious Appearing, Chang thought, the good guys finally had even a better deal than they had when the daylight hours belonged solely to them.

Now, for as long as God tarried, for as long as he saw fit to keep the shades pulled down and the lights off, everything was in the believers' favor.

"God," Chang said, "just give me a couple more days of this."

• • •

Then the fifth angel poured out his bowl on the throne of the beast, and his kingdom became full of darkness; and they gnawed their tongues because of the pain. They blasphemed the God of heaven because of their pains and their sores, and did not repent of their deeds.

Revelation 16:10-11

ONE

FOR THE first time since takeoff, Rayford Steele had second thoughts about his and Abdullah Smith's passenger. "We shouldn't have brought her, Smitty," he said. He stole a glance at Abdullah behind the controls.

The Jordanian shook his head. "That's on you, Captain, I am sorry to say. I tried to tell you how important she was to Petra."

The darkness enveloping only New Babylon, but visible from more than a hundred miles, was unlike anything Rayford had ever seen. By the time Abdullah initiated the descent of the Gulfstream IX toward Iraq, the clock read 1200 hours, Palace Time.

Normally the magnificent structures of the new world capital gleamed stunningly in the noonday sun. Now a stark and isolated column of blackness rose from New Babylon's expansive borders into the cloudless heavens as high as the eye could see.

Chang Wong was Rayford's mole inside the palace. Trusting the young man's assurances that they would be able to see where others could not, Rayford traded glances with Abdullah as he guided the craft into the dark from the whiteness reflecting off the desert sand. Abdullah flipped on his landing lights.

Rayford squinted. "Do we need an ILS approach?"

"Instrument landing system?" Abdullah said. "Don't think so, Captain. I can see enough to fly."

Rayford compared the freakish darkness to the beautiful day they had left in Petra. He peeked over his shoulder at the young woman, whom he expected to look afraid. She didn't. "We can still turn back," he said. "Your father looked reluctant when we boarded."

"That was probably for your benefit," Naomi Tiberias said. "He knows I'll be fine."

The teenage computer whiz's humor and self-confidence were legendary. She seemed shy and self-conscious around adults until she got to know them; then she interacted like a peer. Rayford knew she had brought Abdullah up to speed in computer savvy, and she had been in nearly constant touch with Chang since the lights went out in New Babylon.

"Why is it dark only here?" Naomi said. "It's so strange."

"I don't know," Rayford said. "The prophecy says it affects 'the throne of the beast, and his kingdom became full of darkness.' That's all we know."

Rayford's every visit to Petra had found Naomi growing in influence and responsibility among the Remnant. She had emerged early as a technological prodigy, and as she taught others, Naomi had become the de facto head of the vast computer center. Quickly rising from go-to person to the one in charge, she'd finally become the teacher who taught teachers.

The center that had been designed by Chang's predecessor, the late David Hassid, was now the hub that kept Petra in touch with more than a billion souls every day. Thousands of computers allowed that many mentors to keep up with Tsion Ben-Judah's universal cyberaudience. Naomi personally coordinated the contact between Chang in New Babylon and the Tribulation Force around the world.

Having her join the flight to rescue him from New Babylon had been Chang's idea. Rayford had initially rejected it. He had enough trouble assigning himself the task of traveling more than seventy-five hundred miles from San Diego to Petra, then having Abdullah fly him the last five hundred miles to New Babylon. Combat-trained George Sebastian was better suited, but Rayford thought the big man had been through enough for a while. There was plenty for him to do in San Diego, and anyway, Rayford wanted to save George for what Dr. Ben-Judah called the "battle of that great day of God Almighty," now less than a year off.

Mac McCullum and Albie, stationed in Al Basrah—little more than two hundred miles south of New Babylon—stood ready. But Rayford had other things in mind for them.

Rayford's son-in-law and daughter, Buck and Chloe Williams, both wanted in on the extraction of Chang from the enemy lair—no surprise—but Rayford was convinced Buck would soon be more valuable in Israel. As for Chloe, the International Commodity Co-op always suffered when she was away. And somebody had to be there for little Kenny.

"Store and grab all the equipment you need while I'm en route, Chang," Rayford had said, the phone tucked between his shoulder and ear as he packed. "Smitty and I will come get you in a couple of days."

Chang had explained that the job was too big

and that he and Naomi working together could get him out of there that much faster. "I don't want to miss a thing. She can help. I want to be able to monitor this place from anywhere."

"Don't worry," Rayford said. "You'll get to see her face-to-face soon enough."

"I don't know what you're talking about."

"Her father is one of the Petra elders, you know."

"So?"

"Only the two of them are left in the family. He's very protective."

"We both have too much work to do."

"Uh-huh."

"I'm not kidding, Captain Steele. Please bring her along. It's not like I haven't seen her on-screen already."

"So, what do you think?"

"I told you. We have a lot of work to do."

● ● ●

Rayford felt a tug on the back of his copilot's chair as Naomi pulled herself forward. "Can Mr. Smith see to land?"

"Not sure yet," Rayford said. "It's as if someone painted our windows brown. See if you can raise our boy."

Chang was to be sure the New Babylon runways were clear, but he couldn't talk by phone from there for fear someone would overhear. Naomi pulled a small, thin computer from an aluminum box and attacked the keys.

"Avoid runways 3 left and 3 right," she said. "And he wants to know which you choose so he can be there to meet us."

Rayford glanced at Abdullah. "He's serious, Naomi?"

She nodded.

"Tell him the tower is closed, and it's not like we were going to announce our arrival anyway. We can't see which runway is which from up here, so he's going to have to give us coordinates and—"

"Hold on," Naomi said, keyboarding again. "He's attached everything you need." She passed the machine to Rayford and pointed at the attachment. "It is voice activated. Just tell it what you want."

"It'll recognize my voice?" Rayford said, studying the screen.

"Yes," the computer intoned.

Naomi chuckled.

"Attachment, please," Rayford said.

A detailed grid appeared with an aerial view of the New Babylon airfield.

"I'll set the coordinates for you, Smitty," Rayford said, reaching to program the flight management system.

"This thing will do everything but cook a meal for you, Captain Steele," Naomi said. "You have an infrared port?"

"I assume. Do we, Smitty?"

Abdullah pointed to a spot on the control panel.

"Here," Naomi said. "Let me." She leaned over Rayford's shoulder and pointed the back of the computer at the port. "Ready to land, Captain?" she said.

"Roger."

"Initiate landing sequence," she said and hit a button.

"Runway choice?" the computer asked.

Naomi looked at Rayford, who looked to Abdullah. "Does that thing recognize even my accent?" the Jordanian said.

"Yes," the computer said. "Congestion on runways 3 left and 3 right. Please select from runways 11 or 16."

"Eleven," Abdullah said.

"Left or right?" the computer said.

"Left," Abdullah said. "Why not?"

Abdullah engaged the left autopilot and lifted his hands from the controls. "Thank you," he said.

"You're welcome," the computer said.

Six minutes later the Gulfstream touched down.

• • •

At just after one o'clock in the morning in San Diego, Buck bolted upright in bed.

Chloe stirred. "Go back to sleep, hon," she said. "You stood watch three straight nights. Not tonight."

He held up a hand.

"You need your sleep, Buck."

"Thought I heard something."

The tiny walkie-talkie on the nightstand chirped. Sebastian's telltale code. Buck grabbed it. "Yeah, George."

"Motion detector," Sebastian whispered.

Now Chloe sat up too.

"I'll check the periscope," Buck said.

"Carefully," Sebastian said. "Don't raise or rotate it."

"Roger. Anybody else aware?"

"Negative."

"On it."

Chloe was already out of bed and had pulled on a sweatshirt. She unlocked a cabinet, removed two Uzis, and tossed one to Buck as he headed for the periscope next to Kenny's tiny chamber. He set the weapon on the floor, dropped the walkie-talkie into his pajama pocket, and bent to peer into the viewer. As his eyes adjusted to the darkness he was aware of Chloe opening and closing Kenny's door. Going on four years old,

Kenny slept longer but less soundly than he used to.

"He out?" Buck said, eyes still glued to the scope.

"Dead to the world," Chloe said, draping a sweater around Buck's shoulders. "As you should be."

"Wish I was," Buck said.

"I should think so." She rested her palms on his shoulders. "What do you see?"

"Nothing. George doesn't think I ought to rotate the scope. It's facing west at ground level. I'd love to elevate it about six inches and let it give me a three-sixty."

"He's right, babe," she said. "You know it's got that whine when it moves. Anybody out there could hear it."

"I don't think anybody is out there," Buck said, pulling away and rubbing his eyes.

She sighed. "Want a chair?"

He nodded and returned to the periscope. "Could have been an animal. Maybe the wind."

Chloe pressed a chair behind his knees and guided him into it. "That's why you should just let me—"

"Oh no," he said.

"What?"

He put a finger to his lips and pulled out the

walkie-talkie. "George," he whispered. "Six, seven, eight, nine. Nine uniformed, armed GC directly above to the west."

"Doing?"

"Not much. Kicking at the vents. They look bored. Maybe something caught their eye on the way by."

"Vehicles?"

"I'd have to raise or rotate."

"Negative. Any more?"

"Can't tell from this angle. No more coming past. Only three left in sight now."

"Listen for engines."

Buck sat silent a moment. Then, "Yeah, there's one. And another."

"I hear 'em," George said. "Must be leaving. Can I come over?"

"Tell him no," Chloe whispered.

• • •

What palace personnel Rayford could make out in the eerie sepia-toned landscape through the cockpit window appeared to be in agony. Chang had told him that the people writhed and moaned, but a jet screaming onto the runway also clearly terrified them. They had to think it was about to crash, as some had on runways 3 left and 3 right.

It was as if the people had given up trying to see. Anyone near the Gulfstream IX had stumbled in the darkness to get away from it, and now they huddled here and there.

"That has to be Chang," Rayford said, pointing to a slight Asian hurrying toward them and gesturing wildly to open the door.

"Let me get that, Miss Naomi," Abdullah said, unstrapping himself and climbing past her. As he pushed the door open and lowered the steps, Rayford saw Chang turn to a small group of men and women in dark jumpsuits feeling their way along behind him.

"Keep your distance!" he shouted. "Danger! Hot engines! Leaking fuel!"

They turned and hurried away in all directions. "How did it land?" someone shouted.

"It's a miracle," another said.

"Did you all remember rubber-soled shoes?" Chang said, reaching to help them off the plane.

"Nice to meet you too, Mr. Wong," Abdullah said.

Chang shushed him. "They're blind," he whispered. "Not deaf."

"Chang," Rayford began, but the boy was shyly greeting Naomi. "All right, you two, get acquainted back at the ranch. Let's do what we have to and get out of here."

• • •

"Should I change?" Buck said when he saw Sebastian in fatigues.

"Nah. I always wear these on watch. Let me have a look." He peered through the periscope. "Nothing. Want to raise and rotate it, Buck?"

"Be my guest."

"Clear. False alarm."

Chloe snorted. "Don't be saying that to put me at ease. At least nine GC were out there, and for all we know there were more, and they'll be back."

"Hey," Sebastian said, "why not assume the best and not the worst?"

"Maybe I am," she said. "Priscilla and Beth Ann sleep through this?"

He nodded. "I might not even tell Priss, so I'd appreciate it—"

"If I didn't either? Makes sense, George. Let the little woman carry on, oblivious to the fact that it's time to move," said Chloe.

"Move?" Buck said. "I can't even imagine it."

"Then we sit here and wait till they find us, which they may already have?"

"Chloe, listen," Buck said. "I should have let you take a look at those guys. They weren't even suspicious. They were probably talking about how this used to be a military base. They weren't tense, weren't really looking. They just saw the vents and checked them out, that's all."

Chloe shook her head and slumped in a chair. "I hate living like this."

"Me too," Sebastian said. "But what're our options? GC found an enclave of people without the mark yesterday in what's left of LA. Executed more'n two dozen."

Chloe gasped. "Believers?"

"Don't think so. Usually they'll say if it's Judah-ites. I got the impression it was some militia holdouts, something like that."

"Those are the people we're trying to reach," Chloe said. "And here we all sit, unable to show our faces, raising babies who hardly ever see the sun. Isn't there somewhere in the middle of nowhere where the GC wouldn't even know we were around?"

"The next best thing is Petra," Buck said. "They know who's there, but they can't do a thing about it."

"That's starting to sound more attractive all the time. Anyway, what are we going to do about what just happened?"

Buck and Sebastian looked at each other.

"Come on, guys," Chloe said. "You think Priscilla doesn't know you're gone and isn't going to ask where you've been?"

"She knows I was on watch."

"But you don't come over here unless something's up."

"I'm hoping she slept through it."

Chloe stood and moved to Buck's lap. "Look, I'm not trying to be cantankerous. Buck, tell him."

"Chloe Steele Williams is not trying to be cantankerous," he announced.

"Good," Sebastian muttered. "Coulda fooled me."

Chloe shook her head. "George, please. You know I think you're one of the best things that's ever happened to the Trib Force. You bring gifts nobody else has, and you've kept us from disaster more than once. But everyone living here deserves to know what you guys saw tonight. Not telling people, pretending it didn't happen, isn't going to change that we came this close to being found out."

"But we didn't, Chloe," Sebastian said. "Why stir up everybody?"

"We're already stirred up! I'm with these wives and kids all day. Even without bands of GC nosing around right over our heads in the middle of the night, we live like prairie dogs. The kids get fresh air only if they happen to wake up before the sun and someone herds them out the vehicle bay door. You guys have to sneak around and drive thirty miles, hoping you're not followed, to get to your planes. All I'm saying is that if we're going to have to defend ourselves, we have a right to be prepared."

• • •

Rayford would have to ask Tsion about this one. What was it about the darkness that was so oppressive it left victims in agony? He had heard of disaster scenes—train wrecks, earthquakes, battles—where what haunted the rescue workers for years had been the shrieks and moans of the injured. As he and Abdullah and the two young people tiptoed across the massive runways, around heavy equipment and between writhing personnel, it was clear these people would rather be dead. And some had already died. Two crashed planes lay in pieces, still smoldering, many charred bodies still in their seats.

As he moved from the dead to the suffering, Rayford was overcome. The wailing pierced him and he slowed, desperate to help. But what could he do?

"Oh! Someone!" It was the shriek of a middle-aged woman. "Anyone, please! Help me!"

Rayford stopped and stared. She lay on her side on the tarmac near the terminal. Others shushed her. A man cried out, "We are all lost and blind, woman! You don't need more help than we do!"

"I'm starving!" she whined. "Does anyone have anything?"

"We're all starving! Shut up!"

"I don't want to die."

"I do!"

"Where is the potentate? He will save us!"

"When was the last time you saw the potentate? He has his own concerns."

Rayford was unable to pull away. He looked ahead, but even he had but twenty feet of visibility, and he had lost the others. Here came Abdullah. "I dare not call you by name, Captain, but you must come."

"Comrade, I cannot."

"Can you make it back to the plane?"

"Yes."

"Then we will meet you there."

Abdullah was off again, but their muffled conversation had caused a lull in the cacophony of agony. Now someone called out, "Who is that?"

"Where is he going?"

"Who has a plane?"

"Can you see?"

"What can you see?"

The woman again: "Oh, God, save me. Now I lay me down to sleep—"

"Shut up over there!"

"God is great; God is good. Now I thank him—"

"Put a sock in it! If you can't produce light, shut your mouth!"

"God! Oh, God! Save me!"

Rayford knelt and touched the woman's shoulder. She wrenched away with a squeal. "Wait!" he said, reaching for her again.

"Oh! The pain!"

"I don't mean to hurt you," he said quietly.

"Who are you?" she groaned, and he saw the United European States' number 6 tattooed on her forehead. "An angel?"

"No."

"I prayed for an angel."

"You prayed?"

"Promise you'll tell no one, sir. I'm begging you."

"You prayed to God?"

"Yes!"

"But you bear Carpathia's mark."

"I despise that mark! I know the truth. I always have. I just didn't want to have anything to do with it."

"God loved you."

"I know, but it's too late."

"Why didn't you ask his forgiveness and accept his gift? He wanted to save you."

She sobbed. "How can you be here and say that?"

"I am not from here."

"You are my angel!"

"No, but I am a believer."

"And you can see?"

"Enough to get around."

"Oh, sir, take me to food! Get me inside the terminal to the snack machines. Please!"

Rayford tried to help her up, but she reacted as if her body were afire. "Please, don't touch me!"

"I'm sorry."

"Just let me hold your sleeve. Can you see the terminal?"

"Barely," he said. "I can get you there."

"Please, sir." She struggled to her feet and gingerly clasped the cuff of his sleeve between her thumb and forefinger. "Slowly, please." She mince-stepped behind Rayford. "How far?" she said.

"Not a hundred yards."

"I don't know if I can make it," she said, tears streaming.

"Let me go get you something," he said. "What would you like?"

"Anything," she said. "A sandwich, candy, water—anything."

"Wait right here."

She chuckled pitifully. "Sir, all I see is black. I could go nowhere."

"I'll be right back. I'll find you."

"I've been praying that God will save my soul. And when he does, I will be able to see." Rayford didn't know what to say. She had said herself it was too late. "In the beginning," she said. "For

God so loved the world. The Lord is my shepherd. Oh, God . . ."

Rayford jogged toward the terminal, stepping between ailing people. He wanted to help them all, but he knew he could not. A man lay across the inside of the automatic door, not moving. Rayford stepped close enough to trip the electric eye, and the door opened a few inches and bumped the man.

"Please move away from the door," Rayford said.

The man was asleep or dead.

Rayford pushed harder, but the door barely budged. Finally he lowered his shoulder and put his weight behind it. He bent and drove with his legs, feeling the pressure on his quads as the door slowly rolled the man away. Rayford heard him groan.

Inside, Rayford found a bank of vending machines, but as he reached in his pocket for Nick coins, he saw that the machines had been trashed. Enough people had felt their way here to tear the machines open and loot them for every last vestige of food. Rayford searched and searched for something, anything, they had missed. All he found were empty bottles and cans and wrappers.

"Who goes there?" someone demanded. "Where are you going? Can you see? Is there light anywhere? What has happened? Are we all going to die? Where is the potentate?"

Rayford hurried back outside. "Where're you going?" someone shouted. "Take me with you!"

He found the woman on her stomach, face buried in her arms. She was wracked with sobs so deep and mournful he could barely stand to watch.

"I'm back, ma'am," he said quietly. "No food. I'm sorry."

"Oh, God, oh, God and Jesus, help me!"

"Ma'am," he said, reaching for her. She shrieked when he touched her, but he pulled at the sides of her head until he could see her hollow, unseeing, terrified eyes.

"I knew before everybody disappeared," she said pitifully. "And then I knew for sure. With every plague and judgment, I shook my fist in God's face. He tried to reach me, but I had my own life. I wasn't going to be subservient to anybody.

"But I've always been afraid of the dark, and my worst nightmare is starving. I've changed my mind, want to take it all back. . . ."

"But you can't."

"I can't! I can't! I waited too long!"

Rayford knew the prophecy—that people would reject God enough times that God would harden their hearts and they wouldn't be able to choose him even if they wanted to. But knowing it didn't mean Rayford understood it. And it certainly didn't mean he had to like it. He couldn't make it compute with the God he knew, the loving and merciful one who seemed to look for ways to welcome everyone into heaven, not keep them out.

Rayford stood and felt the blood rush from his head. And that's when he heard the loudspeakers.

"This is your potentate!" came the booming voice. "Be of good cheer. Have no fear. Your torment is nearly past. Follow the sound of my voice to the nearest loudspeaker tower. Food and water will be delivered there, along with further instructions."

• • •

"I'll make a deal with you," Chloe said. "I'll take over the rest of the watch, and you agree that we tell everybody in the morning that we had visitors tonight."

Buck looked to George, who pointed at him. "You're in charge when your father-in-law is away, pal."

"Only because of seniority. I defer to you on military stuff."

"This isn't combat, man. It's public relations. If you want my advice, I'd say do what you want but do it right. Tell them, 'It's only fair we tell you people we saw GC around here last night, but as far as we know there's nothing to be concerned about yet.'"

"Fair enough, Chlo'?" Buck said.

She nodded. "I'd rather pray and pass the ammunition, but yes. Treat everybody like adults and you'll get the best out of them."

"If you're really taking watch, Chloe," Sebastian said, "I'm going home and turning off my walkie-talkie."

"Deal."

TWO

WHOEVER HAD figured out how to rally the panicked souls in New Babylon thought playing music over the sound system would draw them to the loudspeaker towers.

So while Nicolae Carpathia's right-hand man, Leon Fortunato, spoke soothingly—"Tread carefully, loyal subjects. Help one another. Avoid danger."—a recorded version of "Hail Carpathia," sung by the 500-voice Carpathianism Chorale, played in the background:

Hail Carpathia, our lord and risen king;
Hail Carpathia, rules o'er everything.
We'll worship him until we die;
He's our beloved Nicolae.
Hail Carpathia, our lord and risen king.

• • •

Rayford hated that song and the infernal penchant of the Global Community Broadcasting System to play it over the radio at least every two hours. Carpathia insisted upon its performance at his every public appearance. The staged parades and rallies in his honor always began and ended with it.

Something strange was happening here, though. While the people seemed to rouse and slowly, agonizingly move toward the sound, no one sang along.

"Remember," Fortunato intoned, his words pinched when he grimaced from his own pain, "those of us servicing you, bringing you water and food, are also following the sound to the right places. Please be patient and allow push-carts to pass. There is plenty for everyone if we all work together. Now, sing along with the chorale. This takes the place of your worshiping our supreme potentate's image, currently not visible."

The people around Rayford were not encouraged. "I'm not singing," one said. "Death to the potentate!"

"Watch your mouth," another said. "You'll get yourself killed."

"Carpathia can't see any more than we can! He doesn't know who's talking."

"He's no mere mortal. I wouldn't be tempting fate."

"What has he done for *you* lately?"

Personnel inside the palace had a better time of it, Rayford assumed. They could at least feel their way to familiar places, including showers, beds, and refrigerators. Many outside couldn't even find their way back in. Rayford could only imagine the disorientation of zero light anywhere. It was frustrating enough to have been granted even diminished vision.

"There are twelve separate loudspeaker towers," Fortunato said, the music mercifully subdued as he spoke. "When supplies have arrived, please be as orderly as possible. State your name so our personnel can record it on audiodisc, and take your ration of food and water."

"We want answers too!" someone shouted as if Fortunato could hear. "What is this? How long will it last? Why does it hurt?"

• • •

Chloe knew what Ming Toy's response to this new danger would be in the morning. She and Ree Woo would want to marry right away. Everyone but Chloe had been trying to talk them out of it, but Ming had it all planned. She wanted Tsion Ben-Judah to officiate from Petra via video cam. "I know it's a lot to ask of such an important and busy man," she confided to Chloe. "But I have designed the ceremony to last just a few minutes."

"I think he'd do it," Chloe had told her. "I would if I were him."

The same people who urged Ming and Ree not to marry, given where things stood on the prophetic calendar, were the ones who had advised against Chloe and Buck having a child during the Tribulation. But certain matters were private issues of the heart. Chloe couldn't imagine not having married Buck, despite knowing how little time they had. And she couldn't get her mind around the concept of life without their precious little one.

If Ming and Ree wanted a year of marriage before the Glorious Appearing, whose business was it but theirs? It wasn't as if they were unaware of the hardships. Starting a family at this stage was another thing, of course, but Chloe figured that was none of her business either, unless Ming asked.

It seemed Buck was asleep again in seconds. She assumed George was right about his wife sleeping through his leaving their quarters. Priscilla was one of the busiest people in the compound, always up before dawn and rarely fully healthy. She often appeared groggy soon after dinner and was usually in bed by nine.

Chloe was glad to stand watch, if for no other

reason than to keep Buck from having to do it for the fourth night in a row. She enjoyed the routine—checking the motion detector, surveying the area with the periscope. Her daily job was hectic and demanding, spent almost entirely at the computer, contacting and coordinating suppliers and shippers of supplies and foodstuffs around the globe.

That was also her way of keeping up with the news, only the news kept getting worse. More and more of her contacts were being found out, caught by the GC in nighttime raids or at surprise checkpoints. As soon as it was discovered that these delivery people did not bear the mark of loyalty to Carpathia, they were executed.

One eyewitness reported that the Co-op driver of an eighteen-wheeler, laden with copies of Buck's *The Truth* magazine translated into Norwegian, refused to let his cargo fall into GC hands. Distracting checkpoint guards long enough for his backup driver to escape, he set the rig to roll out of control and plunge down a hundred-foot embankment into a deep fjord. Morale Monitors shot him to death.

Chloe also heard of dissidents around the world, Jews mostly, who, rather than being put to death, were transported to concentration camps where they were mercilessly tortured while purposely kept alive.

Occasional reports of miraculous interventions came, like an angel appearing at a guillotine site to warn the uncommitted of the consequences of choosing Carpathia's mark. Besides the fact that by now even the last-minute decision to take the mark was futile—tardy ones were put to death anyway—the angel had pleaded with the undecideds to choose Christ and be saved. And many did.

Chloe wrapped an afghan around her shoulders and moseyed to Kenny's room. His breathing was still deep and slow, and she draped another blanket over him. He did not stir.

Closing his door, she checked the motion detector, then sat before the periscope. With no evidence of anyone in the area, she could raise and rotate it for a full view. She rather liked having the contraption in the middle of her home. It satisfied some inner need to protect—control, Buck would have teased—her friends and loved ones, the more than two hundred who now lived underground in San Diego. All hoped to survive until the Glorious Appearing, but more than that, to also somehow make a difference from their claustrophobic warren.

A unique feature of the periscope was that the viewer did not have to move when it did. A simple control on the handgrips raised and lowered the contraption, as well as made it scan in a circle in either direction. Chloe didn't want to think about the series of mirrors required for that.

As she rested her forehead on the eyepiece and relaxed, letting her eyes adjust to the low light outside, she noticed that George Sebastian had left the scope at ground level and pointing west. The topside lens was camouflaged with fake shrubbery. It could be raised as much as five feet, but it was crucial to do a 360-degree scan at ground level first to be sure no one was in the vicinity who might notice.

The scan could be done all in one smooth motion at virtually any speed, but of course the San Diego Trib Force had learned that slower was better and easier on the eyes and equilibrium. Chloe's method of choice, however, was to move the mechanism one inch at a time. With each mash of a tiny red plunger on the left-hand grip, another one-inch turn of the lens brought a new 45-degree view; thus eight moves covered 360 degrees.

Seeing nothing due west, Chloe began her incremental scan to the right. It was just past three o'clock in the morning in California.

• • •

Rayford had walked perhaps a quarter of a mile north from the terminal, easily slipping past men and women clearly younger than he but who shuffled along with the painful gait of the elderly.

"In our effort to keep you totally informed," Fortunato announced, "we bring some encouraging news. While it remains true that no light is being emitted in New Babylon, this puzzling phenomenon has not affected telephone or radio transmission. Our heating and cooling systems remain functional. Your stoves even work, unless they are solar powered. Electric and gas stoves will still burn and radiate heat, though you will not see it, so be extremely careful.

"Pilots flying from New Babylon or toward her when this darkness occurred report that it is confined to the city. As we do not know how long this will last, be assured that if you can follow a path that leads you beyond our borders, you will eventually reach light."

From all around, Rayford heard determination on the parts of the sufferers. "I'm going," one said.

"Me too. I don't know where or how, but I'm getting to the light somehow."

"Does anyone have a Braille compass? We'll wander in circles without one."

"Attention," Fortunato broke in again, "all senior command personnel are to meet in the potentate's office at 1500 hours."

Rayford studied his watch. *It's one-fifteen. How are they going to pull that off by three in the afternoon?*

"Use audio clocks," Fortunato said. "It is now 1315 hours. At 1430 hours we shall turn off all loudspeakers except for the ones on the tower near the west entrance of the palace. Follow the sound there and you should be able to make your way to the meeting. Elevators are operational. The bottom right button is the top floor. Attendance is mandatory but limited to command-level personnel."

"I'm going anyway," someone said.

"So am I. Get to the bottom of this."

"Find out what the deal is."

"He's supposed to be god incarnate; why can't he do something?"

Rayford blinked, then blinked again. In the distance he thought he saw light. He was getting farther from the plane and from where Chang and Naomi and Abdullah were, but if worse came to worst, he could follow command personnel to the palace entrance at two-thirty and find his people from there. For now, he had to investigate the light.

● ● ●

Chloe was four clicks into her intermittent scan now, looking due east. As she studied the dark landscape she detected a pair of pinpricks of light. She held her breath as they became larger. Whatever they represented was drawing closer. Soon it became clear it was a car or truck. It rolled to within a block of the compound, stopped, and turned around. Now she saw only the red taillights. And there it sat. For ten minutes, then another five.

Chloe hurriedly scanned the rest of the way around. Nothing. One more click and she was back to the east section and the idle vehicle. No way she was going to wake Buck for this. It wasn't as if those in the compound expected no traffic outside. But there wasn't much else in the area, certainly nothing worth stopping for at this time of the night.

Chloe wished the periscope had a telescope feature so she could home in on the vehicle and see whether anyone was emerging. The compound's hidden vehicle bay, used only at night when they knew the area was clear, opened to the east. Dare she head that way for a closer look? An individual service door, hidden next to the big one, would allow her to peek out if she kept the inside lights off. She would be a hundred yards closer. And it wasn't like she was planning to actually venture outside.

Chloe pulled a black sweat suit with a hood from the closet and put it on over her pajamas and sweatshirt. Over thick woolen socks she laced high-top hiking boots. She took the Uzi but not the walkie-talkie. She didn't want any unintended transmission to give her away. And she did not intend to get herself into a situation where she'd need to call for help. The Uzi was just for peace of mind. So was the prayer: "Lord, help me or forgive me, one of the two."

Chloe quietly opened Kenny's door yet again. He hadn't moved. She felt his cheek. Moist with sleep but comfortably warm. She kissed his forehead. Cool and soft.

Shutting his door, she made her way to where Buck slept and planted a knee on the mattress next to his midsection. She leaned to kiss him, holding his head. If he were anything but sound asleep, that would have roused him. In the darkness Chloe was struck by the contrast between her dark clothing and her skin, which hardly ever saw the sun.

She found gloves and a ski mask, and by the time she was in the corridor that led past other underground quarters to the vehicle bay, Chloe was sweating. Their place was in the center of the complex, and four wings led to everyone else's places. She crept past the Sebastians', three other families' places, a bank of single men's residences—including Ree Woo's and her own father's—two more family places, then a mixture of family and single quarters, including Ming's.

Everybody knew Big George was on watch tonight and that Buck Williams, in charge when

Rayford was gone, was first alternate. That must have been why everyone seemed to be sleeping so soundly.

• • •

Rayford broke away from the tentative crowd and headed toward the light. Was it his imagination? Past twenty feet all was foggy anyway, and no one near him seemed able to see anything, let alone what he saw. The closer he got, the more the light appeared to be the silhouette of a person, but he saw nothing else and guessed it was still fifty yards away. When he had worked at the palace and lived nearby, the garages and motor pool had been in that area.

Had someone figured a way to produce light? Rayford had passed through small groups of limping people, and now it appeared nothing stood between him and this . . . this what? Apparition? It looked merely bright from a distance, but soon the color became more distinct. First red, then yellowish, and finally, a deep burnt orange. Yes, clearly a person, specifically a man, tall and lithe. And moving.

Others were within a few feet of the man, using his light to work on vehicles. They seemed in pain like everyone else, but they worked with dispatch, as if invigorated by the light. The glowing man appeared to be able to see as far as he radiated, about three feet. Anyone who needed light had to be that close to him.

Rayford realized it was Carpathia. Dr. Ben-Judah had often taught that this same person came first as a lying snake, then as a roaring lion, and finally as an angel of light. Rayford had to stifle a chuckle. The devil in Nicolae surely wished he could emit more than this pathetic glow that allowed him to identify only those within a few feet of him.

Rayford moved until he was among a small crowd just outside the circle of mechanics trying to ready several vehicles for some purpose he did not yet understand.

"All systems are functional?" Carpathia said.

"Yes, Potentate. The Jeep is operational."

"Turn on the lights."

The mechanic did. "You can hear the drain on the electrical system, so juice is flowing, Excellency, but as you can see—"

"As we can all see or not," Carpathia said, "no lights. Well, if I must, I will walk ahead of the convoy until we pass through the darkness on the way to Al Hillah. I do not care how long it takes."

What kind of a strategy was this? The brass will meet in Carpathia's office, and then he will lead them to Al Hillah? For what? And what about the thousands remaining in New

Babylon? Wouldn't they want to follow, to find relief?

"What's in Al Hillah?" Rayford said.

"Who is asking?" Carpathia said. "And why do you not address me with a title of honor?"

Nicolae was looking in Rayford's direction, but it was obvious he could see no farther than anyone else within range of his hellish aura. As Nicolae moved forward, Rayford moved back and to his left, then circled around behind Carpathia.

"Yeah," Rayford said in a slightly different tone. "What is in Al Hillah, O Great One?"

Nicolae whirled around, and Rayford slipped away again. "I was speaking to the original questioner! Who is asking?"

"Perhaps he fled in fear," Rayford said with a gravelly voice, "Excellency."

This could be fun.

● ● ●

Chloe had known the long passageway to the vehicle bay to be cold and damp most of the time, and perhaps it was now. But in her getup and in her state of mind, moving quickly up the incline past the vehicles and toward where the doors opened to ground level, she had grown uncomfortably warm. She removed her gloves and ski mask, chiding herself for having them on before she needed them anyway. Chloe lowered the zipper on the sweatshirt, then squatted to cool down and catch her breath with her back against the dirt wall between the bay door and the service door.

Being that close to the surface and the outside gave Chloe a delicious feeling of freedom. *Less than a year to real freedom.*

Her knees soon burned, so she slid to the earthen floor and straightened her legs. Setting her weapon aside, she reached for the toes of her boots, alternately stretching her right and left sides. Despite her many serious injuries, she was proud that her duties in Greece had proved she was still in remarkable shape. She zipped her sweatshirt to her neck, pulled the ski mask over her face, raised the hood over that, tugged on her gloves, put the strap of the Uzi over her head so the weapon rested on her right hip and in her right hand, then stood and turned to the service door.

There could be no slight opening of the bay door. That was an all or nothing deal. The glued-on sand and dirt and greenery moved as one, and the thing was either fully open or shut. But the service door, though camouflaged the same way, she could open as slowly and slightly as she wanted. She flipped off the light and gripped the doorknob.

• • •

Rayford hurried toward the palace. He wanted to check on the others and tell them of his plan. He had experienced more bizarre events in six years than he ever could have imagined, and while many had been bigger and louder and wilder, this was unique. These poor people! Yes, they had made their choices, and yes, they had had their opportunities to turn to God. But what a price!

They were in agony. Everywhere he went, more and more people came into the twenty-foot limit of his visibility. Many were dead. More sat rocking or lay weeping. All had given up looking for ways to see anything but a blackness so thick it disoriented them. Those who tried to follow the music or Fortunato's voice limped or shuffled with arms extended to the front or sides, tipping one way and then the other as if drunk or dizzy. They ran into each other, into buildings, tripped over debris, and many simply seemed to run out of gas, slowing, stopping, and tumbling. Rayford wished he could help, but there was nothing he could do.

On his way to Chang's quarters, Rayford came up with an idea and changed course. He stayed on the elevator and reached the top floor of the palace. There he tiptoed past several executives and their aides, who talked on phones or sat before computers, trying to dictate but unable to see whether their messages were getting through.

The phone calls all had the same theme and tone.

Carpathia had a new assistant since the time when Rayford had worked with him. Chang had told him her name. He assumed she was the one on the phone at the desk outside Carpathia's new office. Rayford noticed her double take when she heard him sit on a couch across from her area, but he said nothing and she continued her conversation.

"I don't know," she said with a whine. "He wants me to try to carry on as if I am not suffering like all the others. But I am, Mom. There are little things I can do when he is in here, because he emits this glow of some sort and I can at least find a few things. But he's called a meeting of the brass and they're planning some sort of a pilgrimage. . . . No, I don't get to go, and I don't want to. He's not even telling the rank and file that their bosses are leaving.

"Ooh! Ouch . . . oh, I don't know how to describe it. Cramps, I guess. A headache like nothing I've ever had, and I've had some doozies. . . ."

She sounded American, but her back was to Rayford and he could not see the number on her forehead or hand.

"And it feels as if I'm carrying a huge weight on my shoulders, pressing on my spine. My hips hurt, my knees, ankles, feet. Like your arthritis, I suppose. But, Mom, I'm thirty-six years old. I feel like I'm seventy-five. . . . Yes, I'm eating. I feel my way back to my apartment and I can manage, but when I lie down, I want to sleep for a hundred years. But I can't. . . . Well, because of the pain! No position relieves it. It's like this darkness itself is pushing on me and causing all this, and it's the same for everybody."

Rayford shifted his weight and the woman froze. "Hold a minute, Mom." She turned and Rayford saw the –6 on her forehead, confirming his guess. The United North American States. "Is someone there? May I help you?"

He was tempted to tell her he had some questions about the meeting but that he would wait until she was off the phone. But he knew she knew who was left on the decimated senior staff, and she would not recognize his voice. He wished he could speak soothingly to her, to say something Jesus would say. But she was beyond help now. Rayford had never felt so hog-tied.

"Sorry, Mom," she said. "Now I'm hearing things. I'd better get off. This meeting's coming up, and I don't even know what he's going to want. No one will be able to read anything unless they hold it up to his light, and there are twenty expected. . . . Yes, twenty. . . . I know. . . . Yeah, we're down from thirty-six. Imagine.

"Exciting? No. Not for a long time. He is not the man I thought he was. . . . Oh, in every way. Mean, cruel, vicious, egotistical, selfish. I swear, I'd need a thesaurus. . . . Well, I can't! . . . No! Of course I can't! Where would I go? What would I do? He knows what I know, and he wouldn't be able to let me out of his control. . . . No, now I just have to live with it. . . . I don't know, Mom. It can't end well. I don't care anymore. Death will be a relief. . . . Well, I'm sorry, but I mean it. . . . Now don't, Mom. I'm not planning anything rash. . . . I know you have. We all have. All but Uncle Gregory, I guess. He's still holding out, is he? . . . How does he live? You know what happens if he's found out. . . . No, don't tell me. I don't want to know. That way if somebody asks, I'll be able to tell them I don't know. Just tell him I'm proud of him and keep it up, but be careful. You and Dad be careful too. If you're caught aiding him in any way . . ."

Rayford heard footsteps in the hall, and it was clear she did too. "Gotta go, Mom. Stay well."

She hung up and turned when the door swung open. A big, bony man of about fifty looked wide-eyed at Rayford and his mouth fell open.

He pointed at Rayford's forehead, and Rayford noticed the mark of the believer on him too.

"May I help you?" Carpathia's assistant said. "Who is it?"

Rayford held a finger to his lips and pointed down the hall. He mouthed, "Five minutes," and the man shut the door and ran off.

The woman shrugged. "Thanks for dropping by," she muttered, "whoever you were."

"Whoever it was has left," Rayford said.

She jumped. "And how long have you been here?"

"Long enough to know about Uncle Gregory."

"I'm so stupid! I don't know you, do I?"

"No."

"You're not senior staff."

"I'm not."

"Is anyone with you?"

"No, Krystall."

"How do you know my name?"

"I can help your uncle."

"Tell a soul, I'll deny every word."

"Don't you want him helped?"

"You're trying to trap me."

"I'm not. If I was GC, I would not be able to see, would I?"

"You can't see."

"I can. And I can prove it. Your colors don't match."

"You couldn't prove that by me, idiot. I can't see them either. I dress by sense of touch these days, like everybody else."

"My mistake. Hold up some fingers; I'll tell you how many. . . . Three, and your right hand is facing me, and the three fingers are your pinkie, ring, and middle."

"How do you know that?"

"You mean how can I see?"

"You can't see."

"Then how do I know you're showing me six fingers now, all five on your left and the index on your right, the backs of your hands toward me? I can see by your face you're starting to be convinced. You're hiding your hands under the desk now."

Krystall pressed her lips together and looked as if she was about to cry. Rayford stood.

"Stay where you are," she said, voice quavery, hands in her lap.

Rayford slipped around behind her. "That would be no fun," he said, and she jumped and spun in her chair. "Now I can see your hands again," he said. "They're balled in your lap, thumbs pointing."

"Okay, so you can see me. How?"

"Because this darkness is a curse from God, and I am one of his."

"Are you serious?"

"I can help your uncle, Krystall."

"How?"

"Were you implying he has not yet taken the mark?"

"What if I was?"

"Then it's not too late for him. Is he a believer in Christ?"

"I don't think so. I think he's just a rebel."

"A lucky one, if he acts quickly."

"If you think you're going to trick me into telling you where he's hiding, you're—"

"I don't need to know that. You'd be foolish to risk telling me, and anyway, didn't you tell your mother not to even tell you where he was?"

She didn't respond.

"If you really want to help him, tell him to log on to the Web site of Dr. Tsion Ben-Judah. Can you remember it if I spell it for you?"

"You think I don't know that name and how to spell it?"

"Sorry."

"It's from his Web site that I know it's too late for me and my parents, my whole family . . . who were so proud of me."

"I'm sorry, Krystall."

"You're sorry? How do you think I feel?"

"Ma'am, you're not going to tell anyone I was here, are you?"

"Why would I? They couldn't see you anyway, and what would they do? Feel around for you?"

"Good point."

"What are you doing here?"

"Business. The prospect of helping your uncle was just a bonus."

"Well, thanks for that. You're a Judah-ite, eh?"

"A believer in Christ, to be more precise."

"Tell me something then: what's the deal with it being too late for people who already took Carpathia's mark? We don't still have our own free will?"

Rayford felt his throat tighten. "Apparently not," he managed. "I don't quite understand it myself, but you have to admit, you had plenty of reasons to choose the other way."

"For years."

"You said it, Krystall."

"So the statute of limitations ran out on me when I made the big choice."

"Well, then for sure. Maybe even before that. Who knows the mind of God?"

"I'm starting to, sir."

"How's that?"

"This hurts. It hurts worse than the pain from the darkness. Just learned it too late, I guess, that you don't mess with God."

THREE

THE PROBLEM with the camouflaged service door open just a sliver was that it did not give Chloe the view she needed. While the door faced east, where the suspicious vehicle had stood idling just a block away last time she looked, the opening in the door gave her only a northeast view. The door would have to swing open to at least forty-five degrees to confirm that the car or truck or whatever it was was still there. Dare she risk the door catching a glint from a street lamp or making a sound or triggering some portable motion detector the GC might have brought along?

Chloe allowed herself to wish that the vehicle brought good news rather than bad. Maybe it bore a band of other underground believers who had heard about the Trib Force contingent that had burrowed itself beneath a former military base. Wouldn't that be heaven, to discover more brothers and sisters who could come alongside to help, encourage, and defend? It was Chloe who had stumbled upon The Place in Chicago with its exciting band of self-taught believers. On the other hand, all that activity, their moving in with the Trib Force, was the first step in compromising the safe house. That many warm bodies moving about in an area the GC had believed was quarantined tipped them off and brought them sniffing. If Chloe was to take credit for the new friends, she had to accept the heat for the end of a great safe house.

She couldn't let that happen again. There were too many here, and though the place was under the earth, it had all the advantages the Strong Building had. For one thing, it had George Sebastian, who had expanded on what Chloe—and anyone else who was interested—had learned about combat training from Mac McCullum on their mission to Greece. The rickety exercise equipment George and Priscilla had salvaged from the military base was anything but state-of-the-art, but George thought that was an advantage.

"The newfangled machines do all the work for ya, anyway," he said. He had refurbished and lubricated what was available, and within six weeks several Trib Forcers had spent enough time in a makeshift workout room to start toning neglected muscles. That was just a prerequisite, of course. What Chloe enjoyed most was George's training. A lot of it was just common sense, but a lot of it wasn't. He had been trained at the highest levels and proved to be an excellent teacher. Chloe felt she could handle herself and a weapon in almost any situation.

That training was what niggled at the back of her brain now and told her she was making a fundamental mistake. Not only was she away from her post, but no one would have a clue where she was. She had no way of communicating from a remote location. So if she was going to open the service door wide enough to see a potential enemy a block away or—for all she knew—standing directly in front of her, she had to make a decision. Was she opening the door quickly to step outside and shut it again, or was she going to keep a hand on the doorknob in case she needed to retreat fast?

She pressed her ear against the door to see if she could detect movement nearby, but her Uzi clattered against it, and her ear was covered by her sweatshirt hood and ski mask anyway. She pulled back, feeling like an idiot. *Deep breath. Calm down. Let's just step outside in one smooth motion and shut the door behind us.* Referring to herself in the collective *we* made her feel less alone, but she knew she was kidding herself.

Careful to take full, quiet strides, rolling heel to toe, Chloe pushed the door open, moved out, and shut it behind her. Was the vehicle still there? She'd have to wait a beat. If it was, its taillights were off. Chloe moved to a row of tall bushes that hid her from the east, then spun silently to be sure no enemy had flanked her from another direction. She paused for a moment to drink in the freedom of simply being out in the crisp wee-hour air.

As her eyes adjusted to the dim light provided only by street lamps, Chloe peered through the shrubbery and saw the white GC personnel carrier parked where she had seen it from inside. Not only were its lights off, but it also didn't appear to be idling.

The question was whether it was empty, and if so, how many troops had it brought, and where were they?

● ● ●

Rayford quickly tiptoed to the end of the corridor and found the big man rocking on the balls of his feet and wringing his hands. "English?" he said with a thick German accent.

"Yes. I'm an American."

"Brother, brother, brother!" the man whispered, grabbing Rayford in a fierce embrace. "Who are you? What is your name? What are you doing here?"

The man felt solid, as if he could have been a manual laborer. "I have the same questions for you, friend," Rayford said, extricating himself. "But let's make sure we won't be overheard."

"Good, good, yes. Where?"

"I have colleagues in private quarters here. You need to meet them. We can talk there."

"I'm not sure I can wait that long! This is so exciting. How far?"

"Six stories down and a wing the other way," Rayford said, leading him toward the elevator.

"You live here? In the palace, I mean? You work here?"

"Used to." Rayford looked around and then leaned close. "I'm with the underground in San Diego with connections in Petra. We're getting our mole out of here while we can."

"I was going to ask if *you* were the mole!"

"Used to be one of several. We are down to just this one, or at least that's what we thought. You're from here?"

"Not six miles away, can you believe it?"

At the bank of elevators three executives stood lightly touching each other and feeling for the buttons. Rayford and his new friend looked at each other knowingly and merely moved behind them into the first available elevator car.

"Got to be back up here on time," one executive said.

"Yes," another said. "Wish I had an audible watch."

"I took the crystal off mine. I'm learning to feel what time it is. Problem is, I keep snagging the hands on who knows what, and for all I know, I don't have the right time anymore myself." He pressed two fingers lightly on his watch. "I'm guessing 2:50. Gives us ten minutes."

Rayford noticed the German check his own watch and raise his eyebrows. The elevator stopped two floors down, and the three felt their way off. But as the doors were shutting, Rayford's companion reached out with both hands, tapped the timekeeper on a shoulder, and rubbed his thumb against the man's watch at the same time. The tap made him hesitate, which made the man behind him bump into him. He said, "Hm?" and the third man said, "What?"

The big man pulled his arms back in, in time for the doors to shut unimpeded, and when it was just he and Rayford on the elevator, he burst into laughter. "I think that was the last time he'll have the time right, you know? Now, may I introduce myself?"

"Not just yet," Rayford said. He mouthed, "Most of the elevators and corridors are bugged."

• • •

Foolhardy or brave? Chloe knew that was a matter of opinion and that she would likely hear from many who assumed the former. But she was desperately curious about that personnel carrier, and even more, about the personnel. Keeping to the tree line and away from street lamps, she circled left and headed a block west, moving silently in the night as she had been taught.

She slowed as she came even with the vehicle from about thirty yards to the left of it, chastising herself for not bringing binoculars. And the walkie-talkie. She could have left it off until she needed it, avoiding an inopportune transmission while still having the ability to communicate with Buck or anyone else in a pinch.

So far though, no pinch. Chloe moved closer, telling herself that if anyone sat in the truck the engine would be running or one or more windows would be open. None of that was so, but she didn't want to think she could simply advance past it without knowing for sure. First turning in a slow circle to be sure no one was approaching or that she had not missed anyone, Chloe finally reached the truck and peered in the back windows. No one.

But from there she could not tell if anyone was in the front seat. If anyone was waiting, he or she would most likely be behind the wheel. She approached from the other side, staying below the window level until she could stand quickly and take her prey by surprise, if necessary.

• • •

Rayford was stunned by the increased number of ailing residents who filled the halls as he and his new buddy left the elevator and headed toward Chang's quarters. Couples huddled in corners, weeping. Others crawled, feeling their way to various rooms, pulling themselves up by door handles and running their fingers across numbers before knocking, pleading with friends to be let in.

"This breaks my heart," he whispered to the German.

"Not mine," the man said, "but I'm working on it."

Rayford knocked lightly on Chang's door and heard the conversation inside die. "It's me," he said, just above a whisper. "And don't be alarmed. I have someone with me."

Abdullah opened the door just wide enough to accommodate one eye and the barrel of a .45-caliber Glock. That eye, satisfied with seeing Rayford, surveyed the German side to side and head to toe. Apparently noticing the mark of the believer on the man's forehead, Abdullah swung the door open.

Once inside, it seemed the man couldn't be still. After looking at everyone and the computers and stacks of miniature disks, he said, "I can talk? We are okay here?"

Chang nodded and, though he seemed overwhelmed by the man's effusiveness, he and Naomi kept working.

"Otto Weser is my name," he said. "German timberman, Judah-ite, head of a small band of believers right here in New Babylon."

He embraced Abdullah. "Watch that side arm now, would you?" Otto said, laughing. He nearly lifted Chang off the floor. "Look at us! You are Asian. Our turbaned friend is, what, Egyptian?" Abdullah corrected him. "Ah, Jordanian. I was close. I am German. Mr. Steele, your name is Western and you told me you were American, but your appearance is Egyptian also."

"A disguise."

"And the young lady, you are Middle Eastern too, are you not? Of course you are. I will not hug you without the permission of your father."

Otto pointed first to Rayford, who shook his head, and then to Abdullah, who looked insulted. "Oh, you are old enough even if she is not yours." He turned to Chang. "I know she does not belong to you, unless by marriage."

Naomi approached him, arms spread. "My

father is not here, but if the permission is mine to give, you have it."

"Ah, I love the young ones who appreciate the old movies."

When he had learned everyone's name, Otto said, "I will be brief. I know you are on a mission and you must go. I did not know if I would find any brothers or sisters inside the palace, but I am so glad I did. My friends and I, we consider ourselves fulfillments of prophecy. Do you want to know why? We were holed up in Germany, hiding mostly but fighting the GC when we could, and God—who else?—led me to Revelation 18. It dumbfounded me; what else can I say? You know the passage. I have it memorized.

"I'm no scholar, no student, no theologian, but I try to stay a step ahead of my people so I can teach them a little. Well, Revelation 18 talks about the coming destruction of this city, this one right here. Beginning at the fourth verse it says, 'I heard another voice from heaven saying, "Come out of her, my people, lest you share in her sins, and lest you receive of her plagues. For her sins have reached to heaven, and God has remembered her iniquities. Render to her just as she rendered to you, and repay her double according to her works; in the cup which she has mixed, mix double for her. In the measure that she glorified herself and lived luxuriously, in the same measure give her torment and sorrow; for she says in her heart, 'I sit as queen, and am no widow, and will not see sorrow.' Therefore her plagues will come in one day—death and mourning and famine. And she will be utterly burned with fire, for strong is the Lord God who judges her."'

"Well, you could have knocked me over. 'Come out of her, my people'? What were we to make of that except the obvious? People of God—at least some—were going to be here until just before this happens! Who were they? I could not imagine believers being here, and if they were, not for long. How could they be? If the GC and the Morale Monitors are killing people all over the world for not bearing the mark of Carpathia, what chance would someone stand here?

"We didn't know, but we wanted to find out, and I tell you, playing hide-and-seek with the GC in Germany was getting old. Nearly forty of us packed up and headed this way—no easy trip, I want to say. It has not been easy living here either, but we knew it would not be when we came. We have lost six of our members since we have been here—four all at once, and two, I have to say, were my fault, to my eternal shame. But we will see them again, will we not? And I cannot wait.

"Something else I could not wait for was this plague of darkness. When it came and we realized that everyone was blind but us, I got it in my head I wanted to see this place—the compound, the courtyard, the palace and all—especially the potentate's office. I could not get any of the others to come with me, so here I am, and who should I run into but you? Well, if we are fulfilling prophecy by being at least some of God's people who must come out of here before the end, you are an answer to prayer if I ever saw one. We need a place to go if we are to come out, and what better place than where we will finally be safe? If you have connections at Petra, that is where we want to be, if they will have us."

"Excuse me, Rayford," Chang said. "This is all very interesting and exciting, but I need to show Naomi the, you know, inner workings David set up here, and then I think we need to get going."

"Right," Rayford said, "and I'll feel more comfortable if Abdullah stays with you two. I want to head back to Carpathia's office and see if Otto and I can crash the big meeting and see what's going on."

"Oh! I'd love that! As I said, I wanted to see his office anyway. That's why I was there when you were, but I was so startled to see someone with the mark of the be—"

"Otto," Rayford said, "we've got to move."

• • •

Chloe had crouched by the passenger-side door long enough to almost talk herself out of what she planned. What if she rose into view of a driver waiting for his charges? She likely had the drop on him, and then what was she going to do? Disarm him? Keep him from the radio? Make him tell her where his people were and what they were up to? That would do nothing but give away the underground compound unless Chloe was willing to kill the man and try to run off the rest of them—provided he told the truth about where they were.

She finally told herself that if the truck was empty, she would merely make one wide reconnaissance loop around the compound to make sure the GC weren't close or on to them or about to be; then she would head back for help.

Chloe released the safety on the Uzi, put her right index finger on the trigger, cradled the barrel in her other palm, and rose quickly.

Empty.

And so was she. She had been unaware of the effects of the adrenaline on her since she had ventured out of the service door, but the resultant crash of her system left her nearly immobile. She slumped by the truck to gather herself. Her arms and legs felt rubbery, and had Chloe's senses not been on such high alert, she believed she could have tucked her chin to her chest and slept.

Though she couldn't escape the feeling she was being watched—she imagined at least nine GC with scopes trained on her—she felt remarkably lucky, given how serendipitous her plan had been. That is to say, she hardly had a plan. And while she agreed with the Tribulation Force's motto—"We don't do luck"—it was difficult to attribute her safety so far to God when she felt so foolish for how she had again tested her destiny.

Chloe rose and began her scouting ring of the perimeter. As she moved silently in the darkness, feeling vulnerable and trying to be more thorough than quick, all she was aware of was the pace of her breathing and her thundering pulse.

• • •

By the time Rayford and Otto reached Carpathia's suite of offices, the meeting had begun and the stragglers spilled out of the doorway of his conference room. Rayford saw Carpathia's wretched glow, but it was obvious that only Leon Fortunato stood close enough to the man to take advantage of it.

Rayford gently put his hands on men in the doorway, and they gave way to let him slip through, Otto following. To be safe, they moved to the far end of the room, away from Carpathia.

The potentate asked Krystall to call the roll, which she did almost entirely from memory. When she drew a blank on the last three names, she asked if she could read the rest of the list in Carpathia's light.

"Better simply to have those whose names have not been called identify themselves," Nicolae said.

As they were doing that, Otto touched Rayford's arm and mouthed that he was tempted to call out his own name and see what kind of havoc that might wreak.

"If you gentlemen would kindly attempt to keep your outbursts to a minimum," Carpathia began, "Director of Security and Intelligence Suhail Akbar has the first item."

"Thank you, Excellency. Oh! Forgive me, sir, but I am in pain as well. Ah!"

"Suhail, please!"

"Apologies, Highness, but I don't know what to—"

"Control yourself, man!"

"I shall try, sir. Our primary concern, ladies and gentlemen, besides the obvious, is that a—"

"What's more important than the obvious?" someone with an Indian accent said. "We've got to find a solution to this—"

"Who is that?" Carpathia demanded. "Raman Vajpayee, is that you?"

"Yes, sir, I simply want to know—"

"Raman, I simply want you to be quiet. How dare you interrupt a member of my cabinet?"

"Well, sir, it is most important that—"

"What is most important is that the only response to your offense is an abject apology, and it had better be immediately forthcoming."

"I am sorry, Potentate, but—"

"That was hardly abject. At a time of international crisis, I cannot imagine such insubordination. I am of a mind—"

"To what?" Vajpayee said. "To put me to death as you do anyone who speaks his mind? I tell you, I would rather be dead than to live like this! In the dark! In pain! No relief in sight. And yet you carry on—"

"Show yourself, Raman! Do it now!"

The Indian rushed forward, pushing others out of his way. It was clear to Rayford that he was simply following the sound of Carpathia's voice, unable to see even the glow. "I am here, within arm's length of you! Kill me for daring to speak my mind, or reveal yourself as a coward!"

"Suhail," Carpathia said, "take this man out and execute him!"

"So you *are* a coward! You will not do it yourself! At least give me that much respect."

"I have only contempt for you, Raman. You

have disgraced your position with the Global Community and I—"

"Kill me yourself, you impotent—"

And with that, Carpathia thrust himself toward the Indian, finally allowing both to see one another. As the others listened in horror, the two men struggled, and Carpathia succeeded in getting the man's head in his hands. With a violent twist he broke Vajpayee's neck, and the dead man slid to the floor.

"Any other dissidents?" Carpathia said. "Anyone who would rather be dead than suffer for the cause? Hmm? If not, Suhail, proceed, and when you are finished, get this corpse out of here."

Somehow a shaken Akbar was able to control his own outcries of pain as he reported that an aircraft had landed at the New Babylon airstrip that very afternoon. "We can only assume it was a miracle of autopiloting," he said, "but we have no record of what plane it is and urge caution on everyone's part, as we may have subversives among us."

"If we cannot accomplish having the occupants of that plane identify themselves," Carpathia said, "I will personally inspect it at the end of this meeting."

"That's our cue," Rayford whispered to Otto. "We've got to be out of here before then."

As they began to surreptitiously make their

way out of the room, Carpathia continued. "As you know, I am determined to put an end to our Jewish problem, and if that includes the cowardly Judah-ites who remain hidden in the mountains, so much the better. I am hereby calling for a meeting of all ten heads of the global regions in six months' time. We shall meet in Baghdad to map our strategy to rid the world of our enemies. Meanwhile, we will move our command post into the light at Al Hillah. As many of you know—and if this is news to you, I expect full confidentiality—Al Hillah is the location of our vast storehouse of nuclear weaponry, voluntarily surrendered to us by the rest of the world as a condition of my accepting my position. That will prove most useful to us in this ultimate effort and final solution.

"Until the rest of the world is on the same page with me, I plan to begin amassing fighting forces in Israel. All available military personnel in the United Carpathian States who are not already assigned as Peacekeepers or Morale Monitors will be expected to report for duty in the Jezreel Valley for combat training.

"As for our relocation to Al Hillah, be ready to move out in twenty-four hours. Take anything that will assist you in this transfer."

"What about our workers, our departments?"

"They will stay, and they must not know

where we are going or even that we are going. Is that understood?"

Rayford was just outside the door when he heard that no one had responded.

"Understood?"

"Yes," a few muttered.

"Then go about your business. Mr. Akbar, Reverend Fortunato, and I will make our way to the airstrip."

Rayford motioned for Otto to follow, and he began running toward the elevators. "Call every car and push every button on each. Stall those elevators for as long as you can. I'll take the stairs. I have no idea where my friends are, but I need to leave a note at Chang's place in case they head back there. We have to be out of here before Carpathia finds out the identity of our plane and where we are. Got it?"

"Got it. Thanks for trusting me."

"Were you hoping to come with us? Because unless you can get—"

"No, we'll arrange that later. I wouldn't come without my people anyway."

"If you happen to see any of my friends before I do, send them to the plane."

Rayford bounded down the stairs, drawing screams and squeals from people suffering in the stairwells. They called out, asking how he could run like that in the dark. He hated ignoring them.

He reached the main level, vaulted over several people, and zigzagged between others. He burst out the door and sprinted across the runways toward the plane. If he could get it started and turned around, all he could do was hope and pray that Chang, Naomi, and Abdullah were on their way.

• • •

Buck had been sound asleep for hours before something began troubling him. He grew fitful and was suddenly wide awake. It was guilt. Letting Chloe take watch duty when she worked so hard all day with the Co-op and their son. What kind of a husband was he?

He ran his hands through his hair and sat up, calling out. "How's it going, babe?"

Maybe she was checking on Kenny. Or getting herself some tea in the kitchen. He padded out of the bedroom, stretching. "Chlo'!" he called out. "You've got something on the motion detector here!"

He bent over the periscope and scanned quickly. He saw nothing until he got to the southwest, where he saw a lone figure, armed. He scowled. "Chloe!" he called. "Better call George. I've got a bogey at eight o'clock. Chloe?"

He froze. He stood and moved toward the kitchen. It was dark. And Kenny was crying.

Buck grabbed the phone on his way to Kenny's room and punched in Ming's number.

"Hey, big boy," Buck said, finding the boy standing in his bed, quickly going from crying to smiling.

"Mama?"

"In a minute," he said. "Why don't you lie down and go back to sleep. It's still night."

Ming answered.

"I'm so sorry to wake you, Ming, but I've got a little emergency here."

"Anything, Buck."

"Could you watch Kenny for a little while? I think Chloe is outside."

"Be there in less than a minute."

He thanked her and got on the walkie-talkie. "George, you up?"

FOUR

RAYFORD HAD the engines started and the plane turned around when he saw Carpathia's glow in the distance. The potentate seemed in a hurry, but he was apparently leading Suhail Akbar and Leon Fortunato, and he had to go slowly to light the way for them a few feet at a time. That would not have been as much help without the sounds of the jet engines, however, so Rayford shut down and prayed that this mostly blind threesome would veer off course before his own trio found him.

Rayford turned on his cell phone and called Mac McCullum in Al Basrah to debrief him. "Can you and Albie leave for Al Hillah today?"

"We been sittin' here like a past-due hen."

"I'll take that as a yes. You're pretty hot since Greece. How are you going to get around?"

"With bluster, charm, and only at night, of

course. I figure you pretty much just want to know what NC and his boys are up to."

"Ideal would be your finding out where they're meeting in Baghdad and bugging the place for us."

"Oh, sure. I'll just tell 'em I'm his new valet and can I have a few hours in the meeting room before everyone else gets there."

"If I thought it was easy, I'd do it myself," Rayford said.

"Albie knows everybody. If it's gonna get done, he'll get it done."

Chang, Naomi, and Abdullah appeared, each laden with boxes and cases. Naomi looked ashen. Rayford opened the door and lowered the steps. "Good timing," he said.

"We were on it all the way, Captain," Abdullah said. "Thanks to this young genius."

"Just showing off," Chang said, handing cargo in and helping Naomi aboard. "I wanted to show her how David had bugged the whole place and that we could actually listen in on Carpathia."

"So you knew he was coming," Rayford said, letting Abdullah edge past to the pilot's chair.

"Could we please talk about something else?" Naomi said.

That made everyone uncomfortably quiet. Rayford sneaked a peek. The pale orange silhouette was moving more quickly now. He must have abandoned Akbar and Fortunato or they were ailing anew. The pain didn't seem to reach Carpathia. Maybe God was saving his best till last for him.

Rayford and Abdullah eschewed a formal checklist for a quick confirmation of the cockpit flow by checking the critical switch positions. "Crank 'er up," Rayford said.

But Abdullah just sat there, craning his neck to watch the glow grow larger as it neared the plane.

"What're you waiting on, Smitty? Let's move out."

"A moment, please, Captain. How far do you assume he can see?"

"About as far as he glows. Now let's go."

"A moment, please."

"What are you doing, Mr. Smith?" Naomi called out. "Isn't that Carpathia?"

"He does not know where he is going. But I do."

"Once we start up, he can do nothing," Rayford said. "But I'd rather he not know who we are."

"He won't," Abdullah said.

Rayford leaned past Abdullah and saw Carpathia hurry across the runway about twenty feet behind the craft.

"Here we go," Abdullah said, firing up the

engines and blowing the orange glow to the ground over and over until Nicolae was just an ember in the distance.

Once in the air, Naomi leaned forward. "Can I talk to you?" she said. Rayford removed his headphones.

"Is that stuff normal for you guys?" she said.

"Nothing's normal anymore, Naomi. You've been through a lot yourself."

"I never heard a man being murdered before. And I've never walked by so many hurting people without a thing I could do for them. We're isolated in Petra, and I wanted to be where the action is. But if I never see anything else like this, it'll be all right with me. And we can do more from our computer center than anywhere I can think of."

"I'm sorry it was hard," Rayford said. "It was for me too." He told her of the woman he had tried to help and of his conversation with Nicolae's assistant.

"We'll watch for her uncle's name on the system," she said. "And I suppose we'll hear from Mr. Weser too."

"Hope so. What a character."

She leaned closer, and while she had to raise her voice over the engines, Naomi seemed to speak so only Rayford could hear. "Chang's not doing well, you know."

"Why's that?"

"This has been his home, crazy as it's had to have been. It's got to be strange leaving."

"I should think he'd be glad to be gone."

"I wish I could have met Mr. Hassid, the one Chang talks about so much. What they did in the palace and the setup at our place . . ."

Rayford nodded. "You going to be able to do the same thing—monitor this place—from Petra now?"

"With Chang, yes. It's going to be wonderful to have him in our shop."

"Is he going to be competition?"

"Hardly. I'll just let him do what he wants. He likes the technical stuff, keyboarding and inside the box, more than managing people. But he can teach if he wants to."

Rayford's phone chirped. It was George Sebastian. "Been trying to get hold of you. Your phone down?"

"Had it off for the palace mission. I was going to report in when I knew you guys were up. It's still early there, isn't it?"

"We've got a situation."

"Why are you whispering? Where are you?"

"Outside."

"What time is it there?"

"Just before five in the morning. We can't find Chloe."

• • •

It hit Buck that the figure on the periscope had been Chloe, so where was she? It was just like her to be out without a walkie-talkie or a phone, which he attributed to strategy rather than impetuousness. He would have a hard time convincing anyone else of that, though.

He and George had split up, fully armed and in constant touch with each other. George had found the empty GC personnel carrier—which had to be some sort of a decoy—but no GC or Chloe. Buck hoped he wouldn't have to call for more help and further expose his people or their location.

Two hours later, when the sun left Buck and George with no choice but to retreat inside, they had covered two square miles with nothing to show for it. In the compound, everybody was up, worried, praying, and eager to be brought up to speed. Ming Toy took Kenny and George's daughter, Beth Ann, to her place "for as long as is necessary."

George and Priscilla set up a command center in the workout room. Ree Woo sat at a small folding table in the corner, digging through files to see if any of their aliases had been underused or uncompromised.

Buck admitted he was going to be of little help. "I'm paralyzed."

"Snap out of it," George said. "You do Chloe and us no good that way."

Buck glared at him, knowing he was right. "Easy for you to say, Sebastian. It's not your wife out there."

Priscilla looked away. George let his papers fall on a table and approached Buck. He put a hand on each arm of Buck's chair and leaned close to his face. "I'm only gonna say it once. If it was my wife out there, I wouldn't be sitting in here with my hands in my lap. I owe your wife big time. She risked her life for me in Greece. I can only imagine how you feel. Not knowing anything is worse than knowing the worst, but we know nothing. Maybe you're just a little mad at her because she didn't seem to follow protocol and skipped a lot of steps here.

"Maybe you're feeling guilty about being angry with her because you're scared to death she's into something over her head. I don't blame you. I don't. I'm telling you, we need everybody on this, especially somebody with your brain. Now, you want to find her so we can get her back safe and sound, or you want to assume the worst and start grieving now?"

"George!" Priscilla scolded.

"I'm not trying to be a hard case," George said. "It's just that there's nothing we can do outside in the daylight unless we know the coast is clear and we've got someone with a good disguise and alias. Meanwhile, we've got to rest and strategize, and we don't need Buck sitting here feeling sorry for hims—"

"All right, George, I got it! Okay?"

"You and I are all right then?"

"Of course."

"I mean, you think I was out there in the middle of the night for my health?"

"Not so good news," Ree said. "Chloe's 'Chloe Irene' and Mac's 'Howie Johnson' are no good after Greece. Hannah's 'Indira Jinnah' might still be okay, but only she can use it and she's too far away. Rayford and Abdullah's Middle Eastern brothers IDs may still be okay, but Abdullah is staying in Petra and Rayford will need R and R when he gets here."

"Don't be so sure," George said. "He'll go till he drops."

"Tell me about it," Buck said.

"Has Albie's 'Commander Elbaz' been exposed yet?" Ree asked.

Buck nodded. "Unfortunately, yes."

"Too far away too," George said. "What else have we got?"

"One more. Ming's guy persona, 'Chang Chow.'"

"Let's not risk Ming," Buck said.

"Why not?" George said. "She's still got the uniform. She can cut her hair and—"

"Hey!" Ree said. "You're talking about my fiancée."

"So?"

"She at least ought to be consulted."

"No, Ree," George said. "I thought we'd just drag her in here, hold her down, and cut her hair."

"Cool down, boys," Priscilla said. "Nobody knows who I am. I could be given an alias and—"

"No you don't," George said.

"Shoe's on the other foot now, eh?" Buck said. "Prospect of sending your wife out there—"

"Stop it!" George said. "I'm just saying she's inexperienced and not all that healthy."

"Ming is not very physical," Ree said. "Not trained in weapons."

"Don't give me that," Buck said. "She worked at Buffer."

"Handling inmates at a women's prison is not like rescuing one of our people from the local GC."

"We wouldn't be looking for her to do that anyway," George said. "Buck and I and maybe you, Ree, would have to go get Chloe. We need Ming, or somebody, just to find out where she is."

• • •

Chloe had caught sight of two more GC vehicles, both moving, to the south as she was in the middle of her loop around the compound. As she watched, both trucks stopped and more than half a dozen troops disembarked from each. It became clear that they were walking a carefully planned grid to check for hidden encampments. And the underground safe house was in their path. They may have looked bored to Buck through the periscope a few hours before, but something had sent them for reinforcements.

These guys were serious. They had metal detectors, probes, and what appeared to be Geiger counters. Chloe debated whether she had time to race back to the compound to alert the others. If she erred, she could lead these guys right to her door.

Determined to distract them and knock them off course, she started moving again. She had to make them see her without appearing to want that. She moved stealthily, but with a purpose.

Rather than take a right at the edge of the property and circle back to the entrance, Chloe continued west on the south side. When she heard at least one of the vehicles heading her way, she broke into a trot, then a jog, then a full run. She was not going to outrun a truck, but maybe she could go where it couldn't.

The Uzi, light as it was, weighed her down. Unless she believed she could take on an entire platoon or two of GC with it, it made more sense to ditch it and come back for it later. She would never be able to explain a weapon like that. With the sound of a truck, and maybe two of them, just a block south and closing fast, Chloe detoured and flung the Uzi and her ski mask behind some trees. She picked up her pace and sprinted about a quarter of a mile, succeeding in getting both trucks to bear down on her.

Chloe was out of sight of the underground complex and decided the best approach was indifference, so she kept her head down and kept running. The lead truck pulled up beside her, but she didn't even turn to look. From the passenger-side window a young woman called out, "Need a lift?"

"No thanks."

"Get in."

"No thanks. I'm good."

"We want to ask you a few questions."

"Go ahead."

"C'mon, stop and let us talk to you."

"Talk to me anyway."

"Where you from?"

"About six miles west."

"That was underwater from the tsunami not that long ago."

"How well I know."

"What're you doing down here?"

"Running."

"How'd you get here?"

"Ran."

"Where you going?"

"Home."

"What's your name?"

"Phoebe." *It sounds biblical.*

"Phoebe what?"

"Phoebe Evangelista."

"Ethnic?"

"Husband is." *He's a WASP.*

"Have any ID?"

"Not on me."

"Okay, ma'am, I'm going to have to ask you to stop and let us talk with you a minute."

"No thanks. You can follow me home if you want." *I'll run as far from the underground as I can until I drop.*

"I need to know your original region and see your mark."

"I'm not taking off my hood or my gloves in this weather after working up a sweat."

"What, you've got marks both places?"

Chloe waved her off and kept running. The truck veered off the road in front of her and stopped. Chloe swerved around it and kept going. She heard doors opening and boots on pavement. Soon armed GC in full uniform flanked her, a man on each side, keeping pace.

"Okay," one said, "fun's over. Stop or we'll have to put you in the truck. Come on now, ma'am, you know we can take you down, and there's no need for that."

Chloe kept running. The man on her right tossed his weapon to the one on the left, and the next thing she knew he had both arms around her neck and was drawing his knees up into the middle of her back. He had to weigh two hundred pounds. She staggered and fell. He shifted his weight just before she hit the ground and drove her face into the dirt. Chloe knew she had been scraped deep, and blood ran down her forehead. He slid up and pressed his knee behind her neck, pulled her hands behind her, and handcuffed her.

Desperate to stall them, Chloe let herself go limp. "Have it your way," one of the men said. He grabbed the cuffs to drag her toward the truck. She purposely kept her face down, letting sand and pebbles and pavement tear at her face.

On her stomach next to the truck, she could not be lifted by the handcuffs without wrenching her shoulders out of place, which the GC almost did. "There's an easier way," a young guard said, "if that's what she wants."

He grabbed her feet and bent her legs up to where he could bind her ankles to the handcuffs with a plastic band. He tossed her into the truck.

Chloe was sure she had cracked a rib. During the twenty-five-minute ride to the local GC headquarters, Chloe began to pray. "God, give me strength. Let me die before I give away anything. Be with Kenny and Buck and Dad."

She remembered George regaling them with stories about how he had said absolutely nothing to his captors in Greece. If only she had that kind of fortitude. She would rather banter, anger them, mislead them. Was it better to sit and take it or to shoot back, to let them know she was no pushover?

Torture. Could she handle that? "With your strength, God. Let me trade my body for the ones I love."

At headquarters she was uncuffed, searched, and again asked her name and home region. Chloe said nothing. She gingerly pressed a palm against her face and felt the abrasions on her forehead and cheeks.

"She already told us. Phoebe Evangelista, American."

"Then there ought to be a –6 somewhere under that blood. Get a wet cloth and wash that off."

Someone held Chloe by the back of her head and dragged the cloth across her face. She cried out.

"I don't see anything. Doesn't mean it's not there. We running her name and description?"

"Yeah. Nothing so far."

"Jock will be in at nine. Get her cleaned up and in a jumpsuit. And fingerprinted."

Chloe was tempted to go limp again and make the GC undress her, hose her down, and dress her, but she did what she was told. She came out of the shower with her face stinging, changed into the dark green jumpsuit, and clenched her fists.

When she was led to the photo area and printing station, she kept her hands balled. Chloe looked so different from the girl who had been at Stanford six years before, she wasn't worried about her photo giving anything away.

A matronly Mexican guard reached for Chloe's hand and said, "Right first, please."

Chloe shook her head.

"Come on, honey. You don't want to fight me. You're going to get yourself fingerprinted, so you might as well just let me do it."

Chloe shook her head again.

"I'm going to do this, so how's it going to happen? Do I have to get a couple of guys in here to hold you down? Because if I do, here's what I'm going to use."

The woman showed Chloe an ugly adjustable metal cord similar to the tool dogcatchers use at the ends of poles to snag puppies. "I wrap this about three inches above your wrist. When it tightens, your hand comes open. I don't know who you are or why you're in here, but you don't want to endure this."

Chloe shook her head again, and the woman

spoke into her radio, asking for help. Chloe resisted the two young men, but as the matron had said, it was hardly worth the effort. When that metal loop tightened around her arm, her fingers popped open, and the GC had fingerprints that were sent via the Internet to their databases all over the world.

"We also read your eyes with the camera, honey. If you've ever had a driver's license, been to college, gotten married, anything, we'll find a match."

Chloe only hoped the GC were as shorthanded as everyone else. Maybe it would take long enough that Buck and George and the rest could bust her out. *Who am I kidding?*

● ● ●

Rayford had hoped for a day or two of rest before jetting back to San Diego, but he had no choice but to leave Petra as soon as he could refuel. He was stunned to find Mac McCullum waiting for him.

"Got the word from Buck," Mac said. "Thought Tsion and Chaim ought to know so they could get the folks here praying. Albie's already got a contact on the Al Hillah thing, so he doesn't need me. I'll be your pilot."

"Mac, I can't ask you to—"

"You didn't. I volunteered. Now unless you're gonna be a mule and pull rank on me, saddle up."

Rayford was more grateful than he could express. In the air Mac told him, "You can think, pray, sleep, or talk. I've got this baby on a path to San Diego, and I'm looking forward to seeing those people again and meeting some new ones. My prediction is that Chloe will be there waiting for us."

"I was with you right up until that last," Rayford said. "I've got a bad, bad feeling about this. If Buck and George don't find her soon, or if they find out the GC has her, we've got to get those people out of there."

"And take them where?"

"Petra is the only place I know anymore."

"Chloe ain't gonna give the GC a thing. Unless they saw her coming out of the underground, what've they got?"

"She had to be in the area. Unless she can convince them she came from somewhere else, she sure gives them a place to start looking."

Rayford buried his head in his hands and tried to sleep. No dice. All he could do was pray. Chloe had been Daddy's girl from day one. She loved school, was inquisitive, single-minded, stubborn. She was the last person in the family to come to Christ, and Rayford had no illusions that he was responsible for that. He had taught her to believe only in what she could see and smell and touch.

Chloe always wanted to be in the middle of the

action, and if someone wouldn't put her there, she'd put herself there. He wanted to resent her for it, especially now, but he was overwhelmed with worry and fear. All he wanted was to know she was safe and back with Buck and Kenny. He knew that no matter what happened, they would be reunited someday, and that it would be less than a year from now. But somehow that wasn't as comforting as he thought it might be.

They were destined to be with Christ when they died, and should they survive, they would be with him on earth for a thousand years. But the prospect of dying was still a fearful thing. It was likely that any of the Tribulation Force who died during the next year would be martyrs to the cause of Christ, but their loved ones would still mourn them, still miss them. Worst of all, Rayford realized, he didn't want to think about how his loved ones might die.

The suffering might be short-lived, but no one wants to think of his beloved going through anything terrifying or torturous or agonizing. "Father," Rayford said, "let this be a mission of relocation at worst. I have no reason more valid than anyone else to deserve special treatment, to have my daughter supernaturally protected. You don't need her; you don't need any of us. But we have pledged ourselves to you and trust you know what you're doing."

• • •

Jock turned out to be a tall, heavy man with a uniform that may once have fit him but now encased him like a sausage. He had his underlings bring Chloe from a small cell to a slightly larger room. He pointed to a chair and she sat directly across from him at a metal table.

Jock dropped an accordion file on the table and took off his jacket, draping it over the back of the chair. He sat wearily and let out a loud sigh. "So, Phoebe Evangelista. Where'd you come up with that one?"

Chloe stared at him. She detected an Australian accent and noticed the number *18* on his forehead. On the back of his right hand was a tattoo of Nicolae Carpathia's face.

"Mind if I smoke?"

Chloe raised her eyebrows and nodded.

"Well, what do I care whether you mind or not? I've got a lot of work to do today, young lady, and you're keeping me from it."

"Go do it," Chloe said.

"So, she talks," Jock said, pulling a small cigar from his pocket. "I thought you were going to be one of those name-rank-and-serial-number types, minus the last two. Well, you are my work, and you've been a bad girl. You've been lying to my people, haven't you?"

"Yes."

"You want to fess up, or you want me to tell you what we found?"

Chloe shrugged.

"We're not getting a thing out of you, are we?"

"No."

"Took a while, but we got it. Besides being short of people, our systems are crashing, and—"

"You're breaking my heart."

Jock reached for his file. "Yeah, well, from what we found, I can imagine. I have good news and bad news this morning, Mrs. Williams. Which would you like?"

So, there it was. In a matter of hours, the prints or the eye reading had given her away. "Nothing you can say will be good news."

"Don't be rash. We're reasonable people, much as you and yours would like to think otherwise and persuade all the sheep who follow that kook Ben-Judah."

Tsion has more brains in his eyebrows than any ten GCs I've ever met.

"I have a proposition for you, ma'am."

"I don't want to hear it."

"Sure you do."

"Let me guess. My freedom for a few leads?"

"Well, you can play high-and-mighty all you want, Mom, but I'd think you'd be open to hearing me out when the benefit to you deals with your own child."

FIVE

ALBIE'S BLACK-MARKET world was a shadowy landscape of operators who largely went by nicknames and initials. Albie himself had fashioned his name from his hometown, Al Basrah. People who needed to know who he was knew enough to reach him. Before he became a believer, Albie had been one of the top three black marketers in the Middle East. His conversion to Christ had left only two, and the death of one of them, reputedly at the hands of the other in a deal gone bad, left one. And that was who Albie needed to get ahold of.

He had never liked Double-M, or Mainyu Mazda, even when Albie was of the same ilk and character. Killing was nothing new for Mainyu. It was how he maintained his reputation and control. You wanted something, anything, he was the man. But pity anyone who ever, ever tried to swindle or even shortchange the man. Legend had it that he had personally murdered a dozen people—one of them one of his own wives—who had not lived up to their end of some bargain. None dared calculate how many he may have hired others to eliminate.

Those who claimed to know said Mainyu celebrated each personal killing by adding a tattooed double-M to his neck. He had begun twenty years before when he had strangled a guard in a Kuwaiti prison. He applied the first tattoo himself, the ink a concoction of rubber shavings from the soles of his shoes, paint chips from the prison bars, and blood. A sharpened paper clip heated by a cigarette lighter was his applicator. He put that first double-M directly under his Adam's apple. He added one on either side of the original for each subsequent murder, so people could tell whether he was on an odd or even number by whether or not his tattooed necklace was even on both sides.

The last time Albie had seen Mainyu, his necklace had one more double-M on the left than on the right and his count stood at twelve. The more recent tattoos were clearer and more professionally done, and supposedly the one for his wife had a feminine flair.

Albie put the word on the street that he wanted an audience with Mainyu, and within two hours a note was slipped under his door with an address deep in the street markets on Abadan Island on the Shatt al Arab River in southwestern Iran.

It was like MM to follow the money. Pipelines connected Abadan's huge refinery to the oil fields of Iran. Of course Mainyu did his black marketing in the city's underbelly.

Like anyone anywhere who didn't bear a mark of loyalty to Carpathia, Albie had become nocturnal. He and Mac shared a flat in a forsaken corner of Al Basrah, where the landlord didn't know or care about one's loyalty to the Global Community provided the rent envelope was full and waiting the first of every month. Albie had taught Mac that the best way to get around was on motor scooters small and light enough to be stored indoors or hidden in the woods near where they hid their small plane.

Albie would wait for the sun to disappear before venturing out to a ferry that would get him and his scooter to the island, where he would find the address some thirty miles from home.

● ● ●

When big Jock said something about it probably being past Chloe's breakfast time, her mouth watered. "But as you can understand, ma'am, we don't feed uncooperative prisoners. Oh, at some point, you'll get some sort of nutrition bar that'll keep you alive until your execution." He patted the big file. "I can't say for sure until I hear from International, but this has all the makings of a spectacle. Wouldn't you say?"

"That's not my call."

"But your baby—what's the name?"

Chloe leveled her eyes at Jock and pressed her lips together. How she loved to say her baby's name. *Kenneth Bruce Williams. Kenny Bruce. Kenny B.* But she would not tell this man. There was no official record of Kenny's birth, and the GC didn't even know whether she'd had a boy or a girl.

"Surely there's no harm in my knowing the name."

"Phoebe Evangelista Jr."

Jock looked at the ceiling. "You know what? I am not the least bit amused. I'm not surprised either, because I've dealt with enough of your type. Some say there's something admirable about you people, sticking with something this long even though in the end you're going to lose, and you know it. But I would have thought a religious person—and come on, that's what you are, isn't it?—I would have thought you'd care a little more about the disposition of your child. Is it a girl? How old is she now?"

"Look," Chloe said, "you know who I am and what I am and what I'm not, which is a Carpathia loyalist. That's punishable by death, so why don't you just—"

"Oh, now hold on, ma'am. These things are still negotiable. Don't be jumping to concl—"

"I will not be providing you any information to reduce my sentence. I'm not interested in life in prison. I would not take the mark even if you promised freedom for my family. And everybody knows that even those who take the mark now are executed anyway."

"Oh, where did you hear that? That's terrible. And a lie."

"Whatever you say."

Jock leaned back in his chair and called out, "Nigel?"

"Sir?"

"Could you open a window? It's stuffy in here."

The young guard entered and opened a window behind heavy bars. There would be no escaping.

"It's only fair that I outline what I have to offer," Jock said. "You see, we know more than your name. We know you dropped out of Stanford University six years ago. We know you're the daughter of Potentate Carpathia's first pilot. We know that you know that your father became a subversive and may have either conspired or participated in the assassination of the potentate.

"Your husband is also a former employee of His Excellency and now publishes a contraband magazine. They're deeply connected with Tsion Ben-Judah and the traitor assassin Rosenzweig. And you, Mrs. Williams, are no retiring bride either. No. You run the Judah-ite black market, keeping alive millions without the mark, who have no legal right to buy or sell.

"No ma'am, you should be offered nothing, no plea bargain, no break, nothing even for your child. Because more than that, you were involved in an operation in Greece where you impersonated a Global Community officer."

"How did you know that?" It was out before Chloe could think. Was there a mole in their own operation? She couldn't have been recognized.

"I'll tell you if you'll tell me something."

"Never mind."

"It's the beauty of iris-scan technology. Normal security cameras, like the ones in our headquarters in Ptolemaïs, can get a good enough read on your iris to match it with the one recorded when you enrolled at Stanford. It has four times as many points of reference as a fingerprint, and there has never been a recorded error. Lucky for the one among your number who murdered one of our operatives in that very building that we weren't able to trace you to him. But he's from right here in town, isn't he? How far away can he be? How far from where you were jogging?"

● ● ●

Buck could barely believe what he was hearing. And from Sebastian, of all people, who was sitting there because of the selfless, heroic efforts of the Tribulation Force, Chloe in particular.

"It's not easy to say, Buck," George said. "But we have to weigh the welfare of two hundred people against springing one person in the face of almost impossible odds."

"First," Buck said, "you're assuming the GC has her. She could be anywhere. But even if you're right, how is that any more impossible than the situation you were in?"

"Buck, I know, okay? And there's no way I want to just do nothing. But there's one big difference here too. The prisoner in that situation was a very big and strong man, trained to kill. And, you'll recall, for all Mac and Hannah and Chloe did on my behalf, it came down to me against one of my captors. Even then the odds were bad, and it could have gone either way. Let's say I'd failed and the three of them had been compromised. We lose four people. We blast into local headquarters here, we could wind up giving away everything."

"So, what, we let her rot while we move to Petra?"

• • •

"Here's what I have in mind for your child, Mrs. Williams," Jock said, "in the event you come to your senses and help us a little. I'm guessing you would prefer your son or daughter to remain in the tradition you and your husband have begun. Obviously, that would be counterproductive to our aims. We would like to see all children enrolled in Junior GC before they start school.

"But in your case, we're willing to treat your child as a nonentity until he or she is twelve years old."

"And who would raise him?" Chloe said, wincing, realizing hunger was an effective tactic after all.

"So we're talking about a boy, then. Fair enough. Want to give me a name to make it less awkward to carry out negotiations?"

Chloe didn't answer. These weren't negotiations. All she had to do was protect Kenny for one more year and the GC wouldn't have a chance at him.

"Come now, Mrs. Williams. You're a bright woman. You have to see what a prize you are to us. We have been inconvenienced and, I'll admit it, embarrassed by the Judah-ites. There is little doubt you people are somehow behind our little problem in New Babylon right now. You can help us. I'm not naïve enough to think you want to do that, but I'm trying to give you a reason. You have some huge bargaining chips."

"May I stand?"

"You may, but I need to warn you that we are locked in. I'm three times your size, but just for smiles, let's say you overpower me, get the drop on me. You could break my neck and kill me, but you're not getting out of here."

"I just want to move a little, sir."

"Feel free. And call me Jock."

Yeah, you're my best friend now.

"Hey, you want some breakfast?"

"Of course."

"Me too. What do you like?"

"I'm not fussy."

"I am. I go for the old artery-clogger special. Eggs, bacon, sausage, toast, pancakes with lotsa syrup. Want some?"

He had to be kidding. Chloe stood with her arms folded and turned away.

"Come on! Can't get you to call me by my first name. Can't get you to tell me what you want to eat. How 'bout it? Will you join me? Will you have what I'm having?"

"I told you, I'm not fussy."

"You also told me you were hungry. I'll order for us, eh, Chloe? You mind if I call you Chloe?"

"Actually, I'd rather you not."

"Oh, well, then, by all means. It's all about you. Just let me know all your desires and preferences. If the pillow in your cell is not soft enough, give me a holler. Or call the front desk."

So the gloves were off. Chloe had convinced him she wasn't going to cooperate, so he was done playing good cop.

Or was he? Jock moved past her and summoned Nigel again, and she overheard him ordering the very breakfasts he had described. He turned back to her.

"Food service here is about the same as at any jail, Chloe, but even a hash slinger is hard-pressed to mess up breakfast. Now listen, while we wait . . . I can see you're no pushover. I didn't expect you to be and wouldn't have respected you if you had been. Here's the deal. You know nothing you give us is going to set you free. How would we look to the public? But I can get your execution commuted to a life sentence, and I can get that in a livable facility. You'd have my word on it. It'd be maximum security, of course, but you would have full custody of your son until he's twelve years old."

The fact was, Kenny was safe with Buck, and

if she could maintain her sanity, that might not have to change. If only she could get word to Buck to get everyone out of there and to Petra.

Chloe felt light-headed and hunger gnawed. "And that deal is in exchange for . . . ?"

"Taking the mark of loyalty would be a given. No way we would have any credibility otherwise. That gets you life instead of death. But what gets you the nice facility and custody of your son is information."

"You think I'm going to flip on my people."

"I do, and you know why? Because you're a loving mother. You think your people wouldn't give *you* up in a second to keep their necks out from under that blade? Give me a break."

• • •

Albie shuddered, tooling through Abadan on his scooter, cap pulled low over his eyes. Al Basrah was no better, but this had to be what Sodom and Gomorrah had been like before God torched them. Every form of sin and debauchery was displayed right on the street. What was once the seedy side of town now was the town. Row after row of bars, fortune-telling joints, bordellos, sex shops, and clubs pandering to every persuasion and perversion teemed with drunk and high patrons. Hashish permeated the air. Cocaine and heroin deals went down in plain sight.

The GC Peacekeepers and Morale Monitors had once made a noisy bust or two weekly to keep up appearances. But with their ranks shrunk, they now concentrated on crimes against the government. Skip one of your thrice-daily bowings and scrapings before the image of Carpathia and you could be hauled off to jail. Caught without the mark of loyalty? Zero tolerance. They enjoyed playing with people's minds and telling them they had one last chance. When a gratefully weeping soul eagerly approached the mark application site, he or she was pushed or dragged screaming to the guillotine as an example.

Bad as Abadan had become, there was a worse part of town, and it was where Mainyu Mazda and his kind plied their trade. In the open-air market, where loud haggling and swindling were the daytime sport, were makeshift dens of clapboard squares, which consisted of just walls and a locking door, no roof. A tarp in the corner could be hastily attached to corner posts in the event of rain, but otherwise, black marketeers and their henchmen (one always standing guard outside) held court inside, meeting with people who wanted something, anything, and were willing to pay a lot to get it.

Albie cut the engine but stayed aboard his scooter, straddling the seat and pushing it along with his feet through the narrow alleyways. Amid the sleeping drunks were also crazy men, women of ill repute, men and women with all kinds of wares for sale. All beckoned to the leather-clad, smallish man walking the quiet scooter.

Albie looked neither right nor left, catching no one's eye. He knew where he was going and wanted it to appear so. He couldn't avoid a modicum of pride that his business had never sunk this low. What he had done for years was illegal, of course, and no circumstance justified it. But compared to this, he had had class. He had run an airstrip—that was his front. And his clientele had been made up as much of wealthy businessmen and pilots as it was lowlifes and crooks.

But he knew this world and its language. He needed a bad guy, someone who knew someone. Someone who had an inside track at the palace and knew where the meetings were to be held in Al Hillah. Someone who might even know where the largest ever cache of nuclear warheads was stored. Someone who, before Carpathia and his minions arrived, could get into the meeting room and bug the place, transmitting everything to a frequency accessed by only one person in the world. Only Albie and his people knew that would be Chang in Petra.

Had he more than a day to get this done, Albie

might have been able to do it himself with his own contacts, people less risky, less volatile. But there were times in a man's life when he had to weigh his options and throw the dice. And while that analogy was foreign to his new life, this was one of those times.

• • •

"Please sit at the table while the door is opened briefly, Chloe," Jock said. The smell of the breakfasts overwhelmed her, and she sat with her back to the door.

"Right over here, Nigel, if you would."

Jock sat facing her. He tossed her a cloth napkin and made a show of tucking his over his tie and spreading it to cover the expanse of his chest and belly. Chloe opened her napkin and laid it in her lap as Nigel set the heaping tray between them.

Nigel put a stack of pancakes in front of Jock. A pitcher of syrup. A plate of toast with butter and jelly. A large coffee cup, into which he poured steaming black coffee, and he left the pot there too. A massive plate of scrambled eggs with bacon and sausage links. He set Jock's silver on either side of his main plate, then put knife, fork, and spoon in front of Chloe. And there she sat, only silver before her and napkin in her lap. Nigel removed the tray and left, locking the door.

Jock rubbed his hands together, grinning. "Does this look great or what? I hardly know where to begin." He pulled each plate a little closer, then picked up his knife and fork and began manipulating the eggs into a huge first bite.

"I'm sorry," he said. "Where are my manners? Did you want to say grace? Ask a blessing? No? I will then. Thank you, Excellency, for what I am about to enjoy."

Jock shoveled the bite of eggs into his mouth, stored it in his right cheek, followed it with half a link of sausage, and spoke with his mouth full. "Nigel must have forgot yours, eh, Chloe? Oh, that's right. You haven't been a cooperative prisoner yet, have you? Well, that's your call."

The big man sat there, knifing, forking, spooning, smacking his lips, chugging coffee, and grinning. "Sure you don't want some? Huh? It's good. I mean it. 'Sup to you. Otherwise, Nigel will keep an eye on you and that energy bar will be delivered to your cell, oh, I'd say about an hour, maybe two, after you've given up on it. And *energy* may not be the right word. It's designed to keep you alive until we can put you to death. There's nutrition, but not energy per se. You'll get to love it though, look forward to it. I mean, come on, it's not bacon and eggs, but it's going to be your only treat."

• • •

Albie rolled up in front of a tiny structure that appeared to be a mass of incongruously faded yellow boards wired and nailed together. The padlock was conspicuous on the door, which was guarded by a tall, thin rasp of a man Albie recognized from years before. In fact, if he wasn't mistaken, the name was Sahib and he was Mainyu's former brother-in-law. Former because he was the brother of the wife Mainyu had murdered. Talk about loyalty.

Albie stepped off the scooter and thrust out a hand. Sahib ignored it and squinted at him in the darkness. "Looking to sell that bike? You came to the right place."

"No. I want to see Mainyu, Sahib."

That provoked a double take. "Albie?"

And now the man shook his hand. He held up a finger, unlocked the door, and disappeared. Albie heard a low, intense conversation. A stranger emerged, hard and cold eyes darting before he hurried off.

Sahib came out, shutting the door behind him. "Two minutes, Albie," he said, and made a motion indicating Mainyu was on the phone. "Fifty Nicks to guard your bike."

"Twenty."

"Twenty-five."

"Deal. And if it is not as I left it, I split your skull."

"I know, Albie. Pay in advance."

"Ten now, fifteen later."

"Fifteen now."

Albie peeled off the Nicks. The negotiation, even the threats, was expected. A throat clearing from behind the door spurred Sahib to usher Albie in, but as Albie followed, he saw a small woman striding their way from a similar cubbyhole a hundred feet away. "Wait," he said. "Sahib. Watch the bike."

"I said I would. Oh, this is just a guest who will be joining you."

The young woman, robed head to toe, big eyed and severe looking with a *42* on her forehead, carried a satchel. Sahib pulled her in as he slid out, locking the door.

Mainyu, illuminated by a battery-powered lamp, sat behind a flimsy wood desk, a mug of something before him, his smile exhibiting surprisingly white teeth. "Albie, my friend, how are you?" he said, reaching with both hands.

"I am well, Mainyu. But I must insist that my business with you is private."

"As usual, of course. Please, sit."

Albie sat in a rusted metal folding chair while the woman went around the desk and pulled a wood box from a corner and sat on it, opening her satchel. Albie looked into Mainyu's eyes and cocked his head at the woman.

"Her?" Mainyu said dismissively. "Tattoo artist. She has neither ears nor tongue."

The woman smiled as she removed her instruments and reached in front of Mainyu to direct the lamp more squarely toward him. He lifted his chin, and she swabbed a small area on his neck where a tattoo would even the number on both sides.

"You know what they say about my tattoos, do you not, old friend?"

Albie smiled. "Everybody knows what they say."

"So, true or not, it is effective, no?"

"Effective. Is it true, Mainyu?"

"Of course."

"Who was your latest victim?"

"You mean who will be?"

"Sorry?"

"Sometimes I get the tattoo in advance."

● ● ●

In spite of himself, Rayford had been dozing. And as the Gulfstream rocketed toward the States, he began digging through his bags.

"What's up, Ray?" Mac said.

"What time is it in New Babylon?"

"Coming up on ten o'clock in the evening."

"That makes it late morning in San Diego, and

still no word. Buck promised to call even if they just found out where she was. You remember the main number at the palace?"

"Never knew it. Did you?"

"Once upon a time."

"Should be easy enough to get. But no one is still there, Ray. Need someone at Petra?"

"No. Now do you remember what David or Chang said about making these phones impossible to trace?"

"That I do remember." He told Rayford the combination of symbols and numbers that made the satellite phones appear to be coming from anywhere.

Rayford punched in the number for an international operator. "The Global Community Palace in New Babylon, please," he said.

"I'm ringing it for you," the operator said, "but they have no light there just now, and you may encounter delays."

"Thank you."

"You have reached the Global Community Headquarters Palace in New Babylon. Please bear with us as technical difficulties may make it impossible to answer your call immediately."

And there came "Hail Carpathia" by the big choir again. "Agh!"

"Global Community, how may I direct your call?"

"Krystall, please."

"In the potentate's office?"

"Of course."

"Sir, it's after hours here. Those offices are closed."

"I know that. Her quarters, please."

"Who may I say is calling?"

"I'll tell her."

"I need to know, sir, or I won't ring someone at this time of the night."

"If you have to know, it's her uncle Gregory."

"One moment."

Mac shot Rayford a look. "Uncle Gregory?"

"Long story."

"Long flight. I'll look forward to it."

"Uncle Gregory?" Krystall said, her voice thick from sleep.

"Is this line secure?" Rayford said.

"I think so. I don't know. This isn't my uncle, is it?"

"You know who it is."

"You never told me."

"You know I'm a friend."

"I'll know for sure if you can really help my uncle. I passed along your message."

"You did? Is he following up?"

"I think he is."

"Believe me, if he makes contact, our people will get him everything he needs."

"I'm grateful, but why are you call—"

"A favor."

"I knew it. I can't—"

"Hear me out. I had no idea I would need anything when I talked to you. I just need information that only you can give me."

"I can't be giving you inf—"

"I'm not asking for much, but I don't want to get you in trouble."

"Oh, what's the difference?" she said. "Being in trouble is no worse than being in his good graces around here."

"I need to know if there's been any talk of an important arrest in the United North American States. It would be a young wom—"

"Yes! Yes! Late in the day, a couple of hours after quitting time—we were still working because of the move tomorrow afternoon—Mr. Akbar came in excited about some break in San Diego. Local GC there arrested someone connected with the Judah-ites."

"Any idea whether they are planning to—"

"That's all I know. Really."

"I appreciate this more than I can say, Krystall. Is there anything I can do for you?"

"What could you possibly do for me?"

"I just wish—"

"If you can't send me a pair of eyes, I can't think of a thing."

SIX

THE TATTOO artist snapped on her rubber gloves and asked Mainyu Mazda in an Indian accent if he wanted anesthetic. He pulled back and looked at her.

"You never do," she said. "Head back, chin up."

Albie did not expect a meeting with this man in this part of this town to be other than bizarre, but neither did he dream he would have to compete with a dermatological procedure.

"Go ahead, my friend," Mainyu said, gesturing. "You come to me why?"

Albie leaned forward, forearms on the desk, and told MM of his urgent need in Al Hillah. The woman's battery-powered applicator emitted a loud, rapid clicking as she worked. Mainyu winced but managed to encourage Albie with

"Uh-huhs" and "Hmms." Finally he said, "A moment, Kashmir." The woman pulled away and busied herself with the needle in the glow of the lamp.

"It is no secret that you are not a friend of the potentate," MM said.

Albie smiled. "I hope it is a secret in some places."

"Why do you not let me have Kashmir give you a loyalty mark? Any number you wish."

"You know I cannot do that, Mainyu."

"Oh yes. You are now a Judah-ite and believe in the evil spirits."

"The evil sp—?"

Mainyu waved with the back of his hand. "Don't you people believe that anyone who takes the mark of Carpathia goes to hell, something like that?"

"More important is where our loyalty lies."

MM looked at Kashmir, then leaned back and grinned at Albie. He laughed loudly. "You are not going to start in on me now, are you, old friend? I wondered."

"No, you have made your choice. I am curious as to why you have a *72* and not a *216,* though."

"You think I am a friend of the international regime?"

"Well, I wond—"

"You think my mark is real? You know me better than that." He spat.

"But the penalty for a fake mark is worse than death," Albie said.

"Public torture, I know," Mainyu said. "But the GC is not interested in me except in how I can benefit them. If I were to bear the mark of the one to whom I am loyal, it would have to be the number *1*. What is it our Mexican friends say, Albie? 'Look out for *número uno!'* And if I was not a benefit to the GC, I would be assigned to the Plain of Jezreel like so many millions of others. What kind of business could I do there?"

"How do you benefit the GC?"

Kashmir dabbed at a tiny stream of blood on Mainyu's neck.

"I am a businessman, Albie. I look for the biggest profit for the smallest expense, and right now that is bounty money."

"You—"

"Deliver the disloyal to the Peacekeepers. Of course I do. Tell me, what is the cost of doing that kind of business? Twenty thousand Nicks a head, same price dead or alive. I find the dead more manageable. Once the victim is still, there is no danger, no escape attempt, nothing messy. With the right size plastic bag, even the car stays clean. Follow?"

"So, you are a supplier—"

"To the GC, yes, of course. If low overhead and high profit is the businessman's mantra, what better business is there than something for nothing? They are willing to pay for something I can provide."

Albie wondered how many unmarked victims of Mainyu's were Judah-ites. "My request, then," Albie said, "does it constitute a conflict of interest for you?"

"Of course not, my friend! Not if you brought the money. I am not a friend of the GC. I am merely a business associate. My interest is profit."

"I wasn't sure what such services would cost."

"Oh yes, you were. You are not out of the business that long. And surely you didn't expect me to commit to this without all the money up front, not when it has to be done almost immediately."

"You have the people, the hardware, the—?"

"You know I have everything. It will be done. Provided you have the money."

"Such a job would have cost twenty thousand Nicks a few years ago," Albie said.

"So I assume you brought more, due to inflation and the urgent nature of the request."

Albie hesitated.

"Sure you did, and you will not make the mistake of holding out on me, because you know how easy it would be for me to find out how much you have with you."

"Of course. I brought thirty thousand Nicks."

"Hmm."

"Surely that's enough. Fifty percent more than before has to cover inflation and the rush."

"It's not enough," Mainyu said. "It's twenty thousand short."

Albie assumed the deal was about to go down. They were in the haggling stage, and anything other than a vigorous argument from both sides would show disrespect. "Thirty thousand is all I brought, and all I am willing to pay."

"Uh-huh. And is it all on your person or did you leave some on your bike?"

"You know better than that, Mainyu. Who leaves cash in the alley here?"

Mainyu laughed. "Sahib!"

The tall man unlocked the door and entered.

"How much is our friend paying you to watch his bike?"

"Twenty-five."

"How much does he owe?"

"Ten."

Mainyu turned to Albie. "Do you have thirty thousand plus the ten you owe Sahib?"

"Yes."

"Any more?"

"Spare change for the trip home."

"Let me see the thirty thousand."

Albie reached inside his jacket and produced a brick of bills wrapped in cellophane.

"Now the ten you owe Sahib."

Albie slapped a ten on the table.

"Now your spare change."

From his left pocket Albie produced a wad of bills and coins. "Maybe another fifteen-plus," he said.

Mainyu pressed his lips together and cocked his head, arching his eyebrows at Albie. "We are still twenty thousand apart," he said.

"I said thirty thousand is all I'm willing to pay."

"Then we have a problem. What are we going to do about the other twenty?"

Albie fought a grin. Mainyu had always driven a hard bargain. "You're serious," Albie said. "You won't do it for thirty? You want me to take my business elsewhere?"

"Oh no! And pass up what's before me? No!"

"It'll be done, then?"

"It's already done, my friend. Something for nothing. Fifty thousand and change for virtually no overhead."

"Fifty?"

"Kashmir, call the palace for me, will you? Get Mr. Akbar. Sahib? Remember what I have been teaching you about the business? Creative solutions for getting to where a deal makes sense?"

Sahib nodded. "Yes, Mr. Mazda."

"Your handgun, please."

Sahib produced a .44 revolver.

Mainyu Mazda hefted it and turned it over in his hands. "My old friend and I are twenty thousand Nicks apart, and he is the solution. What is the bounty on unmarked citizens again, Sahib?"

"Twenty thousand."

"That makes fifty. And we don't even have to do the job."

He pointed the barrel between Albie's eyes and pulled the trigger.

• • •

Her cell, Chloe thought, was in a strange location. It consisted of a cage in the corner of a larger room. A metal shelf protruded from the wall. Her bed, she imagined. And a combination sink and toilet stood in plain sight. It was what wasn't there that concerned her. Nothing was movable or removable. There wasn't so much as a toilet seat, a blanket, or a pillow. No reading material. Nothing.

Faint from hunger, Chloe crawled onto the shelf and lay on her side, facing the door. She was supported by woven strips of metal about four inches wide that might have given a bit if she weighed a hundred more pounds. Not even the formerly ubiquitous Nigel was anywhere to be seen. The outer room was bright enough, the sun streaming through the windows and bars.

But the room was otherwise drab, all tile and linoleum and steel in institutional greens.

Chloe wanted to call out, to tell someone she was hungry, but her pride overcame her discomfort. She sat up quickly when she heard the door open, and a man in a custodial-type uniform hurried in. Cleaning bottles hung from his belt next to his cell phone. He carried a rag and had another in his back pocket.

"Oh, hi," he said. "Didn't know we had somebody in custody."

"You're not supposed to," she said, dying to be charming.

"Pardon?"

"I just wandered in here. Locked myself in like an idiot."

He laughed, a smile radiating. "And you had the bad fortune of wearing a jumpsuit today that makes you look like an inmate too. Unlucky."

"Yeah, that's me," she said.

"Maybe they locked you up for your taste in clothes, huh?"

"Must have."

"Well, I'm just getting a bucket over here. Best of luck to ya."

"Thanks."

He grabbed a bucket from the corner under a suspended TV set and headed back toward the door. Then he stopped and turned on his heel. "They gave you your phone call, didn't they?"

"Oh, sure. I've been treated like a queen. I called Santa Claus."

He set the bucket down and moved to within a few feet of the cage. He looked over his shoulder at the door, then turned back and lowered his voice. "No, I'm serious. That's the one thing I don't like here. I mean, people get what they deserve, not taking the mark and all, like you. I'm not so naïve as to think there'd still be a trial for that after all these years, but what ever happened to one phone call? I mean, this is still America, isn't it?"

"Not the one I remember."

"Me either. Hey, you wanna make a phone call?"

"What?"

"You gotta promise not to tell. I'd be in a lot of trouble."

"What, with your phone?"

"Sure. Here." He slid it from his belt and angled it so it would fit between the wires of the cage. "But just one, and you gotta make it quick. Then hide it. Or slide it across the floor like I dropped it or something. I'll come back for it in a while."

"You're serious?"

"Sure. What's the harm? Go ahead. Knock

yourself out. Pretty little thing like you. I'll be back."

Chloe's hands shook as she went to a corner with her back to the door. *How dumb do they think I am? Thing probably doesn't even work, and if it does, not from here.* She didn't care. It was worth a try. She had to talk with someone. She didn't dare risk calling the safe house, assuming this was a setup and that any call would be traced.

Chloe dialed her dad's phone number. He had to be back in Petra by now.

● ● ●

Rayford had awakened Krystall in the palace yet again. "I've been thinking about your request," he said.

"My request?"

"For eyes."

"Don't play with me."

"No, it kept working on me, and I might just know of a pair you could use. You remember, just before you and I spoke, someone opened the door, then shut it again and ran off?"

"How could I forget? That's when you scared the life out of me."

"He's a believer too, and he can see in New Babylon."

"I'm listening."

"I might be able to talk him into coming back

and helping you when everyone else is gone. He can tell you where stuff is, do all sorts of things for you."

"What's in it for you?"

"There might be things in the files I'd like to know about."

"More than you know."

"See? He helps you for a few days, or for however long you want, and you give him access to things that might help me. Deal?"

"What's in it for him?"

"I'll take care of that. In fact, I'll call him right now and see if I can set it up. Well, I'll call him tomorrow. No sense waking him."

"No, why should I be the only one up at this hour?"

"Sorry." Rayford heard a tone that told him he had a call coming in. "Hang on just a second, Krystall." He checked the caller ID. A San Diego area code, but a number he didn't recognize. "I'd better take this. If I can get this deal arranged, I'll have the guy call you."

He punched his call button twice, ending one call and picking up the other. "Steele here."

"Daddy, it's me."

"Chloe!"

"Please, just listen. You still have that record feature on your phone?"

"Yes, but—"

"Turn it on right now. Do it. Did you? Is it on?"

"Yes, but—"

"I know this call is being traced and your phone is going to be useless after this, but I couldn't call anyone else. I'm in the San Diego GC jail, and they're trying to bargain with me to get to the others. Tell Buck and Kenny I love them with all my heart and that if I don't see them again before heaven, I'll be waiting for them there. Dad, this was all my fault, but I was jogging within thirty miles of our place and, oh, listen, I just wanted to tell you that I'm all right for now. I've just been sitting here reminiscing about that wonderful trip you and Mom and I took to Colorado when I was five or six. Remember?"

"Vaguely. Chloe, listen—"

"Dad, I don't dare stay on long. It's important to me that you remember that trip!"

"Honey, that had to be more than twenty years ago. I—"

"It was! But it was so special, and I wish everybody could go there again. If I had one dream, it's that we could all go there right now, as soon as possible."

"Chloe—"

"Dad, don't. You know they have to be listening. Just please give my love to everybody and tell them to pray that I'll be strong to the end. I will give nothing away. Nothing. And, Dad, think of the Colorado trip so I know we'll both be thinking of the same thing at the same time. I love you, Dad. Don't ever forget that."

"I love you too, honey. I—"

"Bye, Daddy."

And she was gone.

• • •

"You're supposed to be the combat guy, George," Buck said. "And all you want to talk about is packing."

"I just want you to know, Buck, that I'm not going to hold you responsible for any mean thing you say to me until Chloe is back safe and sound. Then I'm going to tell on you."

"Yeah, and she'll ground you," Priscilla said.

Buck owed George a smile, and it never ceased to amuse him when Priscilla vainly tried to add to or improve on her husband's humor. It was just that Buck's spirits could not be lifted. His father-in-law had confirmed where Chloe was through his contact at the palace, and the local GC headquarters simply was not a place vulnerable to a raid.

"The best thing we have going for us," Sebastian said, "is that as soon as they determine who she is, she's most valuable to them alive."

Buck knew it was true, but talking about his beloved as a commodity of war left a bad taste.

Late in the afternoon Ming brought Beth Ann Sebastian and Kenny into the workout room. Ree leaped to his feet and uncharacteristically embraced Ming. Buck knew the Chloe situation had sobered him. He wondered if it had even given Ree second thoughts about marriage.

Beth Ann ran back and forth between her parents, showing off. Kenny, frowning, trudged to Buck and climbed in his lap.

"He didn't nap," Ming said.

Buck nodded and held Kenny's cheek to his chest. "Sleepy, bud?" he said.

Kenny shook his head. "I want Mommy."

"She'll be back later."

The boy closed his eyes.

Buck looked at Priscilla, biting his lip and unable to stanch the tears. "This is the part I'm going to hate," he mouthed, his chest convulsing. Kenny roused, but Buck tucked the boy's head under his chin and wrapped both arms around him, rocking. And weeping.

Priscilla pushed Beth Ann toward her dad and leaned close to Buck. "Don't you dare give up, Buck. None of us are."

● ● ●

Chloe wanted to call everybody she knew, but she had little question she'd been set up. It had all been too easy. The global positioning system in her father's phone would tell the GC right where he was. She had assumed Petra, but from the ambient sounds, he was in the air. How long had he and Abdullah been in New Babylon if he was just heading back now? It didn't compute. Of course he would have been informed of her disappearance. Maybe he was on his way home. She only hoped he could get rid of the phone before getting close to California. The last thing she wanted was to lead the GC right to the safe house.

Chloe reached as high as she could and pushed the phone through an opening in the cage. It flew about eight feet before landing on the floor and breaking into pieces. "Oops," she said. "And after that nice man entrusted it to me."

Inside a minute Custodian returned, still dressed the same but this time with no props. No bucket, no cleansers, no rags. No smile either. He knelt to pick up the pieces.

"Thanks for the use of your phone. That was most thoughtful. Maybe you could smuggle me in a cake with a file in it or get word to my people. Sorry about the damage."

"That's all right, doll," he said, not looking at her. "We got what we needed. Looks like Daddy's just off the East Coast. Gotta think he's due to refuel by now. Should be able to alert the most likely airports. You wanna do yourself a favor, work with Jock. He's a fair guy. No, he really is. I'm not saying he's got your best interests at heart, but he's a realist. You've got what he wants, and he knows that's going to cost him."

"Well, then by all means, friend, tell Jock I'm ready to wheel and deal. I'll give him everything he wants, now that I know he's fair. I mean, I heard that from you, and I've known you long enough to trust you completely."

"Be as much of a smart aleck as you want, kid. See where it gets ya. Oh, by the way, Nigel's got your energy bar. Should I tell him you're hungry?"

Chloe sat on the metal bed. She was famished but still more proud than desperate. "Nah. I had a big breakfast. I couldn't eat another thing just yet."

"Maybe some television then."

"Spare me. I've heard enough propaganda to last a lifetime."

"But it's time for the news."

"Oh yes, the eminently objective Global Community News Network. Hey, okay, all right! That's plenty loud enough!"

He ignored her, leaving the volume up and heading for the door.

"Turn it down, please! Sir?"

"Can't hear you," he said. "TV's too loud."

Jock must have been choreographing everything. The five o'clock news was just coming on, Anika Janssen anchoring live from Detroit.

"Good evening. Darkness continues to plague Global Community International Headquarters in New Babylon at this hour. It is confined to the borders of the city and is believed to be an act of aggression on the part of dissidents against the New World Order.

"GC Chief of Security and Intelligence Suhail Akbar spoke with us by phone earlier from the beleaguered capital. In spite of the turmoil there, he reports good news, constituting our top story tonight."

"Yes, Anika," Akbar said, "following months of careful planning and cooperation between the various law-enforcement branches of the Global Community, we are happy to report that a combined task force of crack agents from both our Peacekeeping and Morale Monitor divisions has succeeded in apprehending one of the top-echelon Judah-ite terrorists in the world.

"The arrest was made before dawn today in San Diego after months of planning. I'd rather not go into the details of the operation, but the suspect was disarmed and arrested without incident. Her name is Chloe Steele Williams, twenty-six, a former campus radical at Stanford University in Palo Alto, California, from which she was expelled six years ago after making threats on the lives of the administration."

"Thank you, Chief Akbar. We have further learned that Mrs. Williams is the daughter of Rayford Steele, who once served as pilot for Global Community Supreme Potentate Nicolae Carpathia. He was fired some years ago for insubordination and drinking while on duty, and GC intelligence believes his resentment led to his current role as an international terrorist. He was implicated in the conspiracy to assassinate Potentate Carpathia and is a known associate of former Israeli statesman and now leading Judah-ite Dr. Chaim Rosenzweig. Both are known to serve on the cabinet of Rabbi Tsion Ben-Judah, head of the Judah-ites, the last holdouts in opposition to the New World Order.

"Mrs. Williams is the wife of Cameron Williams, formerly a celebrated American journalist who also worked directly for the potentate before losing his job due to differences in management style. He edits a subversive cyber and printed magazine with a limited circulation.

"Williams, his wife, and her father are international fugitives in exile, wanted for more than three dozen murders around the world. Mrs. Williams herself heads a black-market operation suspected of hijacking billions of Nicks' worth of goods around the world and selling them for obscene profits to others who cannot legally buy and sell due to their refusal to pledge loyalty to the potentate.

"The Williamses, who have amassed a fortune on the black market, have one child remaining after Mrs. Williams apparently aborted two fetuses and an older daughter died under questionable circumstances. The son, whom they have named Jesus Savior Williams, pictured here, is two years old. Acquaintances report that the Williamses believe he is the reincarnation of Jesus Christ, who will one day conquer Nicolae Carpathia and return the globe to Christianity."

Chloe sat staring at a toddler, clearly not Kenny Bruce, who had a Bible in his lap and wore a tiny T-shirt that read "Kill Carpathia!"

"Chief Akbar reports that his forces traced the leading cell of the Judah-ites in the United North American States to San Diego, where Mrs. Williams was apprehended today. Local GC operatives there say she is already, quote, 'singing like a bird, offering all kinds of information on her colleagues, including her own family, to avoid a death sentence.'

"Here's San Diego GCNN reporter Sue West with Colonel Jonathan 'Jock' Ashmore. Sue?"

"Thank you, Anika. Colonel Ashmore, how important would you say this arrest is?"

"It's almost inestimable," Jock said, nervously

tugging at his uniform jacket, which came short of covering his middle. "And Mrs. Williams has proved to be the typical terrorist who knows when it's time to bargain. When the reality hit her that she had been positively identified and we informed her of the overwhelming charges against her, it was only a matter of minutes before she began offering various deals to save her skin."

"Are you at liberty to say what some of those might be?"

"Not entirely, though she has already pledged to enroll her son in Junior GC as soon as possible. She did reveal the whereabouts of a low-level Middle Eastern black marketeer named Al Basrah, after the Iranian city of the same name."

"I believe that's in Iraq, Colonel, but go ahead."

"What?"

"Al Basrah is in Iraq, sir."

"Whatever. Anyway, this character shot himself to death rather than be arrested."

"We are about to show a picture of the dead Al Basrah," Sue West said, "but we warn you that the picture is very graphic."

Chloe stood and stared as the photo was displayed. It showed Albie with a black hole between lifeless eyes, a pool of blood behind his head. It was clearly him. But was it real or doctored?

Chloe shouted, "Jock! Jock! Nigel! Get Jock!"

Her screams became sobs, and she demanded, "Is that true? I want to know if that's true! Is Albie dead? Tell me Albie's not dead!"

But no one came. No one responded. As the TV blared, Chloe slid to the floor, wailing, "God, please! No!"

SEVEN

"GOT ME a friend in Florida," Mac said. "Jacksonville. Co-op guy. We can refuel there and avoid the normal spots."

"And I can put this phone under one of the wheels before we take off," Rayford said. "If they find a mass of metal and plastic on the tarmac, what're they going to do with it?"

"Wouldn't you rather drown it? Won't take but a minute to drop it in the drink."

"What'm I going to do, Mac, roll down my window and toss it out?"

"Nah. There's a dandy little thing we used to do in the military when we wanted to drop something from altitude. You stick it in the speed brake well, which is, of course, closed on the ground. When we get back in the air, I'll activate the speed brake—"

"Which will open the panel. Beautiful."

"Yes," Mac said. "You just take her up, throttle up, activate the brake, and send that phone into the wild blue yonder."

"I don't want to lose any time fooling around."

"Gimme that thing. I'll do it. Won't take more'n sixty seconds."

"I've got to copy Chloe's message first. She's trying to tell me something, that's for sure."

"It's about my turn for a break anyway, Ray. Once you get it ciphered, switch seats with me and I'll study it."

• • •

Chang had arrived at Petra in the middle of the afternoon, and Naomi offered to give him his first look at the place. "I will leave word at the computer center to let us know when they learn anything about Chloe," she said, "but I don't want you to see that place until the end, okay?"

He shrugged.

"Abdullah got someone to take your things to your new quarters, which are not far from his. He will take you there so you can get settled, and then I will come by to give you your first day's tour."

Chang had been determined not to let anyone immediately pair him off with somebody. Especially not Naomi. She had to still be a teenager, which was all right. He was just twenty himself.

And while there was no question about her intellect and technical brilliance, they were going to have to work closely over the next year. Why complicate things?

And yet . . . in person she was stunning. Olive skin and welcoming dark eyes were set off by her long, black hair. Chang found it difficult not to stare. She had a beautiful, shy smile, and she seemed so friendly and selfless. He had never even had a girlfriend, only girls he had been interested in in high school but whom he would never have dared let know it.

On the way to Chang's prefabricated quarters, Abdullah seemed to know everybody and wanted them to meet him. They treated Chang like royalty, but he was so ashamed of bearing the mark of Carpathia that he kept his baseball cap pulled low. His instinct was to remove it and bow each time, but he could not.

"Our man inside the palace," Abdullah called him, and people embraced him or shook his hand, and many blessed him.

To Chang it was a foretaste of heaven. "I wonder what the chances are of meeting Dr. Ben-Judah and Dr. Rosenzweig," he said.

"Oh, I am so sorry," Abdullah said. "I was supposed to tell you. They send their most abject apologies for not greeting you appropriately. They have been meeting with the elders about the issue of Chloe's disappearance, and they have a council meeting later. They request that you join them over manna in the morning."

"Good, yes. Thank you, Mr. Smith. I have something I must consult with Dr. Ben-Judah about."

"I believe Naomi's father would like to meet you too."

He could tell from Abdullah's inflection that he was trying to say something, but Chang would not bite. "Well, I will look forward to meeting him as well."

When they reached the dwellings, shipped in and assembled by a team led by Lionel Whalum, Abdullah first showed Chang his own place. "You can see that I like to live close to the ground. I sit outside near a fire when I eat my manna. And inside, I sleep on the floor. If that is not your custom, you need not do that. Your place is not much different in size from what you had at the palace, but of course it is much plainer and simpler."

"It's perfect," Chang said when they arrived. His luggage lay next to his cot and his computers and file boxes sat by the door. "I will sleep tonight a free man, worried about nothing but the welfare of our comrades."

"I'll leave you to unpack. If you need anything, you can see my place from here. Do you need anything at all?"

"Just one thing. I am a little nervous about the manna. Does everyone care for it?"

"Yes, they do. I am confident you will enjoy it. Imagine, being fed by the King. Yes, it is just sustenance, and yes, it appears to be merely bread. But it comes from the kitchens of heaven. How can it be anything but glorious? We are due a portion just before sundown, so you will know before you join the doctors for breakfast whether you like it or not."

Half an hour later, when Chang had his place situated just the way he wanted it, he heard a knock. "Come in!" he said, but no one did. As he approached the door, he said, "It's open!" Still nothing.

He opened the door to Naomi. "Come in, come in!" he said.

"Oh, I must not," she said. "In my culture it is improper."

"I'm sorry."

"You'll learn. Come, let me show you Petra."

"No word yet on Chloe?" he said as they ventured out.

She shook her head. "It's not going to come to a good end, you know."

"That's my fear," he said. "But we can hope and pray."

Naomi explained that the city was so spread out that it would take days to see it all. "We'll get

ATVs near the tech center. Then let me take you to the Treasury first, then to a few of the nearby tombs—there are many. Finally I'd like to take you to the high place where the missile hit and the spring still bubbles, providing daily water for more than a million people. If I have timed it right, it should then be close to sundown, and we can enjoy our manna with water directly from the source."

Chang was not used to this much walking and climbing, so he was glad when they were finally aboard four-wheelers. He was stunned by Petra's beautiful architecture and wondered how anyone could have carved such structures out of solid rock.

When they finally reached the crest of the high place, where the spring cascaded into cisterns and aqueducts to the entire area, Naomi cut her engine and signaled Chang to do the same.

"Are you thirsty?" she said.

"Always. But mostly I'm trying to get used to not worrying who is watching."

"I cannot imagine. Are you willing to drink from my hands?"

Chang, usually quick and flippant, only smiled. "Whatever is proper in your culture."

She knelt and washed her hands in a brook, shaking them dry. Chang did the same. She took him as close as they could get to the center of the spring. "Ready?" she said.

He nodded, and she thrust her cupped hands into the water, bringing them up to just under his chin. "Hurry," she said, laughing. "My hands are not watertight."

He lowered his face into her hands and took a huge gulp. His throat had been more parched than he knew, and though the water could have been only a few degrees cooler than the air, it felt almost icy. He coughed and laughed and said, "More."

He drank from her hands again, and she said, "My turn."

Chang made a bowl of his palms and let her drink. "Enough?" he said, when his hands were empty. She nodded, and he cupped her face and wiped the dust from under her shining eyes. He spread his fingers and extended his hands, brushing through her hair.

Naomi closed her eyes and lifted her face to the setting sun, spreading her arms and holding her hands palms up. "Here it comes, Chang. Receive your daily bread from the God of heaven."

Chang stepped back, looked up, and extended his arms as the skies seemed to snow bits of soft bread that covered the entire area. Below, the million strong emerged from their quarters with jars and baskets, and gathered what they needed for dinner.

"Just like in the Bible," Naomi said, "we are to

take what we need but not store any. It will spoil and we will have shown our lack of faith in God to provide every day."

Chang sat beside her and scooped manna into his hand. "Do you ask God to bless food that he has just personally delivered?" he said.

She laughed. "Would you like me to?"

"Please." He quickly removed his cap as she began.

"To the great God of Abraham, Isaac, and Jacob, and to the Father of our Lord and Savior Jesus Christ, we offer our humble thanks for everything you provide."

Her young voice was so pure and sweet and her words so perfect, Chang found his face contorting as tears welled.

"Thank you for safety for our mission today and for allowing us to bring Chang here. May he find refreshing peace and rest in you. In the name of Jesus we ask you to bless to our nourishment this gift you have given. Amen."

With tears streaming, Chang turned away and tugged his cap back on. He sat with the warm manna in his hand, unable to eat for crying. He felt Naomi caressing his shoulder. "God bless you, Chang," she said. "Bless you."

He gathered himself and wiped his face with his free hand. "Don't wait for me," he managed. "Go ahead."

"I just might," she said lightly. "I never grow tired of this."

"What does it taste like?" he said.

"Oh no, that is not for me to tell you. I know only what it tastes like to me."

Chang picked two of the small, white disks from his hand and laid them on his tongue.

"Well?" she said.

It was as if he had been struck dumb. "Oh," he said. "Oh."

"That's all you can say?"

He took several more at once. "Oh!"

"I'm guessing you approve."

"I taste honey. Honey for sure."

"Yes."

"Almost like cookies, those sweet wafer things. And they're so filling. I want more and yet I've had enough."

"Imagine," Naomi said. "Everything we need for twenty-four hours comes in three helpings of this."

"Miraculous."

"Exodus 16:31 says, 'And the house of Israel called its name Manna. And it was like white coriander seed, and the taste of it was like wafers made with honey.'"

"I'm impressed," he said. "What, you have the whole Old Testament memorized?"

She laughed. "Hardly, but you know for all of my childhood, I didn't call it the Old Testament.

It was my Bible. I studied it every day. I still do, but it's a whole different thing now, now that I really know God."

"I memorize Scripture too," Chang said. "But I've never owned a Bible. I was raised an atheist, so I have to memorize off the Internet."

"But you do memorize?"

"Doesn't everybody? I mean, Dr. Ben-Judah only reminds us to about five times with every daily message."

"What are you memorizing?"

"New Testament. John. I'm up to chapter three. I'm slow."

"But you have it memorized up to there?" she said. "That's good."

"Well, yeah, I think. But don't test me. I mean, you could test me on chapter three, because that's right where I am, but . . ."

His voice trailed off. Chang could have sat there next to Naomi all night, but she stood and took another drink from the spring. "Let me show you something," she said, reaching for him. He offered his hand and she pulled him up. "You see my garment?"

He shrugged and nodded. Did he see her garment? He had been stealing glances all day. He wouldn't have known what to call it. It was more robe than dress, like something he imagined women wearing in Bible times.

"It is the only thing I have ever worn here. I had it on when we arrived."

"It looks brand-new."

"I wash it out every night, and it is new every morning, like the Lord's compassion."

"Another memorized passage?"

"Yes. Only that was one my father led me to after we survived the bombs."

"You were here for that?"

"We were among the first."

"What was that like?"

"Like a dream, Chang. Sometimes I cannot imagine it really happened."

"What was the passage?"

"Lamentations 3:22-24: 'Through the Lord's mercies we are not consumed, because His compassions fail not. They are new every morning; great is Your faithfulness. "The Lord is my portion," says my soul, "Therefore I hope in Him!"'"

"That's beautiful."

"Isn't it? Well, I promised my father we would be back at the tech center at least by sundown. It's near the amphitheater, so we'll have to hurry."

"Am I going to get to hear your story?" he said.

"Of course. And I want to hear yours. Maybe after breakfast tomorrow."

Chang found the tech center much as he might

have expected, except that it was so incongruous to see the massive network of computers in a building cut from rock. By that time, however, he was much more impressed with Naomi than with hardware and software.

"Can you find your way to your quarters?" she said. "We retire early here and rise with the sun."

"I can, but I'd rather not," he said. "I think I need a guide just one more time, you know, being my first night here."

"I can find you one. Hold on."

"Naomi!" he said. "I'm kidding. Of course I can find it. I'd just rather you walked me there."

"In my cul—"

"Inappropriate, of course. How about my walking you home?"

"That would be acceptable and even chivalrous. My father is waiting for me, and it will be dark by the time I arrive. He will appreciate that I had an escort."

Like Abdullah, Naomi's father tended a small fire outside their place. He was a tall, rotund man with a thick, curly beard. Chang approached shyly, took off his cap in the darkness, and bowed. "Chang Wong," he said.

Naomi's father grasped him by the shoulders and pressed his right cheek to Chang's, then his left. "Eleazar Tiberias," he said with a great, deep voice. "Perhaps you know my lake."

Chang scratched his head and looked at Naomi, which seemed to bring no end of mirth to her and her father.

"I have heard so much about you, young man," the elder said. "I am grateful to you for looking after my daughter, and I look forward with great anticipation to getting to know you better."

Chang breathed deeply of the crisp night air on his way to his quarters. Abdullah's fire was just smoldering now, and the smoke permeated Chang's clothes. He felt so free, so happy, and so enamored that he was sure he would not be able to sleep. He knelt by his bed, hardly knowing what to pray. He tried to remember the verse Naomi quoted, but all he could come up with was "Great is Your faithfulness," so he repeated that over and over as he climbed into the cot. Through the open window he stared at skies so clear he felt as if he could see every star in the universe. But after fewer than sixty seconds he saw nothing but Naomi in his dreams.

● ● ●

Mac studied Rayford's scribblings. "You copied every last word of this conversation, didn't you?"

"I didn't know what else to do," Rayford said. "Clearly the clue is in that Colorado business."

"What do you remember about it, Ray?"

"It was so long ago, Mac. Just one of those

summer things you do when the kids are little. Raymie wasn't even born yet. It was just the three of us."

"Yeah, but after she tells you what to say to Buck and Kenny, she says something about this being her fault. And then the jogging stuff, she's not serious about that, is she?"

"Being thirty miles from home? Nah. Trying to mislead the GC, no doubt, but they're not going to fall for that."

"She promises not to give anything away, and you know, I believe every word of that."

"Me too. They won't get anything out of Chloe."

"So she says the trip was 'so special and I wish everybody could go there again.' But you say it was just the three of you."

"Right. So she, what, wants everybody in San Diego to go to Colorado?"

"Can't be," Mac said. "She says herself she knows the GC is listening in. But she says her dream is that 'we could all go there right now, as soon as possible.' Where did you go in Colorado, Ray?"

Rayford shook his head. "I don't remember. Where do you go there?"

"Been there lots of times," Mac said. "What cities were you in?"

"Just the Springs and Denver, I think."

"You do the cog railway thing?"

"Pikes Peak, sure."

"The place with all those big rock formations?"

"Yeah, Garden of the Gods."

"That cowboy place, the ranch?"

"Flying W, of course. Wouldn't miss that."

"Air Force Academy?"

"Drove by it but didn't have time. We were going to a concert."

"Where?"

"Outside of Denver. And it was outside too. Seemed like we climbed forever, and I had to carry Chloe. I was so out of breath at that altitude."

"Red Rocks?"

"Yes! That was the place. Some country-music deal. Chloe loved it."

"You got it yet, Ray?"

"Got what?"

"What she's trying to tell you."

"No, but apparently you do, Mac. Spill it."

"Red Rocks."

"That's what I said."

"Um-hm."

"Oh! Petra! The GC is on to the safe house, and we've got to get those people out and to Petra."

● ● ●

In the morning Abdullah ushered Chang toward an area near where the elders' council met daily. Fresh manna covered the ground all along the way, and many were out gathering their breakfasts. "I will not be joining you today," Abdullah said, "as Miss Naomi has need of me in the computer center. She requests that you come and help when you are free as well."

"Is there a problem?"

"I'm afraid there is."

Chang stopped. Abdullah sounded so sad, so ominous. "What is it?"

"I'd rather not spoil your breakfast, Master Chang."

"It would spoil my breakfast? I am meeting with my heroes, and I am here where I can go where I please and do what I want, and still there is news that intrudes enough to ruin my day?"

"Please hurry. Let us not be late."

"I need to know, Mr. Smith. Tell me it's not Chloe Williams."

"She is alive for the moment, and except for the fact that the Global Community News Network is spreading the most heinous lies about her, everyone involved speculates that the GC will not execute her as long as they think they can get information from her."

Chang shook his head as they continued walking. "So she would be better off to pretend to be about to cave, to at least be considering giving them something, than to make plain from the beginning that she will not."

"Have you met Mrs. Williams?"

"Of course not."

"But you have dealt with her by phone and via the Internet enough to know—"

"Her personality. Yes. Not only will she not be betraying a thing, but she will also enjoy telling them so."

"My fear," Abdullah said, "is that this will shorten her potential benefit to the GC and thus shorten her life."

"Surely the San Diego Trib Force is planning a raid."

"I do not know. Knowing Cameron, it must be all he can do to keep from trying to blast in there on his own. George Sebastian will want to lead such an effort, and he's the man for it, but this is not like surprising a band of amateurs in the woods, as they did in Greece. You can imagine that the San Diego GC is alert to just such an effort."

"You're not telling me everything, are you, Mr. Smith?"

"I should save some for you to learn at the tech center, not that Naomi is eager to tell you either."

Chang stopped again and put a hand on Abdullah's shoulder. "Forgive my familiarity, but there is no point in withholding information. Please, I must know. Don't make me go in there unprepared."

Abdullah appeared to study the ground. He stooped and scooped a handful of manna but just held it. "The GCNN says Chloe gave up Albie and that he committed suicide rather than be taken in."

"Come on, Mr. Smith. We know that's not true. She would never—"

Abdullah took Chang's elbow and urged him to keep moving. "No one suspects Chloe of having anything to do with it, and anyone who knows Albie does not believe he killed himself."

"Then what is the probl—?"

"There is evidence that Albie may be dead. He and Mr. McCullum had grown close, as you know, and when word reached Mac, he tried several different ways to get in touch with Albie."

"It could be coincidence. He may have been away from his phone. Maybe he—"

"He is never away from his phone. Mac has always been able to reach him."

"But Mac and Captain Steele should be in San Diego by now. Maybe the satellite phone acts up at that distance and—"

Now it was Abdullah's turn to stop. "We are almost there. Around the next bend, Drs. Ben-Judah and Rosenzweig await you. Mr. Tiberias will make the introductions and attend to the meal. Meals are short here because we eat only one food and enjoy springwater with it."

"Thank you, Mr. Smith. I am going to go believing that Albie will still call back."

"All right, if you insist on knowing. . . . Albie's phone was answered, but not by Albie. As you may know, he was on a dangerous mission and may have erred terribly by going alone. The man who answered the phone told Mac that if he wanted to see his friend one more time, he should watch the news. We have watched and recorded that newscast, Master Chang. Naomi will show it to you after breakfast. Now go."

• • •

At 9 P.M. in San Diego, Chloe lay whimpering on the steel bed in her cell. With the setting of the sun the big room had faded to darkness, and now the only light came from the blaring TV. No one had visited her since the phony custodian had come back for what was left of his phone. She had heard her segment of the news a dozen more times—only because she had no choice—but she refused to watch again.

She didn't care about the lies. No Judah-ites would believe any of that, and if they did, Buck could straighten them out in the next issue of *The Truth*. But Albie, poor precious Albie. She hoped and prayed that was a lie too, but how could they have so quickly concocted such a vivid image of a dead man who looked so much like him?

Chloe had not eaten since seven o'clock the night before. She drew her knees up to her chest and wrapped her arms around her shins. She rocked, trying to ease the pain in her stomach. She tried to comfort herself by imagining the operation George and Buck and her father had to be planning that very minute.

Chloe tried to force from her mind thoughts of Kenny, because she so longed for him that her arms ached. Would she ever see him again? How would Buck answer their son's questions about her? Who would take care of Kenny when Buck was away?

She wondered if sleep would ease the hunger pangs and whether it was possible to sleep. She had learned enough about such things from George to know that any attempt to free her would have to come when the GC least expected it, so it could be days, maybe longer. She had to learn to sleep. Somehow Chloe had to keep her sanity in spite of how she was treated.

Any vestige of prisoners' rights had disappeared with the rise of Nicolae Carpathia. *Here we are, a year to go to the end of history, and I could be shot in my cell for not bearing the mark.*

Lonely, hungry, aching for her loved ones, grieving for Albie, Chloe closed her eyes in the darkness, covered her ears, and hummed to drown out the TV. That, she realized, was why she didn't hear the night matron until she was standing at the cage. Chloe flinched and sat up quickly, terrified of the stocky silhouette.

EIGHT

NAOMI'S FATHER greeted Chang the same way he had the night before, cheek to cheek, and while Chang bowed, he did not remove his cap in the light of day. "A word to the wise," Elder Tiberias rumbled in his ear during their embrace, "just about any culture considers it impolite not to remove one's hat in the presence of one's elder."

"Forgive me, sir," Chang whispered, "but removing it would reveal a disgrace."

Eleazar Tiberias shut his eyes and nodded knowingly, as if remembering that he had been told of Chang's dual marks. "I understand."

The older man reached for a basket filled with manna. "Dr. Ben-Judah will be a few moments, but let me introduce you to Dr. Rosenzweig. Come, come."

Chang followed the big man into his quarters,

where he was surprised to see the diminutive Chaim Rosenzweig, who looked more like Albert Einstein than the famous Micah who had stood up to the potentate. Rosenzweig had apparently been in Petra long enough for his hair to grow back, his pigmentation to return to normal, and to look like his old self.

Rosenzweig leaped to his feet, a bundle of energy for such an elderly man. "So you are Chang Wong, the genius mole!"

"Well, I—"

"Do not feign modesty, my young friend. God has used you. Oh, he has used you so mightily! Ah, the rewards that await you in heaven." He took Chang's arm and pressed it against his own side. "Come, let us wait outside for Dr. Ben-Judah. Eleazar, join us, please. Dr. Ben-Judah, as you know, is the leader here, though he is my junior by many years. Oh yes, at least twenty years. He was a student of mine many, many years ago. It is true. Well, Mr. Wong, welcome, welcome, welcome. It is unfortunate you join us on a day of sadness over the loss of one of our members and the capture of another, but we are happy that you are with us."

From a distance, Chang saw the commotion as Dr. Ben-Judah approached. He was flanked by several of the other elders, and they were coming from the direction of the tech center.

Dr. Rosenzweig confided, "Those men will not be joining us, and they are not bodyguards per se. None are needed here, of course. But Dr. Ben-Judah is so popular and beloved, if he is not surrounded by the elders, he would never get anywhere. Everyone wants a moment of his time, but those moments add up. They just want to express their appreciation and their love, but he has so much to do and such a heavy schedule."

"I'm honored that he would take a little time with me," Chang said. "Like everyone else, I want a moment of his time."

"Oh, trust me, young friend, I know him well, and he has been looking forward to this."

The other elders peeled away as Dr. Ben-Judah arrived. "I am so sorry to have postponed and then to be late on top of that," he said. "But it could not be helped. Well, someone introduce me to our newest resident."

Eleazar Tiberias chuckled loudly as Dr. Rosenzweig said, "Oh, I believe you know who this is. Dr. Tsion Ben-Judah, may I present Chang Wong."

Dr. Ben-Judah eschewed the customary Jewish greeting, first returning Chang's bow, then stepping forward to embrace the boy tightly. "Sit, sit," he said. "Sit right here between Dr. Rosenzweig and me. You know, years ago he was my prof—"

"I have told him all about it, Tsion," Chaim said. "Let us pray and eat."

Tsion leaned close and whispered, though loud enough for Chaim's benefit too, "The elderly have no patience!"

Tsion held one of Chang's hands and reached across him to take one of Chaim's too. "Eleazar, join us and take a hand, please."

As the four sat holding hands, Dr. Ben-Judah lifted his face and Chang bowed his head. "Great Father, creator, master, and friend," he began, "as we begin yet another day leading to the glorious appearing of our Lord and Savior, we bless your name. We thank you for our daily bread. And we are humbled as we think of where we were so few scant years ago. Mr. Tiberias, a businessman and devout man of religion. Dr. Rosenzweig, a statesman and scholar and agnostic. I, a student of the Bible but blind to the truth. And Mr. Wong, a brilliant young atheist. Who but a good God would give us all a second chance and redeem us by the blood of your precious Son? We praise you in his name."

Tsion held out the basket of manna to Chang, who took a small handful. The older men all took goodly portions, and Tsion said, "Allow me to show you how I eat my daily provision. I am grateful that mealtime does not consume the time it once did, though I confess there are days when I miss everything that used to go with it. Often my meals here last but five minutes."

He allowed the manna to settle in his right palm, wrapped his fingers gently around it, and formed a circle with his thumb and forefinger. "Like peanuts, no?" he said, smiling, and tapped his thumb knuckle on his chin until the wafers popped into his mouth. "A handful," he said, chewing, "and I am nourished."

Mr. Tiberias stood and gathered leftovers into the basket, then tossed them to the wind, where they scattered on the ground.

"Tell me, Dr. Ben-Judah," Chang said, "is it true about Albie?"

"That he is dead? I am afraid so," Tsion said. "Self-inflicted, no, none of us believes that."

After a few moments, Chaim said, "Tsion, we really must be going."

"Oh, sir," Chang said, "I hesitate to ask because I have been told by everyone how busy you are and how everyone wants a bit of your time. . . ."

"Please, Chang. We feel so indebted to you. Ask anything of me, and if I can comply, I will."

"I need just a moment alone, sir. No offense, Dr. Rosenzweig."

"None taken. Mr. Tiberias and I will prepare for our meeting."

Tsion took Chang behind an outcropping of rock. "What can I do for you?"

Chang took off his cap, exposing the *30* emblazoned on his forehead and the thin, pink line where the Global Community biochip had been inserted. He caught the pity in the older man's eyes.

"I confess it *is* strange, Mr. Wong, to see that when I also see the mark of the believer on you."

"I can't stand to look in the mirror," Chang said. "I don't dare take off my hat here. Yes, it may have kept me alive and yes, I had access where no believer would have dreamed. But it mocks me, curses me. I hate it."

"It was forced on you, son. It was not your choice or your fau—"

"I know all that, sir, but I want it gone. Is that possible?"

"I do not know."

"Sir, I study your teachings every day. You say that with God all things are possible. Why would he not remove this now?"

"I do not know, Chang. I just do not want to promise that he will."

"But what if I believe he will? And if you believe?"

"We can agree in faith on this, Chang, but as much as we believe and trust and study, no one can claim to know the mind of God. If you want me to pray that God will remove it, I will. And I believe he can and will do what he chooses. But I want you to pledge that you will accept his decision either way."

"Of course."

"Do not say that glibly. I can see how much you want this, and if God does not grant it, I do not want to see your faith threatened."

"I will be disappointed and I will wonder why, but I will accept it. Will you pray for me?"

Dr. Ben-Judah seemed to study Chang's face. He pressed his lips together, then looked away. Finally, he said, "I will. Come, sit over here and wait. Much as you want to do this in private, I prefer having men of God agree together in prayer. Do you mind?"

"Of course not. I just hate to have them see me with this—"

"There is no getting around that. It may be part of the price."

Chang nodded, and Tsion moved away to call for Eleazar and Chaim. They came, looking somberly at Chang, who sat on a rock and had begun to weep. Tsion briefed them and asked them to join him in the effort of prayer. The three approached, Ben-Judah in the middle, Tiberias on his left, and Rosenzweig on his right.

Tsion placed his left hand behind Chang's head and the heel of his right hand on Chang's forehead. The other two each took one of Chang's hands and put their free hands on his shoulders. Chang shuddered at the gentle touch from these three men of God, and he felt loved by them and by God. His body stiffened and then relaxed.

"Creator God," Tsion began, so softly Chang could barely hear him, "we acknowledge that you made this young man. You have known him and loved him since before the earth was formed. You, who are rich in mercy, loved us even when we were dead in trespasses, made us alive together with Christ and raised us up together, and made us sit together in the heavenly places in Christ Jesus, that in the ages to come he might show the exceeding riches of his grace in his kindness toward us in Christ Jesus. For by grace we have been saved through faith, and that not of ourselves; it is the gift of God, not of works, lest anyone should boast. For we are his workmanship, created in Christ Jesus. . . .

"Now, Chang Wong, knowing that you were not redeemed with corruptible things like silver or gold but with the precious blood of Christ, as of a lamb without blemish and without spot, believe in God. He raised Christ from the dead and gave him glory so that your faith and hope are in God. We now come together in faith, believing. We pray to the God for whom anything is possible, the God who spared us like Shadrach, Meshach, and Abednego of old from the fire of the enemy and made it so that we were people on whose bodies the fire had no power; the hair of our heads was not singed, nor were our garments affected, and the smell of fire was not on us.

"God, according to your will, we ask that you remove from this boy any sign of the evil one."

Chang went limp and felt as if his limbs weighed a hundred pounds apiece. He perspired profusely from every pore and felt sweat run down his face and arms and torso. The men's hands were wet, but they remained still, unmoving in the silence.

Just when Chang felt that if the men let go he would slide off the rock, Tsion said, "Thank you, gentlemen."

They squeezed Chang's hands and shoulders and stepped back. Now he was supported only by Tsion, who still cupped the back of his head and had his right hand over Chang's forehead. He pressed with that hand and let it slide around to the right so that now he had both hands behind Chang's head.

Chang opened his eyes, blinking against the sun and studying the face of Dr. Ben-Judah as Tsion studied his.

Tsion smiled. "Gentlemen," he said, "what do you see?"

Tiberias leaned in from one side and Rosenzweig from the other.

"Praise God!" Chaim said.

Eleazar lifted his head and roared with laughter in his deep bass voice. "I see only the mark of the believer! I have a mirror in my house. Come, see for yourself!"

• • •

Rayford had never seen Mac so despondent. Or so resolute.

"If somebody's killed that old boy, I'm gonna have to do something about it, Ray," Mac said. "Find me something to do that puts me right in the middle of it, and I'm not kidding."

"Albie and I go way back too," Rayford said.

"I know you do. And I feel like I've known him forever."

"What's your gut tell you, Mac? This just part of the GC's propaganda, or is he gone?"

Mac sighed. "Well, no way he killed himself, but I feel like they got him."

Rayford used Mac's phone to call Buck and tell him they would be putting down at about 10 P.M., San Diego time.

"Buck's phone. Hey, Mac, this is George."

"Well, this is Mac's phone, but it's Rayford. How's it going there, George?"

"Like you'd imagine. Buck's in pretty bad shape. It's all we can do to keep him from heading to GC headquarters by himself."

"Can you guys come get us at ten?"

"Ten? You made good time."

"Not bad. Only stopped once, then detoured a bit to drown my phone. Make Buck come with you. Maybe we can all help keep him cool."

"*You* make him come with me. He's not listening to me, and he shouldn't have to."

"Is he there?"

"He's down with Kenny. The little guy's having trouble getting to sleep without his mom."

"Well, tell Buck I said it's a directive. The four of us need to talk as soon as we hit the ground. Can somebody watch Kenny?"

"Sure. For right now we've got more babysitting volunteers than we can use."

"Hey, you think it's too late to call Lionel Whalum in Illinois?"

"Nah. He's a night owl. 'Sup?"

"I figured out Chloe's message. She's convinced we've got to get everybody out of San Diego and to Petra."

"I was afraid of that," Sebastian said.

"Lionel's the only guy I know with enough

planes, enough contacts, and enough experience to pull off something like that—and fast."

"This place was so perfect."

"Every safe house we've had has been perfect until it all of a sudden wasn't safe, George."

"Can't argue with that."

"Call Lionel for me, would you? I need to try to get hold of Zeke. See if he's ready to come out of mothballs and help us in Petra."

"What're you thinking, Captain?"

"Something for Buck to do so he doesn't go crazy, and something for Mac and me to do so we feel like we're doing something for Albie."

"Hope I'm part of that."

"We wouldn't dream of trying anything without you, George."

● ● ●

"Tired of that TV?" the night matron asked Chloe.

"Yeah. I hope I don't miss it though." Chloe had been watching the congregating of armies from every country in the United Carpathian States, excluding only the city of New Babylon, which was largely ignored on the news. In the flickering light of the TV, Chloe could see the woman was black.

"I'm Florence," she said, jangling to the TV and turning it off with her nightstick. "I'll be the one feeding you tonight if you've been good. You been good?"

"I'm officially hungry, if that's what you mean."

"That's not what I asked you, but I do have your daily energy bar in my pocket if you want it."

"I want it."

"Didn't take long for your tune to change. I heard you was all uppity and smart-alecky before, like nobody had nothin' you needed or wanted."

"I'd like to stay alive."

"For how long? You better be coming up with something Jock can use or you won't make your first hosing down."

"And when is that?"

"Once a week. A week from now."

"I don't bathe for a week?"

"Bathe all you want in that sink. How's that water taste?"

"Not like water."

Florence cackled. "Ain't that the truth. You'll get to like it though. You got to have it. That two hundred fifty calories a day will keep you alive, but you won't be good for much else."

"What else is there in here?"

"Oh, you know, a guard or two might take a liking to you, want a date. You know what I mean."

Chloe laughed. She couldn't help it.

"You think it's funny? What you going to do?"

"That would be worth dying for," Chloe said. "They'd have to kill me first."

"You say that now. But you ain't going to kill me. Look at the size I got on you."

"One of us wouldn't come out of here alive."

"Big talk. You'll be singing a different song when your body weight drops and you be stinking and that jumpsuit is falling off you."

"I'll warn you right now, while I'm lucid, you and anybody else around here would regret trying anything with me."

"That so?"

"That's so, and that includes Jock."

"Jock don't do that kind of thing, but he knows when to look the other way."

"Well, he'll look back to find somebody dead. One of his people or his star prisoner."

"Why don't you just give a little, girl? Tell Jock something. He's not asking for much. And you'd be getting breaks nobody else has got for months. Come in here with no mark and still be alive? That should tell you something. You're in a bargaining position."

"They might as well kill me now."

"Don't think I wouldn't like to."

"You? You don't even know me. I wouldn't want to kill you."

"You just said you would, missus. If I came in that cage."

"Well, yes, if you intended me any harm, I'd defend myself."

"I mean you all kinds of harm. You're either with us or against us now, honey."

"Well, I'm against you," Chloe said.

"Tell me something I don't know."

"Tell me what form these two hundred fifty calories come in."

"You know. The energy bar."

"And that's all I get?"

"That's it. Once a day."

"A person can't live on that."

"You said it, not me. 'Course, the more you tell, maybe the more you get."

"Maybe?"

"But not likely. Like since you didn't earn it today, I'm in charge of it tonight. And you only get one every twenty-four hours. Way you been sassing me, I might just pass it on to Nigel for tomorrow."

Chloe wanted to beg for it, but she would not. She would just fall silent and hope Florence would get some fun out of being the one in charge of the food each day.

"If you're still awake and don't tick me off anymore, I'll bring it by about midnight. Now, in case you want to read or do your makeup, paint your toes, whatever, I'll turn the lights on. And since the TV's off, I'll pipe in a little music to help you sleep."

Oh, please, leave the lights and music off.

Florence waddled to the door, elbows resting on her leather equipment belt, which had everything but a gun—nightstick, can of Mace, ring of keys, empty holster, and for whatever reason, a supply of bullets. She flipped the lights on, all of them, and it seemed to Chloe it was brighter than when the sun had shone through the windows.

She could deal with that. She would turn her face to the wall. And despite her deep, private regret that she had cost herself a bit of food for a few more hours, Chloe would handle that as well. She would pray, think of her loved ones, rehearse her Bible memory verses, and hope to drift off to sleep.

But then came the music, louder than it needed to be. Much too loud. And of course it was "Hail Carpathia" on a loop that would no doubt play all night.

Buck had taught her his alternate words. That might amuse her for a few minutes. What were they again? She walked them through her mind, then began to hum along, then softly sing:

Fail Carpathia, you fake and stupid thing;
Fail Carpathia, fool of everything.
I'll hassle you until you die;
You're headed for a lake of fire.
Fail Carpathia, you fake and stupid thing.

• • •

Chang had raced from Eleazar Tiberias's mirror to the tech center, where he leaped and shouted, exulting with Abdullah and Naomi.

Eventually, however, they showed him the tape of Albie, which sobered him. And despite being fresh from the palace, even Chang was stunned at the gall of the GC to air a so-called news story about Chloe that was so patently invented. He wondered how even GC sympathizers could buy such poppycock. But Naomi showed him samples of e-mails coming in from Judah-ites around the world that showed many were going to need reassurance and to be reminded that the devil is the father of lies.

"Our writers," Naomi told Chang, "here in this section, are composing boilerplate responses, answers to the most common questions. These will be transmitted to the keypunch people, who can pick and choose and shoot them out immediately."

She asked a writer to print out his current list of responses, then pulled it from the printer to show Chang.

> The only thing the news seemed to get right was Chloe's name and age and the fact that she is the daughter of Rayford and the wife of Cameron "Buck" Williams. While it's true

she attended Stanford University, neither was she a campus radical nor was she expelled. She dropped out after the Rapture but had a grade point average of 3.4 and had been active in student affairs.

Rayford Steele did serve, while already a believer, as pilot on the staff of Nicolae Carpathia, providing invaluable information to the cause of Christ's followers everywhere. He was never fired and never charged with insubordination or drinking while on duty. He left after his second wife was killed in a plane crash.

The Judah-ites are anything but "the last holdouts in opposition to the New World Order." Many Jewish and Muslim factions, as well as former militia groups primarily in the United North American States, still have refused to accept the mark of loyalty to the supreme potentate and must live clandestinely in fear for their lives.

Cameron Williams was indeed formerly a celebrated American journalist who also worked directly for the potentate, but he quit rather than "losing his job due to differences in management style." As for his subversive cyber and printed magazine's "limited circulation," that, of course, is a matter of opinion. *The Truth* is circulated to the same audience that is ministered to daily by Dr. Tsion Ben-Judah, at last count still more than a billion.

Rayford Steele, Cameron Williams, and Chloe Williams are not "wanted for more than three dozen murders around the world." The Tribulation Force acknowledges one kill for Cameron Williams and two for Rayford Steele, both in self-defense.

The International Commodity Co-op, headed by Mrs. Williams, has never hijacked any goods, nor does it sell for any kind of profit, but rather trades for the benefit of its members.

The Williamses have amassed no fortune on the black market or otherwise. In fact if not for the generosity of its members, no such Co-op could exist.

Mrs. Williams has never had an abortion or lost a child, and has had but one pregnancy, resulting in a son, now three-and-a-half years old. The Williamses have never claimed deity or special powers for their son, though they do believe Nicolae Carpathia is the Antichrist and that Jesus Christ will one day conquer Carpathia and bring his own kingdom to earth.

Limited contact with Mrs. Williams since her capture has confirmed that she is committed to not bargaining with the GC, and that is

> the policy of the Tribulation Force. Not only is she not offering anything to avoid a death sentence, but she has also been on the record many times in the past regarding her willingness to die for the cause of Christ.
>
> There is no evidence that Mrs. Williams provided any information about Tribulation Force activist Al Basrah, and neither is there evidence to support that he committed suicide.

"Will this do any good?" Chang said.

"Among our people it will," Naomi said. "Even people who know better want to be reassured. Everybody else is preoccupied with troop buildup in the Jezreel Valley anyway."

"What's happening in San Diego?"

"Not much until Captain Steele and Mr. McCullum get there, which should be any minute now. We are gearing up for at least two hundred new arrivals over the next few days, so that should tell you something. Have you talked with your sister lately?"

"No. But I've been meaning to, and now, of course, I have news for her."

"Well, she has news for you too."

"What?"

"Oh, I can't spoil it for her."

"Naomi!"

"Now, no. I can't wait to meet her, and I don't want to start off on the wrong foot by breaking her confidence."

"She told you something she hasn't told me?"

"Not exactly. But my job makes me privy to information I might not otherwise know."

"Such as . . ."

"Such as messages to the leadership. Rather than have them come and read them off the computer, often we print them out and deliver them ourselves."

"And so from one of those you learned something about my sister that she would want to tell me herself."

Naomi nodded.

"Well, I can take care of that in short order," he said, pulling out his phone. "And then when will you have a few minutes?"

"Right now," she said. "But only a few. It's going to be a hectic day."

"You owe me a story."

"My story, you mean? It's really my father's and my story, but it's not a long one, so yes, I'll have time to tell it."

"I'll see you in ten minutes then," Chang said, punching his sister's number.

"Hello, Chang," Ming said when she answered. "Forgive me for whispering, but I am baby-sitting Kenny Bruce, and he is finally asleep."

"Just wondering how you were and how things are going out there."

"I'm sure you know."

"Yes. I have news for you."

"Tell me, Brother."

"God has removed the mark of the beast from my forehead."

"Praise God! Tell me all about it! I can't wait to see you."

He told her what had happened.

"That's too wonderful for words, Chang. Too bad it had to happen on an otherwise unhappy day."

"Yes, and you have news for me, no?"

"What are you talking about?"

"I have no idea. It's just a hunch."

"Oh, Chang. Ree has asked me to marry him, and I have asked Dr. Ben-Judah to officiate when we arrive."

NINE

"LET ME scout the area," Buck said, "make sure they're clear to land."

George, behind the wheel of the Hummer, shot Buck a sideward glance. "Nobody was in the area when we left the compound, there's been no one suspicious along the way, and no one followed us. We came the last half mile in the dirt, using the lights only to make sure we were on track. Buck, the airstrip is as secure as it's ever been."

Buck sighed and shook his head. "When did I become the cautious one? You're the military guy."

"There's cautious and prepared, and there's paranoid," Sebastian said. "I know they've got Chloe, but that wasn't because of some vast stakeout. It was her fault. I'm sorry, but your father-in-law said she admitted that herself. And she has a history of venturing out—"

"But *why* was she out? I saw guys. She must have seen 'em too. And they got her."

"Routine reconnaissance. You said yourself they looked bored."

"Well, they're not bored now, are they?"

"No, Buck, they're not bored now. I'm parking at the end of the runway. You want to go traipsing around in the woods till they get here, be my guest."

"You're not coming?"

"You're the boss. If you tell me to come, I'll come. But you distinctly said, 'Let me scout the area.' Well, I'm letting you scout the area."

"Come with me."

"You're making me?"

"I'm asking you as a friend."

"That's not fair, Buck. Don't play that card."

"Come on. What if I find something? You'll never forgive yourself."

"You're incurable."

Buck knew Sebastian was right. The fact was, he was frazzled and needed something to do. He was ready to head straight to San Diego GC headquarters, guns blazing, and bust Chloe out. "You know Rayford will be up for going after Chloe," Buck said as they tramped through the woods in their fatigues, Uzis at their sides.

"C'mon, he and Mac will have just spent nearly sixteen hours in the air, probably splitting the piloting duties. These guys are going to need to sack out."

"You know Mac's heard about Albie. He'll be wired and ready to go."

"He'll be looking to get back to Al Basrah and find out what happened. Anyway, Buck, even if we do plan a raid, when are we going to do it, and who's going to get our people to Petra in the meantime?"

"I thought Rayford was getting Lionel on that."

"Lionel will organize and supply it, sure. But we've got to lead these people and see the work gets done."

Buck slapped a mosquito. "What're we doing? There's nothing out here. Whose idea was this anyway? You hear a jet?"

"No. Now we're out here like you said, so let's do a job."

"Now you *want* to look for something?"

"I just don't want to waste time, that's all. Let's not get too far from the landing strip."

Buck was suddenly swarmed by bugs. He let his Uzi dangle and smacked his head and face with both hands. "Let's get out into the open."

They emerged at about the midpoint of the strip.

"Now we're going to have to go all the way down to that end when they get here," George said.

"Let's head that way now," Buck said. "You can occupy your time helping me plan the attack."

"On GC headquarters?"

"Where else?"

"What do you know about the place?"

"What do you mean? We've been past there. You've seen it."

"Buck, neither of us has ever been inside. I know it's four floors plus a basement, but I don't even know if they use the basement for prisoners. Do you?"

"Nope, but I remember they have bars on the windows down there."

"Well, that's good. That's helpful. But the more you know, the more you should realize you don't know."

"What kind of GI mumbo jumbo is that?"

The big man stopped. "All right," George said, "look. Here's my take on San Diego GC headquarters. I know it's one of the biggest in North America, but I have no idea how many personnel they have. Do you?"

"No."

"Of the four floors and the basement, I don't know which houses the jail. Do you?"

"No."

"I'm guessing they segregate men and women prisoners, but I don't know for sure. Do you?"

"No."

"Well, if they do, are they all on the same floor or different floors?"

"Couldn't tell you."

"You see where we are, Buck? Nowhere. A military operation, especially a surprise first strike, is a complicated, highly planned maneuver. We'd have one objective and one only, and that is to get Chloe out alive. To accomplish that, we'd have to have someone inside."

"We can't get someone inside!"

"Then how are we going to do this, Buck? Think, man. Think what we'd have to know before we go charging in there. Do they keep high-profile prisoners separate from the general population, and if they do, where?"

"All right. You've made your point."

"I haven't even started, Buck. You guys are all enamored with my military training, but you don't know the half of it. Most of this is just common sense. Besides knowing exactly where Chloe is, we'd have to know the shortest distance in and out. We'd have to know what doors or windows might be vulnerable. We'd have to know how much firepower we'd need, and, Buck, you tell me what that means. What will determine our munitions needs?"

"The size and strength of the doors and windows?"

"Well, that, yeah. But it's their personnel, buddy. How many of them are we going to run into, and what will their resources be? If you could tell me Chloe was in the northeast corner of the second floor and how many GC I'd have to get through to get there, then how many are guarding her and what kind of weapons they are toting, I might be able to plan a mission for you. Otherwise, we're messing around, guessing, and we're likely to get a strike mission force wiped out."

They reached the end of the runway and sat in the grass in the darkness. "Then how does anybody ever pull off a raid like that?"

George cradled his weapon in his lap. "It's never easy, but there are prerequisites, and in the good old days when people weren't identified by a mark, you could usually get somebody into a place. Somebody has to have a thorough working knowledge of the building, maybe even access to the blueprint, the floor plan, the utility systems."

"I can't just do nothing, George. What're we going to do?"

Buck saw the landing lights before he heard the roar of the Gulfstream's engines. He signaled with a powerful flashlight that the area was clear, and within minutes the plane was down and hidden, and Rayford and Mac were disembarking.

The four shook hands without a word; then Buck and Rayford embraced. Neither was much for showing emotion, but they held each other tight for longer than Buck could remember doing before. They loaded the Hummer, but before they got in, Mac said, "I feel twenty years older. Do we have to sit in a cramped space again right away?"

"We're in no hurry," Rayford said. "Stretch your legs."

"I don't mind getting back a little late anyway," Buck said. "We've had no GC activity today, but they'll be snooping around later for sure."

Rayford said, "You don't suppose Chloe got them started in a whole new direction by claiming she was thirty miles from home?"

Buck chuckled. "Hardly, but you got to hand it to her for trying. Actually, it'll be interesting to see where they are tonight. That should give us an idea where they picked her up."

"Now you're thinking," George said. "It'll also give us an idea how long it'll take them to discover the compound and how much time we've got to get out of there."

● ● ●

"I really mustn't be gone too long," Naomi said. Chang sat with her beside a pillar that made up part of the portico in the courtyard of the Urn Tomb. "Now if I had someone like you who could fill in for me, I could be gone longer."

"But with who?" he said, and she laughed. "Seriously, though, I'm curious about your background."

"I love remembering, Chang, though it is also a sad story. My father was a businessman, a restauranteur. He owned several eateries in the area around Teddy Kollek Stadium. Do you know Jerusalem?"

"No."

"He was honest and good and people liked him, respected him. That is very important in my culture."

"Mine too."

"I suppose in all cultures a person's reputation is paramount. But my father took great pride in his many friends and his successful businesses. He provided well for my mother and me. He was also a devoutly religious man, and so our family was too. Synagogue every Sabbath. We knew the Scriptures. We loved God. I believe my father was proud of that, but not in a bad way—you know what I mean?"

Chang nodded.

"About eight years ago—this was when I was eleven—my mother fell ill. Cancer. Cancer of the . . . well, you'll forgive me if I am too shy to mention it. We do not know each other well enough for me to be comfortable about it."

"It's all right."

"She was very ill. My father was so good to her. He had the money to hire help for her, full-time help. But he would not do that. He hired part-time help, but he cut his workday in half and spent every afternoon and all night with her. He was a wonderful example to me and made me want to help even more. We loved my mother, and my father said we should consider it a privilege to serve her the way she had served us for so many years. He made her happy despite her pain."

"He seems like a wonderful man."

"Oh, he is, Chang. He always has been. Even before. Well, just after my twelfth birthday, my mother, she took a turn for the worse and he had to put her in the hospital. The doctors told him there was no hope. But my father did not believe in 'no hope.' He believed in God. He told the doctors and anyone who wanted to grieve my mother too early that we would show them—he and his little girl would show them. And how were we going to show them? We were going to pray, and God was going to work, and my mother was going to be healed."

Chang heard the anguish in Naomi's voice, and then she fell silent. "It's okay," he said. "You can finish another time."

"No," she said, wiping her eyes. "It's just that it does not seem so long ago now. I can finish. I want to. One night my father came home from the hospital late, and he was upset. I did not go with him on school nights, only in the afternoons. I asked him, 'Father, what is it? Is Mother worse?' and he said, 'No, but she might as well be.'

"That frightened me. He had never had a cross word with her, never said a bad thing about her, at least not in front of me. But she told him something that he said was only because of all the drugs she had been prescribed. She wept and told him that wasn't true, that she really believed it. I said, 'What, Father, what?' But he burst into tears and said he had raised his voice and told her that she should stop talking nonsense.

"'I made her weep,' he told me, crying, crying his eyes out. 'The woman I love with all my soul, who is dying before my eyes, I upset her.' And I said, 'But, Father, she upset you too. What did she say?' He said, 'She told me, "Jesus is Messiah." I demanded to know where she had heard such heresy, but she would not tell me for fear I would get someone in trouble, which I would have!'

"I did not know what to think. I gasped when he repeated what she had said. He told me that he had told her that he would not allow me to see her again if she kept up with such nonsense, but that only made me cry. That very night we were called to the hospital, told that if we wanted to see her alive, we must come now.

"All the way he wept and blamed himself for being cross with her. 'I caused this!' he said over and over. He pleaded with God to spare her, made promises to him. I had never seen him so pitiful. We were with her when she died. Her last words to us—and they were to us both, Chang, because she looked directly into my eyes and spoke, and then she looked at my father and said the same thing—her last words were, 'I go to be with God. Study the prophecies. Study the prophecies.'"

"Wow!"

"I did not come to Jesus in the way you might think. The tidy conclusion might be that my father and I went home and studied the prophecies and came to believe the way my mother did. But it didn't happen that way. My father was so heartbroken that he became angry with God and quit studying the Scriptures at all. We stopped praying. We stopped going to synagogue.

"He still loved me and took care of me, but he tried to lose himself in his work. His friends only pitied him, because he was not the same man he had been.

"I could not get my mother's last words out of my head, but my father forbade me to study anything in the Bible, let alone the prophecies. I was sad, so sad, because my life had changed radically with the loss of my mother and, really, the loss of my father as I had known him. Whenever I suggested that God could help us or the synagogue might comfort us or we might find some answers in the Bible, he would not hear of it.

"I was thirteen when the disappearances happened. That got everyone's attention, even my father's. Scared to death, we turned back to God, back to synagogue, back to the Scriptures. I began studying the prophecies, and though I was young, I couldn't avoid seeing what Mother had seen when someone pointed them out to her. My father wouldn't admit it, but I think he started to see it too.

"When we heard that the renowned biblical scholar, Dr. Tsion Ben-Judah, was going to speak on international television about his conclusion about Messiah from the Bible prophecies, we watched it together. The next day everyone was talking about the trouble Dr. Ben-Judah had gotten himself into by declaring that Messiah had already come, but my dad and I were excited about more than that. He found a New Testament, and we began reading it every night.

"When we got to the story of the Jewish man Saul, who became Paul, my father was overwhelmed. We read faster and faster and more and more, and we came to believe that Jesus was Messiah and that he could save us from our sins. We memorized First Corinthians 15:1-4: 'Brethren, I declare to you the gospel which I preached to you, which also you received and in which you stand, by which also you are saved, if you hold fast that word which I preached to you—unless you believed in vain. For I delivered to you first of all that which I also received: that Christ died for our sins according to the Scriptures, and that He was buried, and that He rose again the third day according to the Scriptures.'

"All my father and I wanted to do was what Paul had done. Receive. Receive that truth by which Paul said we could be saved. We didn't know what to say or do, so we just prayed and told God we believed it and wanted to receive it. It was weeks before we read enough and knew enough to understand what we had done and what it all meant. Father finally found in the back of the New Testament a guide to salvation that talked about accepting and believing and confessing. We studied what it called the road to salvation—all those verses that tell that all have sinned and come short of the glory of God, that the wages of sin is death, but that the gift of God is eternal life through Jesus Christ our Lord."

Chang sat looking at her. "It's always something different," he said. "I can't tell you how many stories I've heard about people becoming believers, and each one is unique. I mean, they all get to the same place, but for some it was the disappearances. For you, it was your mother, really."

"We just can't wait to see her again, Chang. And it won't be long."

• • •

Chloe couldn't tell whether she had actually been dozing or was just zoned out when Florence made a loud entrance about midnight. She unceremoniously poked the energy bar through the cage and let it drop. Chloe wanted to leap on it, tear it open, and gobble it down, but her pride was still working. She turned to look, but she didn't move.

"Dinner, honey," Florence said. "I recommend a white wine, like tap water."

Chloe didn't move until she left. She ate half the bar, which was flat and tasteless. But Chloe had always been told the greatest seasoning was hunger. She wrapped the rest, determined to save it for breakfast. But the few calories she had just ingested merely triggered her appetite. She was able to hold out for about another half hour, then ate the rest.

Though she was still hungry, the bar had taken enough of the edge off that she was able to doze. She dreamed first of her family. Buck and Kenny were close enough to smell, but she couldn't reach to hold them, to touch or kiss them. Then images danced of their horrified faces, repulsed by her. Did she have the mark? Was she hideously ugly? They grimaced and turned away.

Chloe ran to a mirror and found herself headless. She fainted, and when she hit the floor, she woke up. She sat on the cot, her face in her hands, rocking. This was going to be harder than she had ever imagined. She would not for an instant be fooled or even tortured into giving the GC an iota of what they wanted. She just prayed that if she was not going to be sprung somehow—and she couldn't imagine how anyone could pull that off—her execution would be quick.

• • •

"I've come to a hard decision, Buck," Rayford said. It was two o'clock in the morning in the underground compound. Rayford sat with Buck in Rayford's quarters, where Buck would spend the night. Ming was staying at his and Chloe's place so Kenny could be in his own bed. Sebastian and a young associate were on watch.

"I don't want to hear it, do I?" Buck said.

"Probably not. But for some reason God put me in this position, and even though I'm biased and have almost as much vested interest as you do, I need to take leadership on this one. Mac is asleep. When he is fully rested, he's going to

Wisconsin to pick up Zeke. He'll drop him in Petra to start work on our next assignment."

Buck hung his head. "Our next assignment is not right here?"

"Hear me out. Mac is going to go on to clear out of Al Basrah and move to Petra. On the way I'll have him call Otto Weser, the guy I told you about. He'll be in the palace and should be able to dig up what's going on in Al Hillah. Carpathia's assistant knows Nicolae's planning a meeting in Baghdad of the ten heads of state from around the world. We believe that's when he'll add all the other regions' manpower to the armies he's already marshaling in Israel."

"Dad, I'm sorry, but I don't really care about anywhere but right here at the moment. It looks like everything is coming together for all kinds of activity over there, but meanwhile, we're hanging Chloe out to dry."

"Buck, we've both been without sleep way too long. Believe me, I've done as much crying and praying and worrying as you have, which is—"

"I doubt that."

"—exhausting. I need to rest, and so do you."

"Dad, I'm not going to be able to sleep."

"I didn't say anything about sleeping. Get your clothes off, stretch out, put your feet up. Give your body a break even if you can't turn your brain off. We need you sharp, Buck."

"You're telling me I'm not going out with George tonight."

"I'm not even letting George go, Buck. Talk about somebody we don't want to burn out. He's got a good team that can track the GC if they show tonight. All we want to know is where they're starting their canvasing. I'm impressed that people have already started packing, getting ready to go. Lionel's got planes and pilots lined up. We have to be ready to go at a moment's notice."

Buck leaned forward and rested his elbows on his knees. "I trust you, Dad, and I know you have Chloe's and my best interests at heart. But I don't get this. When do we start scoping out headquarters, figuring how to get in there or how to get next to somebody who would know something about the place?"

"You and I can see how close we can get tomorrow night. If George is available, we'll take him."

"But time's wasting."

Rayford sat back and sighed. "Job one with me is conserving resources, and that includes human ones. Our minds tell us we have energy because we can think of nothing else, but running on adrenaline like that will wear us down quicker, make us rash, ineffective. Trust me on this, Buck. I want her out of there as much as you do, but she's not the only person we're accountable for."

"But I want to know as soon as the reconnaissance party knows anything about—"

"No, now I've left word that we are not to be disturbed until midmorning except in an emergency."

"Dad!"

"Knowing something you can't act on right away anyway is no help. Now no more talk. Let's get some rest."

• • •

Like everyone else in Petra at high noon, Chang preferred working inside. He had discovered, through much trial and error, that he was able to tap into everything in New Babylon from where he was. The problem was, all the decision makers were gone to Al Hillah. When the plan to beat them there and bug the place had fizzled, he had been assigned to come up with a way that Otto Weser could feed him information. That all depended on what hardware might have been left that could be tapped from Petra.

Chang worried that he might have become too obvious in his interest in Naomi, wanting to spend every spare minute with her. He decided not to assume anything and stayed at his computer over lunchtime. He was hungry, but he could also wait for the evening manna.

Chang was thrilled when Naomi approached

shyly with a basket. "Hey, workaholic," she said. "Don't go starving on me."

"Hi," he said.

"Brought you some honey wafers."

● ● ●

"Hail Carpathia" had become just part of the background for Chloe by now. She guessed it was about four o'clock in the morning. She had tried to keep her ears covered as she dozed, but when she drifted off, her hands fell away. That was why she heard the door and held her breath.

From the heavy footsteps and the jangling keys, she could tell it was Florence. What could she want? It sounded as if she was close to the cage, and Chloe smelled food. A burger with all the trimmings. And the sound of a straw, probably in a cold soft drink. Right then it all hit Chloe as the nectar of the gods.

She slowly turned and in the low light saw Florence sit on the floor and lean back against the cage. Chloe rested on one elbow and let out her breath.

"You awake?" Florence said.

"'Fraid so."

"Want me to turn off that music?"

"Do you care what I want?"

"Don't be sassin' me again."

"If you really want to know what I want, yes, I want the music off."

"I'm not all bad, you know," Florence said.

She set next to the cage her half-eaten burger and soft drink and another tall paper cup with a lid and moved to the door. The music stopped.

When Florence returned, Chloe said, "Thank you."

"Mm-hm," she said, sliding to the floor again. "Just having a burger."

"So I gathered."

"Brought you something."

"You did not."

"See, why you wanna be that way all the time? Can't a person do something nice for somebody?"

"I wish."

"Well, your wish has been granted, if you like chocolate."

"Who doesn't?"

"How about a chocolate shake?"

"I'm still dreaming, right? No more music, and now a chocolate shake in the middle of the night. What's gotten into you?"

"I told you. Ain't all bad. Nobody is."

I can think of someone. "If you're really going to give me a chocolate shake, all I can say is I'm grateful."

"I'm a mama too, you know."

"That so?"

"Mm-hm. Brewster. Almost three."

"Have a picture?"

"I do! You wanna see it, really?"

"'Course I do."

"Jes' a minute. Can't get in trouble turning on the lights when it's only just us." She finished her meal, leaving the chocolate shake on the floor while throwing away the trash. Chloe wanted the shake so badly she trembled. Was it possible she could get next to this woman somehow, mother to mother?

Florence went out again and turned on the lights. When she returned and shut the door, it clearly locked behind her, which Chloe had already learned was protocol. The shake was not going to fit through the mesh of the cage, so if the cage door was going to be open, of course the outer door could not be unlocked. But that also told Chloe that Florence was lying about being there alone. Otherwise, how would she get back out?

"Now if I unlock this cage, which is totally against the rules, you're not going to pay back my kindness by trying something, are you? I'm bigger and stronger than you, but even if you—"

"Yeah, I know. Heard it from Jock. We're still both locked in."

"Exactly."

"So if I behave and take the shake and you lock me back in here, how are you getting out?"

"I buzz 'em, and they let me out."

"So we're not really alone."

"Well, no, not after I buzz 'em."

"What if they see what you gave me?"

"Then I'm in trouble, so if you want it, you better take it now."

"I want it."

"Stay right where you are. Don't be standing up when this door opens or I'll be shutting it again."

Florence unlocked the cage, handed Chloe the shake, then quickly locked it again. It was the first time Chloe had noticed emotion in her. Florence looked excited, maybe scared. Maybe flush with the feeling of doing something nice when she wasn't supposed to.

Chloe sucked eagerly at the straw and was not disappointed. The shake was still cold, thick, rich, and—if anything—too chocolaty. Which, as she used to laugh about with her friends, was like saying something tasted too rich.

Florence stood watching her. "Whoa, girl. 'Member you're doing that on an empty stomach. Better pace yourself."

"I will. And I don't want brain freeze."

Florence laughed.

"And don't forget to show me the picture of Brewster."

"Oh, I will. Soon as you're finished."

Why not now? Chloe wondered as she attacked the straw again. The sugar and caffeine were going to keep her awake, but it wasn't like she had anything to look forward to in the morning. Maybe Jock would show up and eat his breakfast in front of her again.

"Jock," she said, giggling.

"What?" Florence said.

"Eggs in front of me."

"What you going on about?"

"Jock. Jack. Jick. Jeck . . ."

"Hm?"

Chloe was dizzy. The cup was slipping. She reached with her other hand to steady it, but the shake fell to the floor and splashed. It hit her as the greatest tragedy she could recall, and she began to weep.

Her eyes were trying to shut. She forced herself to keep them open and deliberately lifted her chin so she could see Florence, who just stood watching. Florence pressed her buzzer. The outer door opened, and both Nigel and Jock entered, pushing a gurney.

"I'll get this cleaned up," Florence said, unlocking the cage.

"Great work, Flo," Jock said. "Loved the bit about you having a kid."

"Oh, honey, they easy when they hungry."

TEN

BUCK WAS awakened midmorning by soft but insistent knocking on Rayford's door. He reached up from the foldout couch and opened it.

"I was kinda hoping I'd wake your father-in-law," Sebastian said.

Suddenly Buck was wide awake. "What time is it?"

"Almost 1000 hours."

"What's the deal? What'd your guys find?"

"Buck, I got to go through channels."

"What're you, kidding me? You can't tell me anything about my wife?"

"I report to Rayford, Buck. So do you."

"You beat all, George. You know that?" Buck rocked himself up off the couch and banged on Rayford's door. "Sebastian's here with a briefing, Dad. Let's go."

Rayford emerged, looking foggy. "Hey, guys," he said. "How'd you sleep?"

"Same way you did," Buck said. "Now let's get to this."

Buck stuffed sheets and blankets between the mattress and the back of the couch, closed it, and sat. Rayford joined him.

"I have my guy in the hall," Sebastian said. "Wanted to make sure you two were presentable."

"Your call," Rayford said. "Here we sit in our Skivvies."

George opened the door. "Razor?" he said. "You're on."

Razor was Hispanic, early twenties, and very military. He saluted everybody and Buck waved him off. "Come on, come on," he said. "It's just us. What've you got?"

"Sirs, I was on watch, as you know, and noticed motion-detector activity at approximately 0300 hours. One of my team of three is a female, so I asked if she would check the periscope in the Williamses' quarters, due to the fact that a female was in there alone—well, with a baby, and I didn't want to breach protocol by—"

"We know why, Mr. Razor," Buck said. "Please."

"Yes, sir. She checked and reported enemy activity within two blocks of the compound and secured permission from Mrs. Toy for me to enter your domicile."

Buck glanced at Rayford, shook his head, and stared at the floor. *For the love of all things sacred . . .*

"I personally observed similar activity and so marshaled my team. We went out in fatigues and greasepainted faces, armed with lightweight, high-powered automatic weapons. Our objective was to observe, get close enough to listen, if possible, and—if necessary—either defend the compound or somehow misdirect the enemy to a neutral area, thus giving the occupants of said compound—"

"Time to evade," Buck said. "Yeah, what happened?"

"We observed two separate platoons of GC canvassing the area; however, they appeared to have started about two blocks west of us and were proceeding in a westerly direction."

"Meaning they were moving away from us rather than toward us?"

"Yes, sir, but that is not all entirely good news. Observing their direction and relative speed, we were able to flank them, and the two of my party on their south side had enough flora-and-fauna coverage to get close enough to hear them. They came away with the distinct impression that the objective for that particular mission was to begin where they had recently left off—in my estimation, Mr. Williams, what you and Mr. Sebastian had observed approximately twenty-four hours before—and were to survey a wide area leading to where Mrs. Williams was apprehended."

"I'm praying you followed them to that point," Buck said.

"We did, sir. We also overheard them saying that tomorrow night at the same time, they would be backtracking and going past where they started, which obviously would include our compound again. We expect them to be quite thorough, and thus if at all possible, we should be evacuated before 0200 hours tomorrow."

"You have informed the right people, and the move is on pace?"

"Yes, sir, but there's more. Near where they indicated Mrs. Williams was apprehended, our people recovered her Uzi and ski mask."

"What's that tell you, Buck?" Sebastian said.

"She ditched them."

"But we also—at least my people—heard two GC discussing her disposition."

It was all Buck could do to contain himself. "Please, Officer Razor, tell me what you heard about the disposition of my wife."

"They seemed to indicate that she was to be moved, sir."

"When?"

"Within the hour, sir. Something about getting it done before Carpathia starts calling for troops from this region."

"Back to the 'within the hour' business, Razor," Buck said. "Within an hour from now or then?"

"Then, sir."

"All right, quit with the 'sir' stuff, please. I know you were in the military, but I wasn't and it makes me crazy. You're telling me Chloe was to be moved at about four this morning?"

"Yes, s—"

"To where?"

"The best my people could gather, s—Mr. Williams, was 'somewhere back east.'"

"Somewhere back east." Buck stood and held his open palms to Rayford and George. "They moved her somewhere back east, which implies an aircraft—" he looked at his watch—"going on six hours ago. Tell me, Razor, did anyone think to get to GC headquarters and see if there was a chance to abort this move?"

"No, sir."

"No one thought this might be an emergency worth waking Mr. Steele or Sebastian or me?"

"By the time I got the report, sir, um, sorry, the move would have been already in progress."

"You assume."

"Yes, that's an assumption."

"The one time they might be more vulnerable

than another, taking a woman out of a cell, out of a building, into the open air to a vehicle so they could get her on an airplane, and we all sleep through it."

"I apologize, sir, but in my judgment nothing effective could have been accomplished, given when we overheard this and the, ah, assumed timing of the maneuver."

Buck could not stand still. He paced the apartment, looking expectantly at the three others. "We sat on it," he said. "We had a window of opportunity, and we were asleep."

"Buck, please," Rayford said, but Buck would not be appeased.

"Somewhere back east," Buck parroted. "That narrows it down, doesn't it? Maybe if we all just start walking east, we'll overtake them, huh?"

"Thank you, Razor," Sebastian said. "If there's nothing else, you may go."

"Thank you, sirs," Razor said.

"Yeah, thanks for nothing," Buck said.

"I apologize, sir, if—"

"Oh, just go," Buck said.

Rayford nodded at the young man, and he hurried out.

"Buck," George said, "he probably made the right decision. Racing down there in the wee hours, hoping to get there in time to do something without a plan—"

"Would have at least been an effort, wouldn't it?" Buck kicked a chair that flew into the kitchen and banged off the table and a cabinet. "I guess if I ever want to see my wife again, I'm going to have to be a one-man commando unit."

"And get yourself killed," Rayford said. "Now you've vented. That's enough."

"It'll never be enough until I have Chloe back."

• • •

Chloe had fallen off the metal shelf and into the chocolate mess on the floor. Since she was unable to break her fall, her head banged on the tile. She lay there with one leg tucked awkwardly beneath her, her head lolling, and fighting sleep. Whatever had been in the shake had tranquilized her so thoroughly that she wanted only to go with the feeling and sleep the deep sleep of the drugged. It reminded her of how she felt after giving birth to Kenny.

Florence unlocked the cage and knelt to clean up the spill. She rolled Chloe onto her side and pulled her foot down so both legs were straight. She held Chloe with one hand as she cleaned the floor, then let go, and Chloe rolled onto her back.

Her eyes fell shut and her breathing became deep and regular, but she prayed desperately. "God, let me stay conscious. Let me hear. Help me listen."

"That floor dry?" Jock said.

"Give it a second," Florence said.

"Put the sheet down there, Nigel, and take her ankles."

Chloe felt Jock's hands under her armpits and Nigel's at her feet. "On three," Jock said, and they lifted her off the floor and a few inches over to the sheet. Then they lifted the sheet to the gurney, and Chloe was glad her eyes were closed. She had lost equilibrium and felt as if she could pitch off the cart any second.

"Out to the truck quickly now."

The gurney rolled across the big room, through the door, and stopped. Chloe heard elevator doors open. She was rolled aboard, and the car lifted one floor. Soon she was outside and could not open her eyes as hard as she tried. Uncovered, she felt the cold air, but something didn't allow her even to shiver. She wanted to press her legs together and rub them and massage her arms with her hands, but she couldn't move.

"Lord, please. Keep me awake."

"A hearse?" Nigel said. "Whose idea was that?"

"Mine," Jock said, chuckling. "People don't want to look if they think there's a stiff in here."

"You going with her?" Florence said.

"Yup," Jock said, and Chloe heard pride. "It's my deal right up to the end."

"When's that going to be?" Florence said, and Chloe felt the vehicle moving.

"Not sure. They're going to milk it. We may still get some information out of her. Truth serum is next."

"That always works, doesn't it?"

"Usually."

Not this time. "God, don't let me say anything you don't want me to." Chloe was immobile from her toes to her scalp, yet God seemed to grant her wish of consciousness. She could hear and she could smell. Touch and sight were a different matter, but she had certainly felt the chill of the predawn air.

She guessed the mostly smooth ride at a little less than an hour. Then the gurney was lifted out of the hearse, rolled maybe a hundred yards, and carried by hand up some stairs and into what she assumed was a plane. And when the engines began to whine, she knew she was right. Chloe heard the congratulations and good-byes from Nigel and Florence. Then Jock and, she assumed, another man laid her out along several seats with armrests raised. The men somehow belted her in at the torso and the knees by using parts of seat belts from adjoining seats.

From their voices she could tell they sat in the row ahead of hers. She had the impression it was just the three of them and the pilots on a jumbo jet. She didn't know of another plane that had enough seats together to allow her to stretch out.

"How long is this flight anyway?" a man with a Spanish accent said.

"Four hours, I think, Jess," Jock said. "Then we've got about a fifty-mile drive from the southwest. Whole Chicago area was nuked, you know, so we'll be about as far north as we dare."

The conversation deteriorated into the mundane, and Chloe succumbed to the drowsiness.

• • •

Buck knew he was being a nuisance, but he couldn't help himself. While everyone else in the compound was preparing for the big move, he badgered people. Had anyone worked at GC headquarters before becoming a believer? Did anyone know anybody who had or did now? Any connections, any leads, any inside information? Somebody, anybody to talk to who might know someone who could be bluffed into giving out information about Chloe's whereabouts?

He tried calling headquarters himself from a secure phone, pretending to be from GC International. Nobody was buying. He scripted a speech for Ming to try while he played with Kenny. She struck out too.

Rayford finally tracked Buck down and told

him, "Do what you have to do, but be ready to go when everybody else is."

"I'll be traveling light anyway, boss," Buck said. "Don't suppose one of Lionel's guys could just drop me back east somewhere?"

Rayford shook his head and moved on.

"Hey, Dad," Buck said, "your place unlocked?"

"Yep. And empty except for your stuff."

"I'll clear it out now."

On his way to Rayford's place, Buck passed Razor in the corridor. "Sir," the young man said, saluting self-consciously.

"Hey, son, hold up. I owe you an apology."

"No, that's all right. I understand what you're going through."

"That's a reason, but it's not an excuse. I want you to forgive me. I was way out of line."

"Of course, sir. Don't give it a second thought."

"Well, thank you. And can I ask you a question?"

"Anything."

"Where's the name come from?"

Razor flushed and looked down. "Snowmobile accident."

"Ouch. Do I want to hear it?"

"First time on. In Minnesota. Not exactly like Mexico, you know? Didn't see the razor wire. Should have been killed. It caught my helmet and luckily dug in rather than sliding down and slicing my head off. It ripped that helmet off as I went underneath. People watching said the wire somehow wrapped itself around the helmet. The wire never broke, and after I had stretched it as far as it would go, it flew back and came forward again like a slingshot and flung the helmet at me, hit me in the back of the head, and knocked me out."

"But here you are. And no matter how I sounded earlier, I'm glad to have you with us."

Of all things, that crazy story got Buck obsessing about decapitation. Losing Chloe was his main concern, of course, and he worried about her suffering. He couldn't stand to think of her being violated, abused, tortured—he didn't want to even consider all the possibilities. It was no consolation to know that even if she was martyred, he would see her in less than a year. What would that mean to Kenny?

Worst of all, all he could think of was how Chloe would most likely die. Death was death and it shouldn't make any difference, he knew. But if it came to that, if the GC made a public spectacle of her, as they certainly would, there was no way he could watch it. The idea of his beloved dying such an ugly, grotesque death made him ill.

No question she would stay true to her faith to the end. He had heard stories of others, even watched as his old friend Steve Plank thumbed his nose at Carpathia and honored God before he died. Buck also knew that if it came to that, Chloe's body would be new one day in heaven. But still, he was repulsed by the idea that the person most precious to him in the world might die in the worst possible way he could imagine.

If he couldn't push it from his mind's eye now, how would it be if it actually happened? He sought out Rayford.

"I'm really busy," his father-in-law told him, "and you should be too. I'm not saying it'd take your mind off Chloe; it sure hasn't mine. But you'd be more productive."

"I know, but I need a minute."

He told Rayford of his tormenting daydreams. To his surprise, Rayford's lip began to quiver. His voice was thick. "I've been going through the same thing, Buck. I didn't want to tell you."

"Really? This whole idea?"

"Exactly. A father has a different take, you know. Imagine how you feel about Kenny. I was there when Chloe was born. Seems like yesterday she was a little red ball of squealing girl who could be comforted only by being tightly wrapped in a blanket and put on her mother's chest. Then, to us, she was the most beautiful creature we had ever seen. We would have done anything for her, anything to protect her. That's never changed. She's grown up to be a beautiful woman, and somehow, even with all her injuries and disfigurements, I still see her that way."

"So do I."

"So, yes, Buck, I know what you're thinking. We just have to be strong and try not to dwell on it. I don't know what else to do."

• • •

Chang was walking Naomi to her quarters late at night. "I want to show you something on my computer tomorrow," he said. "I discovered that the GCNN production chief's solution to the plague of darkness was, I guess, to feel his way into the control room and find the switch that allows the international network feed to be remotely accessed by three or four of the major affiliates."

"Ingenious," Naomi said. "Isn't it?"

"Oh, I was impressed. But I'm also excited. There is no block on my accessing it too, and I can override the affiliates with the system David Hassid had set up in New Babylon."

"I can't wait to see it."

"It has unlimited capabilities, Naomi. When Cameron Williams gets here, we'll work together and counteract the lies that the GC broadcasts, and we can do it immediately."

"Nothing they can do about it?"

"Not that I can think of, short of starting a

whole new network. They may think they have time to do that, but the end is closer than they know."

● ● ●

"So you drew the short straw, eh there, pardner?" Mac said.

"I am sorry, Mr. McCullum," Ree said, "but I do not understand that expression."

"Well, without getting into specifics, it means you got grunt duty."

They had studied the area through the periscope an hour before and determined they could get the Hummer out of the vehicle bay without being detected.

"Driving you to the plane? No problem. I like to do it. I only wish I was flying you to Wisconsin. I have flown a Gulfstream only once before, and I liked it."

"If you've got so little experience, I'm glad you're not flying me, know what I mean?"

A little more than three hours later, Mac touched down in Hudson, Wisconsin, where he was met by the hulking Gustaf Zuckermandel Jr., better known as Zeke.

"I wish you could meet everybody in Avery," the twenty-five-year-old said. "But even the guy who drove me has already headed back. Took us an hour to drag my stuff into the underbrush."

Mac followed him to his cache of boxes and trunks. "You sure we want to be lugging this stuff all the way to the plane in broad daylight, Zeke?"

"Unless you want to wait till dark, but there's no need. This is the part of the country the GC forgot. I haven't seen a Peacekeeper since I got here."

As they were loading, Mac said, "No second thoughts about leaving? You must be close to these people."

"Lots of second thoughts, but I figure a guy's got to go where he's called. I was called here, and now I'm being called there. Who woulda thought a no-account like me would ever get called anywhere?"

"Well, you're the best document and appearance man I ever saw, and I hear you really blossomed here."

"Oh, that's not true if you want to know the actual fact, Mr. McCullum. Thing is, there wasn't anything for me to do here as far as disguises and documents and such, because we flat didn't need 'em. So I got real involved in the Bible studies, improved my reading and all that, and pretty soon the leader took me under his wing. I never got to teaching or preaching, but I helped out all I could. I liked it, like to stay busy. They gave me that assistant pastor title sort of as a gift."

"Honorary, eh?"

"Yeah, like that."

"Well, I hope you were honored, because that really means something."

"I'm gonna miss everybody, but I got to tell you, I'm ready to get to Petra and just see the place. And to hook up again with Dr. Ben-Judah and Dr. Rosenzweig and you and all the others, well . . ."

"And you've got a big job."

"You're supposed to tell me about it."

● ● ●

Chloe more than woke up after almost four hours in the air. The drugs had worn off and she came to. And she was ravenous. An energy bar and whatever portion of shake she ingested before the Mickey kicked in had been all she'd eaten since seven the evening before she was abducted. That made it easy to pretend she was still unconscious.

"What time is it here?" Jock's companion said as the plane landed.

"Coming up on noon, and I'm hungry," Jock said. "You?"

"Oh yeah."

"I'm going to feed the prisoner finally. Play a little good cop. Shoot her a little truth juice. See if we can't get her to sing."

"She's been a tough bird, hasn't she?"

"Tell me about it, Jess. I'd have been doing the 'Hallelujah Chorus' solo by now."

"What if she doesn't flip? How long do you give it?"

"If you can't get to 'em somehow in the first forty-eight hours, more of the same isn't going to be any more effective."

"Starvation isn't a motivator?"

"Would be for me, but I guess they've proved it with prisoners of war. The ones who can survive that first round of psychological and physical torture aren't likely to ever break, no matter how long you keep it up."

As Chloe was being carried down the jetway, Jock said, "This facility never had woman prisoners before we took it over. We'll keep her in solitary. That's the only real way to keep her separate from the rest of the population."

Chloe was laid out across the backseat of a large SUV, which she noticed had wire mesh on the windows and no locks or door handles on the inside. Jock handcuffed her anyway. "She'll be coming to soon," he explained. "Can't be too careful."

When they stopped along the way, Chloe racked her brain for any idea of escape.

Jock said, "I'll get the food. You stay with her."

Chloe sat up. "I need to use the rest room."

Jock stared at her. "Seriously."

"I'd say."

"Well, I got no matron who can go with you. You'd have to use the men's, and one of us would have to be in there with ya."

"Forget it."

"You want me to buy you one of those adult diapers?"

"How far are we from where I can go?"

"Half an hour."

"I'll wait."

While Jock was inside, she tried to strike up a conversation with the man she had not gotten a look at until now. His mark was a *0,* which meant he was from the United South American States. He was strikingly dark with perfect teeth. "You remind me of my husband," she said.

"That so?" he said.

"Yeah, except he's not ugly."

The man found that hilarious and turned to face her. "You're funny," he said. "Why would you want to antagonize me?"

"You're one of the people who are going to wind up killing me. Doesn't look like I'm going to get to fight back, do any physical damage, so . . ."

"Makes sense."

"Jock calls you Jess."

"Yeah. Jesse," he said.

"Hmm. Named after Jesus. That your real name? Jesus?" Chloe pronounced it in Spanish.

"Matter of fact, yes, and I have a sister Maria."

"Is she also a Carpathianist?"

"Of course."

"How disappointing that must be to your namesake."

Jock brought food and uncuffed her. The men tore into theirs, while Chloe sat behind the cage that separated her from the front seat. She said aloud, "Lord, thank you for this food. I pray that you will help me eat it slowly so it doesn't make me sick, and that you will override any poisons Jock might have put in it. Give me strength to resist any efforts on the part of Jock or Jesse to get me to say anything I shouldn't. In Jesus' name I pray, amen."

ELEVEN

"I LIKED Albie a lot," Zeke said as Mac piloted them across the Atlantic. "He was a good man."

"You got that right, Z," Mac said. "And for the life of me I can't understand it, but I'm afraid he did something royally foolish to get himself killed."

"Doesn't sound like him. You and Captain Steele and everybody used to listen to his ideas all the time."

"But everybody's human. Let your guard down for a second, get overconfident, who knows? He was determined to see this lowlife he used to know, and even when he and I agreed I should go on to Petra and fly Rayford back to the States, Albie still wanted to go through with his little mission. It's just as much my fault. Both of us thought it was something that had to get done—and fast. Now look where we are."

"Rayford said Tsion and Chaim are taking it hard."

"We all are. As much of this as we've gone through, it never gets easier. They're planning a little service for Albie at Petra once everybody gets there from San Diego."

"When will that be?"

"Oh, first wave ought to be arriving around three in the morning tomorrow. You and I got about a thirteen-hour jump on 'em. Once I drop you off, I got to get to Al Basrah and clear out Albie's and my apartment, make sure we didn't leave any clues for anybody. I'll be taking a bigger plane from Petra 'cause I got to bring back this Otto Weser guy and his people."

"Captain Steele told me about him. So you're bringing them back to Petra because of that Scripture about God's people getting out of Babylon before God destroys it?"

"Exactly."

Z sat staring at the ocean seven and a half miles below. "What must that have looked like when it was all blood?"

"You can't imagine."

"Hey, Mac, you think Rayford ought to be trusting Carpathia's secretary?"

"The way he tells the story, I guess. You don't think so?"

"I don't trust anybody who isn't a believer. What if she has second thoughts, sets a trap, gets you and this Otto ambushed?"

"A pleasant thought."

"You said yourself, you can't be too careful."

"Well," Mac said, "we've got to know what's happening in Al Hillah, and as much as possible what's coming after that, and we don't know how else to do it."

An hour later, Zeke dug through one of his bags and brought out a book. He looked self-conscious. "Something I wouldn't even have been able to read when you knew me in Chicago."

"I was gonna say—"

"But now that I'm reading better, I think I can do more things, you know, scientifically."

"Such as?"

"Such as I'm guessing you guys are asking me to come up with new looks and identities for a bunch of people."

"Right. All our old aliases and appearances have been compromised."

"Found this book in an abandoned library just across the Minnesota border. There's all kinds of stuff in here I never even heard of before. New ways to change skin and eye color and all that.

Fake scars and blemishes. How many people are we talking about?"

"I think just five," Mac said. "I think Ray wants getups for him and Buck and Sebastian and Smitty and me."

"Really? That's it? I brought way too much stuff."

"What'd you bring?"

"Everything I had left over from Chicago. GC uniforms at all levels, IDs, documents, stuff for women and men. This is going to be easy. I mean, it'll take time, but I was afraid you'd need ten or twelve. The hardest one is going to be Mr. Sebastian, but I've already got an idea for him."

"Tell me."

Zeke put his book down, apparently so he could gesture with both hands. "The problem with your big people is that no matter what you do with them, you can't make 'em smaller. You can make a small person big with padding and whatnot, but you can't take pounds off the big ones.

"But what I can do, see, is give George a whole new look, the look of an older man. So his size doesn't look so threatening. It looks like it came on him from getting old, rather than from working out and military training. Might even give him a cane, glasses. Make him look like one of those old middle-aged guys who have gone to seed. Chop off that blond hair, give him a rim of white, put some lines in his face. All of a sudden instead of being a guy in his late twenties in perfect shape and huge, he's thirty years older, slowed down by food, maybe diabetes, bad knees, bad feet, stooped a little. Add some padding around his middle, front and back, so he waddles. He's not gonna threaten anybody."

"Brilliant. What do you do with me?"

"Biggest giveaway with you is your Southern accent. Can you fake others? Can you be a Yank or a Brit?"

"A Brit easier than a Yankee, that's for sure."

"If you can be British, I can make you look that way. Tweeds and all."

• • •

Chloe's guess about where she was headed was confirmed when Jock radioed ahead and the SUV was met by a phalanx of GC motorcycles and squad cars. They escorted the celebrated prisoner to the grounds of what had once been known as Stateville Correctional Center in Joliet, Illinois.

The place was a gothic house of horror that had been converted from a state penitentiary to one of the GC's largest international prisons. It had both male and female prisoners. In fact, the female population was second largest only to the Belgium Facility for Female Rehabilitation (Buffer).

The first thing to hit Chloe was the crowd of media trucks jamming the entrance. Cameras pointed toward the SUV from every conceivable perch, and once the vehicle had passed, she looked back to see the crews scrambling for position in the vast courtyard.

The yard had become legendary at Stateville during the last two and a half years. Prisoners were allowed there for only two reasons. They were herded past a gigantic bronze statue of Carpathia three times a day, where they were stopped in groups of thirty to fifty and allowed to kneel and worship, or they were in the yard to be executed. The yard had seven guillotines about thirty feet apart and positioned so that the sun baked them from dawn to dusk.

Jock stopped the SUV just inside the yard. "Look at 'em there, sweetie," he said. "Those blades get sharpened every night, but not a one of 'em's ever been cleaned. No scraping, no washing, no rust inhibitors.

"And you know those slots on each side, where the big blades slide down? Back when we were more humane, those were lubricated every time they were used. No more. Now the blades scrape along the sides, sometimes get hung up, get crooked, slow down. I mean, they still weigh enough that, even on a bad day, by the time they reach your neck, they're gonna dig in at least three inches.

"In the old days, a blade didn't do its job, too bad for us. The sentence was to stick your head in there until the blade dropped. If it somehow didn't kill you, well, you had taken your punishment. And don't think that didn't happen more than once. Lots of people walking around with severe neck wounds.

"But now, blade doesn't kill ya, we just hoist 'er again and let 'er go. Two, three times with a rusty, blood-caked blade that, like I say, is sharpened every night—that'll do the trick."

About twenty feet before each guillotine stood a rickety wood table, also gray and weathered by the sun and wind. Each had two incongruous Bank of England chairs behind it, burnished redwood significantly less wind worn.

"Processors and mark applicators get to sit," Jock said. "The condemned stand in lines. Once their information is recorded and any personal belongings have been confiscated, they're issued a plastic laundry basket they hand to the executioner. He or she sets it on the other side of where the blade comes down.

"Head drops in the basket, body stays where it knelt. Lifers without parole do collection duty. Come on, I'll show you."

"Spare me."

"Oh, you'd like that, wouldn't you?"

Jock got out. "Cuff her, Jess," he said.

Jesse turned and opened the cage. "Hands," he said.

"Better dope me again," Chloe said.

"Say what?"

"You think I'm going to voluntarily be cuffed so you guys can take me somewhere I don't want to go?"

Jock opened the back door.

"Hold on, Jock!" Jesse hollered. "She's not cuffed yet!"

"What the—?"

Jock, seeming to Chloe to show off for the cameras, leaped into the backseat. Chloe sat with her fists balled under her thighs. "You like to be difficult, don't you?" he said.

Jock grabbed her wrists and jerked her hands up and together where Jesse could reach them. As soon as she was cuffed, Jock slid back out of the car, pulling her by the cuffs and letting his body weight drag her out. She came out hands first, head banging the door, knees scraping the floor and then the ground. Jock pulled her to her feet.

Chloe hurt all over, but she was glad she had made them work. Someone else could go gently into that good, good night of death. Not her. Jock clamped a hand around her elbow and led her to the middle death machine. "This is going to be yours tomorrow if you don't cooperate today."

The stench overwhelmed her, and both men covered their mouths and noses with handkerchiefs. Chloe, mercifully cuffed in front this time, bent her elbows and held her nose closed with her fingers.

"As you can see," Jock said, "we don't wash the platforms or the ground either. I mean, who would that benefit?"

The area around the middle machine, like the others along the sixty-yard row, looked to Chloe like a slaughterhouse. The ground around it was black, caked with blood. "See that Dumpster back there?"

Directly behind the middle machine, maybe a hundred feet back, sat a Dumpster that looked half the size of a boxcar. It had no lid. "One collector takes the basket and dumps the head in there. Two collectors drag the body to the same place. See those black trails from each station to the Dumpster? You know what that is."

Chloe knew all right. She tried to hold her breath, but Jock kept pulling her arm so her hands came away from her nose. She prayed he would not take her out and make her look in the Dumpster. "It gets emptied about once a week."

The GC held the media back, but they yelled

questions. "What's that on her jumpsuit? Did she soil herself?"

Chloe, mortified, hollered, "Chocolate!"

Jock whirled and batted her in the forehead with the back of his hand. "You say nothing to anyone but us, understand?"

"They drugged me with a choco—!"

Jock slipped around behind her and clamped his hand over her mouth. When she tried to bite him, he drove a knee into her lower back, knocking the wind from her. "Give me the tape, Jess."

"It didn't have to come to this, ma'am," Jesse said, pulling a three-inch roll of duct tape from his jacket pocket. "I was hoping we wouldn't have to."

Jock reached to pull a length of tape off the roll, freeing Chloe's mouth. "Tell the truth for once! I was drugged! They—"

Jock pressed the tape under her nose so tight her upper lip bulged, and when he pressed the sides against her cheeks, she couldn't move her jaw, let alone speak.

"God," Chloe prayed silently, "help me be strong. I don't want to go easy. I don't want to be beat or scared into submission. And if they kill me, let me speak first. Remind me of all the verses I've memorized. Please, God, let me speak your words."

Jock and Jesse took her back across the yard

toward a steel door in the wall of one of the cell blocks. The door was at ground level, but she assumed stairs would lead below the ground to solitary confinement.

They stopped about ten yards from the door, and the media was about the same distance away on the other side. "Has she spilled any more?" a woman called out.

"Oh yes," Jock said. Chloe vigorously shook her head. "More all the time," he continued. "Of course we had to tell her there would be no trading leniency for, ah, physical favors as it were. She can only help herself by telling the truth. I'm confident we'll get there. We've already gained more knowledge about the Judah-ite underground and the illegal black-market co-op from her than from any other source we've ever had. And as you know, she gave up Mr. Al Basrah, the leading subversive in the Middle East, and he is already dead."

Chloe continued to shake her head, but she had no illusions that would be shown on GCNN that evening.

"That's all for now, folks. We have a few more prerequisites for Mrs. Williams to qualify her for a life sentence rather than death, but our daily executions here will be held tomorrow at ten A.M., regardless. We do not foresee having the full house they did yesterday, with every machine busy for nearly half an hour, but the latest count is thirty-five on the docket, so five for each machine."

The press began to disperse, but still Jock and Jesse stood there with Chloe. "I am going to finish my tour-guide speech, little lady, and you're going to hear me out," Jock said. "Some of the best days of my life have been spent in this yard, seeing people get what's coming to them. Frankly, I was disappointed when I was transferred to San Diego, but the brass assured me a huge Judah-ite cell was suspected there. They told me I could cart them back here if we rooted them out. Here's hoping you're just the first."

● ● ●

Mac was glad to have Zeke for company on the long flight. Though uneducated, the young man was smart and inquisitive. He never ran out of questions or things to talk about.

"Abdullah's kinda tough because he's already so ethnic. He's not good with accents, so I've got to keep him Middle Eastern but obviously something different than Jordanian. Rayford's pretty easy, 'cause I can go any direction with him. Buck's the hardest, with all the facial scars. But anyway, let's say I make you five guys into totally different people. What're you gonna do?"

"I'm not totally sure myself, Z," Mac said. "Rumor has it Carpathia's calling in the ten kings—'course, he calls 'em regional potentates, but we know what's going down, don't we?"

"I do."

"If Otto succeeds in New Babylon, we find out where the big shindig is gonna be before it happens, and we get in there and bug the place. We're not going to try to stop prophesied events, of course, but it'll be good to know exactly what's happening."

"What happens to Carpathia's secretary?"

"Krystall? If I had a vote, I'd say we convince her we know what's going to happen to New Babylon and get her out of there."

"To Petra?"

Mac shook his head. "Much as we might like to do that, God has set that city aside as a city of refuge for his people only. Sad as it is, she made her decision, took her stand, and accepted the mark. Getting her out of New Babylon just keeps her from dying in that mess when God finally judges the city. She's going to die anyway, sometime between then and the Glorious Appearing, and when she does, she's not going to like what eternal life looks like.

"That doesn't mean we can't befriend her and be grateful for her help. Or that we can't feel sorry that she waited too long to see the truth."

"I still wonder if we can trust her though," Zeke said.

• • •

The San Diego evacuation deadline was moved up to midnight, partly because preparations were ahead of schedule and partly to be safe. No one knew for sure when the GC would begin their next round of canvasing.

Buck was in the vehicle bay on a walkie-talkie with Ming, who was in his apartment watching Kenny and also manning the periscope. When she said the coast was clear, Buck sent loaded vehicles to the airstrip, where planes and pilots arranged by Lionel Whalum met them.

At 6 P.M. Ming radioed. "Buck, Chloe's on TV."

"Kenny watching?"

"I'll get him into his room."

Buck sprinted back, and by the time he got to his quarters, Rayford had shown up too. The news showed Chloe trying to communicate to the press and Jock backhanding her. Buck felt murderous, especially when they taped her mouth shut. He was used to the lies, but he couldn't stand to see her mistreated.

"Where's that look like to you, Ray?" he said.

Rayford shook his head. "Studying it."

One of the woman reporters said, "Here in Louisiana prisons are notoriously hard, and none harder than Angola. International terrorist Chloe Williams will rue the day she pushed the Global Community to the point where she was sent here. The guillotine will be sweet relief compared to hard labor for the rest of her life."

"Angola, Louisiana!" Buck said. "That's where I'm going. I want to take Sebastian and Razor, and you'll want to come, of course, Dad. Who else do you think we should—?"

"Hold on, Buck," Rayford said. "We're not going to Louisiana."

"What? You send three of your top people to Greece to get George, and you're going to let the GC do what they want with Chloe?"

"No way she's in Louisiana."

"You just heard it!"

"Think, Buck. They want us to believe she's in Louisiana. They moved her from San Diego to keep away from a raid. They wouldn't be announcing where they took her."

Buck knew Rayford was right. "She's at a prison though, isn't she? They're not faking that."

"I wouldn't put anything past them."

"Ray, I can't fly to Petra and leave her here. If I stay somewhere closer to back east, at least I'd have a chance to—"

"But how are we going to find out where she is?"

"I'd never forgive myself if I jetted off to safety

and left her to die alone. I don't know how you could either."

"I'm not about to, if you must know."

"C'mon, Dad, we're in this thing together. Don't be holding out on me."

"I've got a call in to Krystall to see if she's heard anything. Problem is, it's four in the morning over there, and she doesn't think anybody has a clue anyway. The people who would know are in Al Hillah, and we have no access to them. It's going to look pretty suspicious if Krystall starts asking them about Chloe."

• • •

It was the middle of the evening in Illinois, and Chloe was surprised to have been left alone for hours. She had been right about solitary. The stairs led below ground, and she had been ushered into a small cell with no cot, no sink, no toilet, no chair, no bench, no nothing. Including no light or window. The duct tape had been removed from her mouth, and when the solid metal door was shut, she was in pitch darkness.

A small square hole in the door opened and was filled with Jock's face. "I'm going to let you get some rest," he said, "and I'm going to get some too. Think about anything you can tell me that will benefit you, because when I come back, we're going to see if we need to give you an injection to help you open up. Your little shenanigans today bought you this. You're not going to like it in there if you're claustrophobic or afraid of the dark."

Chloe was both, but she was not about to admit it. She feared she would panic or go mad, but as she heard Jock's footsteps retreat, she was overcome with a sense of peace. "Thank you, Lord," she said. "I need you. I'm willing to die, but I don't want to shame you. I need you to override the truth serum. Don't let me give away anything or anybody, and keep me strong so I won't worry so much about myself. Help me keep my mind, my focus, and my priorities. And be with Kenny and Buck and Dad."

Just thinking about them brought a sob to her throat. Chloe pressed her back against the wall and lowered herself to the cold floor. "God, please, bring to mind Scriptures you want me to hear right now. Don't let hunger or fatigue or fear keep me from remembering. You know who I am and who I'm not. I just want to be what you want me to be. You know better than I that you're working with imperfection here."

She lay on her side with no heart palpitations from the closed-in space or the darkness. That alone was evidence that God was hearing her. She began rehearsing in her mind her memory verses, starting as far back in the Bible as she could remember. But when she stalled, she panicked. "Lord, keep my mind fresh. Don't let me forget. I want to be quoting you when I see you."

Her mind became a jumble. *How will I remember? What if my mind goes blank?* "Lord, please."

And suddenly, light. Was she dreaming? She blinked. The rusted, filthy chamber was bright enough to make her shield her eyes. A vision? A dream? A hallucination?

Then a voice. Quoting her favorite verses. She repeated them, word for word. "Is this your answer, God? You'll speak them and I'll repeat them? Thank you! Thank you!"

Loud banging on the door. "Keep it down in there!"

"Yes, peace, be still." That voice came from the corner!

Chloe pulled her hands from her eyes and jumped at a figure, sitting, a finger to his lips.

"Is it you, Lord?" she said, breathless.

"No one can see God and live," he whispered.

"Then who are you?"

"He sent me."

"Praise God."

"Yes, please."

"Can anyone else see you?"

"Tomorrow. Not until then."

"You'll remind me of what God has promised?"

"I will."

"You make me want to sing."

"Do so."

"Sing with me."

"I am not here to sing but to speak. You sing."

Chloe began singing. "'When we walk with the Lord in the light of his word, what a glory he sheds on our way! While we do his good will, he abides with us still, and with all who will trust and obey.'"

"Shut up in there!"

Chloe sang louder. "'Trust and obey, for there's no other way to be happy in Jesus, but to trust and obey.'"

"If I have to open this door, you're going to wish I hadn't!"

"'Then in fellowship sweet we shall sit at his feet. . . .'"

That brought knocking—it sounded like with a stick—and Chloe laughed aloud. "They don't like my voice," she told her new friend.

"Or the words," he said, and she laughed all the more.

"You going crazy in there?"

"No! Do you have any requests?"

"Only that you knock it off!"

"Sorry!" And she began again. "'Standing on the promises of Christ my King, through eternal ages let his praises ring; glory in the highest I will shout and sing, standing on the promises of God.'"

"All right!" The small door flew open. The room went dark again. "You got a light in there?"

"Sure! The light of God."

"I'm serious! What've you got in there?"

"Just the light of his presence."

"If Jock gets back and finds you with something in there, you'll regret it."

"Regret the chance to surprise him? I don't think so. Do you know how to sing harmony? Sing with me. 'Standing on the promises that cannot fail . . .'"

The guard slammed the door.

TWELVE

RAYFORD HAD only an inkling of what Buck must be going through. It had to be different for a husband than for a father. But he couldn't put his finger on it.

"Here's what we'll do," he told his son-in-law. "I have arranged with Lionel to leave us a two-seater. It's fast, but it holds only so much fuel. We'll have to take on more en route, maybe in Cypress. We'll help get everyone else out of here; then we can sit at the airstrip for all I care. Fly to the Midwest somewhere, the South. Wherever you think we'd be closest to Chloe."

"And do what?"

"We can take that little satellite TV and keep in touch with Mac and Otto and Krystall, see if we can get a clue," Rayford said.

"You just want to be on the same continent when she dies, is that what you're telling me?"

"Well, uh, no—"

"Dad, think about it. I don't fly planes. You don't have a backup pilot. Neither of us is military. You've got a two-seat plane for two guys, so there's no thought of springing Chloe and bringing her along."

Rayford sat and held his head in his hands. "I don't know what else to do, Buck. I'm not leaving the States with her still in custody. But unless we find out where she is, I'm not putting a crew on it either."

"Where're we going to go?"

"How about Wisconsin, where Zeke was? He tells me the GC never nose around. It's fairly central, so if we do get word, we can be on our way quick."

• • •

Jock led Chloe to a dimly lit room about a hundred paces from her cell. "It's just you and me tonight, ma'am. No playing off the other cop, no bright lights in your eyes, no pressure."

But when she saw where she was supposed to sit, a steel chair bolted to the floor with leather straps on the legs and armrests, she said, "No, it won't be just you and me, Jock."

"What do you mean?"

"You alone cannot strap me into that chair."

"I think I could, but you wouldn't like it."

"And I'd make you wish you hadn't done it alone. I'm not getting strapped down for any reason unless I'm overpowered. Uh-uh."

"How about we try this the easy way?" he said. "How about we just talk awhile and see if you need restraining?"

"No truth serum?"

"Not if you cooperate."

"I can tell you right now I won't."

"I can't persuade you to rethink this, be nice, help yourself?"

"No sir. For one thing, I have to use the ladies' room, and I won't even be sitting, let alone strapped in, until then."

Jock sighed and walked her farther down the hall. "As you can imagine," he said, "there's no window in a prison john. The only way out is the way in, and I'll be waiting."

● ● ●

Mac was on the phone to Rayford from high over the Atlantic in the middle of the night. "When is Weser going to be at the palace?"

"By eight A.M. their time."

"I'm guessing top priority is anything on Chloe."

"Right."

"And then Carpathia's plans."

"Exactly."

"I'll try him a half hour after he's supposed to have gotten there. I'll call you as soon as I know anything."

• • •

Chloe emerged from the dingy Stateville bathroom to find Jock with three guards, a woman and two men.

"So it's not just the two of us, Jock?"

"Could have been. When you're all strapped in and not happy, look in the mirror. At least by telling me up front, you saved wasting my time trying to talk you into anything and then having to rassle you into the chair."

As Chloe walked down the hall, the woman grabbed her right hand and twisted it up behind her, while one of the men did the same with her left. She thought about protesting; she had made it clear to Jock she wasn't going easy. As soon as they entered the small room, the third guard bent and scooped her off the floor by her ankles. The wrenching pressure on her shoulders made her cry out, but within seconds she was strapped in the chair.

The guards left, leaving a hypodermic with Jock. He shut the door and approached. "Last chance," he said. "You're not going to tell the truth without this?"

Chloe's pulse sprinted until she noticed her friend from solitary sitting in Jock's chair. "I'm not going to tell you the truth with it," she said.

"Oh, this has broken stronger subjects than you," Jock said.

He began by inserting a receptacle in a vein in her forearm. He did it with such precision it was clear he had experience. Chloe felt no pain, and he deftly taped it in place. Then he inserted a tube that ran to his side of the desk.

Jock sat and Chloe's new friend stood behind him. She fought a grin, peeking at him over Jock's head. "What are you looking at?" Jock said.

"Nobody you know," Chloe said. There was some truth, if he wanted it.

Jock inserted the hypodermic into the tube. "When I push the plunger, it will inject 15 cc's of serum, half an ounce, into your veins. You should feel little more than a relaxed mood. You probably know how this stuff works. It counteracts a chemical in your brain that inhibits over-frankness. But, of course, that is precisely what I want from you."

"I can't wait to hear what I have to say."

"Say enough, and it's life rather than death for you."

"Oh, Jock, I think someone else here needs truth serum more than I do."

"You doubt me?"

"You know as well as I do that no matter what I say, I still die."

"Not necessarily."

"You're a liar. I know that, and that's the truth, and if I'm not mistaken, you haven't even injected me yet."

"No, but enough of this. Here we go."

Chloe's visitor motioned from behind Jock like a music director, and Chloe began to hum. Then she sang quietly. "'There shall be showers of blessing; this is the promise of love. There shall be seasons refreshing, sent from the Savior above.'"

"The serum doesn't act that quickly, so don't assume you're singing the truth."

"'Showers of blessing, showers of blessing we need. Mercy drops round us are falling, but for the showers we plead.'"

"Nice tune."

"Thanks. Nice lyrics too."

Within a few minutes, Chloe felt the effects of the serum. It was strange. A sense of well-being, of trust, that she could feel free to say anything, anything at all. If she didn't know better, she would want to help this man by answering his questions. No harm would come to her, and everything would be all right.

Except that she knew better. She looked past Jock. "How long will you be with me?" she said.

"As long as necessary," the invisible man said.

"Hm?" Jock said. "As long as this takes. I got some rest. I can hang in here as long as you can."

"Bet you can't."

"Try me."

Chloe smiled. "I think you'll find me very trying."

"How are you feeling?"

"Mellow."

"Good. That's progress. What is your name?"

"Chloe Steele Williams, and proud of it."

"What is your father's name?"

"Rayford Steele."

"And your husband?"

"Cameron Williams. I call him Buck."

"Do you have a child?"

"Yes."

"What is his name?"

"His name is very special to Buck and me, because he was named after two dear, dear friends and compatriots who died."

"And what were their names?"

"If I answer that, you will know the name of my son."

"And why should I not know the name of your son?"

"The less you know about him, the harder it will be for you to gain access to him."

"I have told you we mean your son no harm."

"That is a lie."

"Anyway, you mentioned his name to your father on the phone. Kenny."

Jock pushed the hypodermic plunger again, and maybe it was psychological, but Chloe seemed to feel an immediate rush. Strange, but the stuff did seem to be making her tell the truth, even if the answers were not what Jock wanted.

He was more red-faced than usual. Was she making him mad? She hoped so.

"Are you a member of an underground group subversive to the Global Community government and its supreme potentate, Nicolae Jetty Carpathia?"

"Yes."

"Is it true that you do not believe the potentate is worthy to be called a deity?"

"Yes, and beyond that, we believe he is the Antichrist of the Bible."

"Are you aware that that statement alone is punishable by death?"

"Yes, as well as I know that God desires truth, God's law is truth, Jesus is the truth, and if you know the truth, it can set you free."

Where did that come from? Thank you, Lord.

"Are you a member of a Judah-ite faction with a large cell group residing in San Diego, California?"

"Are you asking me who I am?"

"I am asking you are you a—"

"I am a follower of Christ, the Son of the living God. He is the one who is mightier than I, whose sandal strap I am not worthy to stoop down and loose."

"What?"

"Did you not hear me?"

"Did the Judah-ites or a faction of the Judah-ites called the Tribulation Force have anything to do with the darkness that envelops New Babylon?"

"That was the work of God himself."

"Do you or the group you represent seek to overthrow the government of this world?"

"That has already been done. It has simply not been played out yet."

"The Global Community government has been overthrown?"

"It shall become known."

"Do you worship the image of Nicolae Carpathia at least three times a day?"

"Never."

"Will you tell me the whereabouts of your compatriots or any information leading to their capture? Primarily I am talking about your father, your husband, Dr. Tsion Ben-Judah, and Dr. Chaim Rosenzweig."

"I would die first."

Jock pushed the rest of the serum through the apparatus and sat picking at his fingernails for about five minutes. Chloe sang, "'Amazing grace! How sweet the sound, that saved a wretch like me! I once was lost but now am found, was blind but now I see.'"

Jock stood and looked out the door, breathing heavily. Presently he moved to Chloe's chair and removed the surgical tubing and receptacle. He unstrapped her.

"We're finished?" she said.

"No, but you have ingested the maximum dose. I've never seen anything like it. We can sit and chat for a few minutes, and if that last hit kicks in and makes you come to your senses, you let me know."

"Let's talk about you, Jock. What got you so fired up about Carpathia?"

"Oh no, we're not going there. You can just leave me alone. You obviously believe what you believe. That's impressive, I'll give you that. Misguided, but impressive. That's the problem with religious extremists."

"Oh, that's what we are?" she said.

"Of course."

"You'd like to lump us with people who kill in the name of their faith, wouldn't you?"

"You're as extreme as they come, ma'am."

"We don't kill people who don't agree with us. We don't erect statues of our God everywhere and require by law that everyone bow and scrape before them three times a day. We offer the truth, show people the way, call them to God. But we don't force them."

Jock sat heavily. "Do you realize you're going to die tomorrow?"

"I had an inkling."

"And that doesn't bother you?"

"Of course it does. I'm scared."

"And you're never going to see your husband, your baby, your loved ones and friends again."

"If I thought that was true, that would be a different story."

"I get it. Pie in the sky by-and-by. You're all going to be floating around on clouds someday, playing your harps and wearing white robes."

"I hope you're right about the pie but not the harps."

Jock shook his head. "You know we're going to televise this to the world."

"Spread some more lies about me first?"

"We say what we have to say to save face."

"And you need to save face with me because this operation was a colossal failure, wasn't it?"

"Could have gone better."

"Could have? It couldn't have gone worse! What'd you accomplish?"

"Well, when we find out where the rest of the cowards are hiding, we'll have accomplished something."

"You calling them cowards because they're in hiding, or do you mean the rest of the cowards like me? You find me cowardly?"

"Actually no."

"Do I get any last words tomorrow?"

"In your case we might not allow that. I can just hear you trying to preach a sermon, going off on Carpathia, trying to get people saved."

"So, I get to say my last words only if they pass muster with the Global Community."

"Something like that."

"We'll see about that."

"We? Who's we?"

Chloe stood and realized her friend was gone. She plunged on. "Jock, do you realize that the day is coming—and much sooner than you think—when everyone will have to acknowledge God and his Son?"

"Think so?"

"'It is written: "As I live, says the Lord, every knee shall bow to Me, and every tongue shall confess to God."'"

"Well, honey, not me."

"Sorry, Jock. 'Each of us shall give account of himself to God.'"

"My god is Carpathia. That's good enough for me."

"What about when Jesus wins?"

"He wins?"

"'Therefore God also has highly exalted Him and given Him the name which is above every name, that at the name of Jesus every knee should bow, of those in heaven, and of those on earth, and of those under the earth, and that every tongue should confess that Jesus Christ is Lord, to the glory of God the Father.'"

"I hope all that gives you some comfort when you're standing in the hot sun tomorrow morning, smelling that smell, seeing heads roll, and knowing yours will be next. Maybe I'm not the interrogator I thought I was, and maybe you paid a lot of money to be trained and prepped for truth serum. But there's nothing that brings clarity to the mind like knowing you're next in the guillotine line.

"I'll be watching you in the morning, girl. My money says you'll be shaking and wailing and pleading for one more chance to save yourself."

● ● ●

At 8:30 A. M. Palace Time, Mac was still about seven hours from Petra. He called the number Rayford had given him for Otto Weser and identified himself.

"He is risen," the German said.

"Christ is risen indeed," Mac said. "What've you got for me?"

"I gotta tell you, Miss Krystall has been a gem. I wish she was on our side. She let me listen in on a conversation from a man named Suhail Akbar, head of Sec—"

"I know who he is, Mr. Weser. All due respect, cut to the chase."

"Carpathia has assigned him and his people to do two things. First, get the government running in Al Hillah, and second, prepare for a real Oktoberfest for all the leaders of the world in Baghdad six months from now."

"So, not in October?"

"That was just an expression. It's going to be what you Yanks would call a big blowout. All the pomp and circumstance, flags, banners, light shows, bands, dancers, everything. If the lights come back on in New Babylon, the government goes home. But even if they do, the big deal still happens in Baghdad."

"Exactly where? Do we know?"

"It's a brand-new building, Mr. McCullum. On the site where the Iraq Museum used to be, before the war. It's supposed to be state-of-the-art, plush accommodations, room for the meetings and the pageantry. I mean, there are only ten other heads of state, but apparently besides the private meetings with his cabinet, Carpathia wants some festivities open to the public.

"To his people he is referring to the meetings with the sub-potentates, however, as the final solution to the Jewish problem."

"To a German, that has to resonate with your history books, eh, Mr. Weser?"

"Frankly, sir, our history books don't read the same as those of others who write about us, but I know what you mean, yes. We've been down this road before."

"Anything on Chloe Williams?"

"Krystall says she's at Angola Prison in Louisiana."

"She basing that on the same news we saw, or does she have inside information?"

"Let me ask."

Otto came back on a few seconds later. "Both. She says she heard that newscast but that she's also heard Security and Intelligence people talking about Chloe being there. Latest word is that she is to be executed at 1000 hours Central Time."

• • •

"We've got to go and take George and a few others with us, Rayford," Buck said.

"It still makes no sense," Rayford said. "Why would they broadcast where she is?"

"Maybe to trap us."

"Then it's *less* likely she's there."

"You think they're on to Krystall?" Buck said. "Giving her bogus info to test her?"

"Let's get Sebastian in on this."

• • •

Since before dawn, Chang had been at his computer in the tech center. When Naomi arrived, she stood behind him, hands resting lightly on his shoulders.

"Troops, troops, and more troops," he said. "The ones from Greece could overpower Israel, let alone those from all over the Carpathian States. And this is just the beginning."

"What's the latest on Mr. Williams's wife?"

"Everything I'm getting from communications going into the palace from Al Hillah puts Chloe in Louisiana and sentenced to death at six P.M. our time."

"Oh no."

"That's not the worst of it, Naomi. They let that out over international television, and they never tell the truth. If they want to lure the Trib Force, they could have left her in San Diego. Rayford and Buck are in the thick of the evac from San Diego, but they're not going to know what to do now. I hope they can see through this. For all we know, Chloe is an hour from San Diego. All the GC has to do is have her somewhere where a GCNN affiliate can send a live feed."

Naomi pulled up a chair and sat next to Chang. "If ever there was a newscast you'd want to interfere with, it has to be that one, doesn't it?"

"No way I want the world to see it."

"But we *would* want them to see and hear what Chloe might say."

"Definitely. I'll just be ready to flip it when they've lost patience with her."

• • •

Rayford found that Sebastian agreed with him. "No way they're letting out where she really is," he said. "It would be a major gaffe."

"Then where are we?" Buck said. "I'd rather know the worst than not know anything."

"Let's see if Krystall's ready to take a chance," Rayford said. "I'll call her."

When she came on the line, Rayford said, "I need to ask you to do something bold for me."

"I could be executed for what I've given you people already."

"I'm going to trade information with you that will prolong your life."

"What are you talking about?"

"You're a visitor to Dr. Ben-Judah's Web site, right?"

"I told you I was."

"Then you know he has shown from the Bible, in advance, all these plagues and judgments that have hit the earth."

"Yeah, it's spooky."

"It's spooky, but it's real, and we know the

next thing that's going to happen in New Babylon, only we don't know exactly when."

"And what is that?"

"God is going to destroy the entire city in the space of one hour."

"Oh my—"

"He will call his own people—like Otto and his friends—out of there so they will be spared. You need to get out too."

"Where will I go?"

"Anywhere but New Babylon."

"And you're sure this is going to happen?"

"If it doesn't, it will be the first time one of these prophesied events hasn't happened. Now, Krystall, I can't promise you'll be safe just because you leave New Babylon. The rest of the world will suffer as well, but maybe not as severely and quickly as New Babylon. Getting out of there will be your only hope."

"Is Carpathia sending all these armies into Israel one of the prophecies too?" Krystall said.

"Ever hear of Armageddon? This is it. But the end of New Babylon comes first."

"And for that fair warning, you want me to do what?"

"Call someone. Someone who would know. And I want you somehow to work Chloe Williams into the conversation. Tell him you saw it on the news or whatever, but you're just curious.

Is she really going to be executed and where? Can you do that?"

"You don't believe it's going to be in Louisiana?" she said.

"Finding that hard to swallow."

"No promises, but I'll see what I can find out."

• • •

"What're you doing tonight, Jock?" Chloe said as he walked her back to solitary.

"Sleeping like a baby. Big day tomorrow. We tell the world you sang like a canary, but that in the end you refused the mark and wouldn't pledge allegiance to Carpathia. Our hand was forced."

"And you're the hero."

"Probably promoted. Shipped off to International."

"Which is where now?"

"What do you care? You can't tell anybody or do anything about it."

"Then what's the harm in telling me?"

He cocked his head at her. "Rumors say I'll be assigned to the Jezreel Valley."

"Oh? What's going on there?"

"Not at liberty to say."

"But you know?"

"Well, yeah, 'course I do."

"Congratulations."

"Thank you."

"Sky's the limit, huh?"

"I guess," he said.

"Want a little inside information?"

"You're a little tardy with that, but I'm listening."

"New Babylon is never getting back to normal."

"And you know that for a fact."

"Sure as I'm standing here," Chloe said.

"Well, I doubt you're right, but you won't be around to find out. And I will."

"I wouldn't be so sure of that either."

"See you in the morning, ma'am."

Chloe sat in the dark chamber and asked quietly, "Are you still here with me?"

"Always," came the reply. "To the end of the age."

Chloe prostrated herself on the floor and prayed the rest of the time, unable to sleep. She sang, she quoted Scripture, she praised God, and she listened.

Mostly she listened. As he comforted her heart.

THIRTEEN

"I'M NEVER going to let this happen again, Dad," Buck said. They stood outside their two-seater jet in remote western Wisconsin at dawn, monitoring a miniature TV and a radio and waiting for Krystall's call. "We could find out Chloe was half an hour away in St. Paul, and there wouldn't be a blessed thing we could do about it. No car, no disguises, no IDs, nothing. Never again, Dad, and I mean it."

Rayford didn't appear to have anything to say, and Buck felt sorry for him. "I don't know what else could have been done," Buck said. "But anything more than sitting on our hands, waiting for something to happen."

"I don't know why Krystall hasn't called," Rayford said. "She's had all day." He looked at his watch. "It's the middle of the afternoon in New Babylon."

"You'd better hope they're not on to her, haven't bugged her phone or something. They'd know about Otto, know we know where the big confab is going to be, everything."

"I don't know," Rayford said. "David and Chang have always said the GC doesn't tap its own phones."

"So everybody in Al Hillah's been in meetings all day and there's no one to tell Krystall the truth about where Chloe is? You should have given her some kind of a time frame. Doesn't she assume we'd like to know before the execution?"

"It's not like she works for us, Buck. She's been a godsend."

"Interesting thing to say about someone bearing the mark of the beast."

• • •

Mac dropped off Zeke in Petra at about two in the afternoon. Abdullah had already readied the bigger plane for Mac and then took charge of getting Zeke settled. "I plan to get in and get out of that apartment as fast as I can," Mac said. "Then I'm picking up Weser and his clan and getting back here. I'd like to get all that done before the GCNN goes on the air with Chloe.

I won't watch 'em kill her, but I want to see what leads up to it anyway."

• • •

In pervasive darkness, Chloe had no idea of the passage of time. Occasionally she pressed her ear against the steel door to listen for activity in the solitary unit. So far, nothing.

She thought waiting for one's execution would be like waiting to see the principal or facing a punishment you knew was coming, only multiplied on a mortal scale. And yet she found herself relatively calm. Her heart broke for Buck, not so much for the prospect of his missing her, but for how wrenching it would be to have to explain this to Kenny.

He was too young, and there would be no explaining it, she knew. But the daily questions, the need of a boy for his mother, the fact that no surrogate could love him like she did . . . all that worked on her.

Chloe felt the presence of God, though she didn't see the messenger she had the night before. Her muscles ached from the positions she found herself in for prayer and then just trying to get comfortable. Hunger was a distraction she succeeded in pushing from her mind. Soon, she told herself, she would be dining at the banquet table of the King of kings.

Most gratifying was that she had fewer doubts and more assurance as the hours passed. She had put all her eggs in this basket, she had always liked to say. If she was wrong, she was wrong. If it was all a big story, she had bought it in its entirety. But for her the days of questioning and misgivings were gone. Chloe had seen too much, experienced too much. She had been shown, like everyone else on the planet, that God was real, he was in control, he was the archenemy of Antichrist, and in the end God would win.

Early on in her spiritual walk, Chloe had entertained a smugness, particularly when people berated or derided her for her beliefs. She was too polite to gloat, but she couldn't deny some private satisfaction in knowing that one day she would be proved right.

But that attitude too had mercifully been taken from her. The more she learned and the more she knew and the more she saw examples of other believers with true compassion for the predicaments of lost people, the more Chloe matured in her faith. That was manifest in a sorrow over people's souls, a desperation that they see the truth and turn to Christ before it was too late.

She didn't even know what to do with her feelings of love and concern and sympathy for people who had already taken Carpathia's mark and were condemned for eternity. They were beyond help and hope, and yet still she grieved for them. Flashes of humanity in Florence, in Nigel, in Jesse, in Jock . . . what did those mean? She couldn't expect unbelievers to live like believers, and so she was left without the option to judge them—only to love them. Yet it was hopeless now.

While Chloe couldn't understand how there could still be uncommitted people in the world, she knew there were. Those were the ones she would try to reach with whatever freedom God made the GC give her to make a last comment. How someone could see all that had gone on during the last six years and not realize that the only options were God or Satan—or worse, could know the options and yet choose Satan—she could not fathom.

But no doubt this was true. Ming had told her of Muslims who were anti-Carpathia because they were so devout in their own faith. Some practicing Jews who did not believe in Jesus as Messiah also rejected Carpathia as god of this world. George knew of militia types who refused to give allegiance to a dictator yet had not trusted Christ for their salvation either.

Was it possible, after all this time, that there were still spiritually uncommitted people who simply hadn't chosen yet? Chloe couldn't imagine, but she knew it had to be true. Some simply chose to pursue their own goals, their own lusts.

Chloe wondered about the others in Stateville who would die that morning. Many would be bearers of Carpathia's mark, but surely many would not. Would she, as the prize arrest, be last on the docket?

"Clarity, Lord," she said. "That's all I ask for. You have already promised grace and strength. Just let my mind work better than it should under the circumstances."

• • •

Mac dug through his luggage and found his wino outfit. No one cared to look for the mark of Carpathia under the stocking cap of a smelly man down on his luck. It had become the only ensemble Mac dared go out in during the day. He found his scooter where he had left it in the underbrush near the airstrip and rode to the outskirts of Al Basrah, chaining it securely before staggering into town.

Mac was greeted only by real drunks. He acted as if he was just wandering, but he was on a clear route. And when he got to within a block of his and Albie's place, he ducked into an alley and found himself alone. He jogged the rest of the way and started up the stairs when he heard voices. Mac stopped and sat on the landing at the top of the stairs. Two men stood in front of his and Albie's dingy rooms.

"You can't be in here, old man!" one of them shouted. "Get out."

Mac mumbled and let his head fall back, snoring.

The men laughed. "Anyway," one said quietly, "I'm guessing he'll come after dark. Double-M wants him alive."

Mac recognized the nickname.

"I got two guys who can watch the entrance starting about an hour before sundown. You're sure he wouldn't come earlier?"

"He's got no mark, man! Who would risk that?"

When the men moved on and Mac was sure the way was clear, he sprang to his feet and unlocked his door. The place was empty. Not a lick of furniture. None of their stuff. Now it just sat as a trap for him to return to.

Mac bounded down the stairs and ran back to his scooter, sped to the airstrip, and headed for New Babylon. He had arranged with Otto that he bring his people to the New Babylon airstrip. "Better to load up where no one can see us," he said.

The thirty or so men and women in Otto's charge tried individually to thank Mac, but he just smiled and kept moving them into the plane.

He wasn't going to feel at ease again until he was in Petra. Then, with a new identity courtesy of Zeke, he'd be ready for any caper Rayford could think of.

Otto was bouncing on the balls of his feet at the back of the crowd. "Once you're on," Mac said, "we're off."

"Mac, we can't go yet."

"Why? What now?"

"She's dead."

"Who?"

"Krystall."

"What are you talking about?"

"Go see for yourself. After I was here this morning, I went back to our underground place and helped get everybody ready to meet you. When we got here, I told them to wait for you and that you would be the only person who could see enough to land. I went to thank Krystall, and that's when I found her."

"How do you know she's dead?"

"I'm not a doctor, sir, but there was a stench like someone had tossed something in there. She was on the floor with the phone buzzing. I let it lie. I checked her pulse. Come see for yourself."

"Mr. Weser, we don't have time. If she's dead, she's dead, and I'm sorry. And Rayford getting her mixed up in all this may have caused it. But there's nothing I can do for her, and we might jeopardize this mission if you and I go running off with all your people waiting on the plane."

"You think they were on to her? Sent somebody to kill her?"

"I don't know how they would do that if they couldn't see."

"I was thinking maybe they had someone who knew the palace come back and feel his way up there, make sure she was there by talking to her, and then toss poison gas or something in there."

"Could be. That explains why Rayford never heard from her. Did you let him know?"

"I should have, shouldn't I? I didn't know what to do. I was so upset."

"Get aboard. I'll call Rayford."

• • •

Buck looked on as Rayford took a call from Mac and covered his eyes with a hand. "What is it?" Buck said.

Rayford held up a finger to tell Buck to wait, and his knees buckled.

"What? Is Chloe already gone?"

"No, Buck," Rayford said, on his knees in the grass. "But she might as well be." He told him the news.

Buck sat and pulled his knees to his chest. "I can't believe I'm stuck here in the middle of nowhere, waiting for my wife to die, not even knowing where she is."

Rayford looked ashen. "We should get started for Petra."

"But what if someone—"

"No one who knows is going to tell us, Buck. It's time to give it up."

"Give up, you mean."

"Yes, Buck," Rayford said, standing, emotion in his voice. "I have given up. She's in God's hands now. If he chooses to spare her somehow, he's apparently decided to do it without our help."

As Rayford boarded, Buck stood and spread his palms on the fuselage of the aircraft, his head hanging. "Chloe," he rasped, "wherever you are, I love you."

• • •

After a long night of praying, Chloe actually drifted off. She was awakened, she wasn't sure how long later, by the unmistakable *thwock-thwock-thwock* of helicopter blades. More than one chopper. Maybe as many as three. For an instant she allowed herself to wonder if her deliverance had come.

Deep inside she knew her husband and her father, and perhaps many in the Trib Force, would work to free her until the end. But she also knew that without a miracle there was no way they could know where she was. That had been the whole point of her transfer.

Had they somehow found out? She never ceased to be amazed at the resources available to so many of her compatriots. Should she prepare to flee in the event they did break in and look for her? Did they know more than where she was? Did they know the architecture and layout of the prison, where solitary was, somehow which cell she might be in? And how many were there? Could they overpower the GC?

Her questions were answered in an instant when her friend reappeared and the darkness of her cell was turned to noonday.

"May I know your name?" she said.

"You may call me Caleb."

"I am not to be rescued today, am I, Caleb?"

"You will be delivered, but not in the manner you mean."

"Delivered?"

"Today you will be with Christ in paradise."

That drove Chloe to her knees. "I can't wait," she said. "There are so many here I will miss desperately, but not much else. How I long to be with Jesus!"

Besides the choppers, Chloe heard only the loudest noises from outside and none from inside. Vehicles. Metallic hammering. Shouts.

Construction of some sort. In spite of herself, she began to grow nervous. "I want to be the picture of a child of God," she said, trying to control her emotions.

"God will keep you in perfect peace if your mind is stayed on him."

"Thank you, Caleb. But suddenly I feel so fragile."

Finally Chloe heard sounds from inside solitary. A rap on the steel door, the smaller door sliding open. Jock's face appeared. "How we doing this morning, missy? Bathroom break."

"Give me a minute, please."

"Oh, tough girl."

She looked desperately to Caleb.

"'Peace I leave with you,' says your Lord Christ," he said. "'My peace I give to you; not as the world gives do I give to you. Let not your heart be troubled, neither let it be afraid.'"

Chloe knocked on the steel door. "I'm ready," she said.

A guard opened the door. When Chloe emerged, she found Jock in his dress blues, gold buttons, the whole bit. She also faced a woman wearing a GCNN blazer and carrying a leather bag. "My, my," the woman said. "That won't do. Let me know when I can join you in the bathroom. And, Jock, get her a clean jumpsuit."

"Dressing me for the kill?" Chloe said.

"All pageantry, my dear," the woman said. "Justice will be served, but it will be clear you were not mistreated."

"I see," Chloe said, as the woman followed her. "Snatched from my family, starved, drugged, flown halfway across the country, injected with truth serum, and held in solitary confinement overnight is your idea of fair treatment?"

"Hey, I'm just the makeup artist. Call for me when you're ready."

"For what?"

"I'll fix your hair, make you up a little."

"Don't bother."

"Oh, I have to."

"You don't have a choice?" Chloe said.

"If you were presentable, maybe, but look at you."

"Surely I have a choice. I ought to be able to look however I want."

"You'd think. But no."

Chloe caught a glimpse of herself on the way past the mirror. She did look awful. Her face was greasy and smudged. Her hair a tangle. *Bizarre. When was the last time someone fixed me up?* And here it was, free, when her appearance was the last thing on her mind.

"Don't dawdle," the woman called out. "We're on a TV schedule, you know."

Chloe shook her head. TV people. They expected even the condemned to play team ball.

"I'm putting a fresh jumpsuit on the sink! Tell me when you've changed!"

Chloe changed but said nothing. When she came out, the woman said, "You were going to tell me when you were ready."

"No, I wasn't."

"Let's go back in there so I can use the mirror."

"Feel free. I don't need it."

"Come on! I have to get you ready."

"I'm ready."

"Wait, stop! Hold still."

Chloe looked the woman full in the face. "Do you not see the absurdity of this? It's not bad enough that I'm to be put to death? You have to make a spectacle of it?"

"I have a job and I'm going to do it."

"Then you're going to do it right here and right now."

The woman bent to set her bag on the floor and rose with a comb and brush. She worked vigorously on Chloe's hair. Then she used a wetnap to wash Chloe's face and dabbed rouge on her cheeks. When she produced mascara, Chloe said, "No. Now that's it. No mascara, no lipstick. We're done."

"You know, you're really quite an attractive girl."

Chloe arched an eyebrow. "Well, thank you so much. When I look back on this, that's going to be the highlight of my morning." *What a comforting thought. I have a chance at having the best-looking head in the Dumpster.*

When Chloe was delivered back to Jock, he said, "Do I need to cuff you, restrain you?"

"No."

"That's my girl."

She gave him a look.

"Nothing personal," he said. "I'm just doing what I have to do."

"Then make sure I get a few last words."

"If it was up to me—"

She spun and faced him. "It *is* up to you, Jock, and you know it. Anybody who could tell you what to do is thousands of miles away. Take responsibility once, would you? Make a decision here. Announce that I'm going to speak and then let me. In the end I'm gone, and you're headed for your promotion. What's the harm?"

Jock avoided her gaze. He led her up the stairs and into the morning sun. She shielded her eyes. Not only was the Carpathia-run press out in full force, but stands had been set up and apparently the public invited. Chloe wondered what all the noise was about until she realized the crowd apparently recognized she was the main attraction and was applauding and cheering.

The other prisoners, mostly men, were already in their respective rows, waiting behind the tables. Some bounced nervously. Others seemed to hyperventilate. Officials sat at each table, one with a mark applicator. What was the point? At this stage, even the ones who took the mark still endured the blade. Did they think the mark gave them some sort of an advantage in whatever afterlife Carpathia offered?

Cross-legged on the ground around each guillotine sat prisoners in dark denim. These, Chloe realized, were the lifers Jock described as collectors. They would dispose of the remains. They looked excited, smiling, joshing with each other.

Jock led her to the back of the line at the middle table. "Well, I guess this is it," he said, and to Chloe he sounded apologetic. "You can still—"

"We should have made it a bet yesterday," she said.

"Ma'am?"

"You were sure I would be making last-minute pleas about now."

"You win that one," he said. "You're a strange woman."

Chloe was aware of lights on high poles, scaffolding that supported cameras and cameramen, technicians wearing headphones running here and there, people checking their watches. In line at the table to her right, a middle-aged man bearing Carpathia's mark—which meant he had been sentenced for some other capital crime—had fallen to his knees, shuddering and sobbing. He grasped the pant legs of the man in front of him, who laid a tentative hand on his shoulder and looked ill at ease.

An older woman, yet another line beyond, stood with her face buried in her hands, swaying. Praying, Chloe assumed. In every line were Jews, identified with stenciled Stars of David or wearing self-made yarmulkes, some made of scraps of cloth, some of cardboard. The people were wasted, scarred, having been starved, beaten, sunburned.

Chloe knew enough from Buck's research and the inside stuff from David Hassid and Chang to know that Carpathia wanted these to be tortured to within an inch of their lives but not allowed to die before their public beheadings.

Chloe had been as alarmed as anyone when television had gone from bad to worse and from worse to unconscionable. The worst possible perversions were available on certain channels twenty-four hours a day, and literally nothing was limited. But when studies showed that by far the most-watched television shows every day of the week were the public executions, she knew there had been one more far corner for society to turn after all, and it had turned.

The bloodlust was apparently insatiable. It had come to the point where the most popular of the live-execution shows were those that lasted an hour and included slow-motion replays of the most gruesome deaths. When guillotines malfunctioned and blades stuck, victims were left mortally wounded and screaming but not dead. . . . This was what the public wanted to see, and the more the better.

Each execution was preceded by a rehearsal of the misdeeds of the recalcitrant. The more sordid the past, the more satisfying the justice, the logic went. Chloe knew what kinds of stories circulated about her. She could only imagine what was said about the truly guilty.

Chloe watched Jock make his way back toward the stands and a single microphone. What appeared to be a stage manager quieted the crowd, waited for a cue, then signaled them to applaud while he read from a script, introducing Jock Ashmore. He called him one of the Global Community's crack lead investigators, single-handedly responsible for the capture and arrest of Chloe Steele Williams, the highest level anti-Carpathian terrorist apprehended to date. The people cheered.

"Thank you," Jock began. "We have thirty-six executions to carry out for you today—twenty-one for murder, ten for refusing to take the mark of loyalty, four for miscellaneous crimes against the state, and one for all those charges and many, many more."

The crowd cheered and shouted and whooped and whistled.

"I am happy to say that though Chloe Steele Williams did not in the end agree to accept the mark of loyalty to our supreme potentate, she did provide us with enough detailed information on her counterparts throughout the world to help us virtually eradicate the Judah-ites outside of Petra and put an end to the black-market co-op."

The crowd went wild again.

"But more on her when she becomes today's thirty-sixth patient of Dr. Guillotine."

When the crowd finally settled, Jock said, "We begin this morning in line 7 with a man who murdered his wife and two infant sons."

Chloe caught a glimpse of a monitor where the mutilated bodies of the boys were shown in ghastly detail. "God, give me strength," she said silently. "Keep me focused on you."

A woman directly in front of her, pale and sickly and with no mark of loyalty, turned suddenly. "Are you Williams?" she said.

Chloe nodded.

"I don't want to die, and I don't know what to do!"

Thank you, Lord. "If you know who I am," Chloe said, "you know what I stand for."

"Yes."

"Your only hope is to put your faith in Christ. Admit you're a sinner, separated from God. You can't save yourself. Jesus died on the cross for your sins, so if you believe that, tell God and ask him to save you by the blood of Christ."

"I will still die?"

"You will die, but you will be with God."

The woman fell to her knees and folded her hands, crying out to God. A guard pointed to a collector and then to the woman, and the man jumped up and ran toward her. Just as it appeared he was about to bowl her over, Chloe lowered her shoulder and sprang toward him.

Her elbow caught him flush in the mouth and snapped his head back. He flopped in the dirt, screaming and spitting teeth and blood. The woman continued to pray. Finally she stood. The man made a move toward the woman again, but Chloe merely pointed at him and he skulked away.

"I prayed," the woman said, "but I am still scared. How do I know it worked?"

"Let me have a look at you," Chloe said, and she saw the mark of the believer on her forehead. "What do you see on my forehead, ma'am?" Chloe said.

"A mark, as if in 3-D." She reached to touch it.

"I see the same on you," Chloe said. "Only the

children of God are sealed with this mark. No matter what happens to you today, you belong to God."

The crowed roared as collectors dragged the first man to the guillotine by his hair. He dug in his heels; he kicked and screamed. He let his legs go limp and had to be carried into position. The man squirmed and fought so much that extra collectors were called in to hold him down. When the executioner made sure everyone's extremities were clear, he pulled the cord and the great blade fell.

The rusty thing, blackened by blood, flipped at an angle just before it bit into the victim's neck. Chloe recoiled as it sliced only halfway into the man, causing him to lurch and pull back, flailing at the collectors who tried to hold him.

He somehow broke free and spun and staggered, flinging blood and gore. The collectors ducked and laughed and made sport of him as the executioner quickly banged at the blade, straightened it, and raised it again.

Two collectors grabbed the man and pushed him headlong into position again, whereupon the cord was pulled yet again and the job done right this time. The reaction of the crowd showed they thought it was the perfect way to start the day.

"Next," Jock said, "we begin with the first of ten in a row who refused to take the mark, minus our guest of honor, of course, as we save the best till last."

But before he could say anything else, Caleb appeared in all his brightness in the middle of the courtyard, between Chloe and Jock. He appeared fifteen or sixteen feet tall in raiment so white that when Chloe turned to see the crowd's reaction, it was clear it hurt people's eyes.

They shrieked and froze. Chloe saw Jock turn to see what scared them so. He fell, holding the microphone, and stared, seemingly unable to move.

When Caleb spoke, the ground shook and a wind blew dust about. Chloe was sure everyone wanted to flee, but they could not.

"I come in the name of the most high God," he began. "Hearken unto my voice and hear my words. Ignore me at your peril. 'Oh, that men would give thanks to the Lord for His goodness, and for His wonderful works to the children of men!'

"For He satisfies the longing soul and fills the hungry soul with goodness. You who sit in darkness and in the shadow of death are bound in affliction because you rebelled against the words of God and despised the counsel of the Most High.

"Cry out to the Lord in your trouble, and he will save you out of your distress. He will bring you out of darkness and the shadow of death and break your chains in pieces.

"Thus says the Son of the most high God: 'I am the resurrection and the life. He who believes in Me, though he may die, he shall live. And whoever lives and believes in Me shall never die.'

"But woe to you who do not heed my warning this day. Thus says the Lord: 'If anyone worships the beast and his image, and receives his mark on his forehead or on his hand, he himself shall also drink of the wine of the wrath of God, which is poured out full strength into the cup of His indignation. He shall be tormented with fire and brimstone in the presence of the holy angels and in the presence of the Lamb.

"'And the smoke of their torment ascends forever and ever; and they have no rest day or night, who worship the beast and his image, and whoever receives the mark of his name.'"

FOURTEEN

CHANG SAT deep in the bowels of the tech center at Petra, finally understanding the Western expression about having one's eyes glued to the TV screen. He was prepared to take over the broadcast, to yank it off the air before anyone anywhere saw Chloe's execution.

Yet the appearance of this messenger of God, warning the undecided against taking the mark, pleading with them to receive Christ—this was something the globe needed to see and hear yet again.

For months reports had come from around the world that angels were showing up at mark application and guillotine sites. Some accounts were hard to believe, but Tsion Ben-Judah said they fit perfectly with the loving-kindness he knew of God.

Chang glanced over to where the elders sat before a big screen, and beyond them, hundreds of computer keyboarders awaited instructions. The fading late- afternoon sun cast slanted rays through the door a hundred feet from Chang, and he was moved nearly to tears by the gently falling manna. Providing food for his chosen, protecting and thrilling Chang, comforting Chloe, and sending messengers with the everlasting gospel . . . God was the ultimate multitasker.

A phone rang and Naomi answered. Chang read her lips as she leaned close to Tsion. "It's Buck for you."

"Cameron, my friend! How difficult this must be for you. . . . No, I am sorry, son. I know of no instance where the bearer of the everlasting gospel has intervened in the sentencing. . . . Yes, of course God could miraculously deliver, but I caution you to be prepared for either result. . . ."

• • •

Rayford second-guessed his decision to be in the air during the broadcast. He put the jet on autopilot and watched, but he dreaded the moment that was surely to come and wondered when he would recover enough to trust himself with the controls. Well, he decided, he had no choice. Maybe this was the best therapy. Unless he was willing to see Chloe and Buck and himself die the same day, he had to stay disciplined regardless.

Poor Buck. On the phone with Tsion and apparently not hearing what he hoped. Rayford wanted to comfort him, but Buck was not the type who took soothing until well after a crisis was over. Right now he was arguing his case. As the messenger of God stared down at the apoplectic crowd and saw the nine remaining undecideds on their knees, weeping, Buck pressed Tsion.

"But he has his man right there, Doctor! How hard would it be to intervene? Why can't he just sweep her out of there and deliver her back to us? You know he could! He could have arranged for us to get word of where she was too. What have I done or not done that makes me so unworthy of a little consideration?"

● ● ●

Chang turned back to the screen to be sure he didn't miss anything, but he could still hear Tsion earnestly counseling Buck.

"Cameron," Tsion said, "that is your emotion talking. You know as well as anyone that this whole period, the entire Tribulation, is not about us individually. God has a master plan. It is the culmination of the battle between good and evil that has spanned millennia. He is reconciling his people to himself. We should be grateful we have been included. He has a bigger picture in mind, but it is also evidence of his eternal love for us. Trust him, my friend. Trust him no matter what."

• • •

Chloe felt as if she were already in heaven. Caleb's glow had blocked from her vision the hideous death of the first victim. She watched Jock struggle to his feet and dust himself off.

"Please, people, no one leave. We have had reports of these apparitions at other sites, though this is the first visit we have had here. This is a trick perpetrated by the spiritualists within the camp of the rebellion. Perhaps we should ask permission of the intruder if we may proceed with our program." He turned to look at Caleb, pretending to be even more afraid than he was. Chloe could tell he had not persuaded the crowd that this was other than real.

"Kind sir," Jock said, his voice dripping with sarcasm, "may we continue?"

Caleb's voice, louder than ever, resounded off the prison walls. "You have been tried and found guilty for your crimes against the most high God. That you bear the mark of the evil one condemns you to death. Nothing you do can improve your fate. Because you have worshiped the beast and his image and received his mark, you shall drink of the wine of the wrath of God. You shall be tormented with fire and brimstone in the presence of the holy angels and in the presence of the Lamb. And you shall have no rest day or night.

"That which the Lord God even thinks shall surely happen, and what he decides shall never change, for as the Scripture says, 'The Lord of hosts has sworn, saying, "Surely, as I have thought, so it shall come to pass, and as I have purposed, so it shall stand."'"

Jock stared up at Caleb with brows raised, then looked back at the crowd with a shrug. "Ask a simple question . . . ," he said, and they laughed nervously. "I'll take that as an indication that we may proceed, because, hey, bottom line, if he's right and God's got us in his sights, he can pull the trigger anytime he wants. But look who's dying here today. Huh? Are you with me? Who's dying? Let me hear you!"

No one responded.

"The so-called people of God!" Jock said. "The ones who chose him instead of the real god and our supreme potentate, Nicolae J. Carpathia! Come on, people, don't be intimidated by big, shiny, transparent ghosts. Yeah, he's scary. But all he's done is interrupt a TV show and—get this—make it better! Is this great theater or what? The enemy shows up to rattle his saber, but he hasn't changed a thing! You came to see heads chopped off, and that's what you'll see. These people can cry and pray and beg all they want, but they're still gonna die!"

Chloe was thrilled to see the formerly undecided nine rise and find that six of them had the mark of the believer on their foreheads. Something within them must have confirmed this, because they lifted their hands and smiled despite their impending fate. The other three looked miserable, and Chloe assumed they were among the hard-hearted who may have been desperate to change their minds but had waited too long.

Jock, for all his bluster, was either more intimidated by Caleb than he let on or he still had the TV schedule in mind. "Let's shake things up a little, shall we?" he said. "I want one of the ten without the mark of Carpathia at each of the guillotines, all at the same time. Now! Move! Collectors, see to it! We'll do them all at once and get back on schedule. Any of you who still want the mark, say so now."

The woman ahead of Chloe and the six others she had seen with the mark of the believer stayed where they were, while the other three scrambled to the mark applicators.

The collectors grabbed the remaining seven without Carpathia's mark, including the woman ahead of Chloe. She turned and they embraced. "Be strong and trust God," Chloe said. They dragged the woman to the middle machine.

Not one of the seven struggled or fought or had to be forced to kneel and lay their necks in place. "We'll do it on three!" Jock shouted, and the crowd, though still clearly wary of the huge, glowing stranger, began to come alive with anticipation.

Chloe lowered her head and closed her eyes, determined not to be one who watched the execution of children of God. But even with her eyes shut, she noticed something and looked up to see that Caleb had filled the entire courtyard with a light so bright that no one could see anything. It wreaked havoc on the TV cameras, and cameramen and technicians began hollering for help, pleading with Jock to wait.

"We will not be delayed by this trick of the enemy!" Jock said and counted to three. The sickening sound of the heavy blades echoed, and the people cheered, but because of the blinding light, no one saw the deaths, there or on television anywhere in the world.

● ● ●

Chang sat back and studied the screen. He signaled to Naomi to come over. "Did you see that?" he said. "If the angel does that for Chloe as well, we won't need to switch the feed. He'll accomplish the same thing for us."

"But he's gone," Naomi said. "Look."

She was right. The prison courtyard looked normal again. The executions proceeded on schedule for the next half hour, each death preceded by the typical preliminaries—graphic depictions of the condemned's crimes.

With the absence of Caleb, the crowd had returned full-throated—hissing, booing, cheering, applauding. The collectors were filthy with splattered blood and dust, and they seemed drunk with the thrill of their task.

Chloe had stood in the hot sun for more than an hour, mostly averting her eyes from the ghastly panorama of horror. Weak from hunger, parched with thirst, and dizzy from standing, she fought to maintain her emotions. She prayed and prayed that God would grant her an opportunity to speak for him, and that she would be able to articulate what was in her mind.

Chloe missed Caleb. When he was there it seemed she basked in the glow of glory and felt the presence of God. Now she knew God was with her, but it took more faith. She tried to anticipate that she was just moments from the presence of almighty God, and she thrilled to the idea that she would soon fall at Jesus' feet.

But now she stood in the heat of the day, dust kicking up around her, and noticed the sympathetic looks of the mark applicators and the other officials at each desk who had processed the condemned. They had been through this before, had seen the so-called guest of honor ridiculed and humiliated, as if beheading weren't enough.

More than thirty minutes after Caleb had interrupted him, Jock was full of himself. He had warmed to the task and, Chloe assumed, could taste his promotion, could picture himself in the corridors of power in Al Hillah with the potentate himself.

Still facing the crowd, Jock switched to a cordless microphone and began moving toward Chloe. "And now the moment we have all been waiting for," he announced, and the people began to clap.

As he reached Chloe, he touched her shoulder and turned her to face the stands. He stood there with his arm around her, and though repulsed, Chloe was struck by how gentle he was. His fingers were spread, palm open, as he enveloped her shoulder. In her flesh she wanted to wrench away and spit at him, but she was aware of the international television audience and that this was her last opportunity to impact anyone for Christ.

"It's often customary to give a celebrated case a few last words," Jock said. "But I have been debating this. What do you think?"

Some screamed, "Get it over with! Kill her! Let's see that pretty little head in a basket!"

Others clapped and yelled, "Let her speak!"

Jock looked at a stage manager, and Chloe saw the woman signal that he had time to fill.

"I don't know," he said. "Should I or shouldn't I?" The crowd started in again. "While we're thinking about that," Jock continued, "let's watch this tape of the crimes we're avenging today."

The assembled hooted and hollered as monitors showed a lavishly produced history attributing all sorts of evils to Chloe, the Judah-ites, the Tribulation Force, and the International Commodity Co-op. Chloe was surprised to see that many of the plagues and judgments that had come from heaven the past six years were somehow charged against her and her compatriots' accounts.

Finally, the phony charges against her father and her husband were shown, along with the bogus picture of a two-year-old boy she had supposedly named after Jesus and claimed was God reincarnate.

"Despite all this," Jock said, "this little lady did an almost complete about-face when confronted with her own mortality. In order to take some of the heat off her family, particularly her god-in-human-flesh child, she sang like a canary behind closed doors. She gave us so much information that we have to concede that Chloe Steele Williams has done more than we ever could to help wipe out the last vestiges of the most significant rebellion the New World Order has ever faced."

The people cheered.

"So, maybe she's said enough! Maybe she's said too much already! Maybe we should just get on with this! What do you say?"

More applause, stomping, shouting.

"Mrs. Williams gave up her friends and relatives and coconspirators, but in the end she still refused to pledge her loyalty to the real god of this world, the resurrected Nicolae Carpathia."

Boos filled the courtyard.

"And so, Mrs. Williams," Jock said, turning toward her, "unless you're ready to change your mind about that, I believe we're ready to proceed with justice."

Chloe reached for the microphone, but Jock held it tight. "Ah, ah, ah!" he said. "No speaking privileges for you unless you're ready to take the mark of loyalty to the throne of the leader of the Global Community."

But she continued to reach, and now both their hands were on the mike. "Are we witnessing a historic moment here, folks?" Jock said. "You understand, Mrs. Williams, that taking this microphone also means taking the mark of Carpathia?"

She took the microphone, and Jock turned to the crowd with both arms extended, then led them in a huge ovation.

"Sir, you told me if it were up to you, I would get to say a few words. Is it up to you?"

Jock reached for the mike. "That is not the arrangement! You may speak only if you surrender to the mark."

Caleb appeared behind Chloe again and merely raised a finger and gestured no to Jock. Jock froze in place and toppled backward, his arm outstretched, still reaching. In spite of themselves, the crowd laughed while Jock reddened and perspired, rigid.

Chloe turned to the people and spoke softly. "A famous martyr once said he regretted he had but one life to give. That is how I feel today. On the cross, dying for the sins of the world, my own Savior, Jesus the Christ, prayed, 'Father, forgive them, for they do not know what they do.'

"My personal preference? My choice? I wish I could stay with my family, my loved ones, my friends, until the glorious appearing of Jesus, who is coming yet again. But if this is my lot, I accept it. I want to express my undying love to my husband and to my son. And eternal thanks to my father, who led me to Christ.

"A famous missionary statesman, eventually martyred, once wrote, 'He is no fool who gives what he cannot keep to gain what he cannot lose.' He was talking about his life on earth versus eternal life with God. In my flesh I do not look forward to a death the likes of which you have already witnessed thirty-five times here today. But to tell you the truth, in my spirit, I cannot wait. For to be absent from the body is to be present with the Lord. And as Jesus himself said to his Father at his own death, 'Into Your hands I commit My spirit.'

"And now, 'according to my earnest expectation and hope that in nothing I shall be ashamed, but with all boldness, as always, so now also Christ will be magnified in my body, whether by life or by death. For to me, to live is Christ, and to die is gain. . . . For I am hard pressed between the two, having a desire to depart and be with Christ, which is far better.'

"And to my compatriots in the cause of God around the world, I say, 'Let this mind be in you which was also in Christ Jesus, who, being in the form of God, did not consider it robbery to be equal with God, but made Himself of no reputation, taking the form of a bondservant, and coming in the likeness of men. And being found in appearance as a man, He humbled Himself and became obedient to the point of death, even the death of the cross.

"'Therefore God also has highly exalted Him and given Him the name which is above every name, that at the name of Jesus every knee should bow, of those in heaven, and of those on earth, and of those under the earth, and that every tongue should confess that Jesus Christ is Lord, to the glory of God the Father.

"'Now to Him who is able to do exceedingly abundantly above all that we ask or think, according to the power that works in us . . . and to present us faultless before the presence of His glory with exceeding joy, to God our Savior, who alone is wise, be glory and majesty, dominion and power, both now and forever.'

"Buck and our precious little one, know that I love you and that I will be waiting just inside the Eastern Gate."

Chloe bent and laid the microphone on Jock's unmoving chest and without escort found her way to the base of the middle guillotine. As she knelt and laid her head under the blade, Caleb's glow blinded the eyes of the world. Chloe heard only the pull of the cord and the drop of the sharpened edge of death that led to life eternal.

INTERLUDE

FIFTEEN HOURS later Buck staggered from Rayford's plane, jet-lagged and bleary-eyed, but more than anything aching to hold his son. Abdullah had driven to the airstrip just outside Petra, and Ming had ridden along, holding the boy. Buck gathered him up and held him tight, his tears streaming down Kenny's back.

As the five rode toward the Siq that led into Petra, Abdullah radioed ahead their estimated time of arrival. "I hope you don't mind, Buck," he said, "but Dr. Ben-Judah would like to hold the memorial as soon as you and Rayford get there."

Buck was overwhelmed at the turnout. Several hundred had gathered at the high place, within the sound of rushing water from the stream.

Acquaintances had made way for Buck's and Chloe's closest friends to gather in the front. Hard as it was with Kenny's arms still wrapped tightly around his neck, Buck sat on a rock shelf and took in the scene.

Tsion and Chaim stood in the middle, waiting for people to settle. In an inner half circle, facing Buck and Kenny and Rayford, were George and Priscilla Sebastian and Beth Ann. Ree Woo and Ming Toy held hands close by. And fresh in from Illinois were Lionel Whalum and his wife, Felicia, along with Leah Rose and Hannah Palemoon.

Buck nodded to Zeke, who stood near Abdullah and Mac. Not far away Chang sat on a rock with his new friend Naomi. They appeared very comfortable with each other already, which Buck noticed seemed to catch the eye of Naomi's father, Eleazar Tiberias, standing nearby.

Tsion raised a hand for silence. He began quietly, but Buck got the impression everyone could hear him over the rushing water. "I brought with me today my personal Bible. As you can understand, the elders and particularly Dr. Rosenzweig and I are constantly studying the Scriptures and commentaries and Bible dictionaries, trying to make sense of what is happening in these last days.

"These are academic pursuits, and while they bear on everyday life here, they can also be devotional exercises. Every day on every page we see the fingerprints of God himself, working his will in our midst and in this world.

"But today I bring the Word of God that is not just part of my theological library but rather is the text I have studied since a few years before the Rapture. As you know, my life changed when I discovered that Jesus was the Messiah I had so long sought, and I discovered that not only because of the Rapture, but also because I had been commissioned to study the prophecies concerning Messiah.

"To do this, I had to purchase a copy of both the Old and New Testaments, which was to me—at the time of the purchase—more than an embarrassment. I worried I would be an anathema not just to my colleagues but to my God as well.

"I was on to the truth before it was proved to me by the Rapture, and soon after that I made the knowledge of the true Messiah my own faith. And suddenly this book—" he held it aloft—"became my very life's bread. It had gone from a necessary piece of textual research, which I bought apologetic and red-faced, to my most prized possession.

"When my family was massacred, I clung desperately to it for life. It became a physical symbol, a talisman if you will, of the Word of God that signified to me Jesus, the Christ, the Messiah, the Son of the living God, the Lamb who was slain to take away the sins of the world. I once read of a great theologian whose personal Bible became so precious to him that at times he found himself reaching out and patting it, almost caressing it as he would a son or daughter or spouse. That seemed strange to me, but I grew to understand it, to identify with it.

"I love this book! I love this Word! I love its author, and I love the Lord it represents. Why do I speak of the Word of God today when we have come with heavy, heavy hearts to remember two dear comrades and loved ones?

"Because both Albie and Chloe were people of the Word. Oh, how they loved God's love letter to them and to us! Albie would be the first to tell you he was not a scholar, hardly a reader. He was a man of street smarts, knowledgeable in the ways of the world, quick and shrewd and sharp. But whenever the occasion arose when he could sit under the teaching of the Bible, he took notes, he asked questions, he drank it in. The Word of God was worked out in his life. It changed him. It helped mold him into the man he was the day he died.

"And Chloe, our dear sister and one of the original members of the tiny Tribulation Force that has grown so large today. Who could know her and not love her spirit, her mind, her spunk? What a wife and mother she was! Young yet brilliant, she grew the International Commodity Co-op into an enterprise that literally kept alive millions around the globe who refused the mark of Antichrist and lost their legal right to buy and sell.

"In various safe-house locations over the past half-dozen years, I lived in close proximity to Chloe and to her family. It was common to find her reading her Bible, memorizing verses, trying them out on people. Often she would hand me her Bible and ask me to check her to see if she had a verse correct, word for word. And she always wanted to know exactly what it meant. It was not enough to know the text; she wanted it to come alive in her heart and mind and life.

"To those who will miss Chloe the most, the deepest, and the most painfully until we see her again in glory, I give you the only counsel that kept me sane when my own beloved were so cruelly taken from me. Hold to God's unchanging hand. Cling to his Word. Fall in love with the Word of God anew. Grasp his promises like a puppy sinks its teeth into your pant legs, and never let go.

"Buck, Kenny, Rayford, we do not understand. We cannot. We are finite beings. The Scripture says knowledge is so fleeting that one day it will vanish. 'For we know in part and we prophesy in part. But when that which is perfect has come,' and oh, beloved, it is coming, 'then that which is in part will be done away.

"'When I was a child, I spoke as a child, I understood as a child, I thought as a child; but when I became a man, I put away childish things. For now we see in a mirror, dimly, but then face to face.'

"Did you hear that promise? 'But then . . .' How we can rejoice in the *but then*s of God's Word! The *then* is coming, dear ones! The *then* is coming."

Tsion sat and opened his Bible in his lap. "Let me close with this, as we mourn, not as the heathen, but as we mourn the loss of our beloved brother and sister in Christ. The psalmist writes: 'Precious in the sight of the Lord is the death of His saints. O Lord, truly I am Your servant; I am Your servant, the son of Your maidservant; You have loosed my bonds. I will offer to You the sacrifice of thanksgiving, and will call upon the name of the Lord.

"'I will pay my vows to the Lord now in the presence of all His people, in the courts of the Lord's house, in the midst of you, O Jerusalem. Praise the Lord!

"'Praise the Lord . . . laud Him, all you peoples!

"'For His merciful kindness is great toward us, and the truth of the Lord endures forever. Praise the Lord!

"'Oh, give thanks to the Lord, for He is good! For His mercy endures forever.

"'Let Israel now say, "His mercy endures forever."'"

FIFTEEN

*Six Years, Five and a Half Months,
into the Tribulation*

A FEW days after the memorial service, Ree and Ming had been married in a small ceremony officiated by Tsion. Chang and Naomi's relationship had blossomed, but they were counseled to delay their engagement until after the Glorious Appearing.

Over several months, Rayford had reorganized the Tribulation Force. Mac, Abdullah, and Ree became the principal pilots. Lionel Whalum, after months of duty in the air, volunteered to take over the direction of the Co-op with Ming assisting and Leah and Hannah joining the staff.

Chang had come up with a brilliant plan to bug the Baghdad site of the international confab of GC heads of state. By checking the main computer in New Babylon daily, he discovered that Leon Fortunato was having someone remotely transmit records of the daily activity of the government for duplication and dissemination. The big break came when Chang learned the government was bidding out the job of wiring the conference hall for sound for the big event.

He told Naomi of his scheme. "It's brilliant," she said, "and I think Captain Steele will think so too. You'd better include him in your thinking soon, don't you think?"

Late one night, Chang invited Rayford to the tech center. "Here's my plan," he told him. "Ree Woo's identity has never been compromised, and his name is not known to the GC. I have formulated a dossier on him that tells his entire background in technological college and his small sound-engineering firm in South Korea, Woo and Associates."

"Which I assume does not exist."

"Of course. As you can see, I have him registered as a loyalist in good standing from Region 30, with a list of satisfied customers. If you cross-check those customers, their endorsements are all in order. I already know what all the other bids are on the sound job, so I can easily underbid them and get Woo the job."

"Then what?"

"I put in a bunch of caveats about how he prefers to use a small crew and work quickly at night when no other sounds would interfere with his adjustments. Setting up the main room and working with GCNN will be easy. I can teach Ree and you how to do that in a day or two. We tell the GC the job will take about twice as long as it really will, giving you access to the main conference room off the big hall, where we know Carpathia and his cabinet plan to meet with the regional potentates. Bugging that room is trickier, but I can also teach you that.

"I'd love to come and do it myself, but it would take too much for Zeke to make me unrecognizable to people I worked with for so long. So I propose teaching Buck and George how to do the bugging work, and while you and Ree are doing the basic sound stuff in the big hall, they can slip into the conference room and get that done."

"Ree's the only one who's going to look Korean, Chang. The rest of us are too big."

"That's easy. The whole crew has to be approved in advance anyway, so whatever looks and nationalities Zeke can come up with, I can plug them in and have them cleared. I'll have Mr. Woo explain that he's using his all-star international crew to do the best job possible."

"I like it, Chang. Let me make sure everybody's

on board, especially Zeke. He's going to have to make company uniforms and get everyone's disguises and documents in order."

It went off without a hitch. Zeke was masterful in turning both George and Rayford into much older men. Buck he made a ruddy-faced Aussie. All were quick studies in electronics. Chang found Buck the easiest to teach because, he believed, Buck so badly needed to immerse himself in a new project.

● ● ●

It seemed a small break at the time, but in retrospect, Rayford believed it was major. The only representative of the GC cabinet responsible for letting Woo and Associates into the conference hall was a woman who had not been in place when Rayford and Buck had worked for Carpathia.

She was not suspicious anyway, but interacting with a stranger put them both at ease. The rest of the government was still ensconced at Al Hillah, but the woman let on that as soon as the hall was ready for the big meetings in a few weeks, the government would move there and prepare.

Rayford was impressed by Ree's ability to bluff about electronics. He had learned enough from Chang to know the lingo, and he made sure to keep it over the head of the woman with the keys. She rarely stayed long, and since the Woo crew all had ID tags and company caps riding low on their foreheads, they were never carefully checked, and the job went smoothly.

Chang had worked closely with Lionel in bartering for parts, and the men lugged in with them everything they needed to transmit from every station around the big conference table, as well as put video transmitters in half the light fixtures.

Ree Woo and his associates finished the job ahead of schedule, and to their credit, the GC electronically deposited full payment via the Internet. "We are now on Carpathia's payroll," Chang told Rayford.

• • •

Nicolae's cabinet moved from Al Hillah to palatial quarters near the conference hall in Baghdad, and in a matter of days, the heads of the ten regions would join them. Rayford told Buck one night, "It's been months since the world has heard directly from Carpathia. Now at least we'll know what's in that mind of his."

Carpathia had lain low since the darkening of New Babylon. The government was in chaos and many employees had died. The potentate seemed to have done little but instigate the massive troop buildup in Israel. Rayford speculated that Nicolae was actually embarrassed and humiliated by his inability to counteract the latest plague.

"That's when he's most dangerous though, right?" Buck said. "When given time to think and plot. You can bet he's cooking up something spectacular."

Carpathia hinted at that "something" the first time Chang tapped into the conference room when it was just Nicolae and his inner circle. Chang recorded it for Rayford. "I have news," the potentate said. "And it is so dynamic and delicious, I can hardly wait to share it. But I must. I will make you wait until our colleagues from around the globe are here. I have a trio I want to introduce to everyone, three who will help us accomplish our goals."

"Where are they from, Excellency?" came the clear voice of Viv Ivins.

"That is also a secret for now."

"Oh, Lordship, why must you toy with us?" Leon said.

"Be glad I only toy with you, confrere. The rebel forces will rue the day they ever dreamed of opposing me."

● ● ●

Rayford was about to retire late one evening when he received word that Tsion wanted to see him. "He's willing to come to your quarters," Rayford was told.

"Oh no, I'm happy to go to his."

When Rayford arrived, Tsion began, "Before I get to my request, I want you to know that I am at your disposal. The elders and I are fully aware that when you are in Petra, you are the head of the Tribulation Force, and I am merely, how shall we say it, the chaplain of that."

"I'm glad you raised this, Tsion, because I had been meaning to talk to you about your deference to me. It makes me uncomfortable. I do not see Petra as the headquarters for the Tribulation Force. Yes, I feel God has put the mantle of leadership on me in regard to them, but clearly he has chosen you to lead the Remnant of his people, now a million strong. You must not feel you answer to me. You have your elders and your colleague Chaim, and however the Lord leads you through them is fine with me. In fact I prefer it."

Tsion reached and squeezed Rayford's shoulder. "I very much appreciate your confidence, Captain Steele. But you must not denigrate your own leadership responsibilities. I was about to ask you about my next internationally televised message."

Rayford was puzzled. "Your messages have been going out daily via the Internet, haven't they?"

"Of course. But occasionally God lays on my

heart a message that I believe he wants addressed to believers and unbelievers alike. And while I know the Web site is available to all and that many unbelievers stumble across it, if we were again able to pirate the international airwaves, I would be grateful for the opportunity. I believe God has given me a message he wants even the god of this world and his minions to hear. When people hear the truth of God preached on the Carpathia-owned networks, well, it is like taking the gospel into the very pit of hell."

"'And the gates of hell shall not prevail against it,'" Rayford quoted.

"Excellent. So, what do you think? Can we do this, and when?"

"First, Tsion, you don't need my permission."

"Consider it informing you then."

"Fair enough. Just know that we have the best techies in the world here, and that means more than just Chang. He's tops, but Naomi is right there, and they've developed a team that can do anything. They work as much for you as they do for me, so anytime you want them to do anything, just say so."

"You have such wonderful rapport with them, Rayford. And with me. I would prefer to go through you."

"As you wish. All I'm saying, Tsion, is that no matter when we do this, it is pirating. It *is* illegal."

"You have a problem with that?"

"None whatsoever. Not even a second thought. We are at war, and I am prepared to use any means necessary to gain an advantage. All I'm saying is that this does not have to be planned. Chang has built his system in such a way that it's simply a matter of throwing a switch. Then they're off and we're on. Say when and say the word."

"Well, I should think we would want to do this at a most opportune time, when the most people are watching. Maybe during some official pronouncement from Carpathia, or one of the most popular programs."

"You know what those are."

"Don't remind me. I suppose one time is as good as another. How about tomorrow at noon, our time?"

"Consider it done."

"I shall call a meeting of everyone, as I am energized by a live audience."

"A million strong? I can't imagine why. We'll have the cameras set up and Chang in position."

● ● ●

The next day Tsion found himself uncharacteristically nervous. Petra had many newcomers, and he never knew what to expect from the crowd. The elders had prayed for him and encouraged him, and Chaim had introduced him. And sure enough, when he emerged to speak and Master Chang gave the cue that he was on live international television, Petra erupted into an ovation.

It was just what Tsion had feared, and though he called for quiet and tried to transfer this outpouring of emotion to the Lord by pointing up, the people would not be deterred until they got it out of their system. Rayford must have noticed how uncomfortable and displeased Tsion was, for he rushed to the rabbi and whispered, "They are just loving you and thanking you, Tsion! They are so grateful for what you have meant to them. Just acknowledge it and it will subside."

"But Captain Steele! In Isaiah 42:8 God is clear! He says, 'I am the Lord, that is My name; and My glory I will not give to another.'"

"And I'm telling you these people are not trying to glorify you. They are merely thanking you for pointing them to him."

But Tsion could not acknowledge the people, as much as he wanted to believe Rayford was right. He'd rather the earth had swallowed him right then. He merely hung his head and stared at the ground for several minutes until the people apparently grew tired of cheering.

• • •

Chang had ducked back into the tech center once the transfer was made, and he enjoyed listening in on the chaos in Baghdad. "What is going on?" someone shouted. "How did this happen? It's impossible!"

Someone else ordered the control team to shut off all the affiliates. "We can't," came the reply. "All our systems have been overridden."

And so it wasn't just the million strong at Petra who heard the message of God through Tsion that day. It was billions around the world.

● ● ●

"God has laid on my heart a message that I believe he would have me share with you," Tsion began. "I shall not whitewash or sugar-coat it, as we are at the most perilous time in the history of mankind. We are nearly into the last six months of life as we know it. The battle of the ages that has raged since the beginning of time is about to reach its climax.

"The evil ruler of this world, the Antichrist, is spewing his anger and vengeance primarily on God's chosen people. All over the world innocent men and women are being tortured, even as we speak. Their crime? They are Jewish. Some are believers in Jesus as Messiah, and many are not. Regardless, they refuse the mark of loyalty to Nicolae Carpathia, and he makes them pay every day.

"You have seen the footage, and you know the

glee with which the evil one watches his plan carried out.

"Many years ago I began proving the truth of God's Word by telling you in advance of the judgments and plagues to come, things clearly prophesied hundreds, yea thousands of years ago. We saw the fruition of the prophecy of a rider on a white horse, promising peace but bringing a sword. The red horse, World War III, followed that. That brought the black horse of famine, then the ashen horse of death. Next came the martyrdom of many saints before the Wrath of the Lamb earthquake.

"Those six judgments had been foretold in Scripture, and the seventh ushered in the next seven. Hail and fire rained on the earth. Then the burning mountain fell into the sea. Wormwood poisoned the waters, and then the sun, moon, and stars were dimmed by one-third. Demonic locusts attacked those who were not sealed by God, and then we were plagued by an army, two hundred million strong, of demonic horsemen who slew much of the population. The fourteenth judgment ushered in the last seven, five of which have already befallen us.

"Millions suffered from boils, and then the sea turned to blood, then the rivers. The sun scorched people to death and burned a third of the earth's greenery. The darkness that has fallen on New Babylon has been defended, rationalized, and explained away. But no one can account for the fact that it is so pervasive that it causes those caught in it to gnaw their tongues from the pain.

"Many have speculated how long this will last. I tell you nothing in Scripture indicates it will abate before the end. That is why the ruler of this world has moved out of his own kingdom. He may think the day will come when he and his people can move back in, but I proclaim he never will. Two more judgments await before the glorious appearing of our Lord and Savior, Jesus the Christ.

"Hear me! The Euphrates River will become as dry land! Scoff today but be amazed when it happens, and remember it was foretold. The last judgment will be an earthquake that levels the entire globe. This judgment will bring hail so huge it will kill millions.

"I am asked every day, how can people see all these things and still choose Antichrist over Christ? It is the puzzle of the ages. For many of you, it is already too late to change your mind. You may now see that you have chosen the wrong side in this war. But if you pledged your allegiance to the enemy of God by taking his mark of loyalty, it is too late for you.

"If you have not taken the mark yet, it may

still be too late, because you waited so long. You pushed the patience of God past the breaking point.

"But there may be a chance for you. You will know only if you pray to receive Christ, tell God you recognize that you are a sinner and separated from him, and that you acknowledge that your only hope is in the blood of Christ, shed on the cross for you.

"Remember this: If you do not turn to Christ and are not saved from the coming judgment, this awful earth you endure right now is as good as your life will ever get. If you do turn to Christ and your heart has not already been hardened, this world is the worst you'll see for the rest of eternity.

"For those of you who are already my brothers and sisters in Christ around the world, I urge you to be faithful unto death, for Jesus himself said, 'Do not fear any of those things which you are about to suffer. Indeed, the devil is about to throw some of you into prison, that you may be tested. . . . Be faithful until death, and I will give you the crown of life.'

"What a promise! Christ himself will give you the crown of life. It shall be a thrill to see Jesus come yet again, but oh, what a privilege to die for his sake.

"The good news is that I believe that the

enemy, whether he admits it or not, knows his time is limited. That too has been prophesied. Revelation 12:12 says, 'Therefore rejoice, O heavens, and you who dwell in them! Woe to the inhabitants of the earth and the sea! For the devil has come down to you, having great wrath, because he knows that he has a short time.' Lest you doubt me, remember that everything this man has done was foretold. Revelation 13:5-8 says, 'He was given a mouth speaking great things and blasphemies, and he was given authority to continue for forty-two months. Then he opened his mouth in blasphemy against God, to blaspheme His name, His tabernacle, and those who dwell in heaven. It was granted to him to make war with the saints and to overcome them. And authority was given him over every tribe, tongue, and nation. All who dwell on the earth will worship him, whose names have not been written in the Book of Life of the Lamb slain from the foundation of the world.'

"You can have your name written in the Book of Life! That is the good news.

"Now I must tell you there is also bad news. The wrath of the evil one will reach a fever pitch from now until the end. There will be increasing demands for all people to worship him and take his mark. To you who share my faith and are willing to be faithful unto death, remember the promise in James 5:8 that 'the coming of the Lord is at hand.'

"Oh, believer, share your faith and live your life boldly in such a way that others can receive Christ by faith and be saved. Think of it, friend. You could pray to be led to those who have not yet heard the truth. You may be the one who leads the very last soul to Christ.

"Second Peter 3:10-14 says that 'the day of the Lord will come as a thief in the night, in which the heavens will pass away with a great noise, and the elements will melt with fervent heat; both the earth and the works that are in it will be burned up.

"'Therefore, since all these things will be dissolved, what manner of persons ought you to be in holy conduct and godliness, looking for and hastening the coming of the day of God, because of which the heavens will be dissolved, being on fire, and the elements will melt with fervent heat? Nevertheless we, according to His promise, look for new heavens and a new earth in which righteousness dwells.

"'Therefore, beloved, looking forward to these things, be diligent to be found by Him in peace, without spot and blameless.'

"I urge you to imitate our Lord and Savior and say with him, 'I must be about My Father's business.'

"Some have legitimately questioned how a loving and merciful God could shower the earth with such horrible plagues and judgments. Yet I ask you, what else could he have done after so many millennia to shake men and women from their false sense of security and get them to look to him for mercy and forgiveness?

"Think of how merciful he has been. He removed his church before the Tribulation began. He sent two supernatural witnessing preachers to Jerusalem to communicate his love. He poured out his Holy Spirit in power, as he promised through the prophet Joel, to convince mankind of its need to receive Christ rather than serve Satan and his demons.

"He sealed 144,000 Jewish evangelists to fan out across the globe and reach what the Bible calls 'a great multitude which no one could number' with the saving knowledge of the Son of God. He sent three angels of mercy to help people make their decision for Christ. And he has promised to supernaturally warn mankind before he destroys Babylon.

"Most of all, in his mercy, God still allows people to decide their own eternal destiny, whether to choose Jesus Christ as Lord and Savior or to believe Satan.

"The most wonderful news I can share with you today is that God has prompted us to use the brilliant minds and technology we have been blessed with here. Anyone who communicates with us via the Internet will get a personal response with everything you need to know about how to receive Christ.

"Yes, I know the ruler of this world has outlawed even visiting our site, but we can assure you that it is secure and that your visit cannot be traced. We have thousands of Internet counselors who can answer any question and lead you to Christ.

"We also have teams of rescuers who can transport you here if you are being persecuted for the sake of Christ. This is a dangerous time, and many will be killed. Many of our own loved ones have lost their lives in the pursuit of righteousness. But we will do what we can until the end to keep fighting for what is right. For in the end, we win, and we will be with Jesus."

● ● ●

Near the end of Tsion's message, Rayford picked his way through the throng and made his way to the tech center. He stood behind Chang, watching as the young man chuckled and kept track of the frustration in Baghdad and at the affiliate stations around the world.

When he noticed Rayford, Chang said, "Here, listen to this." He clicked on a session he had recorded in the conference room where Nicolae was demanding to know whom to fire or kill because of the TV disaster.

"Where is Figueroa?"

"He has not been seen since we left New Babylon, Excellency."

"What about his people? The Asian kid. The Scandinavian young man."

"The Asian is unaccounted for. The Scandinavian died from the heat, remember?"

"I cannot keep track of everyone who dies from one of these plagues. Who is running television now?"

"It has been farmed out to the affiliates. Things are impossible in New Babylon."

"I *know* that, Leon! I want someone assigned who can put an end to this. What will people think?"

Fortunato cleared his throat. "Begging your pardon, Highness, but they will wonder what some on the cabinet are wondering. They are asking, 'What about the fact that so many of these things we have suffered through were foretold? Is there some truth to all this? Who is Carpathia anyway?'"

"They want to know who Carpathia is?" Nicolae said, his voice rising. "My own cabinet?"

"Yes, sir."

"And what about you, Leon? Who do you say that I am?"

"I know who you are, sir, and I worship you."

"Are you implying there are those in my inner circle who do not?"

"I am telling you only what I hear, Majesty."

"Maybe it is time we tell them, Leon. Maybe it is time they know who I am, if they truly do not know."

• • •

Chang knew he would be unable to sleep. He and Naomi walked toward her quarters, their pace slowing more and more the closer they got. "What an incredible time to be alive," he said.

"Really?" she said. "If I could choose, I'd rather have known Jesus earlier and gone to be with him at the Rapture."

"Well, sure, if we had that choice."

"We had it."

"Yeah."

"Actually, Chang, in my mind the greatest time to be alive will be after the Glorious Appearing. Besides getting to be with Jesus in a time of peace on earth, I'll get to live with you for a thousand years."

Chang was staggered by the thought. He stopped and took both her hands in his. "I wonder what I'll look like when I'm a thousand and twenty years old," he said. "A wrinkled-up little old Chinese man, I guess."

"You'll still be cute to me. I'll be an old Jewish lady with lots of kids between the ages of five hundred and nine hundred-and-something years old."

He cupped her face in the moonlight. "I am so grateful to have found you."

• • •

Buck lay on his cot, across the room from Kenny's, his arms aching from holding his Bible up to read it. He was studying everything he could find on the coming battle. Rayford had promised he would be assigned to Jerusalem, and at first he was disappointed, thinking all the action would be outside Petra or in the Jezreel Valley. But from what he could tell, those were just staging areas for the armies of the world. Much of the conflict would be in Jerusalem.

And there was no place he would rather be.

SIXTEEN

RAYFORD WAS astounded that things could get worse. Just when he thought there was nothing Carpathia could do to top his evil exploits, reports flooded into the computer center that made it clear Carpathia had turned up the heat all over the world. More persecution, more torture, more beheadings.

Tsion's appeal to people to contact the Internet counselors at Petra had generated an overwhelming response. This necessitated that the elders train more counselors and Naomi and Chang train more teachers to get more people up to speed on the computers.

Tsion had been preaching for ages that the world was speeding headlong toward Armageddon, but Rayford had never felt it so personally.

He began really looking forward to seeing his Savior face-to-face and to reuniting with his loved ones and friends.

But there was much to do yet. Mac, Abdullah, and Ree recruited pilots and planes from all over the world to continue the massive airlift to Petra. There were days when Rayford wondered if they could even begin to catch up to the demand. The only prerequisite for a free ride to safety was the mark of the believer. It was assumed a person without the mark of Carpathia would be persecuted or executed.

Most amazing to Rayford, as he studied the Scriptures every day, was that the end of the strange prediction in Revelation 16:10-11 regarding the plague in New Babylon proved true of Carpathia's followers all over the world: "His kingdom became full of darkness; and they gnawed their tongues because of the pain. They blasphemed the God of heaven because of their pains and their sores, and did not repent of their deeds."

How could it be, Rayford wondered, that all these plagues and judgments could fall and yet the vast majority of people would not change their ways?

• • •

Chang had, of course, mercifully ceded control of international television back to the Global

Community. And it was clear from Carpathia's public pronouncements that he was taking the credit for "finally having this thing under control."

"The next time he says that," Chang told Rayford, "I'm going to immediately switch to this commercial we devised last week."

The tape showed a particularly strong clip from Tsion's last broadcast speech and closed with a voice-over: "Proclamations from your potentate are allowed only by the goodwill of Tsion Ben-Judah and your friends at Petra."

Chang had for several days been testing the bugging job Buck and George had done in the private conference room in Baghdad. He got to where he could coordinate the video with the audio, switch to whoever was talking, and even follow Carpathia as he moved at the head of the table. Two of the hidden video devices had the ability to follow a person around the room.

● ● ●

The arrival of the ten regional potentates from around the world was broadcast by GCNN, and Buck couldn't remember such pomp and circumstance since Carpathia had mocked the Stations of the Cross in Jerusalem. Parades, marching bands, light shows, dancing girls, announcements, and pronouncements. Stands full of cheering supplicants lined the routes, as representatives from each of the regions preceded their potentate.

Finally the dignitaries and a few thousand sycophants lucky enough to get tickets were ushered into the great room of the new conference hall, where Carpathia was to hold forth on an exciting new chapter in world history.

The Most High Reverend Father of Carpathianism, Leon Fortunato, was tapped to make the royal introduction, of course. He was in full regalia, which started at the top with a brimless fez of cardinal-red felt with a flat top adorned by a tassel of alternating gold and silver strings with mirrored bits that reflected the stage lights all over the auditorium. He wore a new robe of purple and iridescent yellow with six bars of brocade on each sleeve.

Fortunato was so obsequious and fawning in his introduction that anyone but Antichrist himself would have been ill with embarrassment. Carpathia stood in mock humility, clearly fighting a smile, and bathed in the worship from his toadies.

"Thank you, thank you, thank you, one and all," Carpathia said, arms outstretched. "You are too kind to this humble servant from modest beginnings who has found himself thrust into a responsibility far beyond what he ever dreamed, only to discover by a spark of the divine that he was truly god—even to the point that he resurrected himself from the dead.

"And yet you—yes, each and every one of you—have made my task easier, in spite of crushing opposition and obstacles on every side. Every region has been well served by dynamic sub-potentates who have pulled together in times of crisis and helped make our fractious world a truly global community."

Carpathia was interrupted countless times by tumultuous applause, and each time he seemed to bask in the glow of it. "This," he said, "may be the most momentous and historic occasion in the history of our world. Despite the decimation of our citizenry—and our government—by relentless plagues and what our enemies glibly refer to as 'judgments from heaven,' I have called the top leaders together from every corner of the earth. Tomorrow, in a highly secure, private meeting, I will outline my marvelous, truly inspired plan to once and for all lead us to our goal of true global harmony.

"Our detractors have been given ample opportunity to see the error of their ways and to join our international family. I truly believed for too long that they were merely misunderstanding our aim and were ignorant of the benefits of standing shoulder to shoulder with us. Imagine what we could accomplish with everyone on board!

"Well, that day will soon come, my friends. We shall work together to enlist our enemies as fellow laborers, or we will eradicate them from our midst and be left with only loyalists . . . loyalists who share a common goal and purpose: true utopia, paradise on earth.

"No doubt all—even the opposition—have to agree that we have been fair. We have been patient. We have tried. But the time for tolerance has come to an end. Do you detect an end of patience? I freely admit it. It is time to get on board or be eliminated. Within half a year, I pledge to every loyal citizen of our Global Community, the opposition to peace will be destroyed. You will be living in the peaceful wonderland of your dreams."

Representatives of the sub-potentates from the ten regions, when interviewed by TV reporters, all played a variation of the same tune: "This is the privilege of a lifetime. What I wouldn't give to be in the private conference that follows this."

When the ceremonies were over, so was the broadcast. But the best part would come early the next morning at the meeting of potentates—which everybody in the Global Community assumed, because it was a closed-door session, was also private.

But it was as if selected members of the Trib Force were in the room. Gathered around a big-screen TV deep in the caverns of Petra, Rayford's hand-selected lineup of colleagues watched every moment through the miracle of technology and Chang's expert maneuvering.

Chang sat in the back, manning the controls. Rayford sat with Buck on one side and George on the other. Tsion and Chaim were also there. All would fill in the other key members, who were busy with Co-op and airlift duties.

As the room in Baghdad was filling, Rayford asked Chang to pan the room. "Let's get a look at who's there."

The big conference table had room for three at each end and six on each side. Each spot had a microphone, and all but the three at the far end also had a name card. Only two places were set at the head of the table, one for Carpathia—who was not there yet—on the left and the other for Fortunato—who was nervously tapping his gigantic ruby ring on the first of two luxurious leather notebooks to his right.

To the left of Carpathia's spot and proceeding to the other end were the potentates from the United African States, the United European States, the United Great Britain States, the United South American States, the United North American States, and Viv Ivins.

Each wore the epitome of a themed outfit from his or her respective region, from the colorful dashiki of the African potentate to the wide sombrero and gauchos of the South American and the ten-gallon hat and embroidered cowboy suit of the North American.

Viv Ivins wore her customary powder-blue suit, which nearly matched her hair color, but for the first time her outfit was completed by a gigantic diamond brooch and a blouse so white it played havoc with the video feed.

To Fortunato's right and extending to the other end of the table were the potentates from the United Carpathian States, the United Russian States, the United Indian States, the United Asian States, the United Pacific States, and Suhail Akbar.

Again, these potentates were dressed in their finest regional garb, the most dramatic of which was a jet-black-and-silver kimono worn by the Asian leader. Suhail wore his most formal dress uniform of the Global Community military Peacekeeping forces, topped by a navy cap with gleaming gold braid.

The three chairs at the end of the table opposite Carpathia and Fortunato were filled with three males who looked to Rayford like triplet manikins. All wore plain black suits, buttoned up, with black ties. No jewelry, no headwear, nothing else. They sat with their hands clasped before them on the table, not moving and looking neither right nor left.

"I don't recognize those three, Tsion," Rayford said. "You?"

The rabbi shook his head. "Oddly, they seem to be not even blinking. Everyone else certainly seems to be stealing glances at them frequently. Do you think they are real? Could they be cardboard cutouts?"

"Chang," Rayford said, "focus on just them, could you?"

He did, and also reported, "They are real. I taped them sitting down. You want to see it?"

"As long as we don't miss Carpathia's entrance."

"You won't."

Chang ran back the tape, showing the three taking their seats. They seemed to be one, moving in unison.

"Which door did they come in?" Rayford said.

"I missed that part. They seemed to simply appear."

"Okay, back to live."

A short buzz made Fortunato jump and reach inside his robe, as if to turn off a pager. He stood quickly and straightened his robe, removing his fez. "Ladies and gentlemen," he said, "please rise for your supreme potentate, His Highness, His Majesty, His Excellency, our lord and risen king, Nicolae Carpathia, the first and last, world without end, amen."

Except for the three mystery men, who still didn't budge, all stood, removing headwear. A military man in dress blues opened the door and Carpathia entered, whereupon Fortunato fell, rather loudly, to his knees. Nicolae was dressed in a black, pin-striped suit with a white shirt and a bright turquoise tie.

While Leon knelt, face buried in his hands on the floor and rear end aloft, displaying more expanse of his robe than anyone might have wished to see, Nicolae stopped a couple of feet behind his own chair and allowed the assembled to approach him one by one.

Individually they bowed and shook his hand with both of their own. Many kissed his hand or his ring, and more than one briefly knelt like Leon, whispering expressions of devotion and deference. They returned to stand behind their chairs.

When all had finished there was an awkward silence, as apparently Leon was next on the docket and unaware of his cue. Finally Carpathia cleared his throat, Leon looked up suddenly and clambered to his feet, catching the hem of his robe under the toe of his shoe. A distinct rip could be heard as he straightened up, stumbling and catching himself on Carpathia's chair, which was on rollers and nearly pitched him into his lord and risen king, first and last, world without end, amen.

Fortunato grabbed Nicolae's hand and pulled it toward his lips, almost making Carpathia leave his feet. At the last instant, Leon realized he had grabbed the wrong hand, dropped it, grabbed the other, and loudly kissed the potentate's ring.

"Your Excellency, sir," he said, pulling Carpathia's chair out with one hand and grandly gesturing toward it with the other.

"Thank you most kindly, Reverend," Carpathia said, sitting. "And, ladies and gentlemen, you may be seated."

Leon had left him a foot from the table, so Carpathia grabbed the edge and pulled himself forward. Fortunato, realizing his gaffe, quickly reached behind to push, and now Carpathia's chest pressed against the table. While Leon busily opened one of the leather notebooks and slid it in front of His Highness, Carpathia backed away to a more comfortable distance.

Nicolae thanked them all for coming, as if they had a choice, and said, "Down to business. Let me begin by reminding you that this is not a democracy. We are not here to vote, and neither are you here to give me input. If there is something you believe I need to know, feel free to say so. If you have a problem with my leadership or have any questions about why I have done anything or about the plans I will reveal today, I remind you of the disposition of three former potentates to the south who have been replaced due to their untimely deaths.

"Questions? I thought not. Let us proceed.

"Ladies and gentlemen, the time has come for me to take you into my confidence. We must all be on the same page in order to win the ultimate battle. Look into my eyes and listen, because what you hear today is truth and you will have no trouble believing every word of it. I am eternal. I am from everlasting to everlasting. I was there at the beginning, and I will remain through eternity future."

Nicolae stood and began to slowly circle the table as he spoke. No one present followed him with their eyes. They just sat as if catatonic. "Here is the problem," he said. "The one who calls himself God is not God. I will concede that he preceded me. When I evolved out of the primordial ooze and water, he was already there. But plainly, he had come about in the same manner I did. Simply because he preceded me, he wanted me to think he created me and all the other beings like him in the vast heavens. I knew better. Many of us did.

"He tried to tell us we were created as ministering servants. We had a job to do. He said he had created humans in his own image and that we were to serve them. Had I been there first, I could have told *him* that I had created *him* and that it was *he* who would serve me by ministering to my other creations.

"But he did not create anything! We, all of us—you, me, the other heavenly hosts, men and women—all came from that same primordial soup. But no! Not according to him! He was there with another evolved being like myself, and he claimed that one as his favored son. He was the special one, the chosen one, the only begotten one.

"I knew from the beginning it was a lie and that I—all of us—was being used. I was a bright and shining angel. I had ambition. I had ideas. But that was threatening to the older one. He called himself the creator God, the originator of life. He took the favored position. He demanded that the whole earth worship and obey him. I had the audacity to ask why. Why not me?

"Did I incite insurrection? You bet I did. And why not? What does seniority have to do with anything when we all evolved from the same source? There is plenty for everyone, but if preeminence is to be gained, I shall have it! About a third of the other evolved beings agreed with me and took my side, promised to remain loyal. The other two-thirds were weaklings, easily swayed. They took the side of the so-called father and his so-called son.

"Am I Antichrist? Well, if he is Christ, then

yes! Yes! I am against the Christ who was falsely crowned by the pretend creator. I will ascend into heaven; I will exalt my throne above the stars of God. I will ascend above the heights of the clouds; I will be like the Most High.

"But because he got there first and I was the one with the audacity to challenge him, I got cast out! Where is the justice in that? We have been mortal enemies ever since, that father and that son and I. He even persuaded the evolved humans that he created them! But that could not be true, because if he had, they would not have free will. And if he created me, I would not have been able to rebel. It only makes sense.

"Once I figured that out, I began enjoying my role as the outcast. I found humans, the ones he liked to call his own, the easiest to sway. The woman with the fruit! She did not want to obey. It took nothing, mere suggestion, to get her to do what she really wanted. That happened not far from right here, by the way.

"And the first human siblings—they were easy! The younger was devoted to the one who called himself the only true God, but the other . . . ah, the other wanted only what I wanted. A little something for himself. Before you know it, I am proving beyond doubt that these creatures are not really products of the older angel's creativity. Within a few generations I have them so confused, so selfish, so full of themselves that the old man no longer wants to claim they were made in his image.

"They get drunk; they fight; they blaspheme. They are stubborn; they are unfaithful. They kill each other. The only ones I cannot get through to are Noah and his kin. Of course, the great creator decides the rest of history depends on them and wipes out everyone else with a flood. I eventually got to Noah, but he had already started repopulating the earth.

"Yes, I will admit it. The father and the son have been my formidable foes over the generations. They have their favorites—the Jews, of all people. The Jews are the apples of the elder's eye, but therein lies his weakness. He has such a soft spot for them that they will be his undoing.

"My forces and I almost had them eradicated not so many generations ago, but father and son intervened, gave them back their own land, and foiled us again. Fate has toyed with us many times, my friends, but in the end we shall prevail.

"Father and son thought they were doing the world a favor by putting their intentions in writing. The whole plan is there, from sending the son to die and resurrect—which I proved I could do as well—to foretelling this entire period. Yes, many millions bought into this great lie. Up to now I would have to acknowledge that the other side has had the advantage.

"But two great truths will be their undoing. First, I know the truth. They are not greater or better than I or anyone else. They came from the same place we all did. And second, they must not have realized that I can read. I read their book! I know what they are up to! I know what happens next, and I even know where!

"Let them turn the lights off in the great city that I loved so much! Ah, how beautiful it was when it was the center for commerce and government, and the great ships and planes brought in goods from all over the globe. So it is dark now. And so what if it is eventually destroyed? I will build it back up, because I am more powerful than father and son combined.

"Let them shake the earth until it is level and drop hundred-pound chunks of ice from the skies. I will win in the end because I have read their battle plan. The old man plans to send the son to set up the kingdom he predicted more than three hundred times in his book, and he even tells where the son will land! Ladies and gentlemen, we will have a surprise waiting for him.

"The son and I have been battling for the souls of men and women from the beginning. If you rulers and I join forces from all over the world and act in unison from a single staging area, we can once and for all rid ourselves of those forces that have hindered our total victory up to now.

"The so-called Messiah loves the city of Jerusalem above all cities in the world. He even calls it the Eternal City. Well, we shall see about that. That is where he supposedly died and came back to life.

"This strange affection for the Jews resulted in what he tells them is an eternal covenant of blessing. If we, the rulers of the earth, combine all our resources and attack the Jews, the son has to come to their defense. That is when we turn our sights on him and eliminate him. That will give us total control of the earth, and we will be ready to take on the father for mastery of the universe."

Nicolae had made two rounds of the table and returned to his chair, looking spent. "It is in their Bible," he said. "And they claim never to lie. We know right where he will be. Are you with me?"

"We are with you, Excellency," the South American said, "but where will that be?"

"We rally everyone—all of our tanks and planes and weapons and armies—in the Plain of Megiddo. This area in northern Israel, also known as the Plain of Esdraelon or the Plain of Jezreel, is about thirty kilometers southeast of

Haifa and one hundred kilometers north of Jerusalem. At the appointed time we will dispatch one-third of our forces to overrun the stronghold at Petra, and I shall do it this time without so much as one nuclear device. We shall overcome them with sheer numbers, perhaps even on horseback.

"The rest of our forces will march on the so-called Eternal City and blast through those infernal walls, destroying all the Jews. And that is where we shall be, joined by our victorious forces from Petra, in full force to surprise the son when he arrives."

Fortunato sat shaking his head as if overcome with the brilliance of the strategy. "Questions for the potentate?" he said. "Anyone?"

The potentate of the United Asian States timidly raised his hand. "I don't know about the rest of you," he said, "but our army of hundreds of millions is led by many independent generals who are not easy to meld. Their staffs and their platoons have been devastated and greatly reduced by plagues, boils, and many other unbelievable tortures. Over half my population is dead or missing. How are we going to get these armies and their leaders to follow us?"

Many heads nodded.

"That is a question I do not shrink from, my friends," Carpathia said. "But before I tell you how together we shall accomplish that, let me tell you what your military leaders' first order of business will be. As you will remember, when I first came to power nearly seven years ago, I collected from all the world governments 90 percent of their weaponry. This was stored at a secret location I am now willing to reveal. In massive armories in and around Al Hillah, just under one hundred kilometers to the south of us, we have enough firepower to destroy the planet.

"Needless to say, we do not want or need to destroy the planet. We simply want your soldiers to have more than what they need to wipe out the Jews and destroy the son I have so long opposed. So once I tell you how we will get your military leaders on board, your next assignment will be to get them to Al Hillah, where our Security and Intelligence director, Mr. Suhail Akbar, will see that they are more than fully equipped."

"How long will this take?" the Indian potentate asked.

"You have less than half a year, ladies and gentlemen, so begin today. I have had Carpathian States troops pouring into Israel for months already. And when our Global Community army is in place, I want the armories of Al Hillah empty. Is that understood?"

"Understood," the Russian potentate said, "but like my colleagues, I am eager to hear how we are to persuade discouraged, sick, and injured leaders and troops."

"Reverend Fortunato," Nicolae said, rising. Leon leaped to his feet, his chair rolling back. "Ladies and gentlemen, the time has come to introduce you to three of my most trusted aides. No doubt you have been wondering about the three at the end of the table."

"Wondering why they seem not to have so much as blinked since we sat down," the British potentate said.

Carpathia laughed. "These three are not of this world. They use these shells only when necessary. Indeed, these are spirit beings who have been with me from the beginning. They were among the first who believed in me and saw the lie the father and son were trying to perpetrate in heaven and on earth."

"Leon," Carpathia said, and they walked down either side of the table to the other end. "Excuse me, Ms. Ivins," Nicolae said, and she stood and pulled her chair out of his way.

"Excuse me, Director Akbar," Leon said, and Suhail did the same.

• • •

Rayford jumped when Tsion snapped everyone to attention by calling out, "Chang, get this! This is Revelation 16:13 and 14!"

The camera angle changed, and those assembled in Petra had a clear view of both Nicolae and Leon from behind the three seemingly lifeless bodies at the end of the table.

• • •

The Antichrist and the False Prophet leaned in from either side, resting their elbows on the table and looking into the eyes of the robotlike creatures. Leon and Nicolae exhaled hideous, slimy, froglike beings—one from Leon and two from Nicolae—that leaped into the mouths of the three.

The three suddenly became animated.

Nicolae smiled.

• • •

"Let's see them from the front, Chang," Buck hollered, and Chang made the adjustment.

• • •

The three now bore a striking resemblance to Carpathia. They sat back casually, smiling, nodding to the potentates all around. The leaders looked stunned and frightened at first, but soon warmed to the personable strangers.

"Please meet Ashtaroth, Baal, and Cankerworm. They are the most convincing and persuasive spirits it has ever been my pleasure to know.

I am going to ask now that we, all of us, gather round them and lay hands on them, commissioning them for this momentous task."

The three backed up their chairs to make room for the potentates, Viv, Suhail, Leon, and Nicolae to surround and touch them.

Nicolae said, "And now go, you three, to the ends of the earth to gather them to the final conflict in Jerusalem, where we shall once and for all destroy the father and his so-called Messiah. Persuade everyone everywhere that the victory is ours, that we are right, and that together we can destroy the son before he takes over this world. Once he is gone, we will be the undisputed, unopposed leaders of the world.

"I confer upon you the power to perform signs and heal the sick and raise the dead, if need be, to convince the world that victory is ours. And now go in power. . . ."

Ashtaroth, Baal, and Cankerworm disappeared amid a huge bolt of lightning that struck the middle of the conference table and temporarily blacked out the TV monitor in Petra. As the picture returned, a huge peal of thunder made Chang rip off his headphones.

Nicolae and Leon returned to stand behind their chairs, as did the rest of the potentates and Viv and Suhail. As they stood there calmly, Nicolae said, "Farewell, one and all. I will see you in six months in the Plain of Megiddo on that great day when victory shall be in sight."

• • •

Buck sat stunned but quickly came to his senses. "Somebody read that passage Tsion mentioned!"

"I've got it right here," Chaim said. "Revelation 16:13 and 14 say, 'And I saw three unclean spirits like frogs coming out of the mouth of the dragon, out of the mouth of the beast, and out of the mouth of the false prophet. For they are spirits of demons, performing signs, which go out to the kings of the earth and of the whole world, to gather them to the battle of that great day of God Almighty.'"

"Read the next two verses too, Chaim," Tsion said.

"The first quotes Jesus himself," Chaim continued. "'"Behold, I am coming as a thief. Blessed is he who watches, and keeps his garments, lest he walk naked and they see his shame." And they gathered them together to the place called in Hebrew, Armageddon.'"

SEVENTEEN

RAYFORD TOLD Buck and George to scout out a new meeting room, somewhere in Petra that would not draw curiosity seekers. "It needs to hold maybe twenty, at most," he told them, though he knew it was unlikely to see half that.

He met with Tsion in the tiny living room in Tsion's quarters. "I need you to teach my top guys," he said. "They all know by now what went on in Baghdad, and everybody has questions about what it all means and what our roles should be. Nobody wants to just sit here in safety while the rest of the world goes to hell."

"I can identify with that, Rayford, and I will gladly do it. I have just this morning turned over all administrative and teaching duties of the Remnant here to Chaim."

Rayford shot him a double take. "You did *what?*"

"I do not want to stay here either."

"What are you saying?"

"If I am to teach your top little military band, I want to be part of it. I want to be taught to fight, to use a weapon, to defend myself, to keep my comrades and my fellow Jews alive."

Rayford stood and walked to the unscreened window that looked out on endless skies. "I'm dumbfounded," he said.

"Do not think I have not consulted the Lord on this."

"It's not enough you're a rabbi, a teacher, a preacher? Now you want to be a soldier?"

"Rayford, listen to me. I identify with my Lord, my Messiah. I cannot sit here when Antichrist and his worldwide forces are closing in on Jerusalem. I will not stand by as innocent Jews are killed. The Bible teaches that a third of the remaining Jews will turn to Messiah before the end. That means many, many more than there are now, and they need to be reached. I want to preach in Jerusalem, Rayford. That is what I am trying to tell you."

"You'll get yourself killed."

"I would rather wake up in heaven a few days early and join the army coming the other way with Messiah, knowing I died with my boots on, than sit here in Petra watching it on television."

"I don't know if I can allow it."

"If the Lord allows it, I do not see that you have a choice. Oh, Rayford, sit down. I do not want to go foolishly, to go unprepared. I am just into my fifties now, not an old man. Not young, I know, but I am in shape. If Mac McCullum can do these kinds of things at his age, surely I can too. I know my hands are soft like those of a scholar, but how long can it take to develop calluses and learn to handle a weapon?"

"You're serious."

"I will not be dissuaded. I am more than willing to teach your team what I know about what is going on. But my price is to also become a student of your Mr. Sebastian."

Rayford sat and shook his head. "You may not be an old coot, but you're stubborn."

"Is that not part of the makeup of the warrior?"

"Oh, you're a warrior now."

"I hope to be."

"Have you consulted the elders?"

"Did I inform them? Yes. Were they happy? No. Will they pray about it? Yes. Do I care what they come back with? Only if it is a yes."

● ● ●

Buck couldn't believe it. "But I have to admire his spunk. I'll never forget the night he and I first talked to the two witnesses at the Wailing Wall.

That was before I even knew Dr. Ben-Judah was a believer. I was pretty new at this stuff myself, but I recognized John 3 and the nighttime conversation between Jesus and Nicodemus. It was moving."

"I'd never forgive myself if I let him go and something happened to him," Rayford said.

"He's a tough guy. He stood up to Carpathia on international television, telling what he thought about Jesus being the Messiah. And after his family was massacred, I know he'd rather have been carrying an Uzi than a Bible. He could be a valuable addition to this team. And the only one who can preach and teach. I'd vote for him."

"I'm not taking any vote."

"You just got one. Anybody voting against?"

"I might," Rayford said.

"You're more of a coward than he is."

● ● ●

Mac got a kick out of the whole thing. He was all for Tsion learning to be a soldier and coming with them to Jerusalem. He sat under Tsion's teaching in the private chamber every week for the next several months and learned more about the very last days than he thought there was to imagine. He saw the fire in the rabbi's eyes and knew, Rayford's misgivings aside, that Tsion was going.

Tsion began one evening's lesson by reading Jude 1:14-15: "'Now Enoch, the seventh from Adam, prophesied about these men also, saying, "Behold, the Lord comes with ten thousands of His saints, to execute judgment on all, to convict all who are ungodly among them of all their ungodly deeds which they have committed in an ungodly way, and of all the harsh things which ungodly sinners have spoken against Him."'

"Did you catch that, people? The word he repeats so many times? It sinks in, doesn't it, when a prophet of God refers to the ungodly four times in one sentence? These enemies of ours are the enemies of God. They are out to steal and kill and destroy anything that is of God. But Jesus himself says in John 10:10 and 11, 'I have come that they may have life, and that they may have it more abundantly. I am the good shepherd. The good shepherd gives His life for the sheep.' Oh, to be a shepherd called to give your life for your flock!

"Many of you have asked where I get the idea that one-third of God's chosen people will turn to him before the end. Turn in your Bibles to Zechariah 13. That is the second-to-last book in your Old Testament. In verses 8 and 9 the prophet is talking about the Remnant of Israel: '"And it shall come to pass in all the land," says the Lord, "that two-thirds in it shall be cut off and die, but one-third shall be left in it: I will bring the one-third through the fire, will refine them as silver is refined, and test them as gold is tested. They will call on My name, and I will answer them. I will say, 'This is My people'; and each one will say, 'The Lord is my God.'"'

"Now as I have told you before, calling this final conflict the Battle of Armageddon is really a misnomer, as this is just the staging area of the world's armies. The actual conflicts will take place here at Petra, or near here, as God has proved this city is impenetrable, and at Jerusalem. To be precise, this should be called the War of the Great Day of God the Almighty."

Buck raised his hand. "I've been hearing you teach this stuff for years, and I still don't think I have the sequence down. What's going to happen when?"

Tsion chuckled. "Scholars have debated that since time immemorial. I found that the only way I could make sense of it was to have my Bible and all my books and commentaries open at the same time and try to make a list of the various stages of the events.

"In my opinion, eight events will take place sometime after the sixth Bowl Judgment, the drying up of the Euphrates River. That event, by the way, makes it possible for the kings of the East to bring their armaments of war directly into the plain of Megiddo on dry land, saving them the time of shipping them all the way around the continents. There is no biblical corroboration for this next assertion, but in my humble opinion, this is a trap set by almighty God. He's luring these rulers and their armies right to where he wants them.

"Regardless, once the Euphrates has dried up, we see the assembling of the allies of the Antichrist. Next, I believe, comes the destruction of Babylon. Isaiah 13:6-9 says, 'Wail, for the day of the Lord is at hand! It will come as destruction from the Almighty. Therefore all hands will be limp, every man's heart will melt, and they will be afraid. Pangs and sorrows will take hold of them; they will be in pain as a woman in childbirth; they will be amazed at one another; their faces will be like flames.

"'Behold, the day of the Lord comes, cruel, with both wrath and fierce anger, to lay the land desolate; and He will destroy its sinners from it.'"

"Wow," Buck said. "I don't know if I want to be there to see that."

"You're going to be in Jerusalem by then, Buck," Rayford said.

"Me too," Tsion said. "Following the destruction of Babylon comes the fall of Jerusalem. That will encourage the allied troops of Antichrist, and they will surge to join their compatriots here at what the Bible calls Bozrah. Immediately following that comes what I call the national regeneration of Israel.

"In Romans 11:25-27 the apostle Paul writes, 'For I do not desire, brethren, that you should be ignorant of this mystery, lest you should be wise in your own opinion, that blindness in part has happened to Israel until the fullness of the Gentiles has come in. And so all Israel will be saved, as it is written: "The Deliverer will come out of Zion, and He will turn away ungodliness from Jacob; for this is My covenant with them, when I take away their sins."'"

"Then comes the good stuff," George said. "At least the way I read it."

"Exactly," Tsion said. "The Glorious Appearing. Jesus Christ appears on a white horse with ten thousand of his saintly army, and regardless of what Antichrist thinks is going to happen, his end is near.

"Want to hear a bizarre word picture? When John talks about this in his Revelation, he says in verses 19 and 20 of the fourteenth chapter: 'So the angel thrust his sickle into the earth and gathered the vine of the earth, and threw it into the great winepress of the wrath of God. And the winepress was trampled outside the city, and blood came out of the winepress, up to the horses' bridles, for one thousand six hundred furlongs.'

"Think of that! When Jesus and his holy army finally slay the world allies of Antichrist, the slaughter will be so great that the flow of blood in Israel's central valley could be as high as a horse's bridle. How high is that? Four feet or more."

"And how far is one thousand six hundred furlongs?"

"I am so glad you asked, George," Tsion said, "because I happen to have studied it. It is about one hundred and eighty-four miles, the approximate distance from Armageddon to Edom."

"But that's only six events," Buck said. "Are there really two more?"

"Yes. There is the end of the fighting in the Jehoshaphat Valley, which is basically the area from here to just south of Jerusalem, west of the Dead Sea. Because Petra is safe, all Antichrist's armies can do is fight outside.

"Then, finally, comes Jesus' victory ascent up the Mount of Olives. I want to be there for that."

"You may be there," Rayford said. "But whether you'll still be alive is a different story."

EIGHTEEN

Six Years, Eleven Months,
into the Tribulation

WITH JUST weeks to go to the culmination of the final events, Rayford had finally gotten used to the idea that Tsion was going to Jerusalem.

"That I'm acceding to this doesn't imply that I support it, does it, Tsion?"

"I know you better than that. But I may also know you better than you know yourself. After all this talk, you would be disappointed if I pulled out now."

"Disappointed? Relieved. I somehow feel I'm going to have to answer to God for what happens to you."

"Trust me. I will let you off the hook."

"Let me see those hands, old man."

"I told you," Tsion said, extending his hands. "I am not that old."

"Older than I am, so ancient in my book," Rayford said. "But those are impressive calluses. And George and Razor tell me you're actually starting to hit targets with that Uzi."

"I do not see how anyone can miss. It shoots so many bullets in so short a time, to me it is like using a garden hose. If you miss your mark, just swing it back and forth until you hit it."

"What do you plan to do, seriously, Doctor? Stand somewhere and preach with a weapon hanging from your shoulder?"

"If I must. Rayford, we have known each other long enough that we should be free to be frank. I feel such a compulsion to plead with my fellow countrymen to give their lives to Messiah that I do not believe it would be physically possible for me not to. I must get there, and I must preach. I do not want a disguise. I cannot imagine the GC even caring about me anymore."

"Are you serious? The leader of the international Judah-ites—"

"That is their term for us, not ours, and certainly not mine."

"But, Tsion, everybody knows you. If they thought my daughter was a prime catch, imagine if they got hold of you."

Tsion shook his head. "But if God has laid this

so heavily on my heart, maybe he is telling me that I will be supernaturally protected."

"Well, is he or isn't he?"

"All I know is that I must go."

"I'm sending Buck with you. I promised him duty in Jerusalem. I can't think of a role with more action than what you're going to draw."

"I would be honored to have him as my bodyguard. Is he the military man George is?"

"Who is? But George is otherwise engaged, you know."

"Defending the perimeter here, yes, he told me. My question is, why don't we ignore the perimeter if our borders are impregnable?"

"Because people are seeking refuge here all the time, and they are not safe until they get inside."

"And yet they are safe in the air. How do you figure that?"

"I've quit trying to figure out God, Tsion. I'm surprised you haven't."

"Oh, Rayford, you have just stepped into one of my traps. You know how I love to quote the Word of God."

"Of course."

"Your mention of figuring out God reminds me of one of my favorite passages. Ironically, it leads into a verse that justifies my going in spite of the danger."

"I'm listening."

"Romans 11:33-36: 'Oh, the depth of the riches both of the wisdom and knowledge of God! How unsearchable are His judgments and His ways past finding out! "For who has known the mind of the Lord? Or who has become His counselor? Or who has first given to Him and it shall be repaid to him?" For of Him and through Him and to Him are all things, to whom be glory forever. Amen.'"

"Impressive."

"But, my friend, that leads into the first verse of the twelfth chapter, which is my justification: 'I beseech you therefore, brethren, by the mercies of God, that you present your bodies a living sacrifice, holy, acceptable to God, which is your reasonable service.'"

"Just hope it's a *living* sacrifice, Tsion."

● ● ●

Chang had concluded that Carpathia believed the prophecy about the drying up of the Euphrates, because he had sanctioned sensitive devices in the river that recorded information that was fed into and evaluated by the GC mainframe computer. Chang, of course, was monitoring that from Petra. Nearly four weeks later, he knew when the event occurred before the GC did.

"It's happened!" he shouted, standing at his computer. Everyone nearby jumped and stared, and Naomi came running. "There was water in the Euphrates a minute ago, and now it is as dry as a bone. You can bet tomorrow it will be on the news—someone standing in the dry, cracking riverbed, showing that you can walk across without fear of mud or quicksand."

"That is amazing," Naomi said. "I mean, I knew it was coming, but isn't it just like God to do it all at once? And isn't that a fifteen-hundred-mile river?"

"It used to be."

Mac's and Abdullah's reconnaissance flights over the area showed that weaponry had been taken from the armories in Al Hillah until they had to be empty. Within days, great columns of soldiers, tanks, trucks, and armaments began rolling west from as far away as Japan and China and India.

"And here," Chang told Naomi, "is the break Tsion has been looking for, whether he knew it or not. Look at this." He printed out a directive from Suhail Akbar himself, instructing Global Community Peacekeepers and Morale Monitors to cease and desist with all current assignments and consider themselves redeployed to the GC One World Unity Army. "Your superiors have been similarly assigned, and you will report to them in the staging area in twenty-four hours or face AWOL charges."

"What happens to the streets?" Naomi said.

"I can't imagine, love. The inmates will be running the asylum. But that means people without Carpathia's mark can come out from hiding."

"If they dare. There's still a bounty on their heads. The loyalists will kill them and stack their bodies, waiting for the end of the war to cash in."

"Won't they be disappointed."

• • •

"I must go as soon as possible," Tsion told Rayford. "What is the fastest way Cameron and I can get to Jerusalem?"

"Helicopter, I suppose, if I can find you a pilot."

"What are you doing right now?"

"Uh, well—I guess nothing. Anything else?"

Tsion laughed. "I cannot wait. I have packed foodstuffs and a change of clothes, and if Cameron has done as I requested, he will have done the same. Who would know if a chopper is available?"

"Meet me at the helipad in half an hour."

• • •

Priscilla Sebastian made a valiant effort to distract Kenny Bruce as Buck tried to extract himself from the boy's embrace.

"I'll be back soon," Buck said. "Got to go with Uncle Tsion."

Kenny said nothing. He just hung on.

"Grandpa's going to come see you after he drops us off, okay? You're going to stay with him while I'm gone."

Kenny lightened his grip and pulled back to look at Buck. "Grandpa?"

"That's right."

"Plane ride?"

"I bet so."

"When?"

"Soon. Soon as he gets back."

"I wanna go."

"Not enough room. Now you be a good boy and play with Beth Ann, and Grandpa will be here soon. Okay?"

"'Kay."

• • •

Mac was working with Otto Weser and George on planning the evacuation from New Babylon, as soon as the word came that believers were to move out. No one, not even Tsion, seemed to know how that would be supernaturally announced or even whether anyone outside New Babylon would hear it.

"I know of a few other cells there," Otto said. "I have left instructions with one of the leaders to call me once she gets the word. I don't know what else we can do. I'll tell them to meet us at the palace airstrip and hope we have a plane big enough to get them all out of there."

"All we can do is all we can do," Mac said.

Naomi interrupted their meeting. "Want to say good-bye to Tsion? Everyone is turning out for the farewell."

"He's going already?"

She told Mac why.

"Tsion never lets any grass grow on an idea, does he?"

He and George and Otto followed Naomi to a clearing near the helipad, where it seemed hundreds of thousands had shown up. "Word travels quick round here, doesn't it, Otto?"

"Mr. McCullum, many of these people are weeping. He's only going to Jerusalem, isn't he? That can't be more'n a hundred miles, can it? And surely he's coming back."

"That's what they're cryin' about, Otto. Most folks wonder if he will be back."

Rayford waited on firing up the chopper so Tsion could be heard. The rabbi pulled a white cloth from his pocket and waved it vigorously at the people as Buck boarded behind him. "These people are going to want your neck when you come back without him, Rayford," Buck said.

"Which, of course, I plan to do in an hour or less."

"*I'd* just better not come back without him," Buck said.

"People! People!" Tsion shouted. "I am overwhelmed at your kindness. Pray for me, won't you, that I will be privileged to usher many more into the kingdom. We are just days away now from the battle, and you know what that means. Be waiting and watching. Be ready for the Glorious Appearing! If I am not back before then, we will be reunited soon thereafter.

"You will be in my thoughts and prayers, and I know I go with yours. Thank you again! You are in good hands with Chaim 'Micah' Rosenzweig, and so I bid you farewell!"

He continued waving as he boarded. Rayford noticed the rabbi's tears as he buckled himself in.

● ● ●

"Something's on your mind," Naomi said, as she and Chang walked hand in hand. He had just finished transmitting to Rayford's helicopter a schematic of Jerusalem with various potential put-down spots.

Chang shrugged. "Sometimes I'm glad I'm here and safe and can sleep—unlike at the palace—but other times I feel I'm taking the easy way out. Everyone else is gearing up for the battle."

"Oh, Chang. Don't say that. You put in your years of frontline work. And anyway, you know full well you're much more valuable here in the center than out there shooting or being shot at. I don't know what we'd do without you."

"You were getting along fine before I got here."

She dropped his hand and put her hands on her hips, cocking her head at him. "You have a short memory, Chang Wong. How can you forget that I spent a good portion of every day on the computer with you, though we were more than five hundred miles apart? I would have been nowhere without your teaching me, which is the way I feel now."

"Everything's up and running here. I could be gone a few weeks."

"I wasn't talking technically, Chang. Call me selfish, but I'm glad you're not venturing out. Father loves me, but not like you do."

"I should hope not."

She smiled. "And I enjoy spending time with him, which is something a lot of women my age can't say about their fathers. But I would rather be with you. Remember, we want to survive so we can be together for a millennium. Let's not risk that for the sake of your conscience."

"You don't think I'd be good in combat."

"Actually I do, Chang. I know you're half the size of that Sebastian character and much more rational than Buck Williams. But I believe a person's personality and character come out when the pressure is on, and I've seen you under pressure. With a little training, you could hold your own."

• • •

Rayford was studying Chang's transmissions and trying to discuss with Buck the best place to land. Buck was busy digging through what he'd brought and said, "It's your call, Ray. I can't imagine one spot is going to be any less treacherous than another."

"Remember that all these GC are expected to be in Megiddo tomorrow," Rayford said. "Not today. They might still like a plum arrest."

"I disagree," Buck said. "Their directive told them to immediately cease and desist and head toward where they had to be. I don't know a guy in uniform who wouldn't take them up on that."

"Just take me to the Wailing Wall, Rayford," Tsion said. "I want to be preaching when I get off this thing."

"Could you think of a more dangerous place?"

"Danger is not the issue now, Captain. Time is. The Day of the Lord is at hand. Let us not be setting up camp when the enemy attacks."

"Easy for you to say," Rayford said.

"Not unless I am on the ground. Now, for once, do what I ask."

Rayford came within sight of the Temple Mount. It was crawling with people. "Agh!"

"They will move," Tsion said. "Trust me. Put this thing down, and they will get out of the way. Wouldn't you?"

NINETEEN

THE INSTANTANEOUS drying up of the Euphrates proved good news to only the kings of the East, who transported their weapons directly into Israel across dry land. The rest of the Fertile Crescent was no longer fertile. Irrigation dried up, hydroelectric plants shut down, factories closed. In short, everything that depended on the massive power of the great river was immediately diagnosed as terminal.

Chang's prediction of GCNN's carrying accounts of reporters standing in the middle of the dry riverbed proved accurate. But all the fancy pronouncements and isn't-it-something-that-I'm-standing-here-where-yesterday-I-would-have-been-a-hundred-feet-below-the-surface did not amuse millions who depended upon the Euphrates for their very existence.

• • •

It didn't surprise Buck that Tsion proved to be right. When Rayford lowered the chopper into a clearing at the Temple Mount, hundreds of angry people scattered, raising their fists at him.

Buck grabbed his bag and tucked his Uzi behind his back and under his jacket. He leaped from the chopper and scampered to safety in underbrush near the Wall. He looked back to see Tsion doing the same and was amazed at the agility of this newly trained guerilla.

They knelt, catching their breath and watching Rayford lift off. The chopper whirling out of sight took the attention off them. Buck looked around. "This is where I saw the two witnesses taken into heaven three and a half years ago," he said.

• • •

That old curiosity was back. Rayford couldn't shake it. No way he could be this close to Armageddon—he guessed less than seventy miles—and not do a flyover. It was crazy, he knew. He might find himself in an air traffic jam. But the possibility of seeing an aerial view of what he had been hearing and reading and praying about drew him like an undertow. And if the result was that he plunged into the abyss like a rafter over the falls, it was worth the risk.

• • •

"Cameron, look," Tsion said. "Look at all the unmarked men! They proudly parade around, beaming at each other, as if defying the GC."

Global Community Peacekeeping and Morale Monitor forces were nowhere to be seen, of course. But war was in the air. For all the posturing of the devout Jews at the Temple Mount, it was clear that terror pervaded the place. These people knew where the GC were, and they knew they would soon be Carpathia's targets.

"The old men are at the Wall," Tsion said, "praying fervently and openly as they have not been able to do for so long. How my heart breaks for them. The young men are talking, planning, looking for arms. They are determined to defend this city, as I am."

"But the city is to fall, Tsion," Buck said. "You've said so yourself."

"Only temporarily, and the more of these people we can keep alive, the more can come into the kingdom. That is all I care about."

• • •

Mac was still not sure what to make of Otto Weser. He was a good man, no doubt, but he was amateur in his thinking. He may have been a successful timber businessman in Germany, but Mac would not want to have served under him in combat.

"But don't you see, Mr. McCullum," Otto was saying, "if we are already on the ground at the palace airstrip when the supernatural announcement comes, we'll be that much more ready to quickly get people on board and out of there."

"And what if we never hear that announcement, or people can't get to the airstrip? There we sit with the city coming down around us."

"But will we not be protected as believers?"

"Think, man! If believers were protected, why would God be calling his own people out of there before he levels the place?"

• • •

"I want to wait no longer, Cameron. I'm going to the Wall and I will simply begin preaching."

"But what if—"

"There is no more time to think things through," Tsion said. "We are here for one purpose, and I am going to do it. Now are you going to cover me? Go with me? What?"

"I'll go with you. No one will give me a second glance, once you open your mouth."

Tsion pressed a yarmulke onto his head and handed one to Buck. "No sense getting stoned for a technicality," Tsion said. "We are going to a holy place."

They stuffed their bags between a tree and a black wrought-iron fence. Wearing loose-fitting, canvas-type clothing and jackets, Uzis at their sides, they crawled out of the bushes and jogged toward the Wall.

"Hey, old man, two hundred Nicks for that gat!"

"I'll go three hundred!" someone else said.

"The weapon is not for sale!" Tsion hollered. "Come hear what I have to offer!"

The area before the Wailing Wall was crowded with people in traditional garb, eager to push their prayers into the cracks between the stones. Many began praying even before they got close. The place would have been deserted the day before. And anyone caught in religious clothing, even with the mark of Carpathia, would have been sent to a concentration camp or executed.

As soon as Buck and Tsion began to shoulder their way toward the Wall, men glared at them and grumbled. Tsion did not hesitate. He bellowed, "Men of Israel, hear me! I am one of you! I come with news!"

It was clear people thought it was news of the impending attack, as they immediately began gathering. Tsion climbed a short precipice, where he could better be seen and heard.

"We will fight to the death!" someone shouted.

"I know you will, and so will I!" Tsion said. "You see me with my head covered and no mark on my forehead or hand."

The men cheered.

"Many of us will die in this conflict," Tsion continued. "I am willing to give my life for Jerusalem!"

"So are we!" many shouted in unison.

"We need arms!"

"We need information!"

"What you need," Tsion boomed, "is Messiah!"

The men cheered and many laughed. Others murmured. This was plainly not what they expected to hear.

"Many of you know me! I am Tsion Ben-Judah. I became persona non grata when I broadcast my findings after being commissioned to study the prophecies concerning Messiah."

Many remembered and applauded. Although they obviously disagreed with his conclusions or they would have been believers, they seemed to admire him.

"My family was slaughtered. I was exiled. A bounty remains on my head."

"Then why are you here, man? Do you not know the Global Community devils are coming back?"

"I do not fear them, because Messiah is coming too! Do not scoff! Do not turn your backs on me!" Many did not. "Listen to our own Scriptures. What do you think this means?" He read Zechariah 12:8-10: "'In that day the Lord will defend the inhabitants of Jerusalem; the one who is feeble among them in that day shall be like David, and the house of David shall be like God, like the Angel of the Lord before them. It shall be in that day that I will seek to destroy all the nations that come against Jerusalem.

"'And I will pour on the house of David and on the inhabitants of Jerusalem the Spirit of grace and supplication; then they will look on Me whom they pierced. Yes, they will mourn for Him as one mourns for his only son, and grieve for Him as one grieves for a firstborn.'"

"You tell us what it means!"

"God is saying he will make the weakest among us as strong as David. And he will destroy the nations that come against us. My dear friends, that is all the other nations of the earth!"

"We know. Carpathia has made it no secret!"

"But God says we will finally look upon 'Me whom they pierced,' and that we will mourn him as we would mourn the loss of a firstborn son. Messiah was pierced! And God refers to the pierced one as 'Me'! Messiah is also God.

"Beloved, my exhaustive study of the hundreds of prophecies concerning Messiah brought me to the only logical conclusion. Messiah was born of a virgin in Bethlehem. He lived without sin. He was falsely accused. He was slain without cause. He died and was buried and was raised after three days. Those prophecies alone point to Jesus of Nazareth as Messiah. He is the one who is coming to fight for Israel. He will avenge all the wrongs that have been perpetrated upon us over the centuries.

"The time is short. The day of salvation is here. You may not have time to study this for yourselves. Messiah is God's promise to us. Jesus is the fulfillment of that promise. He is coming. Let him find you ready!"

• • •

Rayford's was not the only craft over the Plain of Megiddo. It was all he could do to pick his way through the traffic, but he also found it difficult to avert his eyes from the ground. He climbed to where he could see the 14-by-25-mile valley in its entirety, some 350 square miles.

The dust seemed to rise a mile as tanks, trucks, personnel carriers, missile launchers, cavalries, and ground troops moved into the area. Rayford had never seen as large an assembly of people in one place. It appeared as if an army of millions was marshaling in the vast staging area. From there he could also see the bustling seaport at Haifa, where great ships filled the harbor and fanned out in massive lines, waiting to disgorge armaments and troops.

From every direction personnel and equipment

flooded into the region. Massive as it was, there seemed no way it could hold more. And yet the armies kept coming.

• • •

Buck feared at first that Tsion was only offending the devoutly Jewish crowd. Many tried to shout him down and many walked away, but others tried to hush the rest, and still others called more to come and hear him. The crowd kept growing, despite the noise and confusion.

Tsion seemed energized. He began quoting Scripture and explaining it, not waiting for the crowd's response. His message went from dialogue to monologue, and yet people seemed riveted.

"Yes, the armies of the world are coming. Even as we speak, they are rallying to the north. They aim to destroy Jerusalem and destroy us. But I beg of you, 'do not fear those who kill the body but cannot kill the soul. But rather fear Him who is able to destroy both soul and body in hell.' Yes, you know of whom I speak. Messiah is coming! Messiah shall overcome! Be ready for his arrival!

"If you want to know how to be prepared for him, gather here to my left and my associate will tell you. Please! Come now! Do not delay! Now is the accepted time. Today is the day of salvation."

Buck was stunned. He had not been prepared for this, but as the Jews gathered around him, looking expectant, he breathed a desperate silent prayer, and God gave him the words.

"When Jewish people such as yourselves come to see that Jesus is your long-sought Messiah," he said, "you are not converting from one religion to another, no matter what anyone tells you. You have found your Messiah, that is all. Some would say you have been completed, fulfilled. Everything you have studied and been told all your life is the foundation for your acceptance of Messiah and what he has done for you."

Buck moved into the plan of salvation, telling these hungry and thirsty men to tell God they acknowledged that Jesus was Messiah. "He comes not only to avenge Jerusalem but to save your soul, to forgive your sins, to grant you eternal life with God."

● ● ●

"Naomi!" Chang called out. "Come watch this."

She joined him to see Carpathia being interviewed by GCNN. It was clear he was not at Armageddon yet, but he was on a colossal black stallion and brandishing a sword so wide and long it appeared its weight alone would have pulled a smaller man from the saddle. He wore thigh-high boots and leathers, and he seemed unable to quit grinning.

"We have the absolute latest in technology

and power at our fingertips," he shouted as the reporter reached as high as she could with her microphone. "My months of strategy are over, and we have a foolproof plan. That frees me to encourage the troops, to be flown to the battle sites, to mount up, to be a visual reminder that victory is in sight and will soon be in hand.

"It will not be long, my brothers and sisters in the Global Community, until we shall reign victorious. I shall return to rebuild my throne as conquering king. The world shall finally be as one! It is not too early to rejoice!"

● ● ●

As word spread that Tsion Ben-Judah was at the Wailing Wall preaching to the Jews, more and more streamed in.

"These Scriptures foretell what is going to happen soon!" he said. "Listen again to the words of Peter: 'The day of the Lord will come as a thief in the night, in which the heavens will pass away with a great noise, and the elements will melt with fervent heat; both the earth and the works that are in it will be burned up. Therefore, since all these things will be dissolved, what manner of persons ought you to be in holy conduct and godliness, looking for and hastening the coming of the day of God, because of which the heavens will be dissolved, being on fire, and the elements will melt with fervent heat? Nevertheless we, according to His promise, look for new heavens and a new earth in which righteousness dwells.'

"That is our promise, what we have been looking for! For how many generations have we prayed for peace? Soon, after the conflict, eternal peace!

"Messiah will return as King of kings. He promised to return, to conquer Satan, and to set up his millennial kingdom, reestablishing Israel and making Jerusalem the capital forever!

"With probably a billion of Messiah's followers already removed from this earth, and with the disappearances of seven years ago that were predicted more than two thousand years before, many Jews and Gentiles have turned to Jesus Christ as the true Messiah.

"Our own prophet Joel foretold of these very days. Listen to the words of Holy Scripture: 'It shall come to pass afterward that I will pour out My Spirit on all flesh; your sons and your daughters shall prophesy, your old men shall dream dreams, your young men shall see visions. And also on My menservants and on My maidservants I will pour out My Spirit in those days.

"'And I will show wonders in the heavens and in the earth: blood and fire and pillars of smoke. The sun shall be turned into darkness, and the moon into blood, before the coming of the great and awesome day of the Lord. And it shall come to pass that whoever calls on the name of the Lord shall be saved. For in Mount Zion and in Jerusalem there shall be deliverance, as the Lord has said, among the remnant whom the Lord calls.'

"You are that remnant, people of Israel. Turn to Messiah today! Listen further to the prophecy of Joel and see if it does not reflect these very days! 'For behold, in those days and at that time, when I bring back the captives of Judah and Jerusalem, I will also gather all nations, and bring them down to the Valley of Jehoshaphat; and I will enter into judgment with them there on account of My people, My heritage Israel.'

"This massive international force that the evil ruler of this world calls the One World Unity Army will break up from its staging area and pass through the very Valley of Jehoshaphat Joel writes of, and when they find the city of refuge impossible to overthrow, the fighting will spill back into that valley."

● ● ●

Rayford had to head back. There was nothing he could do high above the assembled hordes of Antichrist. He knew it was from this area that the great mass would divide two-thirds and one-third, and that the latter would begin its inexorable march toward Petra.

His best guess was that it would take almost a full day for the force to cover that much ground and begin its offensive. In just a few hours, however, the two-thirds assigned to Jerusalem might already be engaged in battle.

• • •

Buck was answering questions, praying with people, and all the while trying to listen to Tsion, who seemed to have found a second wind.

"The Day of the Lord is upon us," he said. "And lest there be any among you who still doubt, let me tell you what the prophecies say will happen after the armies of the world have gathered at Armageddon—which, as we all know, they are now doing. How many of you know Peacekeepers and Morale Monitors who have been called there? See? Yes, many of you. We have no illusions. They are rallying now, planning our destruction.

"And yet the Scriptures say that when they have gathered there, it will be time for the seventh angel to pour out his bowl into the air. Do you know what this refers to, men of Israel? The drying of the Euphrates was the sixth Bowl Judgment of God on the earth, the twentieth of his judgments since the Rapture.

"This seventh Bowl Judgment shall be the last, and do you know what it entails? When this bowl has been poured out, the Bible says 'a loud voice came out of the temple of heaven, from the throne, saying, "It is done!"' How like the pronouncement of the spotless Lamb of God on the cross when he cried out, 'It is finished.'

"'And there were noises and thunderings and lightnings; and there was a great earthquake, such a mighty and great earthquake as had not occurred since men were on the earth.'

"Let me warn you, my countrymen. This earthquake will cover the entire world. Think of it! The Bible says that 'every island fled away, and the mountains were not found.' The mountains were not found! The elevation of the entire globe will be sea level! Who can survive such a catastrophe?

"The prophecy goes on to say that 'great hail from heaven fell upon men, each hailstone about the weight of a talent.' Beloved, a talent weighs between seventy-five and one hundred pounds! Who has ever heard of such hailstones? They will crush men and women to death! And the Scriptures say men will blaspheme God because of the plague of the hail 'since that plague was exceedingly great.' Well, I should say it will be! Turn and repent now! Be counted among the army of God, not that of his enemy.

"Do you know what will happen here, right here in Jerusalem? It will be the only city in the world spared the devastating destruction of the greatest earthquake ever known to man. The Bible says, 'Now the great city'—that's Jerusalem—'was divided into three parts, and the cities of the nations fell.'

"That, my brothers, is good news. Jerusalem will be made more beautiful, more efficient. It will be prepared for its role as the new capital in Messiah's thousand-year kingdom."

By now the crowds at the Temple Mount had ballooned as word of Tsion's preaching continued to spread. Hundreds and soon thousands wept aloud and fell to their knees, repenting before God, acknowledging Jesus Christ as Messiah, pledging themselves to the King of kings.

Buck was weary but kept ministering, amazed at so many, steeped in their centuries-old religion, finally seeing that Jesus Christ fulfilled all the Old Testament prophecies concerning the coming Messiah.

Tsion thundered, "How will we know when this is about to come to pass? It will be preceded by the destruction of Babylon. Yes, the destruction of Babylon! Listen: 'And great Babylon was remembered before God, to give her the cup of the wine of the fierceness of His wrath.'

"Awful! It will be horrible! The loving, merciful patience of God will have been pushed beyond the brink by that wicked city, and he will not hold back his anger. The plague of darkness has not been enough to satisfy his wrath. He will allow her to be attacked and plundered, destroyed in but one hour's time. So great will be the power of the calamity that befalls it that its repercussions will be felt around the entire globe as all nations mourn the death of what had become the capital of the world."

● ● ●

Knowing the time was short and what Buck had promised Kenny, Rayford radioed ahead to Petra and had Abdullah bring the boy to the helipad. He gave Kenny a quick ride, pretty much straight up and straight down, which Kenny loved.

Rayford was grateful the boy didn't ask about the ragtag platoons George and Razor were amassing below at the perimeter of the rock city. Compared to what Rayford had seen north of Jerusalem, it was plain that the few thousand Petra troops would not have a chance without supernatural intervention.

Rayford spent the next couple of hours with Kenny, then ventured out to check on George and his fighting band.

● ● ●

"Mac, come quick," Otto said. "I've got a colleague on speakerphone, but she's nearly speechless."

When Mac arrived at Otto's quarters, he heard the woman try to recount what had happened. "I don't know how much time we have," she said, out of breath, "but it's time to go."

"How do you know?" Mac said.

"An angel," she said.

"You're sure?"

"Bright, white, shiny, big, very big. And it was a man, at least this one was. He was so bright that the darkness in this city is gone. It is as bright as noon here still."

"What did he say?"

"He spoke so loud that everyone here had to hear it, and I will never forget one word of it. He said, 'Babylon the great is fallen, is fallen, and has become a dwelling place of demons, a prison for every foul spirit, and a cage for every unclean and hated bird!

"'For all the nations have drunk of the wine of the wrath of her fornication, the kings of the earth have committed fornication with her, and the merchants of the earth have become rich through the abundance of her luxury.'"

"We're on our way, ma'am. Get everybody to the palace airstrip, and if you hear from any more groups of believers, send them there too."

"That's not all, sir."

"Excuse me?"

"I heard another voice from heaven. It said,

'Come out of her, my people, lest you share in her sins, and lest you receive of her plagues. For her sins have reached to heaven, and God has remembered her iniquities.'"

● ● ●

"I hardly have enough people to encircle this place," Sebastian said.

Rayford avoided George's eyes. "I don't know what to say. The way I read it, we aren't expected to even hold our own."

"I don't want men and women to suffer, though, Captain. I'd rather we just line up above and pick a few off."

"Look at it this way, George. This is where Jesus is supposed to come first. We could be among the first to witness the Glorious Appearing."

"Tell that to a fighting force outnumbered a thousand to one. They may be in heaven before Jesus leaves there."

● ● ●

Mac had no idea what to expect in New Babylon, so at the last minute he enlisted Lionel to also bring in a large jet. Between the two of them he figured he could evacuate up to two hundred people.

When they landed at the palace, he found it eerie. The place was no longer dark, but the wounded souls within the boundaries didn't know what to make of it. They had been in pain and darkness for so long they were disoriented and still hadn't found their bearings. Most still limped and staggered around.

But waiting for the planes of refuge were more than one hundred and fifty believers, cheering their arrival. They carried their belongings in sacks and boxes and were eager to get aboard, which made the whole process quick and easy. Mac and Lionel had their planes loaded and turned around and headed down the runways when two invading armies attacked.

Before Mac was even out of New Babylon airspace, black smoke billowed into the heavens. He circled the area for an hour, and Lionel followed, as their charges watched the utter destruction of the once great city. Within those sixty minutes every building was leveled, and Mac knew that every resident was slaughtered. When the mysterious armies who had invaded from the north and northwest pulled out, they left the entire metropolis aflame. By the time Mac turned toward Petra, the only thing left of New Babylon was ash and smoke.

• • •

Chang watched, confused, as GCNN reports came in of fighting within the ranks of the One

World Unity Army. Carpathia's forces apparently had to strike back at nations who became drunk with power and ambition when armed with resources that had been stored at Al Hillah. The majority of Nicolae's allies banded together to crush the resistance, and by the time all were assembled at Armageddon, they had all been persuaded, by the demons or by Carpathia or by the realities of war, to join together against the people of God.

The sheer number of troops swelled well beyond the Valley of Megiddo and spilled north and south and east and west, past Jerusalem and down toward Edom. Some estimates included an almost unimaginable mounted army alone of more than two hundred thousand. Aerial views shot by GCNN aircraft could show only a million or so troops at a time, but dozens and dozens of separate such pictures were broadcast.

Chang sensed panic on the part of the people at Petra. Those who saw the news could not imagine standing against such an overwhelming force. Those who didn't see the news heard it from others, and the word swept the camp. Many ran to the high places and could make out the clouds of dust and the dark masses of humanity, beasts, and weaponry slowly making their way across the desert.

Chaim took the occasion to call the people

together, just before the evening manna was expected. "My dear people, brothers and sisters in Messiah. Be of good cheer. Fear not. I am hearing wonderful reports out of Jerusalem, where our brother Tsion preaches the gospel of Jesus Christ with great boldness and, I am happy to report, great results as well.

"I only ten minutes ago talked with a very exhausted and still very busy Cameron Williams. He tells me thousands are repenting of their sins and turning to Christ, acknowledging Jesus of Nazareth as Messiah. Praise the Lord God Almighty, maker of heaven and earth!"

The people seemed encouraged and cheered and wept and raised their hands.

"We are not ignorant," Chaim continued, "of what is to come. New Babylon has fallen, utterly destroyed in one hour, fulfilling the prophecies. That leaves only two events on the prophetic calendar, my friends. The first is?"

And the people shouted, "The seventh Bowl Judgment!"

"And the second, oh, praise God?"

"The Glorious Appearing!"

Chaim concluded, "We serve the great God of Abraham, Isaac, and Jacob, the deliverer of Shadrach, Meshach, and Abednego. We lived through the fires of the Antichrist, and we have been delivered from the snare of the fowler. Do not be afraid. Stand still, and see the salvation of the Lord, which he will accomplish for you. For the enemy whom you see today, you shall soon see no more forever. The Lord will fight for you, and you shall hold your peace."

TWENTY

DARKNESS HAD fallen in Jerusalem, yet still the Temple Mount teemed with people. Buck thought Tsion appeared weak and tired, so he broke away and went to their stash to bring him some foodstuffs. But their bags were gone. He ran back to where Tsion held forth, but now he himself felt dizzy with hunger.

"I need something with which to feed the rabbi!" he called out.

"I am fine!" Tsion said and continued preaching.

"Someone, please. A morsel. Bread, fruit."

"Five loaves and two fishes?" someone suggested, and everyone laughed.

An elderly man tossed an apple to Buck. Others passed him a round of bread, crusty and warm. Someone donated a block of cheese. Someone else a couple of oranges.

"Help me persuade this stubborn teacher to take a break!" Buck said, and many urged Tsion to at least sit. And so he did.

Talking now, teaching rather than preaching, Tsion took questions and nibbled between answers. The crowd only grew. "I had no idea how hungry I was," Tsion said. He looked at Buck. "I am grateful, my friend." Someone passed him a container of water, and he drank deeply.

Suddenly someone held up both hands to shush the crowd, and everyone fell silent. The rumble of a moving army was clear. Buck felt the vibration throughout his body.

"We need to get the rabbi to shelter," someone said. "We can meet over there."

Tsion appeared to start to protest, but the audience was leaving en masse, so he and Buck followed. They were led into a massive stone structure that could easily have accommodated a thousand people. About half that many crowded near the front.

"What are we to do when the enemy arrives?" someone asked. "We are more outnumbered than Gideon."

"We can do only what we can do," Tsion said. "If you have an inkling what I am trying to do here today, it is to usher as many of my fellow Jews into the kingdom of Messiah as possible before it is too late. Because of that I feel a compulsion to keep as many candidates alive as I can. If you agree with my mission, go out into the city proper and invite anyone who wants to, to come and join us. The enemy will begin to conquer Jerusalem and plunge people into captivity, but I believe their main objective is the Old City. What better meat to his pride than for Carpathia to think he can invade this holy place and set up his headquarters here?

"If we are attacked before you can return, take what you have learned here and tell everyone you know. They need not come back here to pray the prayer of faith and become a member of Messiah's kingdom."

Someone shouted, "Better yet to have them come back already decided and carrying a weapon!"

"Well," Tsion said. "Yes."

● ● ●

As was so often true when spending the night at Rayford's, Kenny was nearly impossible to get to sleep unless he began by lying atop his grandfather. Rayford lay gingerly on the small cot designated for the boy and reached for him. Kenny climbed aboard and laid his cheek just under Rayford's chin.

Rayford fought fatigue, not wanting to fall asleep with Kenny asking questions, singing, praying.

"Mommy's in heaven," Kenny said.

"That's right. And we miss her, don't we?"

"I do."

"I do too."

"Gonna see her real soon."

"Very, very soon, Kenny." Rayford knew Buck had been showing him the calendar.

"Tomorrow?"

"Maybe. Or the next day. Not too many days."

"Where's heaven, Grandpa?"

"With God."

"And God is with Mommy?"

"Yes."

"And Jesus?"

"And Jesus."

"I want them to come here."

"Soon."

Rayford had arranged with Priscilla Sebastian that she would come by for Kenny before dawn, when Rayford was expected to join the troops on the perimeter.

Kenny soon stopped talking and moving, and his breathing became regular and deep. Rayford prayed for him and waited a few more minutes before delicately sliding out from under him.

A few minutes later Rayford lay on his own

cot across the room and studied the boy. How thrilled Irene would have been with her grandson. Had Kenny grown up during any other period of history, he would be starting school within the year. Rayford wondered what form education would take in the millennial kingdom.

He also wondered how it worked. Would he and Buck and Kenny grow old while Irene and Raymie and Chloe remained the age they were when they went to heaven? And what about Amanda? He feared that reunion with his wife might be awkward, but would those situations matter when everyone was in the presence of Jesus?

Rayford had been so busy for so long that he had not allowed himself the luxury of daydreaming about it. What would it be like to see the Glorious Appearing and then to actually be with Christ? Rayford was more emotional than he had been as a younger man, and often the mere thought of the change Christ had made in him made him choke up.

To imagine the sinless Son of God caring enough about him to die for his sins . . . Rayford could still hardly fathom it. And to have the opportunity to thank him, to worship him, face-to-face. For a thousand years. And then for eternity. He hadn't even begun trying to imagine what heaven would be like.

• • •

In the wee hours of the morning in Jerusalem, Buck and Tsion found themselves taken in by an elderly father named Shivte and his two sons in their forties. They were all thick, beefy men, and soft-spoken.

As soon as Shivte's wife opened the door to her husband's coded knock, she blanched and nearly fainted. "Praise God! Praise God!" she said. "You are Tsion Ben-Judah! And you!" she added, looking first at her husband and then at her sons. "You have the mark of God on you! Can you finally see mine?"

They smiled and nodded, embracing her one by one.

"I cannot tell you how much we appreciate this," Tsion said. "Our belongings have disappeared, and we made no provisions for lodging."

Shivte's wife told him, "We made no provisions for lodging either. But we have blankets and some food."

"The Lord will reward you," Tsion said.

"He already has," she said. "To see you with my men when they came through the door, that is enough for me. I am humbled to offer hospitality to God's servants."

"Tell me how you came to Messiah, ma'am," Tsion said.

She sat heavily. "Micah," she said, and Tsion

and Buck looked at each other. "I had waited so long to take the mark of Carpathia. I did not want to. My men were not going to. They were going to hide out here during the day so as not to be detected by the GC. But I believed someone had to take the mark in order to buy and sell and keep us alive. I was willing, but the idea of worshiping that statue made me want to vomit. Forgive me."

"Please, continue."

"I was at the Temple Mount, planning to go through with it, even though in my heart I believed in the one true God. I did not know what else to do. I worried about my eternal soul, but I believed I was laying down my life for my family, and I could think of no nobler act. I did not realize at that time that I would be selling my soul to the evil one. Not even these men are worth that."

Her husband and sons smiled.

"I was in line that day, Rabbi, actually in line. I don't know how many people were between me and the mark applicator. But I saw a commotion and slipped out of line. I watched from the back of the crowd. I saw the gunshots that did not kill the man of God. I escaped back to our home, and my men will admit they ridiculed me. They had liked my plan of one of us—me—having the mark so we could eat. Now what were we going to do?

"I told them they could go out in the dark of night and find food, but I was going to find out more about the man of God. One of my young friends had a computer, and we found your Web site. That is how I came to believe Jesus was Messiah. Now I was an outcast in my own home. My men were devout enough Jews to resist Carpathia, but they were not ready for Messiah.

"I tried and prayed and pleaded and begged, but finally we agreed to quit talking about it. Enough, they said, and I had had enough of their rejection and ridicule anyway. But still I could pray. And God answers prayer. Here you are, and here they are, with the mark of God."

• • •

Rayford had trouble sleeping and felt compelled to check in with Buck. He tiptoed to the other room so as not to wake Kenny and placed the call. After asking about Kenny, Buck brought him up to date.

"Amazing," Rayford said. "What's Tsion saying about timing now?"

"He expects a predawn attack. Maybe there as well."

"We're kind of on that schedule too, Buck, but the combat part of this is so futile."

"Temporarily, you mean."

"Of course, but I just don't know that I see the

value of risking people's lives when they could stay inside here and—"

"—and wait for Jesus?"

"Exactly."

"Come on, Dad. Who wants to do that? I'd kinda like to have him find me on the job. Wouldn't you?"

"I know, but you should see the crew we're going to have on the perimeter. A couple of thousand I don't know at all. Then Otto and a few of his people, none of them with any business manning a weapon. Ree, Ming, Lionel, Hannah, Zeke. Not exactly soldiers. Mac, of course, and Smitty. They can take care of themselves, and there's no question about Razor and George. Unless George tries to be a hero. He's so military, Buck, you should see him, trying to make the best of it. You can just tell he thinks his street smarts ought to carry the day, but then he realizes how few soldiers are under his command, and those eyes go glassy."

"You've got directed energy weapons and fifty-calibers yet, right?"

"Yeah, but against nuclear power? Come on."

"Do some damage. Stall till the Calvary cavalry gets here."

"The what?"

"Thought of that the other day. Jesus is going to appear from heaven on a horse. That's literal, according to Tsion. Ten thousand saints with him. The Calvary cavalry."

"Too much time on your hands."

"Hey, Rayford?"

"Yeah."

"We can hear the armies coming. Can you?"

"Not the way this city is laid out. Maybe when they get closer. They're sure easy to spot from the high places, though. Pretty ominous. I'd be looking for a way out of here if I didn't know better."

"Sort of like watching a delayed ball game where you already know the final score, isn't it?"

"I guess," Rayford said. "That's the kind of thing only a mind like yours would come up with."

"Thanks, I think."

• • •

Unable to sleep, Chang made his way to the tech center and his computer at about four in the morning. Idly checking the GCNN affiliate feed out of Haifa, he heard a report of troop deployments.

"Supreme Potentate Nicolae Carpathia has made no secret of his strategy," the reporter intoned. "In fact, it seems as if he would just as soon enemy targets know what's coming. I spoke with him late last night at his bunker, somewhere near the Sea of Galilee."

"You see," Carpathia said, "we have such an overwhelming advantage in manpower, firepower, and technology, it really makes little difference what we encounter. I have not hidden that we have two main objectives aiming toward the same goal. We want to lay siege to the city of Jerusalem, where the majority of the remaining Jews reside. And we want to eliminate Petra once and for all, where what they like to call 'the Remnant' remains in hiding like scared children.

"They know we are coming, and they will see us coming, and there is little they can do about it."

"You expect no casualties?"

"Oh, there are always casualties," Carpathia sniffed. "But my people are honored to give their lives in service to me and the Global Community. I will see that they are appropriately rewarded. Of course, there is the possibility of no loss of life or limb on our part. That is, if the enemy sees what is coming and realizes it has no hope. An unconditional surrender would be the prudent course, and naturally I would accept that with utmost face-saving respect for them."

"Seriously? What accommodations would you make in that case?"

Carpathia could not answer over his gales of laughter.

• • •

Rayford was up, dressed, and armed before dawn. He opened the door before Priscilla knocked.

"I'll stay here with him until he wakes up, Rayford, if that's okay."

"Perfect. Thanks, Priss. Make yourself at home."

"Uh, Ray? You're going to be sure my husband comes home tonight, aren't you?"

"As much as it's up to me."

"That's not very reassuring."

"Well, I take it that was a serious question. A serious answer is that there are no guarantees. I'm hoping he'll make sure I come back."

"He feels obligated to everybody," Priscilla said, sitting.

Rayford stood by the open door. "Price of leadership. He volunteered for this command."

"Like there was another choice."

"There wasn't in my mind, Priscilla."

"Well, I'm just saying—"

"I know. Sometimes, though, seems a guy like me trying to keep an eye on a guy who knows what he's doing can just get in the way. You know, of course, that even if—"

"Don't say it, Rayford. Too many of the wives try to comfort themselves with that stuff about how their man will only be in heaven a day or two, maybe less, then he's coming back. That doesn't help."

"It's true."

"I know. But it isn't the living without him that worries me right now. It's his getting hurt, suffering, dying a hard way."

● ● ●

Buck and Tsion and their hosts drank the thickest, bitterest coffee Buck had ever had. It was still pitch-black outside. Shivte's wife was already sniffling and trying to hide it.

"Cameron," Tsion whispered, "I would like you to go with the old man, Shivte, at first."

"Now, wait. I came here to be your bodyguard, no one else's."

"Do me this favor. I worry about him. Even his weapon is ancient. The sons believe the invaders will come from the northwest and try to come through the Damascus Gate."

"Based on what?"

"The Unity Army could probably easily overrun any of the gates, but the Jaffa Gate and the Citadel are well fortified with many rebel troops."

"But beyond that," Buck said, "they could try to storm any of the gates, and the most likely, in my opinion, would be the Golden Gate. Their first priority has to be the Temple Mount, no?"

"I don't know, Cameron. Just do this for me, please. Take the old man to the Citadel. Once he is settled there, then come and find me. I will be with the other two near the Damascus Gate."

Buck would rather have followed his hunch and gone straight to the Golden Gate, but he was here for Tsion, and he would do him this favor. He didn't know why the brothers were even guessing. If two-thirds of Carpathia's troops were concentrating on Jerusalem, it wouldn't take many of them to take over the tiny Old City.

As soon as he and Tsion and the other three men were out the door, they heard gunfire. Tsion and the brothers jogged northwest, Buck and Shivte, west. Rebels ran everywhere, shouting what they knew. The enemy was on the Jaffa Road. Damascus Gate was under siege. The Yad Vashem Historical Museum to the Holocaust victims had been destroyed. Hebrew University, the Jewish National and University Library, and Israel Museum were in flames. The Old City would be next.

Thousands were dead and many more captured and held. Buck knew, if the rumors could be believed, that he and Shivte were in the worst possible place. In essence, they had cornered themselves inside the walls of the Old City.

• • •

Rayford was impressed with Sebastian's strategy, though they both knew tactics were out the window in the face of such odds. The third of Carpathia's troops assigned to Petra carried every type of weapon in the potentate's arsenal. At least two hundred thousand mounted troops slowly moved into position, far outflanking Sebastian's forces and virtually surrounding them and the city.

"I have so few DEWs," George told Rayford. "In retrospect, if I had known they were going to start with this horse trick, I'd have had Lionel find me more."

"What do horses have to do with it?"

"Horses are not armored, and the riders can't really hide. See how lazily they're moving into position?"

Rayford took the field glasses and saw thousands of horsemen cantering into place. They were a mile from Petra's massed troops. "They act like they've got all day."

Suddenly, George seemed animated. "We're going to get in the first blow in this thing, and we're going to have the advantage, at least temporarily."

"How?"

"Those horses are trained to not spook under artillery fire. We could pop a few fifty-caliber rounds at 'em and get them stirred up a bit. Maybe take out a few horses and a few riders. But I'll bet they haven't dealt with DEWs yet. You ready for some action?"

"Sure."

"I've got only about a hundred DEWs, but at least I was smart enough to assign them all positions inside on the rim. I need them pretty evenly spaced, all around the top of the city. Can you handle that?"

"On it. Then what?"

"Tell them all to wait for my command. If we can hit anywhere close to a hundred horses or riders with DEWs from this distance, we could cause a stampede that would put all their horses out of commission for a while."

"Brilliant."

"Only if it works. Thing is, we've got to do this before they really know where we are. We could have them on the run right off the bat and see how they like being on their heels."

• • •

Buck got Shivte settled well inside the crowded Citadel, where it appeared many scared younger men had decided to hole up as well. While Buck could hear activity on the Jaffa Road, the invaders had indeed ignored the Jaffa Gate for the very reason Buck guessed. Why do more work than you had to?

Buck guessed the Damascus Gate was a little over a quarter of a mile away, but getting there through the crowd of petrified and wild-eyed rebels made it seem farther. And of course, Tsion and the brothers were nowhere in sight. "Lord, come quickly."

● ● ●

Rayford scampered to a four-wheel-drive ATV and charged to the nearest high place. It took nearly half an hour with the vehicle and his walkie-talkie to get the hundred or so DEW operators spread out evenly and coordinated.

At George's command, they would fire invisible beams of directed energy at the enemy. In essence, they heated soft tissue past the tolerance point in less than a second, and if the rider or horse didn't elude the ray, their flesh would burn.

With Petra surrounded by a couple of brigades of mounted troops, the result had the potential to be maddeningly confusing to the enemy. The strategy was to try to hit horses only, making them bolt away and causing the steeds around them to do the same. No question some riders, especially their legs, would be hit in the process, hopefully causing them to kick and achieve the same result. If the beam hit higher on a rider's body, he would likely scream and yank the reins. George, Rayford thought, was a genius.

• • •

"Dung Gate is giving way!" someone shouted. "Let's kill us some One World Army!"

Buck prayed it wasn't true. The Dung Gate was the southern gate closest to the Western Wall. It was the long way around to get to the Temple Mount, and that's why he had assumed the Golden Gate on the east side would be the Unity Army's first choice. If they got through the Dung Gate, they might try battering through the Wailing Wall to get to pay dirt.

Unable to raise Tsion by phone or find him or either of the brothers at the Damascus Gate, which seemed to be holding for the time being, Buck ran toward the Dung Gate, a mile away. All along the route he heard rumors and fears. If any of it was to be believed, it wouldn't be long before half the greater city of Jerusalem was in captivity. His goal was to stay alive until the good guys showed up.

• • •

Rayford figured Petra was fewer than fifteen minutes from sunrise when he let George know the directed energy weapons were in place and awaiting his command. "I'd really like to make sure the targets are where I want them before we commence," George said.

"Only one way to do that as fast as you need it done," Rayford said.

"ATV?"

"Too much ground to cover. You'd have to circle the whole perimeter up top."

"Helicopter?"

"Bingo. If you want to risk it."

"They wouldn't believe it was us," George said. "Who'd be stupid enough to make himself that kind of a target?"

"You would."

● ● ●

Buck had run almost half a mile and was sucking wind when he saw Carpathia's Unity Army troops coming the other way. Now he was desperate to find Tsion and get him out of the Old City.

Rebels, some shooting over their shoulders, ran past him for their lives, but Buck noticed the GC were not firing. They were moving in a colossal battering ram that looked as if it would make short work of the Wailing Wall. Now that was a tragedy. After millennia of prayer, could such a sacred site be wasted in just moments?

Suddenly, all those rebels who had flooded past Buck turned and came back. Shouts resounded: "Not the Wailing Wall!" "Not the Wall!" "Sacrifice yourselves!" "Fight to the death!"

The word spread throughout the Jewish Quarter and into the center of the Old City, and instantly hundreds became thousands. Buck joined the fray.

They charged the GC, shooting, throwing rocks, fighting hand to hand. The rebels overcame those on the battering ram and turned it back toward the Dung Gate.

As more and more rebels joined, at least for that brief skirmish, the Jews had the Unity Army on the run. They pushed the battering ram up to the Dung Gate, chased out the army, and managed to shut the gate with the ram inside. Great cheers rose, and so, it seemed, did the rebellion's confidence. Someone assigned a large group to guard the gate, while others were sent to the Golden and Lion's Gates on the east side.

Buck's phone chirped. "Tsion! Where are you? I tried to call you!"

"My phone is dead. I am borrowing this one. Is it true the rebels turned the army away from the Dung Gate?"

"Yes! I'm here now! Where shall we meet?"

"Do you know the Church of the Flagellation?"

"Near the Muslim Quarter?"

"Just west of there, yes!" Tsion said. "Hurry! I have lost the brothers."

• • •

"You know we've always been protected in the airspace around here," Rayford said as he lifted off.

"I'd rather not test that," Sebastian said. "Just

straight up and give me a three-sixty so I can see if the horses are where I want them. Then straight back down."

"Oh no!" Rayford said. "Incoming!"

"What?"

A missile was streaking right at the chopper. Rayford tried to evade it, knowing that was hopeless. A whirlybird simply didn't have the maneuverability or speed to dodge a missile.

"My idea and a bad one, George. Sorry."

"Just stay away from the city, Ray!"

Rayford had toyed with the idea of dropping onto a high place, but if the missile tracked him, it could injure or kill more than just the two of them.

He banked and let the chopper roll out past where Petra troops were stationed, which only brought him face-to-face with the missile that much faster.

"Sorry, Priscilla," Rayford muttered, shutting his eyes as the warhead met the chopper.

● ● ●

It didn't make sense to Buck that he should get to the rendezvous point before Tsion, despite the difference in their ages. Buck figured Tsion had started from at least twice as close. He searched the crowded church, but once again, no Tsion. This was getting old.

"Herod's Gate!" someone shouted, and hundreds of rebels headed toward the northernmost gate in the city. It was amazing to see the zeal in their eyes when their ancient holy sites were threatened. That had to be where Tsion went too. Buck couldn't think of another option.

It was just over an eighth of a mile from the church, but there was no running this time. Buck found himself pressed on all sides, wall-to-wall rebels. Maybe it was for the best. He was exhausted already, and his pulse raced uncontrollably.

He couldn't call Tsion if the rabbi's phone was dead. All he could think to do was bend his knees occasionally and leap high enough to see over the crowd.

But when he spotted Tsion Ben-Judah, he didn't like where he found him.

TWENTY-ONE

THE CHOPPER shuddered and stayed on course.

"Thought we were goners," Rayford said. "I never get used to that."

"Where'd that missile go?"

"Right through us, as usual."

"Nothing usual about that," Sebastian said. He scanned the horizon. "Over there."

Rayford saw a plume of black smoke about a mile south of Petra.

"They may have hit their own people!" George said and got on his radio. "Big Dog 1 to southern perimeter, over."

"Mac here, Dog. What was that?"

"Just missed us. What did it do?"

"Found one of their transports just beyond the equestrian line. Had to have some casualties. They look pretty exercised."

"Wait till they find out it was friendly fire. Attention all DEW operators, open fire immediately!" George ordered.

Within seconds, the black rim of horses and horsemen surrounding Petra disintegrated, and steeds charged away in all directions.

"A masterpiece, George," Rayford said. "Well done."

"Some of that horse meat is probably well done. Hey, Ray, did I hear you mention my wife's name when we were about to buy it?"

"Guilty."

"What's that about?"

"I told her I'd look out for you as much as was possible."

"And that's your idea of looking out for me?"

"As much as was possible. What say we bounce back up and see if we can get them to shoot at us again, maybe take out some more of their munitions on the other side?"

"Not funny, Rayford."

• • •

Every time Buck leaped over the heads of the crowd, he caught sight of Tsion being borne along on the shoulders of zealots. He wanted to scream at them to put him down, but no one would be able to hear above the din. What were they trying to do, get him killed? Maybe they saw him as a hero. Maybe they thought by getting him to the head of the pack he could inspire the troops. Regardless, it was insanity.

Buck lowered his shoulder and bulled his way through until he was almost up to Tsion. "Hey!" he shouted. "Hey! Put him down!"

"He will lead us to victory!"

"He is our leader!"

"Well, he's my responsibility, and you're going to get him killed!"

Buck grabbed Tsion's ankle, which slowed the crowd, and as they lost their grip, Tsion tumbled headfirst. Buck dived beneath him to break his fall, and now both of them were being trampled. It was providential, however, as Unity Army troops had scaled the wall above Herod's Gate and opened fire. Rebels fell all around Tsion and Buck, heads slamming the ground, blood spattering.

Buck wrapped his arms around Tsion's head and buried his own, waiting out the fusillade. With the zing of bullets ricocheting and the explosion of the pavement around him, he tensed for the killing round that would hit his or Tsion's head or neck or spine.

But they were spared.

When the burst let up, Buck dragged Tsion to his feet and hustled him toward the legendary healing pool of Bethesda. "I was not hit, Cameron! No need for healing!"

Millimeters from death and the rabbi jokes.

● ● ●

Rayford and George landed and were racing down to George's post via ATV. "They've got to retaliate," Rayford said. "What form will that take, and what do we do?"

"They've got mortar launchers in range. I want to see if the riders can persuade their horses to return. If they can't, that's going to be chaos. The key is keeping them out of the Siq. I don't want a one of 'em thinking he can infiltrate this place."

"You'd think Carpathia would have learned his lesson. Imagine how much money he wasted trying to get at us here," Rayford said.

"Yeah, but every military commander thinks he's better than anybody else, so whoever's in charge of this offensive is going to have to learn for himself."

"The DEWs and his own missile should have taught him something."

"Should have," George said. "But you can bet he'll try everything in his arsenal before he gives up."

"What would be the hardest to defend against?"

"Sheer numbers. When they start rolling this way, we're going to be chased back inside."

"Where, so far, it's been safe."

"True. But retreating is not my idea of warfare. That missile was God's protection, but wasn't it fun to attack with the directed energy weapons?"

• • •

A young woman gestured frantically from a small cavelike structure near the pools, and Buck hustled Tsion to her. "There is room for two more," she said.

As they pushed their way in to safety, Buck realized about twenty others were in the echoing chamber. "Is it the rabbi?" someone called out.

"I am here," Tsion said.

"Praise God. When do you expect Messiah?"

"Actually, I expected him about five minutes ago. Or maybe I should say he should have been expecting me."

"I want to believe he is coming to save the day and rescue us."

"He is if you are ready," Tsion said.

"I am ready. I just want to be alive when he gets here."

"So do I," Tsion said. "But we did not choose the best place to ensure that, did we?"

"What is this talk of Messiah?" someone

grumbled. "We have been waiting for him to rescue us for generations."

Tsion ran through his teaching as fast as he could. Three of the terrified men and the young woman prayed to accept Jesus as Messiah, but the skeptic did not. "When he comes," he said, "I will believe."

"'Blessed are those who have not seen and yet have believed,'" Tsion said.

The gunfire suddenly ceased. Buck peered out past the woman. Was this it? Had Messiah returned and saved the day?

Young men raced by, screaming. "We have won! We have won! They are pulling back! The gates are secure!"

"Wait! It's a trap! Don't believe it! They are just regrouping!"

Buck and Tsion's bunker mates piled out and warily looked around, weapons at the ready. "I don't like it," someone said. "They have bombs that could annihilate us. What are they doing?"

"Toying with us."

"We should go on the offensive! Open the gates and attack! Kill them while they are retreating."

"They are not retreating. This is a trap. They want us to open the gates. We should regroup while they are regrouping. Be ready for them."

• • •

There was a lull at Petra too, and Rayford took a call from Mac McCullum. "Can you and Razor spare me a minute, George?" Rayford said. "Mac wants me to come and see something."

It was half an hour's ride by all-terrain vehicle to get to Mac, and when Rayford arrived, Mac was studying the enemy through powerful field glasses. "You know they can see us plain as day by now, Ray, just like we can see them. What are they waitin' on?"

He handed Rayford the binoculars. "Looks like they've got most of the horses under control. That must have been a mess. And I know, Ray, that our DEWs caused the stampede. But what's making them squirrelly now? I don't get it."

Rayford studied the enemy in the distance. It didn't appear it was as simple as horses being shy of where they had been burned. They weren't even close to that. It was more like the riders could not get the horses to do anything they wanted them to.

"It reminds me of a verse, Ray. Something Tsion taught us. What was it?"

"I don't recall. Want to ask him? I need to check in on him and Buck anyway."

• • •

The silence was more than eerie. Buck and Tsion moved close to the wall by Herod's Gate. Buck answered the phone and handed it to Tsion.

"Yes, here too," Tsion said. "I have the strange feeling it is the lull before the storm. Horses? Yes. Zechariah 12:4: '"In that day," says the Lord, "I will strike every horse with confusion, and its rider with madness; I will open My eyes on the house of Judah, and will strike every horse of the peoples with blindness."' You know, Mac, that may be what has happened here too."

As soon as Tsion was off the phone, people around him wanted to know what he was talking about. He told them.

"Let's check it out," one said. "The rabbi believes the Unity Army is blind or mad."

"Could be," Tsion said. "That is the only explanation I can think of for what is going on."

Some of the younger men boosted each other and began climbing. Two reached the top of the wall. "I see nothing! They're hiding, maybe."

"Rabbi! Teach us some more."

Buck looked to Tsion, who shrugged. "That is why I came. If they want to listen, I want to preach."

As soon as he began, curious crowds gathered again. And as Buck watched and listened, he was overcome with the privilege of being where he was and when it was. He sensed he could see Jesus at any time. And Chloe.

To hear God's man in God's place at God's time—what an unspeakable privilege. Scared? Of course he was. Wondering if Jesus would really come when he said he would? Not even a question. Buck couldn't wait. He just couldn't wait.

● ● ●

Back with George, Rayford was out of ideas. "Don't ask me," he said. "If you want to fire the Fifties, fire them."

"I know we could kill horses and men from this distance and take out a few of their vehicles," George said. "But I also know that would bring return fire. I'm not concerned about inside the city. But I'm afraid we're vulnerable out here at the perimeter."

"What would be the purpose of going on the offensive when you know you can't win?"

"Exactly. But I just hate sitting here, waiting for stuff to happen. We need to make something happen."

"Fire a Fifty or two and plenty will happen."

● ● ●

One of the young men on the wall interrupted Tsion, yelling, "They're raising some kind of a giant bullhorn. Maybe they want to negotiate."

"You don't want to negotiate with the devil," Tsion said, and the crowd roared.

"Maybe he's offering a truce!"

"A truce," Tsion said, "is worth the character of the man on the other side of the table."

"Attention, people of Jerusalem! This is your supreme potentate!"

"Boo! Boo! Our only potentate is the God of Israel!"

"Shut up! Hear him out!"

"Please listen, citizens. I come in peace."

"No! You come with weapons!"

"Come, let us reason together!"

"Listen. Shh! Listen to him!"

"I come to offer pardon. I am willing to compromise. I wish you no ill. If you are willing to serve me and be obedient, you shall eat the good of the land; but if you refuse and rebel, you shall be devoured by the sword. I will rid myself of my adversaries and take vengeance on my enemies. I will turn my hand against you and thoroughly purge you.

"But it does not have to be this way, citizens of the Global Community. If you will lay down your arms and welcome me into your city, I will guarantee your peace and safety.

"This will be your sign to me. If at the count of three I hear silence for fifteen seconds, I will assume you are willing to accede to my requests.

A single gunshot into the air during that time will be your signal that you would rather oppose me. But I warn you, half of Jerusalem is in captivity already. The entire city could be overthrown easily within an hour. The choice is yours at the count of three."

But before Carpathia could utter the first number, thousands of weapons fired into the air, including Buck's and Tsion's.

• • •

The enemy's attempt to control the horses and surround Petra was still not working. Rayford stood on a precipice and watched through binoculars as more Unity vehicles were deployed. The horizon was full of dust and smoke, and the mass of munitions and hardware looked like a black, roiling mass, filling his vision and oozing toward him like lava.

"I'm going to let them advance only so far," George said. "Then it's DEWs again and fifty-calibers."

"Like trying to dam a tsunami with BBs," Rayford said.

• • •

When the shooting stopped in Jerusalem, the ghostly silence returned. The One World Unity Army did not immediately attack, but Buck almost wished they had. The quiet was disquieting. He feared the next sound would be the proverbial freight train that tornado victims always mentioned, only this twister would consist of an unending horde of marauders who would stomp Jerusalem to dust.

But if that's what it took to usher in Jesus, well, bring it on.

Strangely, the crowd wanted to hear more from Tsion, and Buck was impressed that the rabbi was ready. "It is not too late!" Tsion cried. "Make your stand for Messiah now! Repent, choose, and be saved!" And many did.

• • •

Now even Sebastian seemed alarmed. The massive flow of horses, men, and weaponry advancing toward Petra was so enormous that as it spread and separated and filled in again, it blocked out the horizon, the desert sands, the rocks.

It was as if a cloud of locusts were blotting out the sun. No human could have imagined the scope of the enemy. They had somehow rallied, somehow overcome their madness and blindness, somehow broken out of their lull. And here they came.

They fanned out and flanked Petra on all sides, slowly filling in as far as the eye could see. And while their front lines were still a mile or so from the perimeter, there was no end to the swarm. The eye could not reach the back of column after column after column of millions strong that kept coming and coming and coming.

And when they were in place, they merely stopped and waited. For what was anybody's guess. But even when they stopped, there was no gap, no holes in their coverage, no end of their ranks.

"That, Rayford," Sebastian said, "is just a whole lot of army. If every one of our weapons fired every one of its bullets and each one was a flat-out kill, we wouldn't put a dent in that wave."

"What do you think about riding out there about a half mile and seeing if you can smoke a peace pipe with somebody?"

"You watch too much TV, Captain."

"Seriously, how about another round of DEW rays? See if we can push 'em back a bit."

"If I thought they'd react like dominoes I would. There really isn't far for them to go, because they'll run into their own replacements. Think we can get millions to stampede?"

Rayford shook his head. "I wouldn't mind seeing what that would do to them. Maybe they wouldn't be so eager to get closer."

"But, Ray, there's so many of them."

• • •

Tsion was still holding forth when a sound like a bomb shook the area, and people scattered for cover. Within seconds came the report that a second battering ram had penetrated the Old City. This time the Unity Army had eschewed any gate and had broken through the northeastern wall of the Old City, about halfway between the Lion's Gate and the northeast corner.

Hundreds of Jewish rebels raced toward the site, and to Buck's dismay Tsion took off behind them, not even discussing options. Buck had no choice but to follow, trying to catch Tsion in the melee. By the time he caught up, the battle was in full swing, and amazingly, the Jews seemed to have the upper hand again. They were pushing the army back, and fierce hand-to-hand combat over the battering ram almost saw it fall into rebel hands again.

Just as the rebellion was forcing the army back through the wall, several on the Unity front line turned and opened fire with high-powered automatic weapons, a grenade launcher, and what looked to Buck like a bazooka. He joined in returning fire, and the invasion was briefly squelched, but he was horrified to see more than a hundred dead or wounded Israelis all around him. He wondered how close he had come to deadly fire himself.

The hole in the wall seemed to be secure for the moment, so Buck turned to grab Tsion and pull him back toward the Bethesda pool. But the rabbi was on his knees, feet tucked awkwardly beneath him. His Uzi had slipped off his shoulder, the strap near his elbow now, the weapon dragging.

Buck grabbed the shoulder of his jacket to help him up, but when he pulled, Tsion pivoted on one knee and flopped to the pavement. "Tsion! Come on! Let's go!"

But he was a deadweight.

"Are you all right?" Buck demanded, turning Tsion's face toward him.

"I do not think so, friend."

"Are you hit?"

"I am afraid I am."

"Where?"

"I am not sure."

"Can you move?"

"No."

"Can I move you?"

"Please. You had better try."

Buck didn't have time to even think about being fancy. He grabbed Tsion's weapon and strapped it on his left shoulder, then got around behind the rabbi's head and thrust both hands under his arms. He bent his knees and lifted, walking backward, dragging the older man through the streets. He was grateful the shooting had stopped, if only temporarily.

Buck was cramping, having pulled his friend about an eighth of a mile, but he didn't want to stop until they were safe in the little chamber he remembered at Bethesda. He kept looking behind him to make sure the way was clear, but when he turned back he realized Tsion was also leaving a thick trail of blood.

Buck stopped to rest and check Tsion. He hurried around and opened the man's jacket. There he found the source of blood. Tsion could not have been shot in the heart or he would be dead already. But he had lost a lot of blood, which had flowed from near his sternum, down his belly, under his jacket, over his crotch, and into the street.

Tsion was pale, and his eyes threatened to roll back in his head. Buck leaned close to hear his shallow breathing. "Stay with me, friend," he said.

"Let me go, Cameron. Find shelter. I could do worse than die in the streets of my beloved city."

"You're not going to die, Tsion. You're going to hang on to see this victory, all right?"

"I wish."

"Don't wish! Work with me!"

Buck whipped off his jacket and his shirt, rolled up his shirt, and stuffed it into the wound. The hole was nearly the size of Buck's fist. "I have to get you to shelter," he said. "You up for a few more feet?"

"I am feeling nothing anymore, Cameron. You go. Please."

"I will not leave you here."

"Come, come. I will not be here long. We both know that."

"I'm taking you to the shelter."

"Do not do it for my sake."

"Then for mine."

Buck knew he was doing Tsion no good. The shirt popped out, and a great mass of blood gushed. Tsion moaned. Life seemed to be escaping him. His eyes were watery and pale, his lips blue. He had begun to shake all over.

Buck wrestled him into the shelter and tried stanching the blood flow again, but Tsion reached for him with weak, fluttery hands. He finally got hold of one of Buck's hands and pulled it toward him.

"Do not, friend. Please. It is too late."

"I don't want to lose you here, Tsion!"

"Come close," he whispered. "Listen to me." He was rasping now, taking labored breaths between words. "I can say . . . with Paul, 'I am already . . . being poured out . . . as a drink offering, and the time of my departure is at hand. . . . I have fought the good fight, I have finished the race, I have kept the faith. . . . Finally, there is laid up for me . . . the crown of righteousness, which the Lord, the righteous Judge, will give to me on that Day, and not to me only . . . but also to all who have loved His appearing.'"

"Tsion, don't! Stay with me!"

"Cameron . . . because of Jesus . . . my wife and children . . . forev—"

• • •

Sebastian had ordered another round from the DEWs, and Rayford had to admit it was something to watch as the front line of the pervasive mass fell back in agony, and the ripple effect could be seen for miles. Razor had the fifty-calibers ready in the event of a counterattack, but none came. That just made things weirder. The city of refuge, a million strong, sat like a pea in the middle of an ocean of enemies that seemed waiting to squash it.

Rayford's phone chirped, and he saw on the readout it was Buck. "Talk to me."

Buck's voice was thick. "He's gone."

"Tsion?"

"Hit in the chest. Nothing I could do."

"You need to get back here, Buck. We'll send somebody."

"They'll never get in, and I can't leave him."

"Buck! Come on. He's gone. I hate it too, but

like you said, there was nothing you could do, and certainly nothing you can do now."

"Nobody could get in here, and I can't imagine getting out."

"You all right?"

"Didn't foresee this, frankly."

"Keep your phone handy. No sense doing anything foolish now. We've got to be very close to the end."

• • •

Buck crossed Tsion's feet at the ankles. He closed his jacket over the death wound and pulled Tsion's hands together, interlocking the fingers at his waist. Buck smoothed Tsion's hair, closed his eyes, and took a last look at his face. "You almost made it, friend," he said. He draped his jacket over Tsion's torso and face.

Brandishing both Uzis now, he headed for Herod's Gate, where two young rebels seemed to have a decent vantage point. It wasn't the safest spot, and it sure didn't fit Rayford's advice of not doing anything foolish. But Buck didn't know what else to do.

• • •

Mac was on the phone from the other side of the perimeter. "Rayford, if I was to ask Sebastian to lend you to us, you think that would be doable?"

"He'd probably be glad to get rid of me. Let me ask."

"What's he need?" George said.

"Mac? Sebastian wants to know what for."

"Don't want to say."

"That's not going to cut it with him; you know that."

"I'm supposed to tell him the truth?"

"Never hurts."

Mac whispered, "I need somebody to talk to. Smitty's about two hundred yards to the west, and Otto's drivin' me bats. Plus, for real, we could use some manpower here. Like I could use an ATV to check on my troops, east and west. You got as many Carpathia troops out your way as we do back here?"

"There's no end to them, Mac."

"I'm countin' on Jesus real soon. But in the meantime, could you come?"

TWENTY-TWO

GETTING TO the top of the wall of the Old City, particularly by Herod's Gate, was no easy task. Buck didn't feel that old, but the two rebels already there were at least fifteen years younger. They nodded to him and pointed in the distance.

Unity Army troops were amassing on Jericho Road, on Suleiman Street, and in the garden where the traditional site of Jesus' tomb lay. Foot soldiers stretched as far as Buck could see—from the Rockefeller Museum on his right to the Church of St. Stephen past the garden, even as far as Hel Ha Handasa.

He and the two rebels were in plain sight, but the enemy seemed content to let them stay there. Buck wondered if Christ would return only in the middle of an active siege, or if he might appear any moment. He hoped the Remnant at Petra would not even have to know about Tsion until after the Glorious Appearing.

Buck worried about the troops behind the Rockefeller Museum. They seemed quieter, more clandestine than the others. And they were harder to see. He detected movement, but it was not hurried. He would have to keep an eye on that area.

Buck watched the sky. At the coming of Jesus he expected a heavy cloud cover to roll in, the sun to go dark, the earth to convulse. All that could happen in an instant, he knew, and when he allowed himself to dwell on it, the atmosphere seemed to crackle with tension.

• • •

Sebastian told Rayford to "go ahead and hold Mac's hand. I swear, sometimes he's like an old woman. But let him wait. Go see Chang on your way. You can go up and in and then down and out and avoid the long way around."

"What's Chang need?"

"Just buck him up. The way he was talking to me the last few days, it was obvious he'd rather be out here than in the tech center. Tell him how crucial he is to us, all that. 'Course it's true, you know."

The route Sebastian suggested was tougher

than Rayford expected. He had become fairly proficient on the machine, but the terrain was treacherous. He used the brake and lower gears more than ever and a couple of times found himself in rock formations that didn't allow him through. He had to put the ATV in neutral, ease back down, and try another route.

By the time he got to the tech center, he was exhausted and glad to have a break.

• • •

A lot of quiet talk and planning seemed to be going on inside the Old City. Buck noticed several groups of particularly young rebels making their way toward the walls. He liked his perch and what he could see, but he wasn't so sure it was a good idea to put the front lines up top all the way around. And the more he watched, the clearer it became that that was precisely the decision someone had come to.

There was still a good strike force in the center of the city as well, but it was made up of the older men and some women. The prime fighting men, the teenagers and those in their early twenties, were taking their places at the top of the wall. Something about it niggled at the back of Buck's brain. There was a vulnerability about it, an all-or-nothing quality. He liked the idea of having options, but that was just for himself. He wasn't charged with defending the whole place.

• • •

Chang had resigned himself to his role, but still he appreciated Rayford's comments and the fact that he had taken the time to stop in. Naomi came by, and the three sat before Chang's screen.

"We all believe the Millennium starts soon," Rayford said. "No later than tomorrow. That's why it's important the populace here not know what's happened to Tsion."

"Tsion?"

"He was killed."

"No!"

Rayford told what he had heard from Buck. Naomi hid her face in her hands, and while Chang wanted to comfort her, he too was overcome. "And Buck is all right?"

"So far, but they were in a very precarious location, and Buck still is."

"Can we get him out?"

"Wouldn't be worth the risk. He's pretty self-sufficient. Like everybody else, he's trying to keep Jews alive and, of course, himself, until the event the world has been anticipating for thousands of years."

Chang pointed to the screen, and they watched the latest GCNN newscast.

"Global Community Supreme Potentate Nicolae J. Carpathia has assembled the largest army in the history of mankind. As you can see in this aerial view, the One World Unity Army consists of all the soldiers, livestock, rolling stock, and munitions available anywhere. The fighting force of untold millions covers the plains of Israel from the Plain of Megiddo in the north to Bozrah in Edom in the south and stretches east to west almost the entire breadth of what was once known as the Holy Land.

"The ground forces are supported by air bases as far away as Cyprus and by aircraft carriers in the Mediterranean Sea, and troop transport ships in both the Gulf of Suez and the Gulf of Aqaba off the Red Sea.

"At this hour one-third of Carpathia's forces have surrounded Petra in Edom to the southeast in Jordan, hideout of the Judah-ite rebels. Global Community Security and Intelligence Director Suhail Akbar says Tsion Ben-Judah himself is ensconced at that location, and while the goal of the Unity Army is annihilation, there may be value in taking the leader alive.

"The other two-thirds of the Unity Army is poised to overtake the city of Jerusalem. Potentate Carpathia himself reports that nearly half the city has been occupied and that it is just a matter of time before the Old City is overrun.

"Earlier today in a press conference held while on horseback, the potentate was upbeat about the potential outcome."

Carpathia's face appeared on the monitor. "We are confident that these are the last two rebel enclaves in the world," he said, "and that once they have been thoroughly defeated and our enemies scattered, we will realize what we have so long dreamed of: an entire world of peace and harmony. There is no place in a true global community for rebellion. If our government was anything but benevolent or did not have the attitude of 'citizen first,' there might be cause for dissention. But all we have ever attempted to do was create a utopia for society.

"It is most unfortunate that it comes to this, that we have to resort to bloodshed to achieve our goals. But we will do what we have to do."

Someone asked, "Doesn't the size of your global army seem like overkill?"

"An excellent question," Carpathia cooed, his leathers squeaking as he reset himself on his horse. "No effort in the cause of world peace is wasted. The rebel factions have proved surprisingly formidable. We have decided at the highest levels to be sure we leave nothing to chance this time. We will use whatever we need, everything that is at our disposal, to succeed."

"Is there any truth to the speculation that you are overarmed in anticipation of running into surprising support for the opposition, that perhaps their God might intervene on their behalf?"

Carpathia chuckled. "I do not worry about fairy tales, but even if they did have supernatural help, they would be no match for our fighting machine. By our numbers alone, even unarmed, we could win any war by continuing to replenish our ranks. But we also happen to be fully equipped with the best and latest technology."

"Why not win this war all at once? What's the delay?"

"I am a man of peace. I always believe first in diplomacy and negotiation. The window of opportunity for settling this peacefully is always open. I had hoped that the enemies of peace would be persuaded by our size and would come to the bargaining table. But our patience is running out. They seem markedly uninterested in any reasonable solution, and we are prepared to use any means necessary. So it is just a matter of time now."

● ● ●

By midday, with the sun riding high, Buck was famished. He gingerly made his way down from the wall when volunteers brought foodstuffs in for the fighters. He gulped fruit and bread and cheese, and climbed up again. The army seemed to be taking a lunch break too. Buck wished the rebels had larger weapons. Maybe a surprise attack would do some damage. On the other hand, a sleeping giant was a gentler giant, and perhaps it made sense to leave things as they were.

He hated the idea of just waiting for the other side to attack, but with the front lines atop the wall now, at least that wouldn't be a surprise when it came.

• • •

Rayford started down the back side of Petra, finding it even more harrowing than coming up. He had stayed with Chang and Naomi a little longer than he had planned, so he assumed Mac would be looking for him and that George thought he had already arrived.

From his vantage point he had a good view of the army a mile off. He was reaching for his phone to reassure Mac when it became clear something had happened. The front lines were recoiling again, so George must have initiated another burst of the directed energy weapons.

This time, however, despite the ensuing chaos, the Unity Army didn't take it sitting down. Rayford heard the booms of retaliatory fire, like thunder from a storm head a hundred miles wide. He knew enough about munitions to know that Carpathia's forces were a little far away to be using the mortar cannons and shooting at high angles. He guessed the shells would drop short of the Petra perimeter.

He was wrong. Maybe their cannons were bigger than the typical unrifled short barrels. The shells flew past the perimeter and began dropping all around him. When one exploded right in front of him, Rayford was nearly pitched off the ATV. Grabbing for the handlebar with his free hand, he saw his phone go flying, bouncing a hundred yards down the rocky steep.

And now his vehicle was out of control. He bounced high off the seat and realized he was soaring through the air with only his hands attached to the ATV. He came down hard, and the contraption bounced and rolled sideways. To hang on or not was the only thing on his mind, and quickly that option was gone too. The four-wheeler hit yet again, ripping his grip away. As he bounced and rolled, he kept picking up the sight of the vehicle disintegrating as it smashed into rocks all the way into a valley.

Rayford reminded himself not to try to break his own fall. He tucked hands and arms in and tried to relax, fighting his natural instinct for all he was worth. The grade was too steep and his speed too fast to control himself. The best he could wish for was a soft landing place.

A shell deafened him from about ten feet to his right, knocking him into a sideways roll. Rayford felt his temple smash into a sharp rock and was aware of what sounded like rushing water as he rolled toward thorny overgrowth. Scary as the thorns looked, they had to be softer than what he had been hitting.

Rayford was able to shift his body weight as he slowed and backed into the thorns. It was then he realized what the liquid sound was. With each beat of his heart, galloping now, his life's blood spurted six feet from the wound in his temple.

He pressed his palm hard against his head and felt the gush against his hand. He pressed with all his might and felt he might be containing it somewhat. But Rayford was in danger now—mortal danger. No one knew exactly where he was. He was without communications or transportation. He didn't even want to inventory his injuries, because regardless, they were minor compared to the hole in his head. He had to get help—and fast—or he would be dead in minutes.

Rayford's arms were gashed, and he felt sharp pains in both knees and one ankle. He reached with his free hand to pull up his pant leg and wished he hadn't. Not only had something sliced the flesh from his ankle, but something had taken part of the bone too.

Could he walk? Dare he try? He was too far from anywhere to crawl. He waited for his pulse to abate and for his equilibrium to return. He had to be a mile from Mac and his people, and he could not see them. There was no going back up. He rolled up onto his feet, squatting, one hand desperately trying to keep himself from bleeding to death.

Rayford tried to stand. Only one leg worked, and it was the one with the nearly totaled ankle. He may have broken a shinbone in the other. He tried to hop, but the incline was so great, he found himself pitching forward again. And now he was out of control one more time, trying to hop to keep from falling but picking up speed with every bounce. Whatever he did, he could not take his hand from his temple, and he dared not land on one more hard thing. "Lord, now would be a most appropriate time for you to come."

● ● ●

Chang sensed something was about to give. He had succeeded in intercepting signals from geosynchronous satellites that supported communications among the millions of troops. They were about to move, and his key people needed to know.

He called George. "Expect an advance within sixty seconds," he said.

"We've already been shelled," George yelled. "You mean more than that?"

"Yes, they will be coming."

"Rayford see you?"

"Left a little while ago. On his way to see Mac."

"Thanks. Call Mac, would you? I'll inform the others."

Chang called and told Mac the same.

"Hey," Mac said, "I can't raise Sebastian, and Ray is overdue."

"On his way," Chang said.

He called Buck. "Expect ad—"

But he was cut off. He redialed. Nothing.

● ● ●

"They're coming! They're coming!"

Buck heard a young rebel shrieking just as his phone chirped and he saw an incendiary device hurled over the Rockefeller Museum, right at his position. He saw Unity Army troop movement from every side, and he grabbed his phone and held it up to his ear just as the bomb hit the wall right in front of him and clattered to the ground outside.

He recognized Chang's voice just before the bomb blew a hole in the wall. Rock and shrapnel slammed his whole right side, killed his phone, and made him drop one Uzi. He felt something give way in his hip and his neck as his perch disintegrated.

One of the young boys near him had been blown into the air and cartwheeled to the pavement. Buck was determined to ride the wall as it fell. He reached for his neck and felt a torrent of blood. He was no medical student, but he could tell something had sliced his carotid artery—no small problem.

As the wall crumbled, he danced and high-stepped to stay upright, but he had to keep a hand on his neck. The remaining Uzi slid down into his left hand, but when he stabbed it into something to keep his balance, it fell away. He was unarmed, falling, and mortally wounded.

And the enemy was coming.

● ● ●

Rayford could break his fall only with his free hand, not daring to take pressure off his temple. His chin took as much of the brunt as the heel of his hand as he slid at what he guessed was a forty-five-degree angle. There would be no walking. All he could do was crawl now and try to stay alive.

● ● ●

Buck's feet caught in a crevasse of shifting rock, and his upper body flopped forward. He was hanging upside down from the crumbling wall over the Old City. His hip was torn and bleeding too, and blood rushed to his head.

• • •

Even inside the tech center of a city made of rock, Chang felt the vibration of the millions of soldiers advancing on Petra. He was clicking here and there, flipping switches, and trying to make calls. How far would God let this go before sending the conquering King?

• • •

Fighting unconsciousness, he tried gingerly edging along, one hand ahead of him, the other occupied. Each inch made the angle seem steeper, the way more unstable. With every beat of his heart, every rush of blood, every stab of pain, he wondered what was the use. How important was it to stay alive? For what? For whom? "Come, Lord Jesus."

Dizziness overwhelmed, pain stabbed. A lung had to be punctured. His breath came in wheezes, agonizing, piercing. The first hint of the end was the crazy rhythm of his heart. Racing, then skipping, then fluttering. Too much blood loss. Not enough to the brain. Not enough oxygen. Drowsiness overtook panic. Unconsciousness would be such a relief.

And so he allowed it. The lung was ready to

burst. The heart fluttered and stopped. The pulsing blood became a pool.

He saw nothing through wide-open eyes. "Lord, please." He heard the approach of the enemy. He felt it. But soon he felt nothing. With no blood pumping, no air moving, he fell limp and died.

EPILOGUE

Immediately after the tribulation of those days the sun will be darkened, and the moon will not give its light; the stars will fall from heaven, and the powers of the heavens will be shaken.

Then the sign of the Son of Man will appear in heaven, and then all the tribes of the earth will mourn, and they will see the Son of Man coming on the clouds of heaven with power and great glory.

Matthew 24:29-30

ABOUT THE AUTHORS

Jerry B. Jenkins (www.jerryjenkins.com) is the writer of the Left Behind series. He owns the Jerry B. Jenkins Christian Writers Guild, an organization dedicated to mentoring aspiring authors. Former vice president for publishing for the Moody Bible Institute of Chicago, he also served many years as editor of *Moody* magazine and is now Moody's writer-at-large.

His writing has appeared in publications as varied as *Reader's Digest, Parade, Guideposts,* in-flight magazines, and dozens of other periodicals. Jenkins's biographies include books with Billy Graham, Hank Aaron, Bill Gaither, Luis Palau, Walter Payton, Orel Hershiser, and Nolan Ryan, among many others. His books appear regularly on the *New York Times, USA Today, Wall Street Journal,* and *Publishers Weekly* best-seller lists.

Jerry is also the writer of the nationally syndicated sports story comic strip *Gil Thorp,* distributed to newspapers across the United States by Tribune Media Services.

Jerry and his wife, Dianna, live in Colorado and have three grown sons.

Dr. Tim LaHaye (www.timlahaye.com), who conceived the idea of fictionalizing an account of the Rapture and the Tribulation, is a noted author, minister, and nationally recognized speaker on Bible prophecy. He is the founder of both Tim LaHaye Ministries and The Pre-Trib Research Center. He also recently cofounded the

Tim LaHaye School of Prophecy at Liberty University. Presently Dr. LaHaye speaks at many of the major Bible prophecy conferences in the U.S. and Canada, where his current prophecy books are very popular.

Dr. LaHaye holds a doctor of ministry degree from Western Theological Seminary and a doctor of literature degree from Liberty University. For twenty-five years he pastored one of the nation's outstanding churches in San Diego, which grew to three locations. It was during that time that he founded two accredited Christian high schools, a Christian school system of ten schools, and Christian Heritage College.

Dr. LaHaye has written over forty books that have been published in more than thirty languages. He has written books on a wide variety of subjects, such as family life, temperaments, and Bible prophecy. His current fiction works, the Left Behind series, written with Jerry B. Jenkins, continue to appear on the best-seller lists of the Christian Booksellers Association, *Publishers Weekly*, *Wall Street Journal*, *USA Today*, and the *New York Times*.

He is the father of four grown children and grandfather of nine. Snow skiing, waterskiing, motorcycling, golfing, vacationing with family, and jogging are among his leisure activities.